IT TAKES A THIEF

Liz Wolfe

[redacted]

Medallion Press, Inc.
Printed in USA

DEDICATION:

For John Frey.

Because he convinced me I could do anything I wanted.

Published 2009 by Medallion Press, Inc.

The MEDALLION PRESS LOGO
is a registered trademark of Medallion Press, Inc.

Cover Illustration by Adam Mock

Typeset in Adobe Caslon Pro
Printed in the United States of America

ISBN:9781934755068

10 9 8 7 6 5 4 3 2 1
First Edition

ACKNOWLEDGMENTS:

I want to acknowledge my husband, Keith, for his belief in me, his support, the hours he spent listening to my plot and making invaluable suggestions—and for the name Drake Leatherman.

1

September 16, Outside Bethesda, Maryland

"You lied to them? About your own father?"

"I lied about my entire life to them, Dad. I'm not even using my real name." Zoe didn't expect her father to understand.

"What name are you using?"

"Drummond. I'd been using it for a while when I met Shelby."

"Why were you using a phony name? What's wrong with Alexander?"

"I told you. I was trying to get out of the life. I was going to school to be a CPA. The few thefts I did were just to pay my tuition."

"You hate being a thief that much?" Her father looked genuinely hurt. Zoe knew he'd always thought being a thief was an honorable profession. He had his own code of honor that he lived and stole by. Besides, she'd realized that Zeke had wanted a son to follow in his footsteps. She could steal better than almost anyone, but she couldn't be his son.

"It just isn't for me, Dad. Hey, what happened to that kid you were working with?"

Zeke waved a hand in dismissal. "He didn't work out. No finesse." He stood and walked to the sideboard that held a silver tea service. "What's so bad about me? About your life?"

"Well, we could start with the fact that you're a thief. Then we could add that you raised me to be a thief. Shelby used to be with the FSA and Paige used to be a cop. I don't think they'd really want to work with someone whose father taught her that stealing other people's stuff is an acceptable way to earn a living." Zoe watched her father's hand and saw the telltale tremble. The housekeeper, Agnes, had told her about the Parkinson's her father had developed. So far, it was mild and didn't affect his life very much. And he'd quit doing jobs, so at least she didn't have to worry about him ending up in prison for the rest of his life.

"But you said you were a thief when you met this Parker woman. So, she knows you were stealing." Zeke filled his teacup. "You want some more tea?"

Zoe nodded and held her cup out while he filled it. "I made up a whole life for her. Told her I was an orphan, in and out of foster homes, learning to steal from some other thieves I met. And I really was going to school to become a CPA, so it looked like I was doing it to survive, like I didn't have any other skills."

"Not like your father used to be the best thief in the world?" Zeke asked.

"Exactly, Dad."

"So, what do you do for these people?"

Zoe set her teacup down and leaned back on the sofa. "Right now, I'm just doing paperwork. Keeping their books, taking phone calls. Stuff like that. But Shelby's training me to be an investigator." She grinned at her father. "I'm pretty good at it, too."

"I'm not surprised. I'll bet some of your thief skills come in handy, too."

Zoe frowned at him. She wasn't about to tell him that she'd used those very skills several times already. Besides, Shelby hadn't been exactly thrilled about it.

"I have to get back to work, Dad. I've been here over a week already."

"And you're not going to tell them your real story? Just going to keep using a phony name? Somehow that seems like you don't have any respect for me."

"It's better this way, Dad. There's absolutely no reason they need to know that I'm the daughter of a master thief. Or that I used to be one myself."

‡ ‡ ‡

September 29, Portland, Oregon

Shelby punched the conference button on her desk phone and picked up her coffee cup. "Hi, Ethan. Is this a social call?" She leaned back in her chair and took a sip of coffee.

"Not exactly. I wanted to let you know that I've been reassigned to Langley for a while."

"You're working with the CIA?" Shelby asked. "Must be something pretty important."

"It's important, all right. And it's bad news. The Dominion Order is up to something again."

Zoe's ears perked up at Ethan's announcement. She kept her head bent over the pile of receipts she was logging, hoping Shelby would forget she was there.

"Crap. I thought you took care of them after that last nightmare we went through."

"I thought I had. But they worked too fast for us. By the time we traced the money transfers, all the accounts had been closed. They managed to get to several of the Eastland executives and Order operatives that we captured. When that happened, the others clammed up."

"So, what are they up to now and why are you telling me?"

"First of all, I thought you and Paige and Zoe should know, since you thwarted one of their operations. Not that I think they'll bother trying to find you. They don't seem interested in revenge," Ethan said.

"What are they interested in now?" Shelby asked.

"I'm still trying to find out. We're hearing rumors that they're looking for a thief. And not just an ordinary burglar. It seems they want the best of the best." Ethan's sigh was audible over the conference phone. "I just wish I knew why."

"I'd think you need to find the thieves they're looking for and keep an eye on them. Then if the Order contacts any of them, you could find out what they want to steal."

"That was basically my thought, too. I've got Jeremy Barstow set up. He'll pull a few high-end jobs under our supervision, then when the Order comes calling on him, we should be able to get the information."

"Jeremy's one of the best," Shelby agreed.

"Barstow's a hack, and if the Order knows anything, they won't be interested in him," Zoe said.

Shelby turned to Zoe. "Just because you used to be a two-bit thief doesn't mean you know everything about the thief world. Jeremy worked with me on a mission once."

"Then you were just lucky. Jeremy always worked with partners. He had the brains for setting up a job but he always blew it when it came to actually getting the goods. His partners were the talent. But they didn't get any of the credit and, knowing Jeremy, probably not much of the profit either. And I wasn't a two-bit thief." Zoe clamped her lips together. She'd come close to revealing her real identity. And it was too bad that she couldn't. She'd be perfect for what they wanted.

"Is Jeremy the only one you've got, Ethan?" Shelby asked.

"No, actually, I'm talking with Zeke Alexander. Now there's a thief that would get their attention."

"He can't do it," Zoe blurted.

"He says he can. And the man was the best thief in the world for years. Still is, as far as I can tell."

"Why would he want to help you anyway?" Zoe asked.

"I don't know. He said something about it being time for him to earn some respect. I'm just glad he's considering it."

Damn it. Her father had suggested that she didn't respect him and she hadn't really done anything to tell him otherwise. She couldn't let him do it. Not with the Parkinson's.

"Zeke Alexander has Parkinson's."

"What?" Ethan asked.

"How could you possibly know that?" Shelby asked.

"Because I just saw him a few weeks ago. Zeke Alexander is my father."

‡ ‡ ‡

October 9, Fort Meade, Maryland

"Forrester." Logan tucked the receiver between his ear and shoulder and continued typing a report that was already late.

"I have a message from your uncle."

Every cell in Logan's body went on alert. His uncle, Giovanni Castiglia, had disappeared three months earlier during a visit to his nephew. Logan still didn't know what had happened. He'd left for work that morning after Giovanni had told him he was going to visit several museums. That afternoon, Giovanni had called Logan's cell phone to tell him that he was returning to Italy. When Logan had questioned the abrupt end to his uncle's visit, he'd been told to leave it alone. That he'd be in touch soon. Logan hadn't heard from him since. It was as if the man had evaporated.

Since the death of Logan's parents several years earlier, Giovanni was his only family. They visited each other every year or so, taking turns flying across the Atlantic. In between visits they called and e-mailed frequently. Logan had exhausted his resources in trying to find his uncle. Most of his resources. He hadn't called the authorities. Partially because he knew they would just explain that there was no reason for alarm. Giovanni had told Logan he was leaving, and the eccentric physicist was known to go into hibernation when he was working. Logan also knew that if he raised an alarm he'd probably lose his position at the National Security Agency. The NSA couldn't allow a cryptanalyst to have access to national secrets if his only relative might have been abducted. But even when Giovanni had disappeared into his work, he'd always stayed in contact with Logan. Not this time.

"Take your cell phone outside. I'll call you in ten minutes." The caller disconnected.

Logan locked his computer, slipped his cell phone into his pants pocket, and walked down the aisle. Minutes later, he walked past the security guards in the lobby of the National Security Agency building and out onto the sidewalk. He paced around the corner and waited, checking his watch. How had the man gotten his cell phone number? Two more minutes. Logan pulled his cell phone out and stared at the dark display. The phone chirped, and he flipped it open. The caller ID showed only *Private Number.*

"Yes?"

"He wants you to know that he's all right."

"Where is he? I want to speak to him."

"I'm afraid that's not possible right now. Trust that he is well cared for and will continue to be so. He has a request for you."

"A request?"

"He wants you to join us."

"Who are you?"

"You don't need that information at this time. You will resign from the NSA immediately. We have need of your services for an indeterminate amount of time."

The voice was smooth and unemotional. A bark of nervous laughter escaped Logan, and he cleared his throat. "I can't just leave my job."

"Of course you can. And you will if you want to see your uncle again."

Was this man really relaying a message from his uncle? Or was he delivering a veiled threat? Logan fought down the panic and pushed the confusion aside. There was no real choice to be made, but could he buy some time?

"I'll need to give two weeks' notice."

The man's laughter rumbled in Logan's ear.

"Oh, please. You're a cryptanalyst. One of their best, we understand. The moment you *give notice*, the NSA will send a guard to watch you pack your belongings and then he'll escort you to the door."

Logan couldn't argue with the voice. That was exactly what would happen.

"Meet me in the lobby of the Trump Tower in New York at eight tonight. I'm sure I don't need to tell you to come alone and to not alert the authorities."

"Will my uncle be there?"

"You'll recognize me by a red and black tie. It's identical to the one you're wearing." The caller disconnected.

Logan looked down at his red and black striped tie. How the hell had the man known what tie he was wearing? It had been in his briefcase until he'd put it on for a meeting that morning. He looked at the street and parking lot but saw nothing out of the ordinary. He shook off the creepy feeling and closed his phone. His mind raced over a plan. He opened the phone again and punched in the number of an old college chum.

"Zach Hansen."

"Hey, Zach. That offer of a job still stand?"

"You're kidding, right?"

"Nope. I'm all yours. If you still want me."

"Hell, yes, I still want you."

"I'll need a few months to get everything in order here, but I'm leaving the NSA today."

"Hot damn! I didn't think I'd ever be able to lure you away from your spy job." Zach laughed. "Hey, you aren't in trouble there, are you? Selling national secrets or anything?"

"No, asshole. I'm just burned out on it. And your offer is pretty lucrative." Logan laughed and hoped it didn't sound forced. "Look, the NSA will probably call you. They investigate everyone who leaves. It's no big deal; they'll just ask if you've hired me."

"Sure, no problem."

"Great. I'll call you in a couple of weeks. I'm going to take a vacation, then we'll talk about what you're paying me so much for."

"See you soon, buddy."

At his desk, Logan logged back on to his computer and started a message to his home e-mail address. The few personal documents he had on his computer were sent, then deleted from his hard drive. He typed up his resignation and printed it out on the ink-jet printer on his desk. Another e-mail delivered all his notes about his current project to one of his co-workers. A phone call assured him that his supervisor would be available for the next hour.

He looked around his cubicle. His only personal belongings were a slightly wilted plant, a picture of his Uncle Giovanni and himself when he was about ten, and his coffee cup. He slipped the picture into his briefcase and tossed the cup and plant into the trash can.

The irony of the situation didn't escape Logan. He lived in a world of spies. His job was to find ways to figure out what spies were saying on cell phones and in e-mails. There were others who found ways to keep what U.S. spies were saying on cell phones and in e-mails a secret. The thought that someone had spied on him seemed ridiculous.

He closed his briefcase, slid the resignation into the outer pocket, and walked down the hall, stopping at the desk of his supervisor's secretary.

"Hi, Maxine."

"I told Greg you were coming. He's expecting you. You want some coffee? I'm getting a cup for him anyway."

"Thanks, but I won't be that long." Logan pulled the single sheet of paper from the outer pocket of his briefcase, and opened the office door. He walked directly to Greg Sullivan's desk and held out his resignation.

"Logan, what did you want to talk about?" Greg took the paper from him and scanned it. His face lost all expression for a moment, then he frowned and looked up at Logan. "No way. I don't accept it." He held the paper out to Logan.

"I'm sorry, but I have to do this."

"Why? If you need some time off, we can arrange that. If you're burned out on the job, we'll move you to another position. We'll work out the problem."

"That's not it. I've accepted a position with Micro Technologies. As a software developer."

"A software developer?".

"I majored in computer science. And I've kept my skill set up to date since I've been with the NSA." Logan resisted the impulse to shift his feet.

"You've been with the NSA for almost ten years, with the CIA for two years before that. You're one of our best cryptanalysts. Are you sure you want to end your career with us?"

"I've enjoyed my work here. But I miss software development." He grinned at Greg. "And I won't mind making that kind of money, either."

"There's more to job satisfaction than just money."

"I know. I've thought this through and it's what I want."

Greg laid Logan's resignation letter down, lining it up with the edge of his desk. "I guess there's no talking you out of this?"

"No. But thanks for asking." Logan allowed himself a smile. He and Greg had always been on friendly terms. He admired the man and respected his position. "My desk is clear. I've e-mailed Ron all my notes on my current project. He won't have any problem seeing it through."

Greg held his hands up. "I know when I've lost an argument." He picked up the resignation letter. "I'll put this through. But if you ever want to come back, just let me know. If you're ready, I'll walk you out."

"Thanks. I appreciate that." Greg didn't have to walk him out. He could have called the security guards to escort him to the front door and take his badge.

"Micro Technologies? I've read about them. Pretty

impressive company. When will you start?"

"Not for a couple of months. I have to sell my condo here and get moved to Oregon. And I thought I'd take some vacation time."

"Good plan."

At the front door, Logan shook Greg's hand, gave him the clip-on badge that allowed him entrance to the building, and turned his back on a satisfying and stellar career with the NSA. Within hours his network account at the NSA would be deactivated and an investigation would be started. At first the investigation would be intense, but as nothing was revealed, it would become routine. Eventually, a report would be sent to his supervisor and on to the director of the NSA. It would state that there was no suspicious activity on his part. Nothing to worry about. He wasn't concerned. He'd made sure there was nothing to cause them to look any further.

Logan pushed those thoughts aside and concentrated on what he had to do before his meeting in less than eight hours with a man he didn't know.

‡ ‡ ‡

October 19, Iraq

Rashid Fadhil Ali stood before the small mirror over

the washbasin and lathered his cheeks and neck with aerosol foam. He scraped the razor over his skin carefully, as this was a relatively new experience. Until recently, he'd never shaved his face, only trimming his beard and moustache to keep them neat.

At first he had cut himself often. Especially after the cosmetic surgery that had given his thirty-five-year-old face the loose skin and jowls of a much older man.

Of course, nowadays, more and more Muslim men were shaving. And there was an ongoing controversy as to whether or not shaving was forbidden or only *makruh*, undesirable. If shaving was wrong, he believed Allah would forgive him. He did it only to become a better warrior against the infidels. It was a small price to pay for an afterlife in Paradise.

He finished shaving and splashed water on his face, then patted it dry with a towel. The next step would be laser treatments to create a receding hairline. He ran long slender fingers though his bushy hair. Smooth, supple hands that belied the aged look of his face. They were unadorned by jewelry, but he knew the ring had already been made. It was identical to the wedding band Chief Justice Isaac Jacobs still wore, although his wife had died over a decade ago. He pulled on a shirt and walked down the hall.

"Rashid." Ziyad Al-Din greeted him when he entered the front room. "You are well?"

"Yes, Ziyad, very well indeed. And you?"

"The same." Ziyad took a moment to examine Rashid's face and head. "It is coming along nicely, although I believe we will have to use cosmetics to make you look as old as the infidel Jacobs."

"We still have several months. Perhaps it will not be necessary, but if it is, I will learn how to apply them so that no one will even suspect I am not the Chief Justice of the Supreme Court."

"Very good. You have been chosen for very special work for the glory of Allah."

Rashid shook his head. "I am merely fortunate enough to look somewhat like this man."

"Precisely. It is Allah's will. Why else would the Chief Justice Jacobs look so much like you?"

"I am truly blessed by Allah." Rashid smiled. "Are the plans coming together?"

"Oh, yes. Although we have other matters to attend to as well." Ziyad frowned.

"You appear worried." Rashid shook his head. "I do not know how you manage so many things at one time."

"It is sometimes difficult, but we must all do what we are called to do."

"There is a complication?"

"Not with your mission. That is going according to plan. But Mussad has brought another matter to our attention. A group that is bent on world domination much as the Americans are."

"What? How is this possible?"

Ziyad waved his hand in dismissal. "We will handle it. They are just some upstart group that believes they can create a world order where they are the rulers. They call themselves the Order. Mussad's father is one of them."

"That is a terrible burden for Mussad to bear. To know that his own father is an infidel."

"True." Ziyad nodded. "Fortunately for him, his mother returned to the true belief and raised him as a good Muslim."

"Allah trusts you to see that the world follows the word of the Prophet Mohammad."

"There are many of us to do his calling. You are also one of them."

"I give thanks that I have been chosen for such an honor. I pray to Allah that we are successful," Rashid said. "Our biggest challenge will be to make the switch."

"We are making the plans even now. It is only a matter of learning his ways; then we will find the perfect opportunity to take him and put you in his place."

"How far in advance will we do this?"

"Not far." Ziyad laughed and slapped Rashid's

shoulder. "We can't put you in the position of actually sitting on the Supreme Court. Although there is a certain humor in that."

Rashid smiled. He wouldn't mind sitting in Isaac Jacobs's place. He could hand down some judgments that would serve the infidel Americans well. But that was not his destiny.

His destiny was much greater than that.

‡ ‡ ‡

October 23, Florence, Italy

Drake Leatherman let his stubbled chin rest on his chest. His mouth hung open and a rivulet of saliva and blood trickled down his chin, but he didn't move. As long as they thought he was still unconscious, they'd leave him alone. At least for a few minutes. His shoulders ached from having his hands tied behind the back of the chair, and the six-inch gash they'd sliced into his arm burned. One eye was already swollen closed, and he thought a couple of teeth were loose.

"How's he doing?" Drake recognized the voice of Lieutenant Colonel Robertson again. That stung more than the physical damage they'd inflicted. Hank Robertson had led the Marine Force Recon team that Drake had served on for seven years. What the hell was he doing with the Order?

"He's not exactly cooperating."

"I'm not surprised. He's not your average agent," Robertson said. "Might want to step it up a bit. I'll be back soon."

Drake could hear Robertson's footsteps, then the faint swoosh of the door opening and closing. He brought up a mental picture of the room, trying to determine the best escape route if he got the chance. But the room boasted only one door and a single window too small to squeeze through. He hadn't heard the click of a lock when Robertson left, so at least that was a possibility.

"Yeah, I got something that'll loosen his tongue. Rico, bring me that pipe."

Drake heard the pipe clatter on the concrete floor and barely kept from reacting. How much more time could he buy before they started in on him again? Not that it mattered. In the end they'd just kill him. They'd killed the other agents. The best Drake could do was die without giving up any information. Unless they screwed up and gave him an opening.

One of the men kicked the leg of the chair he sat in. Drake cursed himself silently when his body jerked and his head lifted. He opened the eye that wasn't completely swollen shut and looked at the man.

"Good. You're awake."

"I must have dozed off earlier," Drake said. "How rude of me."

The man laughed. "You got a smart mouth, you know?" He picked up the pipe from the floor.

Drake smiled, even though it made his swollen lip crack and bleed again. "Wish I could say the same for you."

The man grunted and scowled at him. Good. Drake wanted to piss him off. An angry man made mistakes. And a mistake could be his ticket out.

"I don't think you're going to be laughing much longer." The man took a knife from the table and hauled Drake to his feet.

Drake didn't flinch when the man slipped the knife under his belt and cut through it. But when he sliced through his jeans and shorts, Drake's heart beat faster, his breath came in short, shallow gasps, and sweat beaded on his forehead. He concentrated on taking slow, deep breaths.

The man grabbed a handful of denim and cotton and ripped Drake's pants away from his body. He pushed Drake back into the chair and looked at Rico. "Go get it."

"Now?" Rico asked.

"I said to, didn't I? And give me the pipe."

"Sure, Mort." Rico handed him the two-foot-long pipe and moved to the back of the room.

Drake concentrated on his training and tried to ignore that Mort had exposed his crotch and he was defenseless with his hands tied behind him. Mort walked around the chair, slapping the pipe against his palm. He stopped in front of Drake and grimaced.

"Damn, I hate this part."

Drake gritted his teeth when Mort reached down and lifted his penis. He could hardly swallow, his mouth was so dry. Elevated blood pressure caused his staccato heartbeat to thrum in his ears and he forced himself to think. What were they doing? Cutting his dick off wouldn't get them what they wanted. He'd pass out from the pain, then die from the blood loss. He felt a flash of relief. They weren't going to castrate him. Probably.

Mort fitted one end of the pipe over Drake's penis, then shoved it so the three-inch-wide pipe was pressed painfully against his pubic bone.

Sweat beaded on Drake's scalp. He'd been trained to withstand torture. He knew what to do. How to think. How to get through it. But a silent scream of horror reverberated through him as he fought for equilibrium.

"Go ahead," Mort said to Rico.

Rico stepped around from behind the chair. His heavily gloved hand held a large squirming rat by its tail. Drake inhaled sharply, then forced his mind to detach. He looked at the situation logically, refusing to allow any emotional reaction. Rico would drop the rat into the pipe. The rat would find his penis and start chewing on it. At some point, he would lose consciousness from the pain. Drake wasn't a particularly religious man, but he closed his eyes and prayed that he'd be dead before he woke up again. He felt the pipe move and his eyes flew open. The rat was halfway inside the pipe.

"What the hell do you think you're doing?"

Drake jerked his head around at the sound of Robertson's voice.

"You said to step it up a bit." Mort shrugged. "This is how I step it up."

"Put that thing away," Robertson told Rico, then looked at Mort. "And get that pipe off him. When I said step it up, I didn't mean for you to maim him."

Drake watched as Rico moved to the back of the room where he'd left the rat's cage and Mort and Robertson walked to the wall opposite the door. The door Robertson had left open. It wasn't much of a chance. How far could he get with his hands tied behind his back? He didn't even know how many guards he might run into or if he'd be able to get out without encountering doors that required security codes or key cards. But his will to survive clamored for him to take the chance.

Drake took a deep breath and blew it out. Robertson and Mort were still talking. Rico was trying to get the rat back into the cage. He wasn't close enough to the door to try anything subtle. His only option was to make a run for it. It was a stupid idea. He'd never get away. There was no way he could run fast enough with his hands behind his back that they wouldn't catch him.

Still, he was going to try. He might get lucky. Maybe he'd find a place to hide until he could get his hands free.

Drake pushed himself to his feet and ran toward the open door. He made it across the threshold and half a dozen strides down the hallway before the pipe slammed into his shoulder. He turned against the pain just in time to see Mort swing the pipe again. His last thought was that Mort moved really fast for such a big guy.

When Drake woke, his feet were bound to the metal foot railing of a hospital bed, his wrists secured to the side rails. His jaw ached and he moved it cautiously and ran his tongue around his mouth, surprised that he wasn't missing any teeth.

He tried to pull against the restraints, but his shoulder burned and his legs felt weak. Why were they keeping him alive? He opened his eyes to a narrow white room that contained only a chair and the bed he occupied. Lieutenant Colonel Hank Robertson sat in the chair.

"They tell me that most men scream like an eight-year-old girl as soon as they see the rat." Robertson shook his head. "You didn't make a peep. Even when they put the rat in the pipe."

"Yeah, well, I was trained by the best." Drake tried to clear his mind. He didn't know why he was even still alive, and wondered what Robertson had to do with it. Who the hell knew? He'd been sent in to spy on the Order. But his cover had been blown and then Robertson had shown up. He hadn't seen the man since he'd left the Marines and nothing he knew about his former CO could explain his association with these people.

"You still think I'm the best after what you've been through here?" Robertson asked.

"Well, hell, you made Rico pull the rat out of the pipe before it got to me. I don't know how much more a man could ask from his CO."

Robertson shook his head. "I had no idea they were doing that to you. I'd never have let them start if I had."

"I appreciate that." Drake watched Robertson stand and pace across the room. What the hell was his former CO doing with the Order?

Robertson turned at the sound of Drake's voice.

"You can trust me on that." Robertson returned to the chair and leaned forward, resting his elbows on his knees. "I'll tell you everything I can and then you can decide what you want to do."

"Yes, sir." Drake deliberately let his voice take on the cadence and tone of a marine speaking to his CO.

"I'm a member of a group. We're working to make the world a better place."

"Sounds like something you'd get involved with. I remember in the Corps, you were always talking about each of us having an obligation to make the world better."

"This is different. I've been a member all my life, just like my father. And my grandfather. It's something that's been passed down in my family for generations, centuries."

Drake kept his features passive. But Robertson wasn't making any sense and his words confirmed Drake's belief that the man had undergone some fundamental change over the past few years. And Drake was putting the emphasis on *mental.*

"I can't tell you all of it. Besides, you wouldn't understand anyway. But these are good men. I know that's probably a little hard for you to believe right now, considering your recent experience."

"There is that," Drake agreed.

"We're called the Order. The leaders are men of vision. Of knowledge. And the time has come for us to help the world. To make a change. To make life better for every single person on the face of the earth."

Drake watched Robertson in fascination. His former commander sounded like he'd found Jesus or something. Robertson's eyes were lit with an inner fire as he talked, changing subjects frequently, rarely completing his thoughts.

Drake didn't understand most of what Robertson said. But he knew brainwashing when he saw it. He was stunned that his former CO would succumb to brainwashing. The man had been his leader and his mentor when Drake was in the Marine Force Recon. Robertson had trained him to endure pain and discomfort far beyond what he'd ever thought possible. Drake had learned perseverance, loyalty, and dedication from this man.

"So, do you understand how important this is?" Robertson asked him. "How this new energy will help everyone? And there's more than just the energy. A lot more. The Order will soon put an end to poverty and war. For the first time in history we'll live in peace. Permanent peace." Robertson smiled at him. "We could use your help, Leatherman."

"Me? How could I help? It sounds like the Order has everything under control." Drake knew he had to tread lightly. He focused on Robertson, trying to find a shred of the man he had once known.

"The Order is very close to some discoveries that will change the world. But we aren't quite there yet. And there are people, governments that would stop us." He shook his head. "Sadly, our own government would stop us if they could."

"Why would they want to stop you? I mean, it sounds like the Order knows what it's doing. Why would anyone not want an end to poverty and war?" Drake hoped Robertson believed he was buying this.

"The government is fucked up. You've known that since you were in Force Recon. I imagine you've seen even more evidence of it in the CIA."

"You got that right. Bureaucracy, red tape, every decision made by a committee. I'm amazed they ever get anything done."

"Exactly," Robertson said. "And governments are always afraid someone else will take over because they know what a lousy job they're doing."

"And you really believe the Order can change everything? They can come up with this energy source? Stop poverty and war? That would really be something."

"Absolutely. We're close, Leatherman. Real close."

"Then it'd be a shame if anyone stopped them." Drake watched Robertson closely for any sign that he didn't believe him. But Robertson nodded in agreement.

Drake realized that his former CO believed him because he wanted to. Just another sign that Robertson had been thoroughly brainwashed.

"That's where you come in."

"Me? I don't know what I could do."

"The CIA is investigating us." Robertson laughed. "Well, hell, you know that. They sent you here."

"Yeah. The world works in strange ways, doesn't it? I mean, who would have thought I'd run into you like this?"

"Yeah, it's weird, all right. But we worked together real good back in the Marines."

"*Semper fi.*" Always faithful.

"*Semper fi*," Robertson answered. "The Order wants to know what the CIA learns about us. We need someone inside who can get that information to us."

"I see. And that's where I come in?"

"That's what I'd like to happen."

"I don't know. I'm not real comfortable with spying on my own country. I mean, I know the U.S. has some faults, but . . ." He almost held his breath waiting for Robertson to answer. He couldn't appear too eager, but he needed to make Robertson think he was convinced. He knew for sure that his life depended on it.

"I understand and I wouldn't expect any less of you. Hell, I'd be pissed if you caved so easily." Robertson stood and paced across the room again. "I'd never ask you to spy on our country. It's not like that. The only thing I want you to do is let me know what the CIA discovers about us. I wouldn't ask you if I didn't believe it was in the best interest of America. In the best interest of the world. I believe in the Order. We're doing the right thing for the world."

"You make a strong argument, sir."

"I'd like to fix this so you can get back home." Robertson opened the door and turned back to Drake. "Think about it tonight. We'll talk again."

Drake heard the dead bolt slide into place, then muffled voices from the other side of the door.

"You sure you can trust him?"

"I'm sure," Robertson said. "But we don't have to rely on that. We have someone in place who'll let us know if he turns."

2

October 29, German Embassy, Washington, D.C.

Zoe took a champagne flute from a passing waiter and pretended to sip from it while she cased the room. From her position next to a ficus tree, she counted five senators, a dozen congressmen, three Oscar-winning actors, and a rock star with her newest boyfriend. It was an impressive turnout, and the German Embassy knew that the presence of the politicians and stars would ensure coverage in the major newspapers and magazines.

The room twinkled with the flash of jewelry and candlelight; buzzed with the hum of gossip and politics. Chamber music floated through the main ballroom, and tuxedoed waiters moved unobtrusively through the crowd with trays of wine, champagne, and hors d'oeuvres. Guests who preferred hard liquor were served their drinks from the multiple bars placed in various corners of several rooms. The Germany Embassy had made sure everything was perfect.

The small cubic zirconia–studded watch on Zoe's wrist showed nine thirty, and she turned her attention to the wide, sweeping stairway. Precisely on schedule, Honoria Bueller appeared at the top of the stairway on the arm of her husband, Ambassador Heinrich Bueller. Zoe walked toward the rear door of the ballroom, keeping her pace fast enough to discourage anyone from approaching, but not so fast to draw attention. Her eyes focused on a point across the room, lips curved in a smile. Anyone watching would assume she was crossing the enormous ballroom to greet someone.

The fact that she'd done this a hundred times before didn't stop the adrenaline from rushing into her system. She could almost feel the blood pumping into her arms and legs. Her vision seemed sharper as she swept her eyes across the ballroom lit with multitudes of candles and sparkling crystal chandeliers. Her heart thumped a few beats faster than normal and she deliberately slowed her breathing, trying to control it. It was a scary feeling and she liked the intensity. It was better than chocolate. Better than sex—sometimes. Hell, it was probably addictive.

At the far end of the ballroom, she paused at a set of heavily draped French doors and looked back at the room. The guests were turned toward the stairway as the ambassador and his wife welcomed them to the anniversary party. Zoe pushed the doors open and slipped to the other side, closing them quickly and softly behind her. The wide hallway leading to the kitchen was empty, all the kitchen help currently occupied with preparations for the buffet dinner that would be served later in the evening.

She entered the third door on the left, one of three coed restrooms used by the kitchen staff and servers. Setting her champagne glass on the vanity, she lifted the skirt of her heavy satin gown, pulled a slim plastic rectangle from a holder strapped to her left thigh and opened the door a crack. The hallway remained empty as she slipped the cord of the sign over the doorknob. *Out of Service.* That should keep anyone from knocking at the door and wondering why there was no answer.

She flipped the lock to the on position, unzipped the high-necked, long-sleeved gold satin gown and stepped out of it, revealing a beige bodysuit. After hanging the gown over a hook on the door, she pulled off her rings, watch, and fake diamond necklace, placing them on the vanity. The long, heavy wig landed in the sink and she made sure the nylon cap covering her own red curls was secure.

A flat nylon pouch on her left thigh yielded latex gloves. From an identical pouch on the right thigh, she pulled out a dust mask and placed it over her nose and mouth. She snapped the gloves on and climbed onto the lid of the toilet tank.

The ventilation duct cover came off with a couple of tugs. Zoe laid the vent on the vanity and braced her gloved hands on the inside of the duct. She blew out a breath and hoisted her weight onto her arms, lifting her torso into the duct and tucking her knees tight to her chest. Her legs shot out and landed her butt just on the edge of the duct.

The plans she'd been given showed that the duct traveled along one wall of the kitchen to the rear of the building, then joined a vertical duct that led to the second floor. She crawled along the duct, glancing into the kitchen through the regularly spaced vents. When she reached the vertical duct, she braced her back and feet against opposite sides and inched her way to the second floor of the embassy. She paused for a moment, her breath coming hard from the effort, then crawled down the connecting duct past several guest rooms.

The occupants of the second room had evidently elected to spend their evening pursuing personal pleasure rather than attending the anniversary celebration. Stopping at the fourth vent, she took a moment to check out the large guest suite through the ventilation grate. Empty. Just as it should be. She pressed her fingers through the vent cover and pushed it out.

The cover stuck for a moment, then gave, almost slipping through her fingers. Zoe swore under her breath and tightened her grip on the grate, carefully lowering it to the leather love seat under the opening. She scooted forward and leaned out into the bedroom of a two-room suite.

The guests of the ambassador were treated to excellent accommodations. The spacious room boasted a king-sized four-poster bed and triple dresser made of carved, nut brown oak. Solid wood from the look of it. No cheap veneer for the German Embassy. She pulled back inside the duct, squirmed around, and backed out, dropping silently to the love seat.

The only light in the bedroom came from a bedside lamp, but it was enough. She moved cautiously to the double doors that led to the sitting room and opened one door a few inches. Dark and quiet. She pulled the door almost closed and turned her attention to the wall with the Mathias Grünewald painting. It was an original, worth thousands. She ran her fingers over the painting, then pulled her hand back. She wasn't here for it.

Zoe swung the painting away from the wall, looked at the ornate twenty-carat gold *R* on the dial, and grinned. A Remington double-walled safe with a group two combination lock.

Not bad. Better than most personal safes.

Zoe took a breath and blew it out, then lightly touched the black dial with her fingertips. She twirled the dial until she felt the first click. Then she turned it slowly in the opposite direction. Another click. She continued picking up the wheels, her fingers telling her when the drive cam sent the drive pin into contact with the wheel fly. The wheels and notches lined up to let the fence fall. The bolt slid free and Zoe swung the door open.

Velvet jewelry cases were stacked inside along with a sheaf of papers and a wad of cash. She pushed the cash and papers aside and pulled out the jewelry boxes. Ethan had been specific. Rubies, diamonds, and emeralds—only the most valuable jewels. Zoe dropped the appropriate necklaces, bracelets, and earrings into the pouch strapped to her thigh, tossing the less expensive pieces back into the safe.

The last velvet box held a simple platinum chain with a small cross on it. A nice piece, but nothing a self-respecting thief would take.

Just a little something for herself.

Zoe's fingers twitched and a surge of desire pulsed through her body. She'd felt that desire before. Often. And she'd given in to it.

Not tonight. She snapped the case closed and tossed it back inside the safe.

Zoe repeated her actions in the other six guest rooms, then headed back through the ventilation system to the bathroom. Less than an hour had passed since she'd started. She replaced the vent cover, stripped off the latex gloves, and looked at her image in the mirror.

She was covered in dust from the ventilation ducts. Hair, face, and bodysuit. She washed her hands and used damp paper towels to remove the dust from her face and bodysuit. She pulled the wig on over her hair, replaced the rings, watch, and choker, and stepped into her satin gown. Now all she had to do was leave the party, drop the jewels off with Shelby, go home, and hope that the Order took the bait. She hurried down the hall and opened the French doors.

"I beg your pardon," Zoe said as the door to the ballroom bumped against someone. Great. Mrs. Weston-Smyth. Three hundred people at this little soiree, and she had to bump into one of the few she'd actually talked to, just as she needed to make her escape. The woman had cornered her earlier in the evening and asked penetrating questions about Zoe's background. She'd lied, of course.

"Oh, there you are, dear. I was just telling Logan that I wanted to introduce you two."

"Really?" Zoe asked with a bright smile.

Mrs. Weston-Smyth leaned toward Zoe and placed a gloved hand, heavy with jewels, on her arm. "Logan was educated in Switzerland, too. I thought you two would have a lot in common." She gestured toward Logan. "Logan Forrester, Zoe Alexander."

Zoe offered him her hand and gave him a polite smile. Logan was the kind of handsome that usually indicated a lousy personality. Taller than average height, wavy brown hair streaked with gold, dark green eyes. His tux hung from broad shoulders and skimmed over a lean, muscular frame. He smiled and she couldn't help grinning back. She liked handsome men.

But this was a bad time.

"Where did you come from?" he asked.

Zoe leaned forward a little and lowered her voice. "I was looking for the ladies' room and got lost."

"I see." He grinned and reached out to brush his fingers against her neck. "There's dirt on your neck."

Zoe's mouth went dry. She wasn't sure if it was from his touch or that he'd noticed the dirt she'd missed. "I opened a utility closet by mistake and a feather duster fell on me."

"I see. Your name sounds incredibly familiar to me. Have we met before?"

"I'm sure I would remember if we had."

"Come along, they're serving dinner soon." Mrs. Weston-Smyth waved them toward the far end of the ballroom.

"Of course. May I escort you lovely ladies to the dining room?" Logan held out an arm to each woman.

"I'm sorry, I can't stay for dinner. I have another engagement." Zoe affected an apologetic look.

"What a shame," he murmured.

"Oh, dear." Mrs. Weston-Smyth shook her head. "But I understand. When I was your age, I often had several engagements in one evening."

"It was so nice meeting you both. I hope we'll run into each other again." Like hell, she did.

"Oh, now I remember," Logan said.

Zoe turned and looked at him, her face a frozen mask of casual inquisition.

"But it was a man's name that I recalled. Zeke Alexander. Any relation?"

"I really must run or I'll be late. Good night, Mrs. Weston-Smyth." Zoe nodded to Logan. "Good evening."

She moved through the crowded reception hall smiling and nodding, sneaking a glance down to make sure none of the stuff strapped to her thighs was noticeable under the stiff satin gown. The coat check retrieved her velvet stole, and she slipped out the door and into the waiting limo.

Throwing the stole onto the seat, she scrunched up her skirt, ripped off the pouch strapped to her thigh, and tossed it to Shelby.

"There!"

Ethan had asked Shelby to work out of Langley as Zoe's handler since the CIA was involved in the op. Zoe had been more than a little pleased when her boss had agreed. The stealing was no big deal, but the spy stuff was scary, and she couldn't think of anyone she'd rather have telling her what to do.

"Well done, Zoe." Shelby opened the pouch and pulled the jewels out.

"Where's my bag?"

"It's in the trunk," Shelby answered, still examining the gems.

"Hey!" Zoe banged the heel of her palm on the window separating them from the driver. Shelby grimaced and pressed a button to lower the window.

"Stop the car and open the trunk," she instructed the driver. The car slowed and pulled over to the curb. Zoe jumped out, grabbed her bag from the trunk, and slammed the lid. She was unzipping the bag when she got back in the car.

"Really, Zoe, are you always this way after a job?"

"It's the hormonal cascade," Zoe explained to her boss as she rummaged in the bag and pulled out a giant-sized candy bar. "You know, there's the adrenaline rush from the fight-or-flight response to the possibility of getting caught. Then you don't get caught and you have all that adrenaline still in your system. The sugar helps."

"All that chocolate can't be good for you." Shelby wrinkled her nose and dropped the jewels back into the pouch.

"What are you going to do with those?"

"They'll go to a fence who's about to get out of the business."

"Willingly?" Zoe asked.

Shelby laughed. "He was recently found in possession of some rather valuable merchandise. In return for this favor and some information, he gets to spend his golden years in a cozy cottage on the coast of Maine rather than in a prison cell."

"I see. So the word gets out that I snagged the jewels, the fence gets caught with them, everyone gets their valuables back, the fence doesn't go to jail, and everyone's happy."

"It's a sweet deal any way you look at it. So, how did it go tonight?"

"This was really an easy job. I could have done it when I was ten." Zoe frowned in thought. "Actually, I think I did one similar to this around that age."

"It only seems easy to you. To anyone else, it's a big job that you pulled off flawlessly. It'll go a long way to establishing your reputation as a thief."

Her reputation as a thief. Something she'd spent her youth developing and several years eliminating. Her father had tutored her from the age of eight. Or maybe it had been earlier. Six? Five?

She'd accompanied him on her first real job when she was nine. It seemed like a game and the prize for pleasing her father was his attention. Even when Nana

Phoebe had tried to convince her that stealing was wrong, she'd stayed on with her father until he took on an apprentice. A young man who was just about the age her brother would have been had he lived. That's when she knew beyond any doubt that she'd never be good enough for her father. Ever. Because she'd never be his *son*.

After her brief retirement, it was necessary to convince the thieving community that Zoe, the heir apparent to Zeke Alexander, was again active. And that she was as good as she'd ever been. Maybe better.

The weird part was that Zoe could now do the only thing she'd ever been really good at. And she could do it legally. For the government. What a hoot.

"Shelby, do you know anything about Logan Forrester?"

"How do you know Logan Forrester?"

"I hate it when you answer my question with another question. Who is he?"

"Did you meet him tonight?" Shelby asked.

"You're doing it again."

"Did he approach you? What did he want?"

She crossed her arms over her chest and turned to look out her window.

"Crap." Shelby sighed. "Logan Forrester worked with the NSA as a cryptanalyst until a few weeks ago."

"Cryptanalyst? You mean he decodes stuff?"

"Forrester is one of the best. Actually, he *is* the best. He started in the CIA, got through the basic training for field agents at The Farm, and then they discovered his uncanny ability with codes. He was moved to the NSA and quickly became their top cryptanalyst."

"And he's left the NSA? Why?"

"Just up and quit. Said he was taking a job with some computer company for a lot more money. But when his supervisor at the NSA tried to reach him at the new job, he was told that Logan wouldn't be starting the job for another few months. Then his name turned up in connection with the Order."

"That figures," Zoe said.

"How did you meet Forrester?"

"Mrs. Weston-Smyth introduced us. I think she was trying to be a matchmaker." Zoe's stomach twisted remembering his parting question. "He mentioned my father. Wanted to know if we were related."

"Did you deny it?" Shelby frowned.

"I didn't answer either way. It kind of threw me. At first I figured if he was asking about my dad, then I should admit to it. Then I thought that if I jumped at it, he'd think something was wrong. I mean, if I'm really a thief, I wouldn't be too eager to admit who I am right after pulling a job."

"Good."

"Was this planned?"

"For you to meet him? No, not at all." Shelby shrugged. "We believed the Order would have someone at the event tonight. That's why we sent you in to steal the jewels. It was just luck that Forrester approached you."

"What else have you found out about them?"

"What do you know about cold fusion?"

"That it's an impossibility," Zoe said.

"That's not precisely true; it's just never been done on a consistent basis. There are problems with stability and consistency."

Zoe sighed. "I understand that. I just meant that most scientists consider it impossible because of those issues."

"Cold fusion would be an incredible breakthrough. Ideally, it would provide inexpensive energy with no pollution."

"Sounds like a good thing so far. I'm all for it."

"Unless it's developed by the wrong people." Shelby stared out the dark-tinted window for a moment. "In the wrong hands, cold fusion would be a powerful weapon. Countries wanting to get out from under the control of the oil cartels would be eager to buy it."

"So, they'd be buying cold fusion instead of oil." That didn't seem to be a really big issue to her. In fact, considering the price of gas, wouldn't that be a *good* thing?

"It's complicated. They could quickly amass trillions of dollars."

"And with the combination of endless energy and unlimited funds they could become a power to be reckoned with?" Okay, now it wasn't sounding so good to Zoe.

"That's the general idea. Basically, they could hold governments hostage."

"You mean they could hold *our* government hostage. So, that's what the Order is doing?"

"We think that's part of it. We don't know what their agenda is or who's in control of the organization. We don't know a lot about them. We certainly don't know enough."

"Has Ethan sent an agent in? I mean, that's what he usually does, right?" Zoe asked.

"This actually isn't an FSA issue. Well, partly it's FSA, but the CIA is involved, too. And the CIA sent several agents in. Unfortunately that hasn't worked."

"Hasn't worked? As in the agents weren't able to infiltrate the Order, or as in the agents weren't able to get back to the CIA?"

"We've lost all the agents we've sent in but one. He returned in pretty bad shape."

Zoe wrapped the uneaten portion of her candy bar

in the wrapper and tossed it in her bag. "So, what *do* you know about them?"

Shelby pulled a photograph from an envelope and handed it to her, flicking on the overhead light. The photo showed three men in business suits walking toward a limo. The black-and-white photo was grainy, and the features of the men weren't discernible. She certainly couldn't have picked any of them out of a crowd.

"We believe those three men are the top echelon of the Order. The Triumvirate. Our intel is that they're locating and obtaining certain documents from around the world."

"Documents that make cold fusion possible?"

"That's what we believe."

"Maybe you should start at the beginning."

"It's a long, complex story."

"We've got a long drive." Zoe shrugged.

"You're not too tired for a briefing?"

"No way. I'm always wide awake after a job."

Shelby nodded and leaned back. "An Italian physicist, Giovanni Castiglia, has been missing for almost a year. In spite of the fact that he's been known to disappear into his work before, we believe this is different."

"You think the Order took him?"

"It's possible. Castiglia is brilliant. He studied with Albert Einstein when he was young. But more important, Castiglia is Forrester's great-uncle."

"What did he do when his uncle disappeared?"

"Nothing. He didn't report it to the authorities, never even mentioned it to anyone at all."

"So, you think he knows where his uncle is?"

"Possibly. He might have not reported it because he knew his security clearance would be yanked. The government can't afford to have an employee with a high security clearance vulnerable to demands from kidnappers."

"So, did Forrester leave the NSA to find his uncle or was he in on the disappearance?"

"We have no idea."

"But you still think his disappearance is connected with the Order?"

"There's been a rumor about a group of physicists who have worked on different theories for years. These physicists would take on younger scientists and mentor them, eventually passing along all the information they had acquired and developed."

"Like an apprenticeship of sorts."

"It was never publicized because their theories went against what most physicists believed. They basically worked in secret. A massive amount of information was supposedly developed and hidden."

"Where is all this information?" Zoe asked.

"We don't know. It could be anywhere."

"But if this information is really old, what use

would it be? Cold fusion has only been a concept since the early twentieth century."

Shelby raised her eyebrows. "You've researched cold fusion?"

"Not really. I just read a lot. I remember that from somewhere."

"We don't know what's in the documents. It's possible that there's something in the older documents that doesn't pertain to cold fusion but could lead to a method to make it stable and predictable."

"I see. So, this old information combined with newer information, like quantum physics or quantum mechanics, could be a breakthrough?"

"It's possible," Shelby said.

"So, why hasn't someone in this secret society of physicists collected all this data before now?"

"The whole secret society theory is just that. A theory. There's no proof that it ever existed and if it did, it probably fell apart a long time ago." Shelby stretched and settled back again. "Which means the documents could be anywhere. And that whoever has them might not have a clue as to what they are."

"And you think someone has figured it out?"

"The little information we've gotten indicates that to be true. Castiglia has always been a progressive thinker. He's worked on some pretty wild theories. He might be just the physicist they need to put it all together."

"How do they know where the documents are?'

"We don't know that either. If we did, we'd just steal the documents before they did."

"So, that's why the Order is looking for a thief."

"We believe the Order has already gotten some of the documents. But it stands to reason that some of them will be in places with security they can't deal with."

"So, who's been stealing the documents for them?"

Shelby pulled another photo out of the envelope. "Forrester. His basic training in the CIA would have been enough for him to do some of it."

Zoe took the picture and looked at it. Forrester wore a suit and tie along with a stiff expression. Looked like it was probably the photo from his NSA file.

"That's him, all right." She handed the photo back.

"We arranged for your theft to be discovered shortly after you left tonight. Forrester should put two and two together and come to the conclusion that you were the thief. The fact that he asked about your father is a good sign that he's on the trail."

"And then what do we do?"

"At this point, we're just playing it by ear. We need to be really careful."

"Maybe, but careful doesn't always get you what you want. Or need."

"You aren't a real agent, Zoe."

"I know. But I'm a real thief. And that's what they want."

"Zoe, you've got to play this by the book. You need to do what I tell you to do. No deviations, no winging it, no having any good ideas of your own."

"Absolutely. By the book."

She didn't say whose book.

‡‡‡

October 30, Outside Bethesda, Maryland

"Halt!"

Zoe froze in place, one foot lifted off the floor, arms stretched out to her sides for balance. What had she done wrong now? She glanced across the training room at her father. Zeke Alexander leaned against the wall, arms crossed over his chest, shaking his head in what she assumed to be disappointment at her lackluster performance.

"You have to be conscious of every part of your body." He pushed off the wall with a graceful ease a ballerina would have envied. "Use the spray before you trip one of the lasers."

She shouldn't have had to use the spray again so soon. The idea was to spray the aerosol, which illuminated the otherwise invisible laser beams, then to move around, under, and over the beams from memorizing where they were located. The more she could memorize, the farther she could travel before she had to stop to use the spray again. Zoe hadn't traveled more than two feet since the last spray.

She sprayed the aerosol into the air in front of her and grimaced when the fog revealed a laser beam right where she'd been about to step. She concentrated on the pattern of laser beams her father had set up and moved across the rest of the space without hitting any of them, using the aerosol only twice more.

"You aren't concentrating, Zoe." Zeke flipped off the lasers and walked across the floor to take the aerosol can from her. "What's the problem?"

She padded over to a table and opened a bottle of water without answering. She knew exactly what the problem was. She couldn't stop thinking about the Order. She'd have to be at the top of her form in order to steal for them and find out what they were up to at the same time. That meant total concentration. Which was exactly what she hadn't had during the exercise she'd just completed. Naturally, her father noticed. He noticed everything.

"You never should have left the business," her father

said, walking across the room. Slender and fit, the only sign of his fifty-six years were a few laugh lines around his eyes and a shock of silver hair. Zoe had no doubt that he'd gone prematurely gray from his occupation.

"I wanted out." She turned to look at him. "I didn't want to live that life anymore."

"But you're doing it now."

"I'm working for the government now." She didn't have a problem with stealing. Never had. But she knew that's what her father would assume she meant. He'd never think that she had stopped because she'd realized that she'd never be good enough for him. She wasn't in the mood to enlighten him.

Zeke shrugged. "I don't see that much difference. It's still stealing."

"It's legal. And it's not about the stealing. It's about protecting my country. It's about doing the right thing."

"I don't like it, Zoe." He shook his head. "You're a thief, not a spy. What's Shelby thinking?"

"It was my idea, Dad. I volunteered."

"They're lucky. You're a good thief. Petite, powerful, intelligent." He grinned at her, then shrugged. "Intelligent most of the time. And look at you. You're beautiful just like your mother. Except for your eyes. Damn if I know where you got those gold eyes from."

"I told you, Dad. It's a recessive gene." Why had

she thought it would be a good idea to have her father train her? Because he'd been the best in his time. There still wasn't a thief who could do half of what he'd done in his career. Except for her. And Ethan and Shelby thought it would lend credence to her getting back into the business again.

"Are we done here?" Zoe asked.

"For today, yes." He nodded. "But, Zoe, if you're going to do it, you should put in more time. Practice everything until it's second nature."

He was right. Working for the Order, she'd be stealing from places where Shelby and Ethan couldn't protect her if she was caught.

There would be no safety net.

3

November 3, New York City, New York

"It's a mistake," Logan said after a moment of consideration. "You need the best." He leaned over the table and thumped the stack of papers. Background information that had been compiled on a variety of thieves. "Those guys aren't it."

"They have assured me they are capable." Karl Weisbaum stood at the window of the Trump Tower apartment that faced Fifth Avenue.

Logan considered Weisbaum's back for a moment. Tall and distinguished in an elegant and expensive suit, he looked like the international businessman he professed to be. But there was an edge to him that Logan interpreted as dangerous. Much more so than the other two members of the Triumvirate who ran the Order. Axel von Bayem and Pierre Simitiere sat across the room watching, their eyes and expressions unreadable. Logan suppressed a shudder at the power these three men wielded.

"If they were capable thieves, then why have they all done time for burglary? They were caught once; it could happen again." Logan shook his head. "I thought you were serious about this. Maybe I was wrong."

"Don't be stupid, Logan." Weisbaum turned back from the glass wall that looked out over midtown Manhattan. "We must have the items. You know that."

"Indeed I do," Logan agreed. "Which is why I don't understand using second-rate help to get them."

"What do you suggest, then?" von Bayem asked in a slightly accented rumble as he pushed his bulky frame from the sofa and walked to the small bar. "Is there someone you'd recommend?" He splashed vodka into a cut crystal glass and turned back to Logan.

"There's only one person who can do all of these jobs and not get caught." Logan rose from the leather chair. "Zoe Alexander."

"Zeke Alexander has been out of the business for almost five years. Besides, he's getting too old." Weisbaum waved a manicured hand in dismissal.

"He was the first one we thought of," Simitiere agreed. "Too bad he's not available."

"I'm not talking about Zeke," Logan corrected them. "His daughter, Zoe."

Weisbaum frowned. "I heard that she left the

business a while back."

"Besides, she's just a girl," von Bayem protested.

"Well, she's back in it," Logan said, ignoring von Bayem. "I attended a ball at the German Embassy a couple of days ago. Zoe Alexander was there and shortly after she left, a theft was discovered."

"Really? Did she take the silver or something?" von Bayem laughed.

"More like half a million in jewelry." Logan kept his eyes on Weisbaum. "From state-of-the-art safes in rooms in the well-protected guest quarters."

"So, she was a guest of the embassy." Weisbaum shrugged. "That doesn't mean she did the theft."

"She wasn't on the guest list. And none of the guests had ever heard of her, so she didn't come with anyone." Logan paused. "She was there for one reason."

"She might be worth considering," Weisbaum said.

"I don't know. Can she be trusted?" Simitiere asked.

Von Bayem snorted. "Can any thief be trusted? Once word gets out what we're looking for, everyone and his cousin will be after it." He slugged down a gulp of vodka. "I still think you should be doing this."

Logan sighed. "I told you, I'm not good enough. Not for these jobs."

"You got the first of the documents without a problem," von Bayem pointed out.

"Sure. Those were easy. Breaking into homes with practically no security." Logan shrugged. "But now we're looking at museums, laboratories. These are places with sophisticated security systems. It's far beyond my capabilities."

"Come on, Logan. You were trained as a CIA agent. You expect us to believe you can't do this?" Von Bayem laughed and shook his closely cropped head.

"I told you. I only went through the general field training at the CIA. I worked at a desk until I moved to the NSA. I'm a much better cryptanalyst than an agent. Or a thief."

"You better be a good cryptanalyst. Otherwise, we won't have any need for you." Von Bayem grinned and it looked truly evil to Logan.

"I'm the best. If I can't decode the documents, no one can," he assured them and hoped it was true.

"I'm not worried about her being involved," Weisbaum said, ignoring the exchange between von Bayem and Logan. "We can keep her in the dark as to the importance of what she's stealing. Besides, my guess is that she steals purely for monetary gain. I doubt she'd be interested in why we want the items."

"Exactly," Logan agreed.

"But will she be willing to do it? After all, she

just pulled a big job. She's set for a while, I'd think." Weisbaum turned back to the glass wall.

"Oh, she'll want the work. My sources tell me that the jewels were found with a fence. He hadn't even broken them down yet, so it's unlikely that she's gotten any money from them. My guess is that she's planning another job already."

"How do we contact her?" Weisbaum asked.

"You won't find her number listed in the phone book." Logan chuckled, earning frowns from all three men.

"I assume you have a way of getting in touch with her?" Weisbaum asked.

"There's a benefit gala being held this weekend at the Friedlander Museum to celebrate the opening of an exhibit of Japanese artifacts from the Heian period."

"The Friedlander has an excellent security system," Weisbaum said.

"Yes," Logan agreed. "But most of it is concentrated on keeping thieves out of the museum. The benefit gala would provide an excellent opportunity for her."

"You think she'll be there?"

Logan nodded.

"Then make sure you're there as well," Weisbaum instructed. "Find out how much she wants for what we need done."

"I'm trying to find her beforehand, but if I don't,

I'll be at the gala. I'll call you on Sunday."

"No." Weisbaum shook his head. "We'll be in Europe until Tuesday. I'll get in touch with you."

Logan shrugged, his expression carefully passive. "Whatever." He wondered where in Europe they would be, because he was certain that's where they had his uncle, Giovanni Castiglia.

‡ ‡ ‡

"I knew he was the one. He had to be. All the signs were there." Capo stepped out of the shadows of the hallway.

"Christ! I wish you wouldn't do that." Simitiere glared and picked up the cigarette he'd dropped. "Can't you just enter a room like a normal person?"

Weisbaum flinched at the sound of Capo's voice but recovered smoothly. Von Beyam took his drink and sank into the leather sofa.

Capo was no longer surprised by the three men. He'd worked with them long enough to know their every reaction. Yet they rarely were able to predict his. They should have known that he'd be listening. After all, it was Logan. One of the chosen, an important part of the Legacy. Capo had explained that to them often enough. He spared a brief moment to regret that

Logan hadn't been properly prepared. But everything happened for a reason. This was only a part of it. He had to believe that Logan wasn't intended to be prepared. Everything was a part of the Legacy.

The Triumvirate he'd appointed didn't understand the Legacy completely. Even though they'd been prepared by their fathers and had grown up knowing about the Legacy and what it meant. They didn't understand that every single piece had to fall into place. But they were learning. He'd be patient with them for now. It seemed that he alone was able to see the overall picture. None of the others had even recognized that this was the time. None of them had been able to locate the Legacy document. After generations of waiting, this was the time for the Legacy to come into power. To save the world.

"This woman, this thief. She's an important part of the equation," Capo said.

"How do you know that?" von Bayem asked. "You get a vision or something?"

Capo turned slowly. "Do I detect a note of cynicism, Axel?" He smiled and lifted a hand to still the response. "No, I understand your reluctance to believe. Sometimes the father fails to properly prepare the son."

"No, Capo." Von Bayem's hand ran across his close-cropped hair, then patted the top of his head in a familiar gesture. "It's not that. Just my smart-ass mouth. I didn't mean anything by it."

"I understand." Capo turned to Weisbaum. "See that we enlist her services."

"What if Logan can't contact her?" Weisbaum asked.

"Oh, he will. I have no doubt of that. Logan will do whatever is necessary." He turned back toward the hallway. "I need more sleep. These transatlantic flights exhaust me. When do we leave for Italy?"

Weisbaum checked his watch. "In six hours, Capo."

"Good. I need to get back to the lab." There was so much to do, so much to take care of. *All in good time*, he reminded himself. This had been waiting centuries.

‡ ‡ ‡

November 5, Outside Bethesda, Maryland

"You are one tough woman to get a hold of."

A shiver of excitement skittered up Zoe's spine when she heard Logan's soft, masculine voice on her phone. "Maybe that's because I don't want to be gotten a hold of," she replied smoothly.

"I wanted to tell you how much I admired your work at the German Embassy."

"You're mistaken. I don't work at the German Embassy."

He laughed softly. "Well, not officially, of course. I'm speaking of your work at the ball last week. Very impressive."

"I have no idea what you're talking about. In fact, I have no idea who you are." She pressed the *off* button and laid the phone down. It rang in five seconds. She waited until the fourth ring before picking it up. "What?"

"I have an offer for you."

"Not interested."

"You haven't heard it yet," he argued.

"Whatever it is, Mr. Forrester, I can assure you I'm not interested."

"Ah, so you remember me?"

"Of course, I remember you. However, believe me, you have nothing to offer that I'd be interested in."

"I beg to differ."

"I like it when men beg, but it won't change anything."

"You won't even listen to the offer?"

Zoe sighed, making sure he could hear her. "Fine, I'll listen, if it'll get you off my phone."

"I'm in business with some people who need some items procured."

She said nothing.

"I'm convinced you're the one who can procure these items."

"Not interested," she said.

"How much would you want?"

"I said I'm not interested."

"I heard that. But everyone has a price. What's yours?"

"You don't seem to understand, Mr. Forrester. I work alone. By myself, for myself. I'm not interested in work for hire."

"Not even for a million?"

Zoe hesitated, as she'd planned to do when money was offered. Not being prepared to hear that number made it easy.

"How long does it take you to steal enough to make a million dollars?"

"I don't think that's any of your business. I don't do work for hire. Under any circumstances. You need to find someone else."

It was his turn to sigh and he did a good job of it. "Fine. Forget I asked. But how about dinner Saturday night?"

Just the opening she'd been hoping for. "Sorry, I have a benefit gala to attend in New York on Saturday night."

"A gala? Sounds interesting. I don't suppose you'd like an escort?"

"It's not that kind of evening for me."

"Ah, work then. I certainly understand."

"If there's nothing else, Mr. Forrester, I really have to go."

"Of course. Maybe we'll run into each other again."

"Highly unlikely," she said.

"Still, you never know."

"Good-bye, Mr. Forrester." She hung up the phone and waited five minutes, but it didn't ring again. She picked it up and punched in Shelby's number.

"You were right," Zoe said when Shelby answered.

"Forrester contacted you."

"Just a few minutes ago. I told him no, and alluded to the gala I'll be attending on Saturday night."

"Are you really sure about this, Zoe? It's not too late to back out. The FSA or CIA could send in a seasoned agent," Shelby suggested.

"They don't have an agent who can do what I can do. It won't work."

"You could train them."

"Shelby, it takes years. I can't train an agent to be a thief in a few weeks. Dad trained me for four years before I ever did my first job."

"Fine, you're right, I suppose. What if Logan doesn't show?"

"He'll show. He sounded desperate."

"And how are you going to get him to make you another offer?"

"Easy. I'm going to let him rescue me."

‡ ‡ ‡

November 7, New York City, New York

Zoe pulled on a dark blue bodysuit and regarded herself in the mirrored closet door of her suite in the St. Regis Hotel. Her back was bare to her waist except for several thin cords that crisscrossed over it. She pulled on the sheer kimono-style jacket and turned to check out her rear view in the mirrored closet doors. The diaphanous Japanese print swirled about her calves and did nothing to hide her body. She slipped her feet into flat ballerina slippers, momentarily regretting that she couldn't wear the kind of heels that would make the outfit even more stunning. But she knew exactly what she would be doing tonight, and heels were out of the question. The salon had twisted her red hair into a French braid, leaving a few wisps to curl around her face. The cosmetician had applied creams, powders, and pencils until she barely recognized her own face.

She picked up the specially constructed bamboo purse and pressed a fingernail into the recessed slot under the handle. A slender drawer slid smoothly out of the bottom of the purse. All for looks tonight. The only thing she'd be snagging was Logan's attention. The phone rang and she answered it to hear the concierge say that her limo had arrived. If it wasn't for dealing with the Order, she could get used to this lifestyle. She thanked the concierge and headed to the lobby.

Fifteen minutes later Zoe slipped into the elegant crowd in the main room of the Friedlander Museum and looked for Logan. She moved from room to room, pretending to view the displays, but after almost an hour of mingling she still hadn't spotted him. The sparkly spandex was starting to itch; the pile of make-up felt heavy on her face. She felt the beginnings of a frustration she associated with failure.

"I hope whatever you're stealing is really small if you plan to hide it somewhere in that outfit."

Logan's breath whispered across the back of her neck, and the hairs on her arms stood up. The frustration eased. Her quarry had arrived.

"What makes you think I'm here to steal something?"

"I see." Logan moved to stand beside her. "So, it's merely a coincidence that an internationally known thief is attending an exhibit of priceless Japanese artifacts?"

"Internationally known?"

Logan grinned. "Well, not by the general public,

of course, but certainly the major law enforcement agencies."

"Wouldn't it be foolish for such a well-known thief to attend a function and then commit a theft?"

"Foolish?" He shrugged. "Perhaps. Or daring."

"There's another term for a daring thief."

"What's that?"

"Convicted felon." She turned her attention to the glass case before them.

Logan grinned. "You arrived rather late. The gala will be over in an hour or so."

"Then I'd best enjoy the exhibits before we're all ushered out. Excuse me."

Zoe turned and walked across the room to stand before a display of metal war fans. Taking a glass of champagne from a passing waiter, she moved from one exhibit to the next, comparing the floor plan with the one Ethan had sent her. It all checked out and she relaxed a bit.

She had another half hour to get Logan where she wanted him. She wandered about the spacious main room of the museum, chatting with other guests about the exhibits. Logan was never far from her, and that was exactly what she wanted.

The gala was winding down and everyone was being directed from the small exhibit rooms back to the main gallery where there would be a series of speeches thanking everyone and acknowledging the more generous patrons of the Friedlander. Zoe waited until the room was almost empty, then slipped behind an exhibit, making sure Logan saw the move. She ducked under the red velvet rope and ran silently down the hall to the double doors leading to the small gallery that held the priceless *emaki*. The thousand-year-old picture scrolls weren't being displayed tonight. The Friedlander wouldn't take a chance with such a valuable exhibit.

The doors to the gallery were locked, but in deference to the socialites in attendance, no guards had been posted. Zoe pulled her lock picks out of the lining of the bamboo purse and quickly unlocked the door. Slipping into the room, she removed the kimono duster and knotted it around her waist to keep it out of the way.

From the schematics of the alarm system that Ethan had provided, she knew that cutting the white wire was all that was necessary to deactivate the alarm. But it had to look complicated to Logan. He had to believe that she'd made a mistake. She moved to the display case and ran her hands over it to locate the thin wires, which is what she'd have done if she were really going to steal the *emaki*.

Considering the value of the exhibit, Zoe didn't think the museum had installed adequate security. They were probably counting on exterior security to keep thieves out, which wasn't altogether wrong. Most thieves would wait and break into the museum after hours. She would have.

She barely heard the door open and close. He was quiet, she'd give him that.

"Beautiful, aren't they?" Logan asked.

"What the hell are you doing here?" Zoe whirled and planted her fists on her hips in an imitation of outrage.

"Just watching."

"I don't need an audience. Leave."

"I'd rather stay. Always wanted to see a master thief at work."

She shot a glance toward the door, trying to look nervous. Which wasn't all that hard, considering what she was attempting. Ethan had offered to set the ruse up with the museum, but Zoe had refused. The more people involved, the more likelihood of it looking like a setup. Logan had to believe everything that would happen tonight, and you just couldn't beat reality. She turned back to the display case and knelt down, feeling for the wires at the bottom of the case.

"Then don't get in my way. Open that door a crack and see if anyone's around. If you're going to stay, at least you can be helpful." She snipped the red wire, then stood and lifted the glass.

Alarms jangled and even though she was prepared for them, adrenaline still shot through her body. She dropped the wire cutters and sprinted for the door, grabbing Logan's hand to pull him out of the room. He looked stunned, which was just as she'd intended.

Zoe pulled him down the hallway and shoved him into the men's room ahead of her. She could hear boots pounding down the hallway as she yanked open the door to one of the stalls. Stepping up onto the toilet seat, she launched herself into the air and threw out her arms and legs. Her toes pressed against the rear of the stall, her palms against the door, wedging her into place.

"Drop your pants and sit down," she ordered Logan.

"What?"

"You heard me. Do it!" She inched her way up to the top of the stall, which rose almost to the ceiling. "And lock the stall. Look like you're taking care of business."

Logan unbuckled his belt, dropped his pants, and started to sit.

"Briefs, too."

He scowled at her.

"The idea is to appear that you're in here for a legitimate reason," she explained. "You want them to think you're taking a dump in your shorts?" She settled her palms against the door frame, careful that they weren't in the way of the door opening.

"Who?" Logan asked just as she heard the door to

the men's room swing open.

She shook her head and pursed her lips to let him know to be quiet. Logan dropped his briefs and sat down just before a heavy hand banged on the stall door.

"Hey, anybody in there?" a male voice called.

"Well, yes, actually," Logan answered.

"Open up."

"Excuse me. I'll be done in a moment."

"Open up now!"

Logan reached out and flipped the locking lever on the stall door, letting it swing open to reveal two guards.

"You see anyone come through here?"

"I'm not exactly in a position to see anyone, but I haven't *heard* anyone come in. What's this about?" Logan asked.

"One of the alarms got tripped." The guard looked around the stall suspiciously. But he didn't think to look up, which Zoe had counted on.

"Well, no one's in here with me. Now, if you don't mind?" Logan's voice held just the right tone of indignation and she grinned down at him.

Her arms and legs trembled with the effort of keeping her body in place. She remembered her father chastising her for skipping a couple of gymnastic training sessions. Okay, she'd skipped seven. Over the past month. She pressed her hands and feet harder against the laminate and promised herself that she'd never miss another one.

The guard looked down at Logan's pants and underwear pooled around his ankles. Logan put his hand over his stomach and groaned. She silently cheered the ad lib.

"Yeah," the guard said. "Sorry."

Zoe listened to the guards check the other stalls and then leave. Her arms and legs were visibly trembling from holding her position for so long.

"You can pull your pants up now," she said. "Then get out so I can get down."

Logan zipped up his pants and looked up at her. "I'll catch you."

"No, just get out so I can get down."

Logan reached up, put his hands around her waist, and lifted her down. He let her body slide down his.

"That wasn't necessary," she said. Pleasant, though.

Logan grinned at her. "What happened?"

"The schematics I had for the alarm system were wrong." She unwrapped the kimono from her waist and pulled it back on. "Or they changed something at the last minute."

"So, will you try again later?"

She frowned at him. "I doubt it. They'll step up security now."

"The *emaki* would have brought you a tidy sum."

"Yeah, I could use it, too. Check to see if anyone's outside."

Logan opened the door, looked down the hall, and shook his head. "All clear."

She linked her arm with his, scooted them out of the men's room, and strolled down the hallway back to the main gallery. Most of the guests had left. She picked up a champagne glass and sipped until they heard the announcement that the gala was over and the building would be locked in fifteen minutes.

"I guess they want everyone to leave, then," Logan said.

"No doubt." She set the glass down and they strolled to the front door. As soon as they were outside, she pulled her arm away from his and headed for the line of cabs pulled up to the curb.

"What's your hurry?" Logan grabbed her arm and pulled her back. "It's still early. Let's go have a drink."

"I don't—"

"The job's over. For tonight, anyway. And you're completely hyped-up." He pulled her along toward a cab. "Besides, I find you interesting."

Just what she wanted. She let him hand her into the cab.

"Here we are," Logan said as the cab stopped in front of the St. Regis. Zoe wondered if it was just a coincidence or if he knew she was staying there.

Logan paid the cab driver and led her through the revolving doors, across the lobby to the bank of elevators. They stepped inside and rode up in silence. Zoe breathed a silent sigh of relief when they got off on the eleventh floor instead of the fifteenth, where her room was located. Logan slid his key card into the lock and pushed the door open. Zoe walked inside, and behind her Logan flipped a couple of switches that turned on lights and started the gas fireplace. The setup made her jittery, looking a little too much like a seduction scene.

"What would you like to drink?" Logan asked. "Brandy, wine, champagne?"

"Brandy sounds good."

"So tell me about tonight." Logan splashed brandy into an oversized snifter and held it out to her, taking a seat on the sofa facing her.

"What about it? Other than the fact that it was a bust?"

"Yes, that must have been hard to take, considering."

"Considering what?" She frowned at him for good measure.

"I understand the fence you used for the German Embassy heist was arrested before he could move the jewels."

"Really?"

Logan smiled. "I just assumed that with that loss, the job tonight was important."

"I have a buyer who will be very disappointed about tonight." She lifted a shoulder in what she hoped was a sign of indifference.

Logan swirled the brandy in his glass and sipped. "I thought you didn't do work for hire."

"I made an exception. Why all the interest in my career?" she asked.

"I thought I'd made that obvious."

"You're referring to your offer?"

"I figure that with two jobs that didn't work out, you might be getting a little hungry."

"What makes you think that?"

"Well, your bank accounts show that you're getting a bit low on resources."

She hadn't expected him to check out her bank accounts. Damn it! Was nothing sacred anymore?

"It appears you've been checking me out pretty thoroughly," she said. "Tell me why you need a thief so desperately."

"The Triumvirate doesn't need *a* thief. They need the *best* thief."

"The Triumvirate?"

"The Triumvirate is the governing body of the group."

"And they need a good thief." She held up a hand.

"The *best* thief."

"You're the best in the business right now." Logan sipped his brandy. "Since your father retired, anyway."

"I was trained by the best," she acknowledged.

"You were out of the business for a few years."

"That's the gossip, anyway."

"Oh, it's more than gossip." Logan splashed more brandy into their glasses although she'd hardly touched hers. "You worked for a security company for several years. After they laid you off, you enrolled in college for a while."

"You *have* done your homework." She sipped the brandy. "However, you haven't answered my question. Why do you need the best thief so desperately?"

Logan shrugged. "What we need to procure is very important. We don't want to take a chance with a less skilled individual."

"You've got my interest," she said.

"Great. What's your price?"

"Not so fast. First of all, I want a face-to-face with the powers that be. Then, when I know exactly what's involved with the job, I'll let you know what my price is. My terms are cash. Half up front, half on delivery of the item. And expenses, of course."

"There will be a series of jobs. And a face-to-face meeting might be a problem for the Triumvirate."

Logan frowned.

Zoe shrugged. "I like to know who I'm doing business with. That's how I work."

"Then I'll see what I can do."

She took another sip of the brandy, set her glass down, and stood. "It's been a pleasure. You know how to contact me."

"I'll see you to your room." Logan stood and gestured to the door of his suite.

"My room?"

"Fifteen twenty-nine, I believe. You've been there for the past two days and plan to check out tomorrow."

She arched an eyebrow at him and hoped he couldn't see that she was freaked out at how much he knew.

Logan grinned. "We like to know who we're dealing with, too."

4

November 10, New York City, New York

THREE DAYS LATER, ZOE DROVE to Manhattan and checked into the St. Regis again. Ethan had suggested she wear a wire to the meeting with the Triumvirate, but she'd refused and Shelby had agreed. These people seemed to be extremely cautious. They might have her searched, and if they found a wire, she'd probably get a nice little plot in Arlington Cemetery. Killed in the line of duty and all that.

She took a quick shower, twisted her hair into a loose knot, put on the designer suit, and looked in the full-length mirror.

She looked mature, polished, in control. She could get used to this expense account thing. Then she remembered why she was wearing such a great outfit. She panicked at the thought of meeting the Order and ran some cold water to splash on her face, then remembered her makeup.

No problem. She was fine. She could handle it. She checked her new handbag. Wallet, mirror, comb, cell phone, a new PDA with nothing on it yet. She left the hotel room and walked the few blocks to her meeting with the Triumvirate.

Before she could even check out the lobby in the Trump Tower, Logan was at her side.

"Ready?" he asked.

"Of course." She pushed the button for the elevator and looked at him. "You're looking rather dapper."

"I could say the same, but somehow *dapper* doesn't seem to cover it." The elevator doors slid open and he gestured for her to enter.

The elevator zoomed up, stopped with a stomach-curdling smoothness, and opened. Logan took the lead off the elevator, walked down the hall, and pressed the doorbell at the third door on the left. The door was opened by a woman in a black dress and white apron who ushered them past the marble entryway to a spacious area that Zoe supposed would be called the great room. A tall, slender man entered the room from a hallway and nodded.

"Ms. Alexander. A pleasure. Karl Weisbaum." He stubbed out a cigarette in a crystal ashtray and waved them in. The room looked like a page out of a magazine. Burgundy leather sofa and two matching chairs. A love seat in a rich tapestry fabric with matching ottomans. The coffee table and side tables were carefully mismatched antiques. The art on the walls appeared to be original masters and fresh flowers were in all the right places. But the candle arrangement on the mantle had never been lit and there wasn't a single item out of place anywhere. No one lived there.

"Allow me to introduce my associates, Axel von Bayem and Pierre Simitiere." Weisbaum crossed to the living area and gestured to the seating arrangement. "Won't you be seated?"

"I don't expect to be staying that long," she said.

Weisbaum's eyebrows lifted, Simitiere snorted, and von Bayem frowned.

Weisbaum gestured toward the bar where von Bayem was pouring a clear liquid from a crystal decanter into a glass. "May we offer you a drink?"

"No. That won't be necessary. Forrester tells me you have some items that you need procured from secured locations."

"Right to the point, I see." Weisbaum exchanged a look with Simitiere.

"That's the way I like it, too, Ms. Alexander," Simitiere said. "What do you need to know?"

"Before we go any further, I'd like to take the precaution of a search." Von Bayem slugged down some of the clear liquid and maneuvered his bulky frame between Zoe and Weisbaum.

"I'm not sure that's necessary, Axel."

"I don't mind," she said, thankful that she'd refused to wear a wire. Von Bayem turned to Zoe and held out a beefy hand, which she interpreted as a gesture toward her handbag. She handed it to him, and caught a whiff of alcohol on his breath. He pawed through the small purse, tossing out a pen and a package of tissues. When he came to the PDA, he turned it over curiously, then smacked it down on the marble-topped side table until it splintered.

That pissed her off. It didn't help when he did the same thing to her cell phone. But she didn't say a word. When he was finished, he frisked her in a professional manner, then turned away to pour himself another drink.

"My apologies, Ms. Alexander," Weisbaum said.

"Not a problem."

"Logan tells me that you insisted on meeting with us."

"I like to know who I'm working for."

"Really?" Weisbaum asked. "I'd imagine that's rather difficult at times."

"I don't do much work for hire, so it's usually not an issue." She shrugged. "If I can't meet a prospective client, I usually won't take the job. But, I can assure you, I'm discreet."

"Yes, I'm sure your clients have a need to remain anonymous."

"Exactly. So, tell me, what are you collecting?"

"A variety of items, actually. You would be informed about them on a need-to-know basis." Weisbaum laid a folder on the coffee table and pushed it across the table to her. "The locations of some of the items are in that folder."

"And?" she asked.

"I'd like you to look them over. Make sure you're certain you can gain entrance."

Zoe pushed the folder back to him without opening it. "I'm sure."

Simitiere raised an eyebrow. "Without looking at them?"

"If I can't get in, it can't be done. Forrester told me you wanted the best. I'm it."

"I thought your father was the best."

Zoe nodded and smiled. "He was. He's retired now."

"I see. So, what's your price?"

"That will depend. For each job, I'll need details about the location and the item to be retrieved. After I review that, I'll let you know what my price is." She glanced at the broken phone and PDA. "And I'll expect expenses to be covered, of course."

"Are you really in a position to be so demanding, Ms. Alexander?" Von Bayem frowned at her.

"Those are my terms. Take it or leave it." She

scooped the pieces of her PDA and cell phone into her handbag, smiled at the men, and walked out.

‡ ‡ ‡

November 11, Outside Bethesda, Maryland

Zoe wiped the sweat from her forehead as she approached the end of her fifth lap around the perimeter of her father's estate in the West Virginia countryside. Four miles. She gasped for breath as she slowed from a run to a jog and finally to a walk. She hated running. But running was the answer when everything else failed. It was the way out of a really bad situation. So she ran. Every morning. Okay, she skipped one day a week. Maybe two.

When she reached the gate, she pressed a button on the six-foot stone fence and waited for the gates to open, then trotted to the oversized mailbox at the end of the driveway. The mailbox yielded a few bills, a clutch of advertising mailers, and a package wrapped in brown paper with a foreign postmark. She stuffed the bills and mailers under her arm and examined the package as she walked back to the house. It was addressed to her with a return address of the small village in Greece where her father's family lived.

She'd never met anyone from the family except her

great-aunt Phoebe. Nana Phoebe, as Zoe had always called her. The others refused to move to America, and her father had always had one reason or another not to take her to Greece. But Nana Phoebe had come to live with them when Zoe was still a baby. A tiny, elderly woman full of energy and opinions, she'd taken care of Zoe when her mother had been bedridden during her last pregnancy. And she'd stayed to care for Zoe after her mother had died giving birth to the stillborn son that her father had wanted so badly. When Zoe was six, Nana Phoebe had returned to Greece for three years. When she came back, Zoe had been in training with her father, much to Nana Phoebe's dismay. That time, she'd stayed until Zoe had decided to give up being a thief. After Nana Phoebe returned to Greece again, they had corresponded until her death three years ago. She often wondered how much the woman had figured in her decision to leave the business.

Zoe was glad that Nana Phoebe had never known that she'd become a thief again. No matter how justified the circumstances, she would have been disappointed. But who in the family would be sending her a package? She opened the front door of the house and stopped in the entryway. The package was tattered, like it had gone around the world a couple of times before reaching her. The first postmark was three months earlier, the final postmark just a few weeks ago.

Zoe heard her father's footsteps on the marble staircase and quickly tossed the package into a Chinese urn, laying the other mail on the glass-topped table. Hiding the package from her father was an automatic reaction, and it took her back to her teen years. He'd always insisted on knowing where she was, what she was doing, and who her friends were. She'd never felt like she had even a moment of privacy until she'd left eight years ago. Now she'd been back only a few weeks and she felt like she was seventeen again.

"Today, we work in the gym," Zeke said as he picked up the stack of mail and riffled through it.

"Have Agnes bring some tea. I'm going to change."

"Tea will dehydrate you. You should have water."

"Then tell her to bring some water, too. But if I don't have a cup of tea, I'm not working."

Zoe ignored her father's snort and climbed the marble stairs to her suite on the second floor. She stripped out of her running clothes, pulled on a pair of gym shorts and a sports bra, then trotted to the back stairs. The gym occupied the back quarter of the house and was open from the ground floor to the third. Her father had designed the gym when he had the house built. The polished hardwood floor was partially covered in gymnastic pads and held a variety of equipment. Free weights, machines, floor pads, a balance beam. A rope hung from the ceiling. A cargo net stretched from the roof to the floor in one corner. No expense had been spared, and he'd kept updating the equipment over the years. Zoe ran down the stairs and poured herself a half cup of the rich, fragrant tea Agnes had delivered to the room. She'd only taken a couple of sips when her father entered.

"First, you climb the net," he instructed.

Zoe took another sip of tea, set the cup down, and bounded to the net. She didn't feel like climbing the net but there was no point in arguing. She climbed up the net and back down, did it another four times at his instruction, then moved to the rope. Her leg coiled around the rope and she climbed hand over hand to the top, then back down again. Next was the balance beam.

"No!" Zeke yelled at her when she was poised on her hands and her legs wavered, threatening to topple over. "Walk the entire length of the beam on your hands."

Zoe would have sighed but it was too much effort. She pulled her legs back into line and concentrated on her balance as she completed the length of the beam. Her shoulders and arms ached with the effort, and she was reminded of her position in the stall of the men's room at the Friedlander. If she'd been in better shape then, it wouldn't have been so hard. Still, did anyone over the age of fifteen really do this? She was almost twice that age. At the end of the beam, she slowly lowered herself to her feet and executed a near-perfect one-and-a-half-gainer dismount. Just to prove that she still could.

"You landed that better when you were thirteen," Zeke said.

"There's a reason for that. At thirteen, you don't have anything else to think about."

"So, what are you thinking about now?"

"The usual stuff." Zoe took a towel from her father and wiped the sweat from her forehead, then hung it around her neck. "Will I meet the man of my dreams? How will I explain my father to him? Will the Triumvirate buy my bullshit act?"

"They'll buy it." Zeke nodded. "And what's to explain about your father?"

"That's a joke, right?"

The door at the far end of the gym opened, and Agnes entered and stood silently. She wore her blue dress with the lace collar that was reserved for trips to town and church. Zoe quirked an eyebrow at her father.

"Oh, yes. I promised to take Agnes into town for shopping today." He lifted a hand to acknowledge the housekeeper.

"Shopping?" Zoe asked. "She always has the groceries delivered." In the entire time Agnes had worked for them, Zoe had only seen her leave a handful of times other than her weekly church attendance.

"She doesn't like the quality of vegetables she's been getting." Her father shrugged. "She wants to talk to the store manager."

"I'm going to take a shower and call Ethan." Zoe waved to Agnes and trotted toward the other door. After snagging another cup of tea and a container of yogurt from the kitchen, she waited in the entryway until her father's car rolled down the driveway. Pulling the package from the urn, she sprinted up the steps, closed her bedroom door behind her, and twisted the lock. She used her nail scissors to cut the brown paper at one end, making sure to preserve the return address, and pulled a stack of letters from the wrapping. A single sheet of notepaper fluttered to the floor. She laid the stack of letters on the bed and picked up the note.

It was from one of her cousins and said only that she thought Zoe might want the enclosed letters that were left by her great-aunt Phoebe. There was a short line of apology for taking so long in sending them to her and then her cousin's signature. She picked up the stack of letters and untied the string that held them together. Most of the letters were addressed to Nana Phoebe at her father's address, with a few to Nana Phoebe's address in Greece. The postmarks were mostly from Italy and were dated from twenty-five years earlier to the year before Nana Phoebe's death. Zoe quickly sorted them into date order and opened the earliest one. All were signed with an initial *M* or *N*. It was difficult to read the scrawl. After reading a few of them, Zoe deduced that the writer was a single woman with a young son and living in not very good surroundings. A friend of her great-aunt, or possibly a family member?

The letters pulled Zoe in and she wished she could have read her Nana Phoebe's responses to the woman. But she could imagine what she would have said to the young woman. She would have told her to be strong. To take the moral high road. That was Nana Phoebe. The letters jumped a few years and the woman was now referring to her child as a young boy. Her circumstances had changed for the better. Zoe checked the post dates. The next letter was eleven years later. Now her son was studying at a university. Her eyes skimmed the letters and then suddenly her hands trembled. Her breath came in short gasps, and her eyes blurred as she read.

I know I promised to never speak of this, but I need to know how Zoe is faring. It's been so very long since I've seen my little girl. Although by now, she would be a young woman, wouldn't she? I have dreams of her, but she's still a little girl in the dreams. I need to know that she is doing well. I can't believe all that I've missed with her.

Birthdays, school, parties. Please tell me about her. Send a picture if you can.

Zoe's hand trembled. It wasn't possible that the woman was writing about her. Was it? No. It couldn't be. Because that would mean that the woman writing the letter was her mother. Her mother was dead. Zoe quickly scanned the last letter.

You are right, of course. As you have always been. I certainly meant no disrespect to you. I am grateful for your assistance. It is only a mother's guilt. Please give my darling Zoe a special hug and kiss from her mother, even though she can never know of me.

Zoe flipped the envelope over and read the smeared and faded postmark. It was dated April tenth, seven years prior. Almost a year before Nana Phoebe's return to Greece. Zoe remembered that she had made the decision to go back to college shortly before that. She looked through the letters again because she simply couldn't believe that her mother was alive.

But she couldn't see any other answer. How many nights had she cried herself to sleep, mourning the untimely death of the woman who meant everything to her? How many times had she thought about how different her life would have been if she'd had her mother?

And all these years, she'd had a mother. A mother who had chosen to leave her daughter behind to be raised by her father, the master thief. A father who had made it obvious that he wanted a son to follow in his footsteps. A father who'd had no choice but to settle for a daughter.

The phone rang and Zoe jerked. The letter she held fluttered to the floor when she reached for the phone.

"Hello?"

"You have a fax number?"

Forrester. Talk about lousy timing. She pushed the letters out of her mind. "Yeah, if that's as good as your technology is."

"You have a different preference?" he asked.

"Depends on what you want to send me."

"I have the information you want on the first heist. General location, some pictures."

"Can you upload them to a secure site?"

"Sure. Hold on a second."

Zoe could hear the soft tapping of keys on the phone line. "Okay. I've uploaded the documents to a secure FTP site. Here's the ID and password." He rattled off the information. "You got that?"

"I assume they want an estimate from me about the first job?"

"Hardly. They want a number and a guarantee."

"Oh, the number I can give them. But, Forrester, you should know, there are no guarantees. Not in this business."

‡ ‡ ‡

November 12, Outside Bethesda, Maryland

"Three hundred thousand dollars plus out-of-pocket expenses?"

"You have a problem with that, Ethan?" Zoe held the phone between her ear and shoulder and scrubbed her wet hair with a towel.

"No, of course not. Not with the three hundred thousand. But you're going to charge these guys that much and then want them to pay for your cab fare?"

"You know, Ethan, there's a reason you're not a thief." Zoe threw the towel on the bed and sank down beside it. "On a job like this, pocket expenses could be anything from a cup of coffee to a demolitions expert. If I didn't specify that, they'd have pegged me for an amateur."

"I see."

"Do you? Maybe you want to take a couple of days and run this by whatever geek crunches your numbers for you?"

"Calm down, Zoe. I was just asking."

"Speaking of asking, I need a favor from you." She could almost feel the coldness over the phone, but waited for Ethan to speak.

"A favor?" he asked.

"Nothing big. I need to find someone."

"Zoe, all you need to find is whatever the Order wants."

"Ethan, this is important."

He sighed heavily. "So, who is it? Some guy you were dating?"

"Not exactly." Her voice wavered a little and she hoped he didn't hear it. There was silence for so long that she thought maybe he'd hung up.

"I'll see what I can do. What's the name?"

"She'd be in her early fifties now. Born in San Giusto in northern Italy. Her hair used to be dark and curly. She speaks Italian, English, German, and French. Her family probably still lives in San Giusto, although it's possible they won't know where she is, or even think that she's alive."

"Do you have a name?"

"Her maiden name was Mira Romero. I doubt she's using that now, and I have no idea what name she might have changed to."

"I'll see what I can do. Who is she?"

"She's my mother."

There was a span of silence before Ethan spoke. "Zoe, your mother died when you were a child."

"Evidently not," Zoe said and her voice shook again. "I just received some letters from my great-aunt

Phoebe. She and my mother corresponded for years after her supposed death."

"Does your father know about this?"

Did he? She couldn't imagine that he knew his wife was still alive. She remembered how he'd been after her death. Distant, distraught. She didn't even remember him speaking to her for almost a year. If Nana Phoebe hadn't been there to care for her, to comfort her, Zoe didn't know what would have become of her.

"No, I'm sure he doesn't know." But Nana Phoebe had known that her mother was alive. Nana Phoebe had lied to her and to her father. At the very least. Knowing Nana Phoebe, she'd probably been instrumental in her mother's disappearance.

"Zoe, I think we should talk about this. Before we start looking for her."

"Just find her."

Another heavy sigh from Ethan. "There's not enough to go on, Zoe. What was the return address on the letters?"

"There isn't any. Just an Italian postmark."

"That could help. Send the letters to me and I'll see what I can do. But I still think you should wait until this op is finished."

"I'll scan the postmarks and send them to you. But, Ethan, I want you to start working on this now. Not later."

"Fine. I'll see what I can do. Call me when you have a confirmation on the job."

"I should hear back from Forrester in a day or two. So, you see what you can come up with by then. You call me with some information and I'll tell you what's happening with the Order." She hung up the phone as Ethan was voicing his objections.

5

November 15, Outside Bethesda, Maryland

"WHAT ABOUT THE DOGS?" ZEKE tossed the photos on the table and leaned back in his chair.

"Shelby said she has a solution for that," Zoe replied. She picked up the photos and examined them carefully. "Looks like they have four Dobermans. That's a little worrisome."

"Worry precipitates failure," Zeke said. "Plan your work and work your plan."

"Yeah, I know, Dad." How many times had she heard that from him? But he was right. Worrying didn't fix anything. A good, workable plan did.

"How are you going to nail four of them before they alert someone?"

"I'll have someone with me, so it shouldn't be a problem." She spread the photos out so she could get an overview of what the compound looked like.

"What?" Zeke laughed and pulled a chair up to

the table. "You're working with a partner now?"

"Not exactly." Damn, why did he always make her feel like she had to defend everything she did? "The Triumvirate is insisting that Logan come along for the ride. I thought I might as well put him to use."

"They don't trust you. That's an insult. You shouldn't put up with that." Zeke rose and paced across the dining room, his feet silent on the hardwood floor.

"Dad, it's not insulting. It's not like this is a regular job. The work I'm doing now is different from just stealing for collectors."

"*Just stealing for collectors?* You make it sound like child's play." Zeke turned from gazing out the glass-paned French doors.

"It was child's play for you." Zoe grinned at him.

"No, it wasn't. It was a profession. It took talent and skill. And a certain kind of honor."

"Dad, there's nothing honorable about stealing." He started to speak and she held her hand up. She wasn't in the mood to hear her father's speech about what he considered honor. "I don't care who you're stealing from or why. It's wrong."

He turned back to the door. "You're doing it."

"Don't remind me." Zoe leaned back in the chair and looked at her father's back. "Although I think stealing for national security mitigates the crime a bit."

"Are you expecting Ethan or Shelby?" Zeke asked.

"Shelby said she was coming over today."

"I thought so. The van is here." Zeke continued watching the van as it rolled up the driveway and pulled around to the back of the house. "Do they really think that fools anyone?"

"It's procedure, Dad." Shelby always arrived in a van marked as an electrical company or a plumber or a construction company. If anyone was watching the house on a regular basis, they'd think the place was falling apart. That thought brought her up short. Was the Triumvirate watching the house? Logan had checked out her bank account earlier. What else were they looking at? Standing, she rolled her shoulders and shook off the creepy feeling. She turned at the sound of Agnes's harsh whisper and grinned.

Agnes hated that Shelby came in through the kitchen door. Visitors were supposed to enter the front door and give her the chance to announce them. Zoe snickered as she watched Agnes arguing with Shelby. Finally Shelby rolled her eyes and stood obediently at the kitchen door while Agnes walked across the spacious dining room to stand before Zeke.

"Miss Parker is here to see you and Miss Zoe."

"Thank you, Agnes. Please show her in."

"Zoe. Mr. Alexander." Shelby nodded, laid an aluminum briefcase on the dining table, and gestured to the young woman who accompanied her. "This is

Robyn Lee. She'll be briefing Zoe on the tech for this op."

Zoe nodded to the young woman. She was young and attractive although she didn't seem to do much to capitalize on her looks. Her thick, dark hair hung straight to just above her shoulders, and her dark eyes were covered by small, thick glasses in black plastic frames.

"Hi, Robyn." Zoe turned to Shelby. "What kind of tech ops are we talking about?"

"First of all, we've got tranquilizers for the dogs." Robyn set a case on the dining table and unzipped it. "There's a couple of ways to go with that. We can inject it into meat that you can feed the dogs, but I don't recommend that. Most guard dogs are trained to not take food from anyone but their handlers. Plus you have the problem of keeping the meat refrigerated. If the meat's out for too long, it could make the dogs sick and that's not what we're after." Robyn glared at Shelby when she rolled her eyes.

"The best way is to inject the tranquilizer directly into the dog. This can be done from close range with a pistol." She pulled a pistol from her case and handed it to Zoe. "Don't worry, it's not loaded."

Zoe took the pistol and examined it. There was a space where she assumed the tranquilizer dart was inserted. "What's the accuracy on this?"

"Good question," Robyn said. "With the pistol,

you need to be fairly close. No more than twenty yards. After that, the accuracy sucks. But we also have this." She pulled a short rifle from the case. "Accurate up to seventy yards. And it has the advantage of having a scope with night vision."

"That's a lot of equipment to carry in." Zoe hefted the rifle. "Will I need to reload for each shot?"

"No. Another advantage is that the rifle holds six darts. Plus, it's not like these things are top secret or anything. After you've used it, you can just toss it, so you don't have to carry it around with you."

"Actually, we'd prefer that you bring the equipment back with you," Shelby interjected.

"But the best part is this." Robyn pulled out a small black oblong object that looked like a remote control device. "Just push this button and it emits a sound in a very specific ultrasonic range. It should bring the dogs to their knees." She shrugged. "I have to tell you that it doesn't always work. Every dog's brain is a little different. But it works on most large dogs."

Great. Hopefully the dogs she would encounter had exactly the right brain waves. "What else?" Zoe asked.

Shelby stepped forward. "We don't have any way of knowing what the documents look like or what they might contain, so there's no way to have a dummy ready for you to substitute. You'll need to photograph the documents as you're stealing them."

"That could be tricky. They're insisting that Logan accompany me. I don't know how much time I'll have to do anything."

"If we don't know what you're stealing for the Triumvirate, there's no point."

"Yeah, I get that, Shelby. I'm just saying it's a tight situation and you'd better have some nifty little spy camera for me to use."

"Oh, I do," Robyn said and dug in the case again, coming up with a pair of stylish glasses with amber lenses. "These are designed to increase your ability to see in the dark. Not really night vision, but they help by about ten percent. We've inserted a camera here." She pointed to the piece that would rest across the bridge of Zoe's nose.

Zoe peered closely but couldn't detect anything unusual. "How do I take the picture?"

"They're very pressure sensitive. Just pretend to adjust the glasses and you'll feel a click here." Robyn indicated the bridge of her nose.

"And just how do I explain the fact that I have night vision glasses?" Zoe asked.

"That's the beauty of them. These are readily available from catalogs and several online stores." Robyn grinned at her. "Of course, those don't come with the camera." She shoved the equipment into the case and zipped it closed. "Any questions?"

"When do you leave?" Shelby asked.

"I'm meeting Logan Thursday morning at La Guardia. Evidently we have a private jet for the trip to Mexico City."

"I'll have the equipment placed in locker one seven nine at the airport in Mexico City." Shelby handed her a key. "Tell Logan that you had an associate deliver the equipment earlier."

"Really, Shelby. I could have figured that out for myself."

"Don't get your feathers ruffled, Zoe. I'm trying to make sure you don't make any mistakes that could get you killed. If I tell you stuff you already know, just deal with it."

"Ethan told me you'd be overprotective." Zoe tried not to grin at the look of outrage on Shelby's face and turned to Robyn. "Thanks for all this."

"There's one more thing," Shelby said. "I need you to come to Washington. There's someone you need to meet."

"Why didn't you just bring him with you today?"

"He's in Walter Reed Medical Center and won't be able to leave for another week. Can you meet me there tomorrow afternoon?"

"Sure, but who am I meeting? What's it about?"

"His name is Drake Leatherman, and he's the only agent who has infiltrated the Order and came back."

"I see."

"We're continuing to watch Montoya's compound, and I'll send the latest intel to you Wednesday night."

"Sure. Up-to-date information is always useful." Zoe gathered up the photographs and plans she'd been looking at earlier. "Thanks for everything. And Robyn, it was nice meeting you."

Zoe climbed the marble stairs to her suite. Her stomach rumbled and she remembered that she hadn't had anything but tea and toast for breakfast. And she'd skipped lunch. But the thought of putting food on top of the cold knot in her stomach was less than appealing. She'd always felt a little tense before a job. But not like this. This was fear, plain and simple. She'd never really been afraid when she did a job. Sure, there was the possibility that she'd get caught, but that only served to sharpen her game. This was different. If she failed this time, there were serious consequences.

Her death not the least of them.

‡ ‡ ‡

November 17, Outside Bern, Switzerland

Shahid Nassar parked his rented car in a visitor space close to the entrance of the International Research Institute. The glass doors slid open as he approached, and closed behind him.

"William Russell to see Dr. Stubeck," he said to the uniformed guard. He still wasn't used to seeing women working in positions like this, but he'd learned to school his features so his surprise or dismay didn't show. The woman picked up a phone and spoke quietly, then looked at him.

"Take the elevator to the third floor, Mr. Russell. The receptionist will assist you."

The short security gate swung open, and Shahid walked through and onto a waiting elevator. No doubt the guard was watching a monitor to be sure he went where she'd directed him to go. He stepped off at the third floor and presented himself to the receptionist. Dr. Stubeck arrived in a few minutes.

"Mr. Russell." The doctor held out his hand, which Shahid shook. "I'm pleased to see you again. I think I have some very good news for you."

"You mentioned a demonstration?" Shahid followed him down a short hallway and into his office.

"Exactly. We've refined the Neurotox virus in a way that I think will impress you." The doctor waved toward a guest chair and took his own seat behind his desk. "The result will still be disseminated intravascular coagulation, but it will be even faster than we'd originally thought."

Shahid nodded. "It is most important that the

effects be immediate and dramatic."

"We've added a fast-acting neurotoxin. I believe it will accomplish what you're looking for."

"When may I see a demonstration?" Shahid asked.

"Right now." Dr. Stubeck turned on a television set and punched a button on the remote. "This was videotaped last week. We used a total of ten subjects."

Shahid nodded. He found it interesting how the doctor referred to his victims as subjects. As though they were less than human. Probably it made it easier for the doctor to do what he did. Shahid had no such compunctions. He was well aware that his intent was to kill certain other human beings and he would not try to make it sound otherwise.

The tape began and showed the people in a large bare room, but for two sofas, several chairs, and a couple of tables. The tables held an assortment of cookies and snacks and a few two-liter bottles of soft drinks.

"The virus is being administered by food and drink?" Shahid asked. "This is unacceptable. We must have an airborne delivery."

"Of course," Dr. Stubeck nodded. "The food and drink were only there to put the subjects at ease. Here's the actual delivery of the virus."

Shahid heard a hissing sound and could just barely see a mist shooting out from several nozzles in the ceiling. Within minutes, the people began to react.

"This is the initial phase. The subjects are experiencing extreme pain as the Neurotox activates the clotting factors in the blood all over the body."

Shahid watched the television without any expression.

"As blood clots form, all the clotting factors are used up. Moments later the subjects bleed freely until they die."

Shahid wondered at Dr. Stubeck's cheerful tone. He seemed delighted to have created such a dreadful virus. And he didn't even know whom it would be used against. The people Shahid would kill with the Neurotox were sacrifices. They were infidels and they would serve as a message to other infidels. Stubeck was willing to provide the means for their destruction without any understanding of whom the victims were or why they must die. He glanced at Stubeck, then turned his attention back to the television. Perhaps when they were successful Stubeck would be enlightened.

Two of the people began bleeding from their eyes and noses, then their hands moved up to clutch at their chests. Uncontrollable trembling followed. After five minutes, the first two had soiled themselves and lay crumpled on the floor. Shahid watched as the others followed. All ten of them were dead within twenty minutes. He was pleased.

"It is ready for delivery?"

"Not quite." Dr. Stubeck shook his head. "I mean, it works the way it is, but I'm trying to get it more stable. Right now it's intolerant of extreme cold, and I understand that could be a problem for you."

"Possibly." The plans for delivering Neurotox hadn't been finalized, but it was at least probable that they would have little control of the environment at some point.

"It will be ready in another month," the doctor said. "I'm trying to stabilize it within an acceptable range. Say between ten and twenty-six degrees Celsius?"

"That should be acceptable," Shahid agreed. "The next payment will be transferred later this week."

Now to give Ziyad the good news.

‡ ‡ ‡

November 18, Walter Reed Medical Center,
Washington, D.C.

"My new handler?" Zoe asked Shelby. "I don't want a new handler. I want you."

"Leatherman will be better. He's more familiar with the Order than anyone else. You need him to be your handler. Besides I have to get back to Portland."

"Why? Can't Paige and Mac just take care of business there?"

"A new case has come in that needs my attention. Look, Zoe, I wouldn't do this if I thought it was shortchanging you in any way. But the truth is that Leatherman would be your handler whether I'm here or not. All I'd be doing is holding your hand."

Zoe followed her down the hall of the hospital to one of the patient rooms. She knew Shelby was right and she didn't want to be a baby about it, but still she didn't like it. Shelby knocked, then opened the door when a man's voice answered. Zoe's eyes widened when she saw a tall man with his back to them. The hospital gown gave her a view of his taut butt and well-formed legs. His dark hair was buzzed close to his head and he had a large, muscular frame, with not an ounce of extra fat on his frame. She cleared her throat and looked out the window while the man turned around.

"Hey, Shelby. I thought you were the doctor coming back in." He climbed into the hospital bed without bothering to hold the gown together. Zoe looked at him briefly, then at the window again, trying to give him some privacy while he maneuvered himself back into the bed.

"Drake Leatherman, Zoe Alexander," Shelby said as Drake stretched his bare legs out and pressed the button to raise the head of the bed.

"Hey, Zoe." He grinned and his eyes ran the length of her body.

"Nice to meet you," Zoe said.

"You're going to be Zoe's handler for a while," Shelby said.

"Handler? No way." Drake shook his head and laughed. "Shelby, I'm an agent, not a handler."

"You're going to be on desk duty for the next three months. You have to be doing something. Besides, you're the best person for this."

Drake crossed his arms over his chest, smiled at Shelby, and shook his head slowly.

"Zoe is going undercover with the Order," Shelby explained.

His dark eyes narrowed under lowered brows, and he turned his gaze to Zoe. "Don't do it."

Shelby ignored Drake's objection. "I need you to fill her in on the Order. Everything you know about them."

"I know they're dangerous. I know they're ruthless. I know they will eat you for breakfast." He sat up and swung his legs off the bed. "Trust me, you don't want to go anywhere near them."

"That might be true," Zoe said. "But I'm doing it anyway and I'd appreciate your help." She'd already argued with Shelby about Drake being her handler. She'd lost. And she had to admit that Shelby had a point. Drake knew more about the Order and the Triumvirate than anyone else. And Shelby had promised that she'd still be around.

"I'm a sucker for a beautiful woman." Drake grinned briefly, then lowered his brow. "But, no."

Zoe smiled tightly. Under other circumstances she'd be tempted to engage in a little flirting with him. Not that she'd ever been any good at it. Besides this wasn't exactly the best time.

"The Order is looking for a thief to steal some documents for them. Zoe is, ah—" Shelby cleared her throat. "Zoe is well trained. She won't have any problem convincing them of her ability. And we've got a solid background set up on her."

"We had solid backgrounds set up on all the agents we sent in, Shelby. I'm the only one who came back, and I've been in this damn hospital almost a month recovering from the experience." Drake flexed a fist, drawing Zoe's attention to a thick scar that bisected an intricate tattoo encircling his bicep. "If those agents were found out, she doesn't stand a chance of convincing them she's a thief."

"There's a difference," Zoe said.

Drake arched an eyebrow in disbelief. "Really? What's that?"

"I really am a thief."

Shelby filled Drake in on Zoe's background and the agent finally nodded. "You might have a chance.

A slim chance. Still, I can't say I think it's a good idea."

"So what can you tell me about them?" Zoe took the chair next to his bed.

"Not much. Not enough." Drake looked at Shelby. "I can't believe you're doing this."

"Shelby told me about the Triumvirate that runs the Order. Did you meet any of them?"

Drake nodded. "All three of them."

Zoe gritted her teeth. "Anything you'd like to share about them?"

"They're all mean men."

Shelby spoke before Zoe could tell Drake exactly what she thought of his reluctance. "What do you know about the villa they have in Italy?"

"It's enormous. There's an underground area that we think is at least as big as the house, but we don't know what they're doing there. I was held there, but I wasn't able to see much of it," Drake said.

"Could that be where they're carrying out the cold fusion research?" Zoe asked.

Drake nodded. "We believe they house up to twenty people there."

"Possibly against their will," Shelby added.

"If they're trying to develop cold fusion, they'd need scientists and physicists, right?"

"Exactly. None of the top scientists or physicists

are missing, though. Other than Castiglia," Shelby said.

"Maybe Castiglia is the only physicist they need, although that seems unlikely. And scientists and physicists could be missing whom you don't know about," Zoe said.

"What?" Shelby frowned at her.

"Just because you're really good at something doesn't mean that you're necessarily famous for it." She shrugged. "I'd bet that there are plenty of scientists and physicists you don't know about who could understand those documents."

"You know, Shelby, this probably isn't going to get you anywhere," Drake said.

"How's that?" Shelby asked.

"She's just going to be treated like hired help by them. They aren't going to invite her into the inner sanctum and share all their secrets."

"We're not sending her in to spy on the Order. Her job is to steal for the Order and secure copies of those documents for us. At least with that, we can have our own scientists working on cold fusion."

"Except Forrester has already gotten his hands on some of the documents. Your scientists won't have those."

"We have to start somewhere." Shelby lifted her hands, palms up. "This is where we start."

"When?" Drake asked.

"I'm doing my first job for them on Thursday. Stefano Montoya's compound in Mexico," Zoe said.

Drake turned his attention to Shelby. "I still don't like it. It's too dangerous."

Zoe stood up and scowled at Shelby. "I've had enough of this. My time would be better spent going over those aerial maps and floor plans. I don't need a handler to steal. I know what I'm doing." She had her hand on the door handle when Drake responded.

"Wait."

Zoe turned back to him.

"Fine. I'll tell you everything I know about the Order."

"Good." Zoe crossed the room and sat in the chair.

"I just don't think it's going to help you in the long run."

6

November 20, 35,000 Feet over the Southern United States

"Do you want to use the bed?"

"Excuse me?" Zoe turned to Logan, who was removing his seat belt. What the hell was he suggesting?

"Do you want to use the bed for a nap? It's a long flight. Figured we might as well get some rest."

"Oh." Zoe looked toward the back of the Gulfstream V, the Triumvirate's private jet. Maybe there was something in the bedroom that would tell her more about them. "Sure. Good idea." She unfastened her seat belt.

"I'm going to go over the plans again."

Zoe opened the door at the back of the sleek jet. The bedroom held a queen-sized bed, a small desk with several drawers, and a chair. She closed the door behind her and flipped the lock. The desk drawers held nothing but stationery. The drawers under the platform bed revealed extra sheets, blankets, and pillows. The space was compact and neat. Nothing else to investigate.

Disappointed, Zoe stretched out on the bed and consciously relaxed her body, starting at her scalp and moving down to her toes. She concentrated on her breathing, letting the stress dissolve and dissipate. When she thought about the heist, she acknowledged the thought without dwelling on it. Soon the edges of her thoughts softened and blurred. She concentrated on calm and serenity. After half an hour, she pulled a soft wool blanket over her, letting the hum of the plane lull her to sleep.

She woke two hours later to a soft knock on the door. Remembering that she'd locked the door, she leaped off the bed, flipped the lock, and opened the door to Logan.

"I thought you might want something to drink."

"Sure. That sounds good." Zoe cleared her throat and blinked the sleep from her eyes. "How long until we arrive in Mexico City?"

"Almost two hours. You want Kona Blend, Vanilla Hazelnut, or French Roast?"

"Actually, I'm not much of a coffee drinker. I don't suppose there's any tea on board?"

"Peppermint, Earl Grey, or English Breakfast?"

"All the comforts of home," Zoe said. "English

Breakfast would be nice, thanks."

"I'll heat up some water."

She ducked into the small bathroom, splashed water on her face, and ran her hands through her hair. Her eyes looked a little dilated, and she could feel the buzz of anticipation running through her limbs. She dried her face on a thick guest towel and joined Logan in the main cabin.

The jet was appointed like a luxury hotel. The main cabin held eight leather seats, a wet bar stocked with expensive liquor and fresh snacks, and a table that could be raised and lowered. Zoe sank into one of the seats and looked at the plans spread on the table.

The Triumvirate had furnished her with aerial photographs of the compound they were breaking into. Of course, she'd been studying the photographs Ethan had given her for the past week. The photos the Triumvirate furnished were as good as the ones from Ethan, and Zoe wondered where they'd gotten them.

Logan set a cup of tea on the table and eased into the seat next to her. "So, how do we go about this?"

Zoe sipped the tea and pointed to a small road on the map. "We'll travel over this road. From the airport, it's about two hours to the compound. We should arrive sometime after midnight tonight." Her finger traced the road to the compound. "Everyone is usually in bed by eleven. At midnight, the guards lock the front gate, set the alarms, and put the dogs out."

"Strange," Logan said. "Why not have guards around the clock?"

"Most likely Señor Montoya doesn't think there's a need. And, in general, he's right." She leaned back in her seat. "What do you know about Montoya?"

"That he's a businessman, used to be involved in some drug cartel."

"That was quite a few years ago. Which is to our advantage. Montoya is nearly eighty. He ended his involvement with the drug cartel eight years ago. I guess he thought he had enough money." She shrugged. "Since he's not active, no one has any reason to attack him. The security around his compound isn't as tight as it used to be."

"So, he just sits in that compound out in the middle of nowhere all the time?"

Zoe shook her head. "No. He's become a patron of the arts. He actually spends most of his time traveling. He donates generously to the ballet, museums, symphonies, that sort of thing."

"I assume he's not in residence now?"

"Exactly. Only his servants. Still, we can't be too careful."

"If he's not in any danger, why the elaborate security?"

"Art. Montoya is not only a benefactor, but a

collector. He has probably five to eight million dollars of art in the compound."

"I see. And is this how you know so much about him and his security?"

Zoe grinned. "You could say that." That and the fact she'd gotten information from Ethan and Shelby. "I have some sources."

"I'll bet you do." Logan considered her for a moment. "So, after we get to the compound, what do we do?"

"I'll deactivate the alarm, we'll tranq the dogs, I'll open the safe, and then we're done.

"You make it sound easy."

Zoe stood and stretched. "It's not the hardest job I've ever done."

"From the money you're asking, I'd thought it would be more difficult."

"Oh, it's not easy, by any means. There's lots that could go wrong. But it won't. Because I'm good at what I do. Worth every dollar."

The speakers in the walls of the plane crackled and they both turned toward the pilot's voice as he announced their approach to Mexico City. "I'm going to change before we have to buckle up for landing." Zoe carried her small suitcase into the bedroom and laid it on the bed. She pulled out black knit pants, a thin black turtleneck, and a colorful vest. After they left the airport, she'd only have to exchange the colorful vest for the utility vest in the locker and change her shoes to be dressed for the job. She folded her jeans and sweater, tossed them into the suitcase, and joined Logan in the main cabin just as the pilot asked them to return to their seats and fasten their seat belts for landing.

They passed through customs smoothly, mostly because they each carried only one small bag. Less than an hour after landing, they were standing in front of the car rental desk.

"The Triumvirate would have arranged a car for us," Logan said.

"I like to make my own plans." Zoe placed her driver's license on the counter. "I have a car reserved."

The woman smiled, typed her information into the computer, then handed Zoe a set of keys. "Thank you. The car is on level two parking. A dark blue Lincoln."

Zoe thanked the woman and walked to the escalator. On the second floor, she turned away from the parking garage and headed for a bank of lockers. She pulled out a key and opened a locker. "Here." She handed Logan a nylon bag and pulled out another one for herself.

"What's this?" Logan asked.

"Equipment that we'll need. We couldn't exactly go through customs with this stuff." Zoe led the way to the parking garage and pulled a map from her suitcase before she threw it into the backseat with the other bag.

"Nice," Logan said, settling into the passenger seat of the Lincoln town car. "I was expecting some little economy car."

"Enjoy it while you can." Zoe pulled out of the garage and headed south. Half an hour later she turned onto a small dirt road for a few miles, then pulled into the bare yard of a small house.

"Why are we stopping?" Logan asked.

"We're trading cars. Where we're going we need four-wheel drive. Leave your suitcase and bring the bags." Zoe waved at the man who stepped out of the house. He spoke to her in heavily accented English, and ignored Logan. Zoe followed the man around to the back of the house to a beat-up Jeep.

"Perfect. We'll be back before dawn." She slid into the driver's seat and motioned Logan to the passenger side. The Jeep started easily and she checked the map again, then pulled out onto the road. After a couple of miles, she turned onto another dirt road that was little more than a trail. They bounced over the desert for an hour, then Zoe turned off the dirt road into the desert and doused the headlights.

"There it is." Zoe pointed to the dark silhouette of Montoya's compound. "It's almost one, so the guards should all be in their quarters by now." She pulled up behind a group of cactus and palo verde trees and stopped the Jeep.

"It's a fortress," Logan said. "Didn't look so imposing in the photos."

"I guess it's meant to intimidate people from wanting to break in." She hoisted a bag from the back of the Jeep and tossed it to Logan. She opened the other bag and pulled out two small cases. Opening one, she slipped the glasses on and held the other one out to Logan. "Thought you might want to try these. They're supposed to improve your night vision."

"Where'd you get these? From Spies 'R' Us?" Logan opened the case and took out the glasses. He examined the yellowish lenses for a moment, then slipped them on. "I don't see much of a difference."

"Really?" Zoe pulled a coil of rope and a folded grappling hook from the bag. "I can tell a difference. Unless it's just the power of suggestion."

Logan opened his bag and pulled out a short rifle. "What's this?"

"Tranq gun for the dogs. We each have one." Zoe pulled hers out and checked the loaded darts. "It's important to quiet the dogs before they make enough noise to cause a guard to come out to see what's going on."

"Great." Logan examined his dart rifle, then slung it over his shoulder. "What happens after we get in?"

"You follow me. Stay close and don't make any noise. The safe is located on the ground floor in a room next to Montoya's extensive selection of wines. Unless the servants are helping themselves to his booze, we shouldn't be interrupted."

"So, basically, if everything goes as planned, we won't have any problems?"

Zoe nodded. "Exactly. Just remember, it never goes as planned."

"Great," Logan said again.

Zoe headed for the compound at a trot, leaving Logan to follow her. When she reached the eight-foot stucco wall that surrounded the compound, she dropped the rope and grappling hook, and pulled a pair of wire snips from her back pocket.

"Stay right behind me," she told Logan, then walked cautiously toward the front gate. She stopped at the brick column and ran her hand lightly over the surface. When she found the right spot, she pulled a fake brick face away to reveal a keypad. She used the wire snips to pry the cover off the panel, then aimed a small penlight at the exposed wires. Red, blue, and green wires, just as she'd expected. It was the hallmark of the Centurion security system. The older alarm system was encouraging. If there had been any break-in attempts, Montoya would most likely have upgraded his system. No break-ins meant the staff of guards had probably become lax, which would make her job easier. She clipped the red wire and looked at her watch to make sure she waited exactly ten seconds, then clipped the green wire.

"That was easy." Logan followed as she trotted along the outside of the wall.

"That's why he has the dogs." Zoe paused to pick up the rope and grappling hook.

"Wouldn't it be easier to shoot the dogs from the front gate?"

"There are video cameras at the gate. And there could be a guard who watches them all night." Zoe rounded the corner and walked to the center of the rear wall. "We'll climb up to the top of the wall. Then I'll call the dogs with this whistle. When they get here, I have another whistle that might immobilize them for a few seconds."

"Might?"

"Be prepared to shoot. If the whistle works, great; if it doesn't, be prepared to shoot sooner."

She threw the grappling hook to the top of the wall and jerked on the rope to secure it. After hoisting herself to the top, she motioned for Logan to follow. They both crouched on the wall and pulled the short rifles off their shoulders.

"Get into position and try not to move any more than you have to. Most dogs have lousy eyesight.

Mostly, they see movement. So if we can stay still while we're taking the shots, we won't alert them."

"Are you sure?"

Zoe rolled her eyes at him. "No, I'm making it up. You take the two on your side. Ready?"

Logan nodded and Zoe blew on the whistle. Within seconds, four Dobermans appeared from around a corner of the house. Their noses were lifted to the air, deep growls rumbling from their throats. Zoe blew the second whistle that Robyn had given her. Nothing. She blew it again.

"Damn it!" She tossed the whistle and fired a dart into one of the dogs. The dog jerked and turned his head to snap at the dart embedded in his shoulder. Another dog yelped when Logan's dart found his hindquarter. They fired again. Logan hit his dog, but the last Doberman streaked toward the fence.

"My gun is jammed!" Zoe tried to ignore the snarling dog and pull the jammed dart from the rifle. The dog stood directly beneath them and his snarl turned into a bark.

"Shoot him!" Zoe whispered hoarsely.

"He's too close." Logan trotted down the fence a few yards, then turned, aimed, and shot the dog in the shoulder. The dog stumbled and fell to the ground. Logan walked back to Zoe and waited while she rearranged the grappling hook and dropped the rope into the courtyard.

"We have about an hour before the dogs wake up." Zoe dropped to the ground inside the wall and sprinted for the shadows at the rear of the house. Logan was close behind and bumped into her when she stopped.

"Sorry," he mumbled. Zoe handed him a flashlight and he flicked it on.

"Not now."

"Sorry, again." He turned it off.

She crept along the wall, stopped at a door, and pulled her lock picks out of her belt pouch. "Now."

"What?"

"Light," she whispered. She fitted the slender rods into the lock and jiggled them until she felt the lock mechanism move. The door swung open into a spacious room filled with comfortable chairs and a sofa, two card tables, and a pool table. Zoe headed for the bar on the far wall. Behind the bar, a door was partially obscured by a low cabinet filled with glassware. Zoe motioned to Logan and they moved the cabinet to one side. She used her lock picks again to open the door and stepped into a dark, musty room.

Logan flashed the beam around the room, settling the light on the large safe. Zoe breathed a sigh of relief when she recognized the ancient Mosler safe. She took a moment to appreciate the painting on the door, the intricate gold script that proclaimed the ownership by Merchants Bank. She knew the safe had a burglary rating of TRTL-60. It would resist entry for sixty minutes of assault with hand or electric tools, picking devices, grinders, drills, or torches.

Fortunately she wouldn't be using any of those.

"You can open that thing?" Logan asked.

"This is the easy part." Zoe took a deep breath, blew it out, and focused her attention on the dial. She touched it softly and moved it back and forth a fraction of an inch, getting a feel for the mechanism. Then she slowly turned it, her entire being attuned to the sensation of the dial under her fingertips. When she felt the first click vibrate through her fingertips, she stopped and reversed the motion. The second and third clicks fell into place, but she almost missed the fourth one. For a moment, she thought it might be a fake notch on the periphery of the wheel. But, finally, she felt the faint click and proceeded on to the final turn of the dial. When the bolts fell into place, she threw the handle and swung the door open.

"What exactly are we looking for?" she asked.

Logan pushed past her and looked at the safe's interior. There were three shelves on one side and six drawers on the other. The shelves held several envelopes and three handguns. Logan reached for the guns and Zoe grabbed his arm.

"Put these on first." She handed him a pair of

latex surgical gloves, then pulled a pair over her own hands.

Logan tugged the gloves on, pushed the guns out of the way, and opened the envelopes, tossing each one aside after examining the contents. He pulled the top drawer open to reveal an assortment of jewelry. The second drawer held neatly stacked bundles of American dollars. Logan looked at her before he closed the drawer. She shrugged. The cash didn't interest her.

Logan drew a sharp breath when he opened the third drawer. He slowly pulled out a cardboard tube and pried the plastic end off. Zoe peered around his shoulder as he drew a roll of paper a few inches out of the tube, then pushed it back in. Zoe's hand stopped halfway to the special night vision glasses she wore. The paper had looked old and crinkled. Logan closed the drawer and turned toward the door.

"Aren't you going to check it?" Zoe asked. How the hell was she going to get pictures of the damn thing if he didn't show it to her?

"No need. I'm sure this is what we're after."

‡ ‡ ‡

November 24, Langley, Virginia

Drake knotted a blue silk tie around his neck, turned

his collar down, and tugged the knot loose, unfastening the top button of his pale blue shirt. He hated wearing a tie, but faced with several weeks of desk duty, he didn't have a choice. He ran a hand over his closely cropped hair and picked up his jacket as his cell phone beeped. Private number. It had to be Hank Robertson. He hesitated a second, then flipped the phone open.

"Hello?"

"They finally let you out of the hospital?"

"Hey, Hank. About time I got out, too. I was going nuts in there."

"I didn't think they'd keep you in so long."

"Well, you know how doctors are. I thought it would be best to play along with them. But I'm feeling good. Back to normal."

"Good to hear. I thought maybe the guys had been a little too rough with you."

That was an understatement. "No problem. Nothing I haven't dealt with before." Except for the two broken ribs, the concussion, the slices they'd taken out of him. When he got his former commander out from under whatever brainwashing they'd done, he was going to give him hell about those injuries.

"That's good. You're on desk duty for a while?"

"Probably a few weeks. The CIA likes to make sure, you know?"

"Not much different from the Marines, huh?"

"Not much."

"I know you hate it, but it's the perfect opportunity to find out if the CIA has any new intel on us." Robertson laughed a little. "And I'm sure they do. It's just a matter of what they know and what they've figured out. You just report to me and we'll decide where to go with it, okay?"

"You can count on me." Drake resisted the urge to wipe the sweat from his forehead. He wouldn't be at all surprised if they'd bugged his apartment while he was in the hospital. He'd done a cursory sweep, which had turned up nothing, but he had the constant feeling that he was being watched, listened to.

"I'm really pleased you're trusting me on this one. I know it's a leap of faith for you."

"Hey, I've trusted you from the moment I joined Recon Nineteen" And he had. Seven years in the Marine Force Recon, all of them under Lieutenant Hank Robertson, known to his men as Hard Nose. He'd trusted the man with his life and he'd never been wrong. Robertson had saved his ass more times than Drake could count.

"I want you to understand it, Drake. I just don't know how to put it into words. My father told me about it from before I could walk or talk so I've just grown up knowing about it. Knowing how right it is."

"That's good enough for me."

"Is it?" Robertson paused. "I'd hate to be wrong about that."

"Have I ever let you down, Hard Nose?" Drake used Hank's nickname from the Marines deliberately.

Robertson chuckled. "No, you haven't. No matter what I asked."

"Nothing's changed, sir." But it had. Everything had changed. Drake had no idea how his lieutenant had become involved with the Order. The man was different. He totally believed in what the Order was doing. Whatever that was.

But Drake knew one thing for sure. You never left a man behind. Robertson had saved his life, and now Drake would do whatever it took to save Robertson's.

Or he'd die trying.

‡ ‡ ‡

November 25, Outside Bethesda, Maryland

Zoe paced across her bedroom and lifted the phone for the fifth time, then set it down again. She twisted the cap off a bottle of water and took a gulp. It was well past noon. Had she given the CIA anything useful?

She picked up the phone again and punched in Ethan's number.

"Hello, Zoe. Nice of you to call."

"Yeah. Nice to hear your voice, too. So, did the photos help?"

"Actually, they did."

"Well, you could have let me know. I had to talk pretty fast to get Logan to open the document so I could take the pictures."

"I was going to call you later today."

"And? What was on the photos? I couldn't really see what I was photographing."

"Basically, it's a document. Old, from the looks of it."

"It looked like it was on some kind of parchment."

"That's what the analysts thought. The script is a little faded but we got enough to know that the entire thing is encoded."

"Encoded? Why would it be encoded? And what was it?"

"We won't know for a while. We have some of the best cryptanalysts at the NSA working on it now. Unfortunately, the best cryptanalyst is working for the Order."

"Right. You think that's why Forrester is involved with them?"

"Of course. At least that's why they wanted Forrester. We don't know what his motive might be.

Although I still think it has something to do with his uncle."

"I haven't heard from Logan yet. I figure if they want me to do another job he'll call. But if I blew it somehow . . ."

"You didn't blow it, Zoe. You got the document. You'll hear from him. But if you wanted to know about the photos, why didn't you just ask Shelby?"

"Shelby went back to Portland over the weekend. I didn't want to bother her. And, besides, I wanted to ask if you'd found my mother." Zoe gritted her teeth when Ethan sighed.

"It's not that easy, Zoe."

"Well, make it easy, Ethan. Or not. I don't really care. I just want to know where she is and how to get in touch with her."

"Zoe, I think you should let this go until after this job. The last thing you need right now is a distraction."

"The last thing I need right now is bullshit, Ethan." She waited through the long silence. "It's just that I thought she was dead most of my life. I know I can't drop everything and go talk to her."

"Fine. I have a lead."

"What? Where?"

"Don't get excited. It's just a lead. I still have to check some things out. Besides, you won't really have time to follow up on anything until this is completed."

"I understand that, Ethan. I'm not going to do anything until this op is finished. So, what kind of lead do you have?"

"We found a Mira de Luca residing in Florence, Italy. We don't have complete information, but it appears that she might be your mother. She has a son, Matteo de Luca, age twenty-four."

Zoe's breath left her body in a silent whoosh. Her mother and brother. If it was really them. In Italy. "What's the address? The phone number?"

"Zoe, you're involved in a very delicate operation for the CIA. I don't think it would be good for you to divert your attention to this matter just now. I really would prefer that you not contact her until this job is finished. After all, a lot is at stake here," Ethan cautioned.

He was right about this not being a good time. She didn't know how she would react to finding her mother and brother, but she knew it would be emotional. And she needed to stay focused on the job right now. "Ethan, I completely understand the seriousness of the situation, and I'm not going to do anything to mess this up. I promise that I won't contact her until I'm done. Happy now?"

"Not really."

"I didn't think so. Give me the information."

"I only have her address."

"Good enough. What is it?" Ethan recited the

address, although Zoe could hear the reluctance in his voice. "Thanks, Ethan. I really appreciate it, you know?"

He cleared his throat. "I'm holding you to your word that you won't try to contact her until this is over."

"Of course. And in the meantime, you'll work on getting more information for me, right?"

"Sure." Ethan sighed. "Call me when Logan contacts you."

7

November 28, CIA Headquarters, Langley, Virginia

ETHAN HUNG UP THE PHONE and turned to stare out his window. He was still uncomfortable about putting Zoe in this position. Sure, she was an excellent thief, but she wasn't an agent. She didn't have the instincts of an agent who had been in the field for even a short time. It was a risk sending her in to steal for the Order. But he had to do something. They'd already lost two agents trying to infiltrate the Order. Drake had escaped but at the expense of several broken ribs, a concussion, and a dislocated shoulder.

Zoe wouldn't have much of a chance if they discovered her affiliation with the CIA. Hell, she wouldn't have any chance at all. But he needed to know the Order's agenda. The information they had gathered so far indicated the Order was a force to be reckoned with. He'd sacrifice any agent he had to in order to ensure the safety of the United States. He wouldn't enjoy it, but he'd do it without blinking.

Ethan swung his chair around at the knock on his door. Before he could say anything, the door opened and Drake stuck his head in.

"Hey, Ethan. The receptionist said I could come back."

Ethan motioned Drake into the office. "Come on in, Drake. We may have to cut it short. I just found out Senator Hemings has scheduled a meeting in a few minutes."

"I would have thought he'd be too busy after winning the election."

"You'd think," Ethan said. Senator Hemings wasn't letting that stand in the way of his work as the chairman of the Intelligence Adherence Committee. In spite of what had to be a packed schedule, he was still doing his committee work and requested regular meetings with a variety of CIA officials, and he continued to attend congressional sessions. Ethan wondered if the man was really human.

"I suppose he wants to make sure we're still adhering to all the rules." Drake snorted.

Ethan waved a hand. "They don't understand that our kind of work can't always be accomplished within the boundaries of rules. But I'll meet with him and tell him what he wants to hear."

"What he wants to hear or what you want him to

hear?"

Ethan smiled thinly but didn't answer. "How do you feel? Ready to work again?"

"More than ready. Not really thrilled about desk duty, though."

"I know. But it's necessary. We're not going to send you back out until we're sure you've recovered. Besides that, I need you as Zoe's handler."

"Yeah. About that, Ethan. I really don't think I'll be effective as a handler."

Ethan swiveled his chair to stare at Drake. "You can stop right there. You will be Zoe's handler because you have more firsthand information about the Order than anyone. Zoe is an excellent thief, and that's the only reason we have this opportunity. But she's not an agent."

"Right. I understand that. But I just don't know that I'll be any good at directing someone from the sidelines."

"You'll have plenty of resources for that. But we need your input. There will be times when we need to give her direction. You'll be a key player in that."

Drake clenched his jaw causing a cheek muscle to jump spasmodically. "I guess there's no talking you out of it."

"No." Ethan shook his head and hid a smile. "There isn't." He turned toward his telephone as he heard Susan's voice.

"Mr. Calder, President-elect Hemings is here to see you. He's on his way in."

On his way in was Susan's way of letting him know that Hemings wasn't about to cool his heels outside. He'd been the same way before he'd won the election. Ethan straightened his tie and stood behind his desk. "We'll talk more about this later, Drake." He glanced at his watch. "Evidently, handling the situation with the Order doesn't keep me busy enough. The director has decided I have time to play congressional liaison." Ethan didn't care for Jefferson Hemings and refused to refer to him as President-elect Hemings.

The door opened as Ethan was speaking, and Hemings stepped in without knocking. Hemings was tall enough that most people had to look up at him, and at sixty-three he still had the imposing physique of a man who worked out regularly and strenuously. The first black senator from Virginia, Hemings had served three terms before he'd campaigned for the presidency.

"Good morning, Senator Hemings." Ethan nodded at Drake. "Do you know Drake Leatherman?"

"You're the one who came back from the Order, right?" Hemings asked.

"Yes, sir." Drake shook the senator's hand. "Nice to meet you. And congratulations on winning the election." He took a step toward the door.

"Thank you. Why don't you join us? I'm impressed with your abilities. And I understand you're back at work already?" Hemings sat down and placed his briefcase on his lap.

"Yes, sir. Desk duty for a while, though."

"I know that has to be hard. But take the time to recover fully. Tell me; were you able to learn much from your infiltration of the Order?"

Drake sat back down. "Not as much as we'd hoped, sir. But we'll keep working on it."

Senator Hemings nodded. "I read about your success last year in Italy. The information you were able to provide helped us take down that arms dealer."

"Thank you, sir. Just doing my job."

"Ethan, what are the plans for further infiltration of the Order?" Hemings held up a hand. "I'm only asking because of the committee. I understand that when we aren't able to infiltrate and obtain information in the usual manner, there's a tendency to want to use more unorthodox methods."

Ethan laughed and sat down behind his desk. "Of course, the temptation is always there, Senator Hemings."

"Please. Call me Jefferson."

Ethan nodded. "The CIA is being very circumspect in this situation. Of course, we're concerned about what the Order is up to. We want to know more. But we also realize that they haven't actually *done* anything at this point. We're absolutely playing by the rules."

"That's good to hear. But we still can't confirm that they're responsible for the abduction of Giovanni Castiglia?"

"No. We suspect, naturally, but we don't have any proof. No intel that would assure us they are responsible."

"I see." Hemings leaned back in his chair and tented his hands, his fingertips tapping together. "Any word on Forrester?"

"Nothing new. We're still researching him and the possible reasons for his leaving the NSA."

"Good. Information is vital. And I want to assure you that the committee has not been formed in order to deter you from your task. We just want to make sure that everything is being handled properly."

"Absolutely, Senator. And it is. Was there anything specific you wanted to see while you're here?" Ethan asked.

"If it's not too much trouble, I'd like to take a look at the Satellite Observance Operations. The committee doesn't really have an interest in that area, but I've always been fascinated by it personally."

"Of course. I'd show you myself, but I have another meeting soon." Ethan picked up the phone and pressed a button. "Susan, would you ask Jeremy to take Senator Hemings on a tour of the Sat Ops room?" Ethan had already known that Jefferson Hemings had an interest in the Satellite Observance area and had arranged to have Jeremy Olson standing by to conduct a tour. Hemings would be out of his office and safely in the hands of an agent who knew exactly what to show him and what to avoid. His office door opened and Jeremy stepped inside.

"Jeremy. Thanks for coming. This is Senator Jefferson Hemings. I'd like you to show him the Satellite Observance operations room. Answer all his questions and give him full access to everything."

Jeremy shook Senator Hemings's hand. "Glad to be of service, sir. If you'll follow me?"

When they were out of the room, Ethan turned to Drake. "I don't want you to say a single word to Senator Hemings that you haven't cleared with me, understood?"

Drake lifted his eyebrows. "What are we hiding from him? He's going to be president soon, you know."

"He isn't the president yet." Ethan smoothed his thin hair. "Specifically, I don't want Hemings to know that we're using Zoe on this. If or when that becomes necessary, I'll take care of it."

‡ ‡ ‡

November 30, Florence Italy

Capo removed the roll of parchment from the safe and laid it on his desk. He closed the safe, spun the dial, and swung the painting back into place. The parchment crackled as he unrolled it, but he wasn't concerned. It wasn't the original. That was kept in a much safer place than his office. He'd gone to some lengths to ensure that the copy looked as old as the original, which had been penned in the early eighteen hundreds. This copy wasn't complete, either. He'd left out the illustrations and quite a bit of the text. There was just enough here to show everyone that the time had come and that he was the one chosen to bring it all to fruition. A soft knock sounded at the door and Capo glanced at the clock.

"Come," he said. He rolled the parchment up and secured the leather thong around it.

"The Triumvirate is waiting in the conference room, sir."

"Very good, Esteban." Capo handed the young man the parchment. "Have this put in the frame and placed in the auditorium. Let the others in a half hour before the meeting starts."

"Yes, sir." Esteban took the roll of parchment. "Will there be anything else, sir?"

"No." Capo shook his head. "Not until tomorrow.

I'll meet with the Triumvirate and then we'll join the others." Capo watched Esteban walk down the hall. The young man handled the parchment with the respect it deserved, and Capo knew he would personally place the document in the glass-enclosed frame and set it upon the stand near the entrance to the auditorium. Capo closed the door to his office and locked it, then opened the door on the other side of the room and stepped inside the conference room.

"Gentlemen," Capo said as he took his seat at the round conference table. The three men shifted in their chairs. "We are getting close to our goal. Everything is falling into place just as the Legacy foretold." The Legacy had pointed out each one of them to him as the men he would need to run the Order in order to succeed. But only he was privy to the whole truth. He was the Chosen One. This was the legacy of the Brotherhood. It was his duty, his privilege to bring it into focus, to make it happen.

"How much will you be announcing to the General Order tonight?" Weisbaum asked.

"Not everything. Not that they aren't to be trusted, of course. But it's better to feed them the information as they need it."

"I agree," von Bayem said. "Too much, too soon, and some of them are likely to rush to the conclusion."

"Exactly. And the Legacy warns us against that."

Capo smiled at the men. "Tonight we will only tell them that we have found the man who reads the corrupted language and the woman who will deliver the secrets."

"It still amazes me that the Legacy mentions them specifically," Simitiere said. "Just proves how right this is. How it is meant to be."

"Precisely, Pierre. Zoe Alexander will deliver all the documents to us, and Logan Forrester will tell us what they say. Then we will be ready to work on the first phase."

"How long before the energy source is developed and useful?" von Bayem asked.

Capo considered him from under lowered eyes. Von Bayem was most interested in the energy source. Although it was only a part of the overall plan. An important part, to be sure. Development of an inexpensive energy source would give them power. The power of having something that everyone wanted. "After we have all the documents and they have been interpreted, it shouldn't take more than a few months. All the information is there."

"You aren't going to mention our recently acquired spy?" Simitiere asked.

"No. There's no need to. We know that the Legacy tells us that we must have him. And the General Order knows that it is mentioned in the Legacy. But there are some who might have a problem with spying. They might not be able to see the necessity."

"It's all for the greater good of the world," Weisbaum said. "But I agree. Some might not see it that way. Especially the Americans."

"That will all change. Within our lifetimes, men, women, and children will cease to identify with a certain country. Everyone will become citizens of the world. A united world that will live in peace. Working together to make a better world. We will cure disease and eliminate prejudice."

The three men nodded their agreement.

"Gentlemen, we are building a utopia. Let us never lose sight of our goal."

Von Bayem lifted his glass to Capo, and Weisbaum and Simitiere nodded. Capo was pleased at their agreement, but not surprised. He expected no less. They had all been indoctrinated, first by their fathers, and later by him. They truly understood and believed. He'd made sure of it. Going over the Legacy with each of them until they knew in their hearts that it was the right time and that he was the leader to follow. The Legacy documents had revealed each of them to him, and he had followed the instructions from the Legacy to bring them fully into the fold.

It was too bad that he couldn't have had the Ascendants here to speak to the General Order. But it was too difficult to gather the thirty men and women without undue publicity. The Ascendants were always in the public eye. Men and a few women in positions of power all over the world. Presidents, premieres, sheikhs, princes, some powerful men in the Universal Banking Association, heads of multinational corporations. They were the kind of people the press paid close attention to. Separately, they influenced the face of the world. Together they were becoming indomitable.

Even the General Order consisted of men and women who were powerful in their own right. Senator Hemings, in particular, was a most valuable asset. Descended from Thomas Jefferson, an original member of the Brotherhood, and his slave Sally Hemings, Senator Hemings had been prepared by his father for his destiny, both as the future president of the United States and as a member of the Order. In just a couple of months, the Order would boast a U.S. president among its ranks.

"Let's go tell the General Order our good news." Capo stood and walked to the door, the three men falling in behind him. They took the elevator down to the auditorium in silence. When the elevator opened onto the sublevel, they walked to the end of the hall and entered the small chamber that led to the auditorium stage. Capo straightened his tie and led them through the double doors. The Triumvirate stood behind him as the heavy velvet curtains opened.

Immediately the people surged to their feet applauding. Capo held up his hands to quiet them. These were only a fraction of the twelve thousand who made up the General Order. There were another hundred thousand or so beneath the General Order who believed in the Order and the utopia they were about to achieve. And under that were half a million who were just beginning to be indoctrinated. Capo smiled at the tip of the iceberg as they stopped clapping and settled into their chairs.

He knew he was the single perfect snowflake that had drifted down from heaven to rest at the very top of that tip.

‡ ‡ ‡

December 3, CIA Headquarters, Langley, Virginia

"Yes, Robyn?" Ethan said when he picked up the phone.

"Tech op is complete for Agent Alexander."

"Ms. Alexander. She's not an agent."

"If it walks like an agent and talks like an agent and uses my tech ops . . ." Robyn chuckled. "Do you want me to report to Agent Leatherman, too? I mean, since he's her handler?"

"Yes, please do. Thanks, Robyn." Ethan hung up the phone. Robyn seemed confused about reporting to both him and Drake and rightfully so. Normally she'd report the completion only to the handler. But Ethan had only named Drake as Zoe's handler because he had some experience with the Order. And because it was a way of keeping Drake on desk duty a little longer. He wanted to make sure there were no psychological repercussions from Drake's experience with them. He was concerned about Zoe flying to Italy for the Order and had considered pulling her out. In spite of Robyn's tech ops, Zoe was *not* an agent. He supposed the upside of that was that there was probably less chance of her actually being exposed to the Order.

His phone rang again and he pushed thoughts of Zoe and the Order from his mind. "Hello?"

"Ethan, there's a briefing in conference room ten in five minutes."

"What's it about?" Ethan asked the division chief, Kevin Bolton.

"More terrorist activity, what else?"

Ethan sighed and hung up the phone. Was there anything else? Everyone had become so attuned to the threat of terrorism that it seemed like everything was blown out of proportion. Still, the CIA couldn't ignore even the smallest incident. So every hint of terrorist activity was taken seriously and thoroughly investigated. He logged off his computer and grabbed a cup of coffee on his way to the conference room. Probably, he could have gotten out of the briefings since he was only here to deal with the Order. But he knew he might hear some information that could relate to the Order.

Several other senior agents and supervisors were already there. Ethan had just taken his seat when Kevin entered from a side door and sat at the head of the conference table. He clicked the remote to the LCD projector connected to his laptop, and an image displayed on the screen on the wall behind him.

"This is Ziyad Al-Din. We've been watching him for a while. Our latest intel indicates that he's the head of a new terrorist cell, Jammat al-Qadar. Ziyad's move up through the ranks has been swift by taking on jobs like the bombing in Italy last May."

"Do we know the purpose of the new cell?" one of the agents asked.

"Unfortunately, we don't know much. But we think he's been put in charge of something that's important."

"Important? Just how important?" Ethan asked.

"Again, we don't know. The NSA has been able to capture only a few of his cell phone communications, and the analysis indicates the Jammat al-Qadar are planning a big event. It's our job to find out what it is and stop it."

"What do we know?" another agent asked.

Kevin clicked the remote and another picture flashed up on the screen. "This is Mussad Abdullah. A known associate of Ziyad's. He's also known as Antonio Cimino, son of Vito Cimino, who lives in Florence. Mussad's mother took him and returned to her homeland when he was three. He didn't see his father for years."

"So, we can assume his loyalties lie with his mother's people?" Ethan asked.

"Exactly. Although recently he's been visiting his father every few months, sometimes more often. The NSA has picked up several e-mail communications they believe originated from him."

"What's our objective?" one of the men asked.

Bolton closed his laptop. "We know that Ziyad makes regular trips to Italy. Mostly Florence and Rome. We don't know what he does there, but we suspect he's meeting with other terrorists. Possibly passing on information that they don't want to trust to e-mail or phones. All of you are involved in, or supervising, missions that put agents in Italy. For the time being, we want everyone to watch for Ziyad. If he's spotted, we want as much intel as possible on what he's doing there, who he's meeting with."

"So, this is just a heads-up?" Ethan asked.

"Pretty much. We'll be sending an agent there to work the op full-time, but extra eyes and ears are always beneficial. Once we can pinpoint his activities, we'll arrange for something deeper."

"You mean infiltrating his organization?" one of the men suggested.

"Possibly. For now, just ask your agents to be aware that he's out there. That's all." Bolton stood as the men gathered their notes and left the conference room. "Ethan, can you stay a moment?"

"Certainly." Ethan sat back down and waited until the others had filed out of the room. Bolton walked over and took the chair next to him.

"I want to send Drake to Italy."

"He's still on desk duty."

"Take him off. I've spoken to him and to the doctors. He thinks he's ready to return to the field and the doctors agree."

"Physically, I'd agree. He's recovered from the beating he took. But psychologically, I'm not sure. I think something like that can take a while to work itself out."

"I know. And it's not that I disagree with you. But we need him there. He can use the same cover he used last year when we took down the arms dealer. He's fluent in the language and easily passes for a native Italian. And last year's op put him in contact with several persons whom we believe are involved in terrorism. He could be a key factor in leading us to Ziyad."

Ethan considered the request. If it could be called that. Director Bolton seemed determined to put Drake on the op and unless Ethan could come up with a very good reason not to, it would happen.

"I've assigned him to be Zoe Alexander's handler. He has more knowledge of the Order than anyone."

"He can still do that. This op won't take all of his time. In fact, he'll mostly be hanging around, being seen in the right places with the right people. He'll make himself available and we'll see who contacts him. He can still handle her work with phone calls."

Ethan nodded. It could work. If he could convince Bolton that Drake needed to make Zoe his priority. And Zoe was already in Italy doing another job for the Order. He didn't think that she would have an opportunity to meet with Drake while she was there, but at least he would be someone she could contact if there was trouble.

"As long as Zoe is still his priority, I think it could work," Ethan said. "But there's another problem. The Order appears to be headquartered in Florence. I have no doubt they'd kill Drake if they spotted him."

"True. But it's unlikely that they hang out with the crowd Ziyad is involved with."

Ethan nodded and stood. "I'll let Drake know. Frankly, he's been chomping at the bit to get back in the field."

‡ ‡ ‡

December 5, Iraq

Ziyad Al-Din stood when Shahid Nassar entered and said, "As sala'amu alaikum." *Peace be upon you.*

"Walaikum as sala'am," Shahid responded automatically. *And unto you, also peace.* "Please, be seated."

Ziyad gestured toward a pair of chairs in front of his desk. He rose and walked around the desk to take the chair next to the one in which Shahid sat.

"It is almost ready," Shahid said. His excitement was apparent to Ziyad. "I cannot explain all the details, for I do not have the scientific background. But the scientists have performed the necessary tests and assure me that it will perform exactly as we wish."

"Did you witness the tests yourself?" Ziyad asked.

"Of course. They exposed ten victims. They all showed evidence of infection within minutes and were dead within half an hour. Two of them hemorrhaged from the ears and eyes less than five minutes after exposure. All of them had hemorrhaged within fifteen minutes."

Ziyad allowed himself a smile. "That is very important. We want the American people to see their leaders suffer and die. That will send a crucial message."

"The infidels will be thrown into a panic."

"And there is no known preventive? No way for them to save anyone exposed?" Ziyad asked.

Shahid shook his head. "How could there be? This mutation of the virus has never been created before. Most scientists don't even believe it to be possible."

"This is good. This is exactly what we need."

"I assured Dr. Stubeck that as soon as I reported to you, the monies would be transferred."

"And they will." Ziyad nodded. "Another fifty million euros now, and a hundred million more when we take possession of the product, as we agreed."

"Dr. Stubeck assured me that he can stabilize the virus," Shahid said. "He said between ten and twenty-six degrees."

"That range will be easy enough to work within." Ziyad spoke with assurance. He had known they would have to deal with the delicacy of the mutated neurotoxin and had expected to have a much more narrow range to work within. This was good news, indeed.

"This is good," Shahid said. "Our next issue is the detonation device."

"Exactly," Ziyad agreed. "There is nothing on the market that currently meets our needs. This is a problem."

"That does not mean that it is not readily available. We only need to find the right source."

Ziyad smiled. "I assume you have a source?"

"Of course." Shahid paused. "I must make some connections. But I believe that I have a source that will be able to accommodate us."

"The detonation device must be small enough to be contained in this." Ziyad drew a white pen from his pocket and handed it to Shahid. Chief Justice Isaac Jacobs was known to always use an identical pen. Every photograph Ziyad had seen of the man showed the distinctive Waterman L'Etalon pen in the breast pocket of his suit coat. It was another way to convince everyone of Rashid's impersonation of the man. And no one would think to examine it.

8

December 5, Langley, Virginia

DRAKE PUNCHED A NUMBER INTO his cell phone and pulled a suitcase off the top shelf in his closet.

"Yes?"

"Hey, Hank, Drake here."

"You have something for us?"

"Not much, actually. I called because I just found out I'll be out of the country on a project for a while so there won't be much chance to get that data you wanted." Drake was careful to not use any words that would alert any of the computers the NSA used to routinely monitor cell phone conversations. He was also using a new cell phone that had been purchased in a different name.

"I see. How long will you be gone?" Hank asked.

"No way to tell at this point, but I had a chance to do a preliminary search and I haven't found much that's new since the last time we met."

"I'll have to let the leader of the project know and see if he has any further instructions for you."

"That sounds good. I'll be in Italy, so I thought we might get together and I can share the small amount of research I've been able to do so far."

"I'd like that," Hank agreed. "And you can tell me about your current project."

"Sure. Although I doubt you'll find it very interesting."

"You never know. I might."

"I look forward to our meeting. The more I've thought about your project, the more interested I am in it."

"I'm not surprised. Something like this doesn't come along every day."

"I'll call you when I get in," Drake assured him.

Hank punched the *end* button on his phone and then a speed dial number. "Mr. von Bayem, I just heard from Drake."

"He has information?"

"Possibly. I'll be meeting with him tomorrow. They're sending him to Italy on an op, so unfortunately he won't be at CIA headquarters to gather information for us."

"That's unfortunate. But it's possible we can obtain the information through other channels."

"Good. Sir, I'm getting the impression that Drake

might like to have a closer association with us. And I believe we could use someone with his abilities."

"That's a possibility. But I'll have to be assured that he's trustworthy first. And that's your job."

"No problem."

‡ ‡ ‡

December 8, Sardinia, Italy

Zoe slid open the metal drawer, wincing when it squeaked, even though she and Logan were the only ones in the basement of the museum. A cloud of dust rose from the tattered envelope she took out and opened. Damn. There had to be fifty pages. She'd never get them all photographed before Logan came in to see what was taking her so long. She pulled a gold lipstick case from her pocket and aimed the hidden lens at the top page. She'd just have to get as many as she could. She was on the third page when the pop and clink of breaking glass startled her. She quickly slipped the lipstick camera into her pocket and shoved the papers back into the envelope.

"What happened?" she asked Logan when he joined her.

"No idea. I was standing at the stairs when I heard the glass break."

Zoe heard the distant tinkle of more glass breaking and seconds later an alarm. "Damn it!" She pulled Logan back into the small room in the basement of the Castel Sardo Museum.

"Did you trip an alarm?" he asked.

She rolled her eyes at him. "Hardly. My guess is that someone broke into the museum to steal something."

"Probably that jewel display on the main floor."

"The jewel display isn't worth that much money. Although amateurs wouldn't know that, which explains them setting off the alarm." Zoe could hear footsteps on the floor above them. Had to be the thieves. Not enough time had passed for the police to have arrived. "We need to get out of here."

"Maybe we should just stay here until they're done," Logan suggested.

"No good. The police will be here soon, and they'll likely search the entire building."

"Good point."

"Follow me and stay as quiet as you can." Zoe stuffed the envelope of papers inside her jacket and zipped it up. She climbed the stairs and cracked the door that led to the main floor. The museum was lit only by moonlight shining in through the windows, but it was enough to see that the thieves had left. The side walls of the museum consisted of tall windows.

Shards of glass lay beneath one, and more glass glinted in the moonlight on the floor in front of the jewel display. The far wall was empty where two small paintings had hung. A Bellini and a Masaccio. Great. The antique jewelry was one thing, but the paintings by renaissance masters would make getting off the island with the documents impossible.

Zoe ran across the marble floor with Logan right on her heels. She opened a door at the back of the museum, trotted down a dark hallway and through the third doorway on the right. She wove through the tables in the staff room and slipped through the exit door to the outside.

She sprinted to the end of the alley and peered around the corner. "Damn it."

"What?" Logan tried to look around her, but she pushed him back.

"The street is crawling with police. Every cop in Sardinia must be here. And they'll be suspicious of anyone in this neighborhood at this hour." She peeked around the corner again, then pulled back and turned to Logan. "Just play along with this, okay?"

Before he could answer, she pulled him around the building and onto the sidewalk. Her arms wound around his neck and her body snuggled up against him while her lips captured his mouth. Logan seemed frozen, his hands hanging at his sides.

"Kiss me," she demanded. Logan complied and if she hadn't been watching for the police, she might have enjoyed it. Maybe she did enjoy it, just a bit.

"Hey, what are you two doing here?" the policeman asked in Italian.

Zoe pressed her knee into Logan's upper thigh hard enough to make him groan and ignored the policeman until he tapped her on the shoulder. She moaned as she pulled her lips away from Logan's and turned her head toward the policeman.

"What?" she asked, pretending to not understand the man.

"You are American?" he asked in heavily accented English. "Why are you here?"

"Here in Sardinia?" Zoe asked. "We're on our honeymoon." She giggled and put her left hand around Logan's waist. Standing on tiptoe, she kissed him on the cheek, using the movement to cover pulling Logan's left hand behind his back with hers. She didn't want the policeman to notice the lack of wedding bands.

"It's beautiful here," she gushed.

"*Si.*" The man nodded. "We have had a problem. You must go back to your hotel."

"A problem?" Logan asked. "What kind of problem?"

"Nothing to worry about. A burglary. That is all."

He shook his head. "Just go back to your hotel." He smiled at them. "It is where you wish to be anyway, no?"

"You got that right." Logan pulled Zoe close and grinned at the policeman. She giggled and hid her face in Logan's shoulder. "Come on, honey. Let's let the men do their job."

Zoe gave the policeman a little finger wave as they walked off, then watched as he waved at the policeman halfway down the block and pointed to them. Logan started to pull away but she pinched his side. "Not yet. Not until we're out of their sight."

Logan leaned down and kissed her lightly, laughing when she frowned at him. "Just keeping up the act. That's what you wanted, isn't it?"

"Over here." Zoe pulled him down the next street they came to. After they walked another block, she stopped. "We're in trouble."

"Not really. The cops bought the act. They think we're honeymooners."

"Not that. We aren't going to be able to get off the island with these documents," she explained.

"Why not?"

"The first ferry leaves tomorrow morning at seven. If they haven't found the thieves by then, they'll be searching every person who leaves the island. How the hell are we going to explain that we just happen to have Arturo Fazio's papers on us?"

"Can't we hide them?"

She shook her head. "By morning, the curator will have gone through the entire museum and they'll know that the papers were taken. They'll be searching everyone who leaves the island."

"You think they'll even check in the basement where the papers were?"

"The thieves took two incredibly valuable paintings by renaissance masters. If I were the curator, I'd check everything in the building, wouldn't you?"

Logan sighed. "Yeah, I guess I would."

"The Triumvirate is going to be pissed about this," Zoe said.

"Worried about your fee?"

"Actually, I'd expect the Triumvirate to do something a little more drastic than refuse to pay me."

"Good point."

They walked into the hotel and took the elevator up to the honeymoon suite. When Logan closed the door behind them, Zoe unzipped her jacket and pulled the envelope out, tossing it on the desk. "Got any ideas?" she asked.

"Actually, I do." Logan pulled the satellite phone from his briefcase and punched in a number. "I'm calling the Triumvirate."

Zoe sat at the desk and considered her options.

She still needed to photograph the rest of the document. And that wasn't going to be easy now. Maybe after Logan went to sleep. The night before, he'd slept on the sofa, leaving the bed for her in spite of her protests that she'd be more comfortable on the sofa. The sitting room and bed area were separated by a short wall and she could possibly take the photographs while he was sleeping, but only if she got the documents into the sleeping area first. She took her vest off and threw it on top of the envelope, keeping an eye on Logan as he paced across the room, talking on the phone. After a few minutes, she gathered up her vest with the envelope and walked into the sleeping area. She laid the vest on the bed with the envelope carefully concealed under it, making sure the vest looked like she'd just thrown it on the bed. For good measure, she took off her shoes and tossed her socks on top of the vest. Not enough. She glanced into the sitting area to make sure Logan was still on the phone, then pulled off her pants, turtleneck, and underwear and threw them on top of the pile. She'd just pulled on the thick terry robe and slipped the lipstick case into the pocket when Logan walked in.

"Oh, sorry."

"No problem. What did they say?" Zoe cinched the belt around her waist and turned to face him.

"We're supposed to meet a man at the bank in

three hours."

"The bank?"

"*Nazionale Banca d'Italia.*"

"At four in the morning?"

Logan shrugged. "That's what Weisbaum said."

"Then what?"

"Then we go back to Florence."

"Whatever they want." Zoe shrugged.

"Is there a problem?"

"No." Zoe moved to the small coffeemaker on the counter, measured coffee into the basket, and pushed the button. "I'm just used to completing a job. This doesn't feel complete. You want some coffee?"

"No. I'm going to take a shower and grab a few minutes of sleep before we have to leave."

Zoe watched the coffeemaker and listened to Logan. The bathroom door closed. The shower turned on. Still she watched the coffee dripping into the pot. When she was sure he was in the shower, she walked back to the sleeping area, pulled the envelope out, and spread some of the papers out on the bed. She quickly clicked off the photographs, then returned the papers to the envelope, pulled out more, and spread them out.

She never even heard Logan behind her before she flew through the air to land on the pillows at the head of the king-sized bed. In spite of the soft landing, the air whooshed from her lungs.

"What are you doing?" Logan demanded.

"Nothing. What is *wrong* with you?"

Logan threw himself on top of her with his forearm pressed into her throat, almost cutting off her ability to breathe.

"I saw you taking pictures." He pulled the lipstick case from her hand. "Now, who are you really working for?"

"You've lost your fucking mind, Forrester." Zoe pushed at Logan but his weight alone held her pinned to the bed.

"Really? Then what's this?" He held the gold lipstick camera up.

"Fine. It's a camera. It's not a big deal." She plucked the lipstick from his hand.

"Not a big deal? You're taking pictures of what you're stealing for the Triumvirate and it's not a big deal?"

"I'm curious, is all. If I'd known you were going to be this weird about it, I wouldn't have done it."

"And everyone carries a camera in a lipstick tube."

"Oh, for God's sake, Logan. You can buy those on a hundred different Internet sites. It's not like it's a top secret thing."

"So, you just like to play spy?"

"Like I said, I'm curious. I'm stealing shit that I

don't know what it is for somebody that I don't know who they are. Makes a girl wonder. That's all."

"I don't believe you."

Logan's face was just inches from hers. Zoe laughed in spite of his arm across her throat. "You really think I work for someone? Who? Maybe the FBI or the CIA?" She snorted. "How the hell do you think a thief gets a job with them? Just fill out an application? What would I put under *former employer*?"

Logan eased up on her. She pushed at his shoulders and he rolled off to one side. She was definitely going to ask Ethan for a bonus after this. Zoe sat up as much as she could with Logan still on part of her robe, and looked at him. "You're really into this, aren't you?"

"Into what?" Logan pushed himself up and moved away from her. When he turned away, she popped the bottom off the lipstick case and dropped the memory chip into her pocket.

"You know. All the cloak-and-dagger stuff." She shrugged. "I thought you were just another hired hand like me." She pulled her robe closer together.

"My involvement doesn't concern you. And what's in the documents doesn't concern you, either. What were you going to do with the pictures?"

"There were a couple of possibilities." Zoe gave him a smile that was almost a smirk. "Depending on the significance of that document."

"Like what?"

"Look. I'm in this for the money. I don't get paid the full amount until I deliver. I just thought that having some photographs might be good insurance."

"Insurance?"

"Well, it's not like I can go to the Better Business Bureau if they stiff me, is it?"

Logan stared at her until she wanted to squirm.

He held his hand out. "Give me the camera."

"No way. I paid fifty bucks for this."

"Zoe." He motioned with his hand.

"It's mine. And I won't use it again."

"You want Axel to find that on you?"

"I guess not." Zoe handed the lipstick case to him. "Are you finished with the shower? I'd like to take one before we have to leave."

"Go ahead."

By the time Zoe stepped out of the shower, she had almost convinced herself that Logan wouldn't tell the Triumvirate about the photographs. He'd even seemed concerned about Axel finding the camera on her. That meant something. Didn't it? She supposed she'd find out soon enough when they returned to Florence. Her only other option would be to ditch Logan and head back to the CIA. She didn't like giving up. She didn't tolerate failure in herself. She'd take her chances with Logan and the Triumvirate.

Zoe and Logan were standing outside the building that housed the *Nazionale Banca d'Italia* five minutes before the appointed time. She had to wonder about a banker who would open up at this hour. Evidently the arm of the Triumvirate reached far and wide. A car pulled up and a short, heavyset man emerged.

"Mr. Forrester, Ms. Alexander?" he asked. They nodded in unison and the man unlocked the door and gestured them inside, glancing down the street before he relocked the door after them.

"Looking for someone?" Zoe asked.

"What?"

"You were looking down the street. Were you looking for someone?"

"Oh, no. I'm just not accustomed to opening the bank at this hour."

"I can imagine."

"Allow me to introduce myself. Alberto Bonacelli." He held out a hand and Logan shook it.

"This way," he said and walked across the polished marble floor past the counter and unlocked a door. The room contained a square table with two straight-backed wooden chairs. The back wall held an array of safety-deposit boxes in four different sizes. Zoe figured about half of them were unused as they had both keys hanging from the locks. Bonacelli pulled one of the largest boxes from the wall and set it on the table.

He turned one of the keys in the lock and removed it.

"We don't need one this big." Zoe pointed to a smaller box. "That size will be fine."

Bonacelli glanced at her, then smiled and pulled the second key from the lock. "It doesn't matter. We'll use this one." He handed her the second key. "Normally, I would encourage you to take your time; however, I would appreciate your speed tonight." He closed the door behind him, leaving Zoe and Logan alone in the room.

Logan opened the lid of the box while Zoe unzipped her vest and pulled the envelope out. She placed the envelope inside, closed the lid, and turned her key in the lock. Logan opened the door and motioned to Bonacelli.

"Very good." Bonacelli turned his key in the lock, then replaced the box in its place.

"Isn't there some paperwork we need to fill out?" Zoe asked.

"No. It will not be necessary." Bonacelli escorted them to the front door, unlocked it, and waved them out.

"That was too strange," Zoe said, tucking her hands into her pockets. "Why didn't we have to fill out paperwork?"

"My guess is that he has an arrangement with someone on the Triumvirate."

"Isn't that convenient? But why? This is a tiny

branch of a large bank. And it's on a small island. He gave me the key so I'll have to come back to get the documents." She shook her head. "Just doesn't make sense."

"I've learned to not question the contacts the Triumvirate seems to have." Logan stopped and looked at her for a moment. "I'd suggest you do the same."

‡ ‡ ‡

December 9, Florence, Italy

Zoe took a sip of the bitter espresso the maid had brought her and wished it was tea. But the maid had informed her it was espresso or nothing. She'd taken the strong coffee drink to give herself something to do with her hands while she tried not to think about what Logan might be telling the Triumvirate. He'd left her in a sun-drenched sitting room while he talked to Weisbaum. She looked out onto the flagstone patio and wondered if the Triumvirate lived in the villa or just used it as an office. The place was enormous and opulent. When she'd followed the maid from the entryway to the sitting room, she'd glanced into two large dining rooms, a parlor, and a ballroom. The floors were marble or hardwood, many covered with luxurious oriental carpets. The furnishings looked old and seemed to span a couple of centuries. She set the espresso down and stood just as the maid arrived.

"Please follow me," she said in German-accented English. Zoe followed the middle-aged woman down several long hallways until they arrived at a set of tall double doors. The woman knocked softly, opened the door, and gestured to Zoe.

Zoe's heart slammed against her rib cage as she entered. Karl Weisbaum stood by one of the tall windows, a phone held to his ear. Axel von Bayem and Pierre Simitiere stood before a large, ornate desk, intently studying some papers that they passed back and forth to each other.

"Zoe, come in," Weisbaum said. He set the phone on the desk and took the seat behind it. "Would you care for more espresso?"

"No, thanks. I'm hoping to catch some shut-eye soon." She walked over to the desk and sat in one of the chairs before it.

Weisbaum nodded. "I would imagine between the jet lag and the lack of sleep last night that you could use some."

"Where's Logan?" she asked.

"Logan has other work to attend to." von Bayem said. "Why?"

Zoe shrugged. "Just curious."

"You aren't paid to be curious."

"Axel, stop." Simitiere smiled at her. "Forgive him. He has no manners. Logan told us about last night."

"Did he?" Zoe was glad she was sitting because her legs felt watery and weak. But Simitiere didn't seem angry. Even von Bayem was no more gruff than usual. Relief flowed through her. Logan hadn't told them about her lipstick camera.

"You handled the situation very well."

"Did they catch the other thieves?" Zoe asked.

"No. I understand they are still searching everyone who leaves the island. I'm sure they'll find them in a few days." Weisbaum smiled. "The funds for this job have been wired to your account."

"Really? I thought you'd want me to go back and pick up the envelope before you paid me."

"No. That won't be necessary. Transportation has already been arranged."

"I see." Her hand slipped into her pocket to pull out the key Alberto Bonacelli had given her. "Don't you need this to open the box?"

Weisbaum glanced at the key, but made no move to take it. "We have another job lined up for you. It's close by and we should have the details by tomorrow."

"What is it?" She dropped the key on his desk.

"We'll give you all the information soon." Weisbaum stood up. "In the meantime, enjoy your stay in

Florence."

"Sure. You know where to reach me." By the time Zoe reached the door, the maid had appeared and escorted her to the front door. She politely refused the car they had waiting for her and walked the six blocks to the Hotel Medici, alternately giving thanks that Logan hadn't said anything about her camera and wondering just why he hadn't.

9

December 10, Florence, Italy

Zoe sat on a cold iron bench nibbling at an Italian ice and watching the house across the street. Twinkling white lights were strung across the roof and around each window. Through the large window in front she could see part of a fireplace mantle covered in greenery and big red bows.

No one had come out of the house in the three hours she'd been sitting there. She was wasting her time. Besides, she shouldn't even be here. She'd promised Ethan that she wouldn't try to contact her mother until after this was over. Not that she was going to contact her mother. She was just sitting there watching the house. Just in case she came out. Just to get a glimpse of her. There was no harm in that, was there? She shifted on the bench, tossed the remnants of her Italian ice in the trash bin, and opened her backpack. She might as well use the time wisely.

In thirty-six hours she was going to break into the *Istituto e Museo di Storica della Scienza*, the Institute and Museum of the History of Science. Her objective was a document by Augustino Columbo. All she knew about Columbo was that he had studied with Einstein for several years in Prague, and the two men had stayed in contact after Einstein moved to America. Of course, she would be photographing the document for Ethan before she turned it over to the Triumvirate.

Ethan had been a bit more upset than she'd thought was really warranted about the lipstick camera. Evidently they actually cost more than fifty bucks.

She opened up the floor plan for the first floor of the museum. This job could be a wild-goose chase. Supposedly the document was hidden in the silk lining of a box that held instruments that had belonged to Columbo. How could the Triumvirate know that?

"So this is where you've been hiding." Logan dropped to the bench beside her.

"Hiding? I just wanted some fresh air. This looked like a nice place. Where have you been the past two days?"

"Working." Logan shrugged. "And checking up on some things."

"Really?"

"You know I spent hours on the Internet and couldn't find one single place that sells a camera disguised as a lipstick case."

Zoe smiled in spite of the chill of dread moving up her spine. "Maybe you just don't know where to shop."

"That's possible. Or maybe you're a spy."

"That's ridiculous. You're the one who approached me, remember?" She folded the plans and stuffed them back into her pack. "In fact, I refused your offer, didn't I?"

"Yes, you did. It was a great ploy."

"Logan, I don't have time for this. I'm trying to get ready for a job." She started to stand, but Logan jerked her back down on the bench.

"They might be watching us, so just listen to me." Logan smiled but it didn't reach his eyes. "And don't look around."

"I wasn't."

"You were about to."

He was right but she wasn't going to admit it. "So, what did you want to say?"

"I haven't told the Triumvirate anything about you. That alone should convince you that I'm not out to expose you."

"Why?"

"I have my own reasons. I just wanted to make it clear that I'm not working for them or against them."

"That's cryptic enough. Why tell me this?"

"Because you're working for the CIA and eventually you'll find out some stuff. If you don't get killed first."

"I'm not working for anyone but myself. And I'm not going to get killed."

"I just don't want you telling the CIA anything about me."

"I wouldn't know how to go about telling them anything."

"Look, I'm proposing a truce. I don't tell the Triumvirate anything about what you're doing, and you don't give the CIA any information about me and what I'm doing."

"What you're doing with the Triumvirate is of no interest to me. I'm here to steal what they want and to make a lot of money doing it. I don't care what it is they want as long as I can procure it and get paid."

Logan stared at her for a moment, then shook his head and laughed. "You aren't going to admit to working for the CIA, are you?"

Zoe pulled her gaze away from Logan and automatically focused on the house she'd been watching all morning. Admitting to working for the CIA was out of the question. Logan seemed sincere, and that fit with the background on him she'd gotten from Ethan.

The door to the house opened and a young man stepped outside, then turned back. Her breath almost stopped.

She could see a woman inside the house talking to the man. That could be her mother and the man could be her brother. She couldn't see either of them clearly. The man waved and bounded down the steps to a blue Alfa Romeo, got into the car, and drove away. Her eyes shot back to the door, but it was closed.

Zoe almost forgot to breathe. Ethan was right. She should have left this until the job was over. The realization that she might have just seen her brother and mother shook her. And she still had to deal with Logan's accusation.

She took a deep breath and tried to forget about the man and woman. Tried to concentrate on the moment. There were two other cars parked on the street. Earlier there had been only one. The black sedan was new. She might not be an agent, but she was used to casing a place. It had been over an hour since she'd even seen a car drive down the street. The black sedan pulled out and drove slowly. The windows were tinted, making it impossible to see the driver or passengers. Zoe frowned at the car, then looked at Logan.

He turned to follow her gaze just as a window rolled down and a rifle barrel emerged. Logan pushed Zoe off the bench and fell on top of her. Shots whizzed overhead as the sedan drove by.

Logan pushed himself off her, grabbed her arm, and hauled her off the ground.

"What—" Her question was cut off by Logan pulling her along beside him, deeper into the park. When they were no longer visible from the street, he stopped.

"Friends of yours?" he asked.

"I don't have friends."

"Let's get out of here." He pulled her through the park, emerging on a street just two blocks from her hotel. There was no sign of the black sedan, and they slowed their pace to a stroll.

"You want to come back to my room?" she asked.

Logan grinned. "Any other time, that would sound like a good idea. But I don't know if they've bugged your room. Let's stop up there and have some coffee." He nodded toward a small café. When they reached the door, he held it open for her.

"Make mine tea." Zoe walked past him and headed for the restroom. She locked the door behind her and turned the water on. For a moment she was afraid that she would throw up. Who had shot at them? And why? She splashed water on her face and used a paper towel to wipe it off. Her reflection in the mirror showed a pale face and a tightness around her mouth. She tossed the paper towel in the trash bin. Hiding in the restroom wasn't going to fix anything. She unlocked the door and walked to the table where Logan sat.

"You have any idea who that was?" he asked.

"No clue."

"Your hands are shaking." Logan put his hand over hers.

"No shit. I don't get shot at all that often. In fact, I do everything I can to prevent it."

"I'd think a CIA agent would be a little more used to it."

"I'm not a CIA agent. If I was, I'd probably be handling this a lot better."

"So what are you?" Logan paused while their drinks were placed on the table. "Who are you?"

"I'm pretty much who you think I am. Zoe Alexander, daughter of Zeke Alexander. A thief." She sipped the tea he'd ordered for her, then put the cup down. "You said you aren't working for them or against them. I assume you're here because of your uncle?"

"My uncle?"

"Giovanni Castiglia."

Logan sipped his coffee, then put it down. "Yes, he's my uncle. My only chance of finding him is to work with the Triumvirate."

"How did you get involved with them?"

"It's a long story. How did you get involved with the CIA?

Zoe looked at him and weighed the value of telling

him what she was really doing.

"If we're going to trust each other, I think we need to be honest," Logan said.

"Sure. You go first."

"You are such a bitch." His smile softened the comment on her character.

Zoe shrugged and played with her cup, centering it precisely on the paper doily, rubbing the small drip of tea from one side.

"Fine. After my uncle disappeared, I did everything I could to locate him. Without involving the authorities. I knew that my clearance would be yanked and I'd lose my career with the NSA if they even got wind that my uncle had been abducted."

"He was abducted? I thought he had just disappeared."

"Uncle Giovanni often went into hiding of a sort when he was working on something. I guess he liked the solitude. But he'd always stayed in touch with me. E-mails, an occasional phone call. This time, there was nothing. So I was worried."

"So you just assumed something had happened?" Zoe asked.

"Yeah, I assumed. But there was no ransom demand, no contact from anyone. Then I got an e-mail from him. He told me that he was all right but that he needed my help. He said I would need to come to him and that someone from the Order would contact me."

"How could you be sure it was really from your uncle?"

"We have a code phrase that we've used since I was a little kid."

"Couldn't they have tortured him to get the code phrase? Isn't that the way it's done?"

"Sure. But no one even knows that we have one. Besides that would mean that they had taken him to get to me." Logan shrugged. "That seemed just a bit far-fetched."

"But you still don't know where your uncle is?"

"No. I quit my job at the NSA when they contacted me. When I asked about Uncle Giovanni, Weisbaum just told me that he was fine and that I'd be able to see him soon. That was a while ago."

"So you have no way of knowing if he's even still alive?"

"At least I know that. Once a week, I get a short phone call from him. Very short. We barely have time to say hello and it's over."

"It seems like they want you for some reason." Zoe tore open a packet of sweetener and poured it into her cup. "Any idea what it is?"

"Yeah. They want me to decode documents. That's what I've been working on the past couple of days. Most of them are written in some kind of code.

All of them different."

"And they'll just string you along until you've decoded everything? Then what? Kill you and your uncle?"

"I'm working on preventing that. Trying to convince the Triumvirate that I'm on their side, that I want in on what they're doing. If I can get them to trust me, I might be able to get to Uncle Giovanni."

"I'm surprised you didn't tell them about my camera then. Exposing a traitor would earn you a few trust points, wouldn't it?"

"Possibly. On the other hand, I was the one who insisted we needed you, so it could work the other way, too. And I figure it doesn't hurt to have the CIA working on them, either."

"Then why didn't you just go to the CIA when the Order first contacted you?" Zoe followed Logan's glance at the door of the café. The fact that he looked there several times every minute make her uneasy.

"I was with the CIA for a while before I moved over to the NSA. I know how they work. They would have tried to get Uncle Giovanni out alive, but it wouldn't have been their first priority. They want to take the Order down, and if someone dies in the process, they figure it's just collateral damage."

She didn't know a lot about how the CIA worked, but it made sense. "What makes you think I won't tell the CIA what you're doing?"

"It doesn't matter if you do. They're already involved. That doesn't change what I'm here to do. Of course, if they know that I'm decoding the documents, they might not like that."

Zoe had to make a choice. Confirm that she was working with the CIA or continue to deny it. All she had to go on was her instinct. She put her cup down, looked at Logan, and went with her gut.

"They've already figured that out," she admitted.

"So what's your part in our little drama?" he asked.

"Pretty much what you see. The CIA recruited me to steal for them. This is just one more job." She decided there was no reason to get into her entire background.

"I don't think so." Logan grinned at her. "This is more than stealing. This is spying. The CIA doesn't send amateurs out in the field."

"I'm not exactly an amateur. I've been stealing most of my life."

"But you're relatively new at the spy thing."

"I had some training."

"That doesn't make you a spy. That just gives you the basics."

"It's enough for what I'm doing. All I have to do is steal what the Triumvirate wants, then I photograph it before I turn it over to them. The rest is up to the

CIA."

Logan looked at her for a moment. "So, do we have a truce?"

"I don't see why not. You do your thing; I'll do mine. We help each other out when we can and stay out of the way when we can't."

"Now if we just knew who was gunning for us this morning."

‡ ‡ ‡

December 10, Florence, Italy

Mussad jerked at the sound of Akbar's gun. He looked out Akbar's window as the man pushed the woman to the ground and fell on top of her.

"Idiot!" he yelled at Akbar as he sped off. "We were supposed to just watch them. What were you thinking?"

"That I could solve the problem right now." Akbar glared at Mussad. "And I would have if you hadn't hit that bump."

"And that is why this was not the place to take them out. Ziyad is going to be very displeased." Mussad drove to the corner, turned, and drove to the next corner before he slowed the car.

Akbar paled at that comment and Mussad snorted.

"I should make you tell him yourself how you bungled it."

"It could have worked. And if it had, Ziyad would have been pleased with me."

"He will not be pleased. Now they are forewarned. It will be more difficult to kill them." Mussad was pissed. Now he would have to tell Ziyad what Akbar had done. Not that Ziyad would blame him. Hopefully. He would have to make sure Ziyad understood that Akbar was acting on his own. But the real problem was that now the two infidels would be watching for something to happen. He took a deep breath. He could still do it. It would be a little more difficult but he would make it happen. Anything to take down The Order.

He only wished he could kill his father as well. He was ashamed that the son of a whore had fathered him. But it must be all part of Allah's design. Because he had found out about the Order and their evil plans from his father.

Mussad parked the car in the hotel garage and got out. He'd need to return the rental car and get another one. He didn't really think the couple would report the incident to the police, but he couldn't take that chance. Ziyad insisted on caution whenever possible. And he was right. There were too many times when caution wasn't possible if they were to attain their objective. Akbar continued on to their room while

Mussad stopped at the concierge's desk to request a different rental car. By the time Mussad arrived in the room, Akbar seemed to have realized that he'd made a mistake. He sat on the edge of the bed watching Mussad nervously as the call was made to Ziyad.

As soon as Ziyad answered, Mussad told him about the incident. Fortunately Ziyad wasn't terribly upset.

"It is disappointing, but not a disaster."

"I fear they will be prepared now that they have been shot at," Mussad said.

"This is true. But still it will not stop us. Allah will give us a way to kill them. And that will slow down the Order in their evil quest."

"Yes, it will slow them down. I only wish there was a way to stop them."

"Of course," Ziyad said. "That is the ultimate goal. But we must get there in increments. And that means we need more information about what they are doing."

Mussad was silent. More information could only come from his father. After a moment, Ziyad confirmed his fears.

"Tell Akbar to return home. I want you to contact your father. Tell him that you want to come for a visit."

"Must I see him?" Mussad asked, hating the whine

in his voice.

"I know you do not wish to. But it is necessary. We must know more and Vito Cimino is the fastest way to get information. If you pretend to be the loving son, he will tell you everything. Perhaps not all at once, but eventually. Convince him that you are interested in joining him in The Order."

"Yes." Mussad straightened in his chair. He should be delighted to be of use in this manner. "I will do it for Allah."

"Good. And you need not stay with him long. As soon as you have gleaned enough information from him, you will return. You can always visit him again later."

"It will be done, Ziyad."

‡ ‡ ‡

December 15, Florence, Italy

Drake stepped out of the miniscule shower stall and grabbed a towel from the rack. As Dante Russo, he would be expected to stay in one of the nicer hotels in Florence, frequent the elegant restaurants, and wear expensive clothes. But first, he wanted a couple of days to check out the situation. To see who the active players were and how he might use them to obtain the information he wanted.

He wrapped the threadbare towel around his waist and walked into the poorly lit bedroom. A glance at his watch told him that Angelo wouldn't be back with his coffee for another five minutes. If the little monster came back at all. He dropped to the sagging bed and folded his legs into a full-lotus position. Taking a deep breath and blowing it out, he cleared his mind of everything. Thoughts of the Order, the CIA, his mission, his very surroundings, dropped away as the seconds passed. He forced himself to think about his breathing, concentrating on the feeling of air bellowing out his lungs then whooshing out his nostrils. His mind floated and his body relaxed completely. In a few minutes he was rejuvenated from the transatlantic flight, the jet lag washed away, his mind clear and sharp. He took another deep breath, stretched his limbs, and rose from the bed just as a knock sounded at the door to his room. He thought he could smell the coffee through the flimsy door.

"*Café*, just as you directed." Angelo held out the large paper cup to Drake.

"*Graci*." Drake took the hot cup and handed the child a couple of euros. The boy's eyes lit up at the money and he smiled. "Bring me the same thing tomorrow morning at eight."

"*Si*. Would you like *canolo* or *pasticiotto* as well?

My mama makes excellent *pasticiotto.* I bring you some with your coffee?"

"*Si.* I would love some of your mother's *pasticiotto.* With ricotta cheese, *si*?"

"*Si.* Ricotta. She make the best."

"*Buon.* Eight, then. Do not forget." He ruffled Angelo's curly dark hair with one hand and lifted the coffee to his lips with the other. Angelo scampered down the dirty hallway, no doubt to tell his mother to make *pasticiotto* with ricotta for tomorrow morning. Drake returned to the bed, pulled his cell phone from his briefcase, and punched in Zoe's number.

"Hello?"

"Hey, Zoe. Drake here. Can you talk?"

"Would I have answered if I couldn't?"

"Where are you?"

"At a café on De Panzini, why?

"How did the job go? I heard there was a little problem."

"You could say that. Some dumb ass decided to break in on the same night. I understand they got away with some jewels that were on display and a couple of valuable paintings. It played havoc with getting off the island."

"Ethan tells me that you had to drop the document at a bank in the middle of the night?"

"Yep. That part was weird, but mostly because we

put the document in a safety-deposit box. Then when we met with the Triumvirate, they weren't at all interested in me retrieving the damn thing. They didn't even ask for the key."

"Sounds like they had an arrangement with the bank, or at least with the bank manager."

"I guess. But if that's the case, they must have an ongoing thing with them because the manager obviously had an extra key to that particular deposit box."

"You think that's significant?"

"Well, why would they have an arrangement with that particular bank? I mean, it's a very tiny branch in Sardinia. Sardinia is a tourist area. It just kind of made me think that it was the bank in general. Like maybe they have an arrangement with the mother bank that extends to every freaking branch. Geez, Drake, what the hell would I know about it?"

"You sound a little tense," Drake said sipping his coffee.

"Yeah, well, Logan and I were shot at today in a park. Kind of shook me up."

"What were you two doing at a park?"

"I was going over the plans for the next job. Logan showed up to talk to me."

"How did Logan know you were at the park?" Drake asked.

"I don't know. I didn't think about it."

"Had you been there before?"

"Sure. It's not far from the hotel. I like to walk, and it's a nice spot."

"Still how did he *know* you were there?" Drake paused but there was no answer from her. "He might have bugged you. And they might have bugged your room. Have you made any calls from your room?"

"No. I called Ethan from a pay phone on the street."

"Good. Don't make any calls from your room. We need to talk. I'll meet you tomorrow at the Boboli Gardens. Go to the amphitheater and wait for me. Nine thirty. And be sure to erase this number from your call history."

"Sure. But, Drake, what are you doing in Italy?"

"Be there. At nine thirty." He punched the *end* button. What the hell *was* he doing in Italy? Besides trying to hook up with some terrorists and hoping he could rescue Hank Robertson from the Order without the CIA discovering that he'd lied to them?

‡ ‡ ‡

December 16, Florence, Italy

Zoe arrived at the Boboli Gardens shortly after nine and paid her admission fee. She took a pamphlet with a map of the gardens and strolled along the walkways toward the amphitheater. The place was almost empty that early and Zoe regretted she didn't have the time to fully enjoy all the statuary and neatly manicured lawns bordered with hedges. When she reached the amphitheater, she sat in front of a statue and read the rest of the pamphlet. In minutes, Drake approached from the Pitti Palace. Before she could say anything, he signaled her to silence with a finger pressed to his lips. She picked up her backpack and followed him out of the amphitheater and along a path, then behind a thick hedge.

She watched as Drake took the backpack from her, opened it, and dumped the contents on the ground. He pawed through everything, examining books, pens, her wallet, makeup case. Then he examined the bag itself, running his hands over every inch of it. He removed her jacket and gave it the same attentive examination, then motioned for her to take her shoes off. She complied and after looking at them closely, he handed them back and knelt to run his hands slowly over her pants. When he reached her hips, she batted his hands away, but he frowned at her and continued. She stood still while his examination moved to her torso and chest. Her face flamed when her nipples stiffened as his hands swept across her breasts.

"You're clean," he announced.

"What was that about?" she demanded, stuffing her belongings back into the backpack.

"I was checking for a bug. The Triumvirate or Logan could have planted one on you."

"I can't imagine what for."

"Ethan told me that Logan found the lipstick camera. You really think he hasn't said anything to them about that?"

"He told me he didn't. And if he did, they haven't mentioned it, and they still have jobs for me to do."

"Just because they don't trust you doesn't mean they won't use you, Zoe."

"I'm doing the next job alone, so they must trust me to some degree."

"Doesn't make sense that Logan wouldn't have told them about the camera, unless he has a different agenda from the Order."

Zoe only debated for a moment. It wasn't just that she was supposed to trust Drake because he was her handler. Or that she knew she was absolutely out of her depth with the Order and could use all the professional help she could get. It was also her instinct that made her tell Drake about Logan's motives.

"He does." But even though Logan had said that it didn't matter if the CIA knew what he was doing, she still felt like she was ratting him out. "The Order has his uncle, Giovanni Castiglia. His only goal is to get his uncle away from them."

Drake barked a short laugh and shook his head.

"I believe him. He was afraid that if he went to the CIA, they would consider his uncle's death as acceptable collateral damage."

"So you told Logan that you're working for the CIA?"

"No. I'm not stupid, Drake. He figured that out from the camera. And probably from the fact that I'm just about the worst CIA agent ever."

"That's probably what's saving your life. These guys have been able to sniff out every agent we've sent in. You don't behave like an agent, so they aren't concerned."

Zoe grinned at him. "Well, as long as there's an upside to my ineptness."

Drake returned the grin. "Ninety percent of a successful op is doing what works. Where's your next job? And when?"

"Tonight. The Institute and Museum of the History of Science. You ever heard of Augustino Columbo?" Drake shook his head. "He studied with Einstein for several years in Prague. After Einstein moved to America, they stayed in touch. Evidently the man was brilliant."

"What are you stealing?"

"The museum has a box of instruments that belonged

to Columbo. According to the Triumvirate, there's a document hidden in the lining of the box. I'm to take the document and leave no one the wiser."

"You'll be photographing it?"

Zoe nodded. "I have the photo glasses from Robyn and one of those little credit card–sized cameras since I'll be working alone this time."

"And this Augustino Columbo was one of the scientists working on cold fusion?" Drake asked.

"Evidently."

Drake shook his head. "I don't know if I really buy Ethan's theory about them creating cold fusion."

"Why not?"

"Well, for one thing, there've been a lot of people working on it over the years. It's actually been done, just not controlled. I don't see how a bunch of documents from dead scientists would contain any information that would make it work."

"You never know. They could have been working in a different direction. Or it could be some combination of processes that will make it feasible."

"Yeah. Maybe. But I also don't believe that the Order would be that interested in it."

"In your debriefing, you said they mentioned an energy source."

"They did. I'm just not convinced it's something as benign as cold fusion. The thing about cold fusion is that it can't be used as a weapon. It doesn't put out enough energy at one time to be used like that. I think the energy they're developing goes a lot further than cold fusion."

"Like what?"

"I wish I knew."

10

December 19, Florence, Italy

DRAKE SAT AT A CORNER table on the patio of La Trattoria with a *caffee corretto* in front of him. As much as he liked the rich dark coffee with a splash of cognac, he hadn't touched the cup. The servers here knew him as Dante Russo, as did many others in Italy and several other European countries. He leaned back in his chair, legs stretched out, appearing to be totally at ease. Inside, he was vibrating with tension.

He would remain at the café until midnight, which was only another ten minutes. He lifted the coffee and glanced around casually. He'd chosen the corner table so he could observe the rest of the outdoor tables and the front door of the café. No one new had entered the café or patio in over half an hour. At three minutes before midnight, he drained the last of his coffee and stood, pulling several euros from a gold money clip.

As he dropped them on the table, a man sat down in the chair opposite him.

"Dante Russo?" the man asked.

"Depends on who's asking."

"A mutual friend told me I could find you here."

"Yeah, until midnight."

"It is not quite midnight." the man said in English with only a slight French accent.

Drake glanced at his watch and sat back down. "You have two minutes."

"I believe it will be worth your time. I have a client looking for a special device."

Drake lifted an eyebrow. "Go on."

"I believe it will need to be manufactured. Do you think you could handle that?"

One corner of Drake's lips lifted. "I can handle anything."

"You seem very sure of yourself."

"I am," Drake acknowledged. "Getting stuff is my business. Whether it already exists or has to be invented."

"This would have to be manufactured to exact specifications, although I don't believe it would be terribly difficult."

Drake's eyes never left the man's face as he waited for more information. When nothing was said, Drake glanced at his watch and stood. "Midnight. See you around."

"Wait."

"Why? You going to get around to telling me exactly what you want anytime soon?"

The man shifted in his seat. "I wanted to make sure you could deliver before I explained the particulars."

"I can deliver."

"I need a detonation device. But it needs to be in an ink pen."

Drake sat down again. "Sounds simple enough."

The man drew a pen from his breast pocket and laid it on the table. Drake picked up the white and gold cigar-shaped pen. "Waterman L'Etalon. Very nice." Drake knew the pen cost over four hundred dollars. He rolled the pen in his fingers. He'd always liked expensive, well-made accessories.

"The device must be in a pen identical to this. The operation must be simple and natural."

"So, you want the device to detonate when the pen is used? Say, when the cap is removed?" Drake unscrewed the cap and removed it.

The man nodded. "That would be excellent."

"Distance?"

"Pardon?" the man asked.

"How far from the device will the remote detonator be?"

"Probably no more than a few meters."

"Suicide mission, huh?" Drake smiled.

"Actually, I don't concern myself with those details. I simply procure what my clients want."

"Yeah, me too. That kind of shit fascinates me, though. From a distance of course."

"Can you supply the item?"

"Can you supply the money?"

"Money will not be an issue," the man assured Drake.

"Perfect." Drake pushed a business card across the table to him. "Have a hundred grand, American, deposited in this account by noon tomorrow."

"A hundred grand?"

"A good faith deposit," Drake explained. "You didn't think I'd go to all the trouble of hunting down a source without a deposit?"

"Of course not, Signore Russo. It will be done."

Drake leaned back in his chair and motioned to a server for two *caffee correttos*. "As soon as the money is wired, I'll find someone to produce the mechanism. Then I will give you a price. If we can come to terms on money, we have a deal."

"Money will not be a problem," the man assured him again.

"You have a name?" Drake asked. "And a number where I can reach you?"

"Jean-Luc Fournier." He pulled a card from his pocket and handed it to Drake. "You can reach me at this number."

Drake pocketed the card. Of course, Jean-Luc Fournier wouldn't be his real name, but it was a place to start. "I hope this isn't a wild-goose chase, Monsieur Fournier. I'd be real unhappy to discover that your clients don't have the money to pull this off."

Both men paused as the server delivered two *caffee correttos* to the table. Drake nodded to the server and lifted his cup.

"I can assure you they have the money." Jean-Luc leaned forward and lowered his voice further. "Middle Eastern oil money. I hope you have the resources. My clients do not deal well with disappointment. And they have a deadline to consider."

"I never disappoint, Monsieur Fournier. Ever." Drake took another sip of his coffee, then dropped a few more euros on the table.

"How do I contact you?" Fournier asked.

Drake smiled at him as he stood. "You don't."

‡ ‡ ‡

December 19, Florence, Italy

Zoe stopped at the pay phone outside the small café

and punched in her calling card number, then Ethan's cell number. Her stomach rumbled when the café door opened and the aroma of fresh pastries wafted past her.

"Hello?"

"Sorry to wake you, Ethan," Zoe said. "The job went without a hitch last night and I've uploaded the photos to the FTP site."

"What was the document you stole?"

"No idea. It was encoded. I imagine Logan is working on it."

"Are you coming back to the states now?" he asked.

"Evidently not. The Triumvirate wants me here. They said it would be better for me to be close by. Sounds like the other jobs will all be in Europe. Either that, or they just don't want to let me out of their sight." That thought made her a little queasy.

"Have you spoken to Drake?"

"We met yesterday. Haven't you heard from him?" She would have thought that Drake would want to let Ethan know about Logan's motive for working with the Order.

"Not yet. I'll probably have an e-mail from him when I get into the office. Stay in touch with him, Zoe."

"Will do. I'll call again when I know what's

happening." She hung up the phone and followed the delicious smells into the café, where she ordered a cup of tea and a brioche. She felt a moment of guilt as she bit into the crusty pastry, but she'd made use of the gym in the hotel three times since she'd been here. Maybe she'd take a run later today as well. She glanced through a small tourist guide while she finished her tea. She had no plans for today, no job tonight. She could be a regular tourist and walk around Florence, take in some of the sights.

Within half an hour, Zoe found herself in front of the house she believed her mother lived in. The blue Alfa Romeo wasn't parked at the curb. Did that mean her brother was gone? She took a deep, calming breath. She didn't know if the man was actually her brother. She wasn't even certain that the woman who lived here was her mother. Mira de Luca might not be an unusual name at all. There could be a lot of women with that name. But this was the address Ethan had turned up. And he hadn't mentioned any other leads.

The idea that her mother could be just a few yards away filled her with a nervous energy that was difficult to contain. She sat on the cold bench and stared at the house, unable to take her eyes off it, willing someone to open the door. She tapped her foot on the concrete walk until her shin burned. The curtains were open at one window, but she didn't see any movement in the room. Probably no one was even at home and she was just sitting there staring at an empty house. She should leave. Walk around the city, maybe. Or return to the hotel. She stood and moved to the sidewalk.

Then she was suddenly running across the street and bounding up the steps to the house. Her cold fingers lifted the door knocker and let it fall against the brass plate.

She shouldn't be here. She'd promised Ethan that she wouldn't do this. And he was right. She had no business trying to find her mother when she was involved in an op. Zoe was half-turned away from the door when it opened.

The woman stood several inches taller than Zoe. Her trim figure was outfitted in a soft green cashmere sweater over darker wool pants. Her hair was more strawberry-blond than Zoe's red, and pulled back into a low ponytail. Zoe focused her eyes on the shiny black pumps that peeked from under the bottom of the woman's pants. She wasn't entirely sure she was even breathing. She looked up into green eyes that felt achingly familiar.

The woman smiled at her and Zoe felt a lump form in her throat. At forty-nine, Mira de Luca hadn't changed that much from the twenty-four-year-old mother who had disappeared from Zoe's young life. The word that whispered from her lips surprised Zoe.

"Mom?"

"Dear God." Mira's hand fluttered to her throat. "Zoe?"

Zoe steeled herself against the tears that pricked her eyes, against the urge to reach out to the beautiful woman in front of her. Any doubt that this woman was her mother evaporated when Mira said her name. Oh, God. What had she done? Why had she been so impulsive? Why hadn't she waited? Mira reached out a hand, but Zoe stepped back before the hand could brush her cheek

"Please, come in." Mira stepped aside.

Zoe hesitated. She'd never been so unsure of what she should do. Of what she wanted. But the burning need to know overcame her reluctance and she walked into the entryway. She'd come to find out why her mother had abandoned her, and she wasn't going to cut and run now. Mira led her through the wood-paneled entryway and into a parlor splashed with bright, contemporary colors. Floor-to-ceiling windows looked out onto a small patio and garden. Zoe chose a large, square chair and sat on the edge of the seat.

"How did you find me?" Mira asked.

"I'm surprised you recognized me."

"Your eyes." Mira's lips quavered when she smiled. "Not very many people have such unusual eyes." She laced her fingers together, then released them, finally resting them on her knees. "Your brother has the same eyes."

"Right. My brother. He would be about twenty-six now."

"Yes, in May. Zoe, I have so many questions." Mira never took her eyes off Zoe. "How did you find out that I was alive? How did you find me?"

Zoe hadn't considered that her mother would have questions. She was quickly realizing that she hadn't considered much at all before she'd knocked on the door. But she wasn't about to answer her mother's questions before she got some answers of her own. She'd had plenty of questions since she'd received Nana Phoebe's letters, but now they had all distilled down to a single intense need.

"I only have one question." Zoe forced herself to meet her mother's gaze. "Why did you leave me?"

Mira sat motionless for a moment, then brushed at the tears that trickled down her cheeks. "I was so afraid."

"Of Dad?"

"No. Well, yes. I was afraid of what he would do to Matt." She tried to smile. "That's your brother's name."

"Why would he do anything to his own son?" Zoe asked.

"He wouldn't harm him. Nothing like that. But

Zeke had always talked about how wonderful it would be to have a son." Mira pulled a tissue from the silver box on the table next to her chair. "He wanted a son to follow in his footsteps."

"And you had a problem with that?"

"Of course, I had a problem with that." Mira seemed surprised at the harshness of her own voice and cleared her throat. "No mother wants to see her son become a thief. What kind of life would that be for him?"

Zoe knew exactly what kind of life it was. "Yeah, I guess it would be pretty awful."

"Your father was away when I went into labor. On one of his *jobs*, as he called them. Your Aunt Phoebe made all the arrangements. When Matt was only two days old, I traveled to Greece by ship. I was met by a friend of Phoebe's. She arranged for me to travel to Italy, where I stayed with friends of hers for a short time."

"You haven't answered my question." Zoe had a stranglehold on her emotions and she wasn't sure how much longer she could hold them in.

"As I said, I knew Zeke would train Matt to follow in his footsteps. I couldn't live with that."

"What about your daughter?"

"He wouldn't do that to you. You were his special little angel. He loved you so much, and I knew he would take care of you." Her hands fluttered in a helpless motion. "I didn't think I had a choice. I couldn't take both of you and I knew you would be all right."

"You were wrong."

The phone rang and Mira glanced at it, then picked up the receiver. Zoe watched as Mira spoke quietly. The break in their conversation cracked her composure. She needed to get away. She needed to think. Following that instinct, she stood and walked to the front door.

"Wait. Please," Mira called after her. "What did you mean by that? That I was wrong?"

Anger flared inside Zoe and her throat ached with unshed tears. She jerked open the door and walked down the steps to the sidewalk ignoring her mother's pleas to stay.

‡ ‡ ‡

December 20, Florence, Italy

"Ethan, Drake here. I think I've got a lead on something this terrorist cell is doing."

"Tell me."

"I was contacted by a man who has a client that wants a detonation device in an ink pen. He said his client has Middle Eastern oil money."

"That could be our group, then."

"He was very specific that the pen has to be a white Waterman L'Etalon. I'm thinking that we might want to go ahead and give them a detonation device. See if I can get any closer to them."

"I hate to put something like that in their hands."

"I know, Ethan, but they'll get the device somewhere, whether we supply it or not. And we might be able to track them from the money transfer."

"I'll see if Robyn can put a tracking device in the pen. She's been working on a miniature model that might work."

"Is there any other intel on the cell?" Drake asked.

"Not enough. Bolton has a lot of agents sniffing it out, but so far we only know what you were briefed on."

"Right. Mussad Abdullah, also known as Antonio Cimino, son of Vito Cimino and a Middle Eastern woman."

"You've had contact with Mussad Abdullah?" Ethan asked.

"No, but I'm checking out Vito."

"Our latest intel is that Mussad, aka Antonio, is currently paying a visit to his father."

"Interesting. Why would a man raised as a devout Muslim spend so much time with his infidel father in

Italy?" Drake asked.

"Maybe you can arrange to run into him somewhere."

"Sounds good. How soon can Robyn have the pen ready?"

"Shouldn't take long. How did you leave it with the guy?"

"He's transferring a hundred grand to the Dante Russo account, as a security deposit. I told him I'd find a supplier after I receive the money."

"That should give us plenty of time to produce the device. I'll have it shipped to your hotel. Have you talked to Zoe lately?"

"Not since we met at the Boboli Gardens. She's supposed to contact me when she knows about the next job for them."

"Keep an eye on her. She doesn't have the experience to deal with the Order if they suspect her."

"If it even looks like they're onto her, I'll pull her out."

"Good. I don't need her spilling any information to them."

"Sure. No problem." Drake hung up, shook his head at Ethan's lack of concern, and booted up his computer. He typed in the address of the bank account he'd given Fournier and smiled when he saw the deposit. He punched Fournier's number into the cell phone he used as Dante Russo and waited.

"Russo, here. I have the security deposit."

"Excellent. How soon will you have a supplier?"

"A few days. I'll call you with an amount."

‡ ‡ ‡

December 21, Florence, Italy

"Antonio, come, have some breakfast." Vito Cimino waved his son over to the table.

Mussad barely understood the Italian his father spoke, and he hated being called Antonio. It was the name his infidel father insisted on. But for now, he would have to put up with it. Ziyad wanted to know more about the Order. Taking that information back to Ziyad would mitigate the shame he felt because of his father. And it served Allah.

"You should eat," Vito said. "You are too thin."

Mussad smiled at his father, even though it was an effort, and tried to keep the disgust off his face as he watched his rotund father shovel the sausages and eggs into his mouth. Obviously his father had never been taught to stop eating before he was truly full. And of course, he was eating pork and drinking coffee, both of which were *haram*, forbidden. Mussad was reluctant to eat the eggs, in case they had touched the sausage, thus rendering them *haram*, as well. But the eggs were in a separate serving dish, so he spooned some onto his plate and took a slice of toast.

"How is your work, Father?" Mussad asked in English.

Vito set his fork down. "I would prefer you speak our native language."

"I am sorry, Father. I remember very little of our language." Mussad was proud that he didn't choke on the lie. "I thought it would be easier for us to use English. I know you are fluent in that language, as well."

Vito grunted. "My work goes very well. Senator Hemings will become president of the United States in a month. It is a huge benefit to the Order."

"I'm surprised he won the election. I didn't realize he had that much support. Unusual for a black man. How is his election a benefit to the Order?"

"Senator Hemings is a member of the Order."

Mussad looked up at his father. "I did not know that. It must be very exciting for you and your colleagues."

"*Our* colleagues. You are a part of the Order, too."

Mussad pushed the eggs around on his plate. He wanted nothing to do with the Order or with his father. But that would not get him the information he needed.

"Of course, Father."

Vito nodded. "Hemings is descended from Thomas Jefferson."

Mussad almost sighed. His father had the annoying habit of relating every Order member to his origination in the Brotherhood. "But Hemings is a black man."

"Of course. He was the product of Jefferson's affair with his slave Sally Hemings. One of several children, as I recall."

Mussad had to assume that it wasn't something Hemings was proud of since the man had not used the information in his campaign for presidency. "It will be a great achievement for the Order to have a member in control of America."

Mussad knew quite a bit about Hemings's politics. The infidel was no different from any other American, worse than most. Always on television talking about how terrorists—*his colleagues*—were wrong and had to be stopped. But that didn't matter. Ziyad had plans that would eliminate Hemings, along with a number of other political leaders in America. Mussad thought it could not come soon enough. He allowed himself a smile. Ziyad's plans would not only cripple the American government, but they would also strike a blow to the Order. Not a death blow, most likely. But possibly enough to make them realize that their plans to rule the world were worthless. Though he knew they would never realize they were misguided. They weren't like Mussad and Ziyad and the others. He and his friends were following the teachings of the Prophet Mohammad. They were showing the world that Allah was the only way. And if they didn't understand that, then they were infidels.

They deserved to die.

‡ ‡ ‡

December 21, Florence, Italy

Logan finished typing the translation of the coded document he was working on and clicked the *save* icon. After decoding half a dozen documents, he now understood why the Order had wanted him for this project. The documents were written in a variety of codes. Some were simple, others extremely complex. He'd encountered codes that were based on number theory, ancient languages, one was even done with a scytale. It would have taken weeks to find a rod the exact circumference to decode the strip of paper. But Logan had written a program years ago that could calculate the circumference with a few measurements. In spite of his expertise with computers and technical encrypting, his specialty was in mathematics and ciphering basic codes. The ones created by humans when they needed to keep secrets, rather than the ones created by machines built by those humans. And there was plenty of that here.

The documents he'd worked on had all been different. All coded by different people with different mind-sets. None of them had been that difficult—yet. But they'd all been ingenious in one way or another, and there were more to come. The documents had been encoded by men who were geniuses, and that lent a certain difficulty to deciphering them. Each man had used his own unique abilities to write the code for his document.

Logan rose from his seat and stretched. His upper back ached from the hours he'd spent hunched over the documents in spite of the ergonomic chair. The room's ornate décor contrasted with the chair and workstation he used. Louis XIV? he wondered. Whatever the period of décor, it featured a lot of gilt and fanciful scrolls. An intricate tapestry hung from an equally fancy rod on one wall; paintings in heavy gilt frames covered the others. The oak parquet floor was dotted with plush carpets. Logan doubted they'd been bought at a local rug emporium. He poured a cup of hours-old coffee from the automatic coffeemaker and took it back to his desk to continue working.

The fact that he didn't understand a tenth of what the documents contained made the work just that much more difficult. There were documents that dealt with physics that went well beyond his knowledge, and others that seemed almost biblical. Flowery prose that spoke of what was to be, what might be, and puzzling references as to how to make sure something did or did not happen. And none of it got him any closer to finding his uncle.

"Perhaps you would like a break from your work?"

Logan set his cup down and turned to see Weisbaum in the doorway of his work area. "Yeah, a break would be good right about now." He refused to let Weisbaum see that his unannounced entry was unnerving.

"How are the documents coming along?" Weisbaum asked.

"Not so bad. I've decoded about six of them. Still have a stack to go."

"The Order is pleased with your work. That is why we have decided you deserve a boon."

Logan didn't know what to say. The way Weisbaum was talking sounded like something from a historical novel. It was so at odds with the number theories, frequency analyses, and key codes he'd been working with that it almost didn't make any sense to him.

"You would like to see your uncle, yes?"

Logan snapped to attention. "Yes. Very much so."

"Follow me," Weisbaum instructed.

Logan rose and followed Weisbaum out of the room and down the thickly carpeted hallway. The sound of their shoes echoed hollowly when they stepped down the marble staircase to the empty foyer. Weisbaum opened the double doors to one of the parlors on the ground floor and moved to the ornate fireplace on the opposite wall. He held a hand up, motioning Logan to stay where he was. Logan stopped and watched Weisbaum, not that he could see much in the dim light of the room. After a moment, the wood panel to the right of the fireplace slid open. Logan shivered, sure that he could feel a cool draft from the opening. Weisbaum motioned him forward and entered the small doorway.

Logan had to duck to avoid hitting his head as he followed Weisbaum. After about a dozen steps down a narrow staircase, Weisbaum opened a door, which let a sharp shaft of light into the narrow corridor. He hurried to catch up to Weisbaum.

He stepped through the doorway into a square room, no more than twelve by twelve feet. The walls were a utilitarian beige, and there was a nondescript vinyl sofa on one wall, two straight-backed wooden chairs and a round table on another. He couldn't imagine what the purpose of the room would be. Or what the hell it was doing underneath the mansion.

"Make yourself comfortable, Logan. Your uncle will be here shortly."

Hc almost snorted at that comment. He hadn't had a comfortable moment since his uncle had disappeared. He waited for a few minutes, then got up and walked around the room, seeming to be passing time waiting for his uncle, but actually looking for hidden bugs and cameras. He didn't find any that were readily identifiable. He sat at the small table and ran his hand underneath it, then moved to the sofa. He didn't see anything that looked like it could be a microphone or a camera, but what the hell did he know? He paced the room for a few more minutes, then settled in a chair at the table again.

"Logan."

He turned at the sound of his uncle's voice. "Uncle Giovanni!" Ho rose so quickly the chair almost fell over.

"Come. Give me a hug. It's been too long." Giovanni held out his arms and Logan walked into them. He enveloped the older man and fought back the tears that burned his eyes. He'd never really been sure he would see his uncle again.

"You okay, Uncle G?"

"I'm fine, fine. And you. How are you doing?"

"I'm good." Logan wanted to ask his uncle a million questions, but the thought that the room could be bugged held him back.

"Come. Sit. We have much to talk about." Giovanni sat on the sofa and angled his body toward the other end, waiting for Logan to sit. "I'm sorry I have had so little time to talk to you.." He waved a hand. "I should have contacted you after I left your place. But I've been so very busy."

"After you left? You were kidnapped. Abducted." Logan stopped, thinking about the possibility of bugs again. The hell with it. This might be his only chance to talk to his uncle. The least he could do would be to find out exactly why he was here.

Giovanni laughed. "I can see how it would appear. But these people, they have only brought me to where I need to be. This is the most amazing place, Logan."

"How's that?"

"Here, I have everything I need to do my life's work. The lab is incredible. Everything I need. Everything I've ever wished for."

"The lab?"

"And the living quarters are exceptional, as well. We all have separate rooms, private baths. All our needs are seen to."

"Who are you talking about, Uncle G?"

"The other scientists." Giovanni smiled at him. "This is what we have all hoped for." He waved his hand again. "Not just the lab and the rooms. The chance to work on what is really important. We're doing something that will help the entire world."

"What? How?"

"Energy," Giovanni said. "Clean, safe, inexpensive energy. For the entire world. It will change life as we know it."

"You're talking about cold fusion?" Logan searched his mind for references in the documents he'd decoded. Although he understood the basics of cold fusion, he didn't have an inkling about the specifics, but certainly some of what he'd read could apply.

"No. Cold fusion isn't enough. Sure, it can be done. But there's always the problems with regulating it and containing it. This is better than cold fusion."

Logan didn't want to ask how. That would only result in hours of dissertation from his uncle. "It seemed that you had been kidnapped. Abducted. I mean, you were just going for a walk one morning and then you were gone."

"No. No kidnapping. Just a misunderstanding. They were only getting me to the place where I can do my work." Giovanni reached out and grasped Logan's hand. "You need to trust me. These are good people."

Logan looked down at the wrinkled hand that held his. It looked the same as when he'd been a child and hung around his uncle while he did his experiments and made endless notes about them. He knew that his uncle's work was his life. It didn't surprise Logan that he would willingly go along with anyone who enabled him to do his work. He knew that Giovanni wouldn't even see the possibility that he was being used. How could he explain this to his uncle?

"Uncle Giovanni, I'm really happy that you're doing the work you want to do. I'm just a little concerned." He grinned at his uncle. "I can't accept that they just took you off the street."

"No, no. Not like that at all. I came willingly. How could I not? They have offered me everything I ever wanted." Giovanni smiled at him. "And I told them you would be the best to figure out the coded documents. They came to you, no?"

Logan nodded. Yes, they came to him, although it wasn't as benevolent as his uncle seemed to think.

"They pay you good money, no?"

Sure. He was getting three times what he'd been earning at the NSA. Not that a government salary was all that much.

"And you are helping the entire world." Giovanni slapped his leg. "That is the best. Doing what you are meant to do and getting a good salary and doing good for the world all at the same time? How could it be any better?"

Logan nodded. He made the decision to hold his

thoughts for now. After he'd had more time with his uncle he could broach the subject. And if he knew more about what they were doing, it could help convince his uncle to leave. "Of course. This is important work." He paused. "But what are the documents I'm decoding? What do they mean?"

"We won't know until we put them all together." Giovanni shrugged. "I know they all lead to the same thing. The energy source that we want."

"Where the hell do they come from?" Logan asked.

"All over. For many years—decades, even longer—some scientists have pooled their knowledge. They hand that knowledge down to younger scientists. But over time there often appeared to be people, groups, even governments that didn't want us to share our findings. So the information was written in code sometimes."

"I see."

"And now is the time for it to all come together." Giovanni clapped his hands together like a child. "Now we will free the world from the wrong way of doing things, the wrong way of thinking."

Logan tried to smile at his uncle. *Wrong way of thinking?*

Giovanni reached a hand into his pocket and drew out a small, faceted crystal globe that hung from a silver chain. He dangled the globe so that the light hit it and blazed out in a prismatic display of colors. "You remember this?"

Logan's face relaxed into a genuine smile. "We used to play some kind of game with it when you visited, didn't we? What was it? A word game?"

"That was one of them." Giovanni nodded. "There were many we played."

"I loved it when you came to visit." Logan sat back in his chair. He felt more relaxed than he'd been in a long time. A very long time. He remembered playing outside the guest cottage while his uncle worked. He would spend the entire day with him, until his mother called them to dinner.

"Yes. I enjoyed it, as well." Giovanni held the globe higher so that Logan had to lift his eyes to watch it. "Remember the beach?"

Logan nodded.

"Can you hear the waves crashing on the shore? Feel the warmth of the sun on your face?"

Logan's eyelids fluttered and closed.

"Remember how happy you were? Remember what I taught you? How you're special. Chosen for a special place in the world? To do special work?"

"I remember."

11

December 22, Florence, Italy

Zoe parked the Kawasaki Ninja 240R at the top of a hill and took off her helmet. She opened the saddlebag and pulled out a Nikon monocular. From the hill, she had a clear view of the Triumvirate's mansion. She hadn't realized just how large the structure was when she'd been inside it. From here she could see that it extended back much farther than she'd expected. But more interesting was the activity at the front entrance. A steady stream of cars pulled into the gated driveway. They each stopped in front of the door, let several people out, and then drove on. She focused her monocular on the limousine that had just arrived. Three men and a woman, all dressed in business suits, emerged. The car drove off and another one immediately took its place.

She continued to watch for another half hour as car after car arrived and departed. Perhaps the

Triumvirate was having a party? Zoe couldn't imagine that, and besides, there was something strange about what she was looking at. She focused her monocular on the next car and watched as three more men got out and entered the mansion. That was it. There were hardly any women in the groups. She'd seen maybe three women and at least fifty men. So, maybe a business meeting? Even so, there should be more women.

Zoe slid the monocular into her fanny pack, rode her motorcycle around so that she was less than a hundred yards from the back of the mansion, and parked behind some bushes. She slipped through the shadows to the back of the wall that surrounded the mansion. As she'd expected, a motion detection device was mounted on the top of the eight-foot-high stone wall. Anyone climbing over the wall would break the photoelectric beam and set off an alarm system. Almost anyone. This is where her diminutive stature worked in her favor. Along with all the gymnastics training she'd done over the years.

She climbed up the wall easily, finding plenty of finger- and toeholds for her small hands and feet. When she reached the top, she quickly assessed the electronics. There were two electronic beams. One about ten inches above the wall, the other about thirty inches. That posed a problem. While she could slide under the lower beam, it would be almost impossible to get into a position to do that without tripping the beam. The higher beam would make stepping over it impossible with her twenty-six-inch inseam. That left going in between them.

She reversed her steps to the ground, backed up a few paces, and considered the wall. If she could get a perch high enough and close enough, she could dive in between the beams. Of course, she'd then be diving down eight feet or more to the ground. Not great, but with a tuck-and-roll maneuver, she'd be all right. Probably. The real problem was that there was nothing to get her up to the right height and distance. A tree grew a short distance from the wall, but even though it would take her to the right height, it looked too far away for the dive she'd need to take. But there was nothing else, so Zoe climbed up the tree.

From this height, she had an excellent view of the grounds inside the wall. One corner held a stack of firewood. It looked to be a couple of cords and was stacked to within a few feet of the top of the wall. That would be good for getting out, but she first had to get in. The branch she stood on was higher than the top beam. There was no way she could get close enough to dive between the beams. But she might be able to dive over the top beam. That meant she'd be falling to the ground from a height of about eleven feet. Not all that different from dismounting from the uneven parallel bars. Except that she'd be landing on hard ground rather than the closed-cell foam pads used in gyms.

There was no other way. Zoe edged out onto the limb as far as she thought it would hold her weight. She bounced on the limb a couple of times, wincing at the creaking of the wood. She backed up several steps and took a deep breath, then blew it out. She balanced herself, took a final glance at the ground on the other side of the wall, and ran lightly down the branch. When she reached the point she'd chosen earlier, she launched herself into the air and sailed over the wall, clearing the beam by inches. Zoe tucked into a ball then extended just in time for her feet to hit the ground.

The shock of her landing reverberated from the soles of her feet through her ankles and up her shins. She took a minute to catch her breath. She'd tied her boots as tightly as possible around her ankles, and even though she wanted to unlace them, she knew better. The pain was abated by the fact that the alarms hadn't been activated. Now to get into the mansion.

All the windows on the back of the mansion were wired with alarms. She might be able to circumvent them, but it would be tricky. She headed along the side of the building and was rewarded with a partially open window on the ground floor. There was no sign of alarms, probably because the window was too small for anyone to get through but a child—or her.

She jumped up and grabbed the edge of the windowsill with both hands, then pulled her body up. Peering through the partially open window, she recognized the small guest bathroom. She balanced on one hand and pushed the window farther open. Her arms quivered with the strain when she straightened them and pulled one leg up and through the opening. Resting her hip on the windowsill, she pulled the other leg inside. She had to turn sideways to get her hips through the opening. Her shoulders were an even tighter fit and she almost ripped her shirt squeezing through.

She opened the door a crack and looked out. The wide hallway was dim, lit only by a bright light that splashed from a set of open French doors. If she remembered correctly, those doors led to an enormous ballroom. She slipped down the hallway and stopped behind a statue where she could see part of the interior of the ballroom.

Rows of folding chairs were arranged in semicircles facing a raised platform where an older man stood at a podium and spoke to the group. Zoe had never seen him before. The Triumvirate sat in chairs positioned behind the speaker. She scanned the room, which was only half-full in spite of having so many people in it. These people were obviously involved in the Order. And she knew Ethan would want to know who they were. Unfortunately, there was no roster conveniently lying around.

The ballroom was open to the second floor and Zoe saw an ornate railing that ran the length of one wall. At either end were heavy velvet drapes.

She slipped from her hiding place, ran silently down the hallway, turned left, and moved down another hallway to the wide curving staircase that led to the upper three floors. At the second floor, she turned right and hugged the wall until she reached the velvet drapes. She pulled her credit card–sized camera from her fanny pack and clicked off photos of the people attending the meeting. She included a few of the older man and the Triumvirate on the platform for good measure, although she mostly got photos of their backs. Everyone began applauding, then they rose from their seats and milled about. Time for her to disappear.

She ran down the stairs and headed for the guest bathroom. She twisted the knob, but it didn't move. Someone called out that they'd be out in a moment. She could hear people talking as they left the ballroom. And there was no place to hide until the person in the bathroom came out.

She slipped down the hallway and opened the door to the room where she'd always met with the Triumvirate. She flipped on the light, left the door open, and dropped into the chair in front of the desk.

Slouching down, she propped her feet on the desk and rested her head on the back of the chair with her eyes closed. She heard the door close just moments later.

"What are you doing here?"

"Waiting for you, obviously." Zoe turned her head to look at Weisbaum, but didn't take her feet off the antique desk.

"Do you mind?" He glared pointedly at her feet.

"Sorry." She took her time putting her feet on the floor. "So, what's next?"

"That hasn't been decided yet."

"Well, I get bored just hanging around all day, you know?" She grinned at him. "And I don't like to stay around too long in a place where I've pulled a job."

"You assured us that no one would even know that you'd taken the document from the museum."

"Probably they won't, but you never know."

"How did you get in?" Weisbaum asked.

"Through the front door."

"That's impossible."

"Well, not if it's standing open."

"The door was open?"

"Didn't I just say that? Must have been because of your party." She waved a hand and stood. "I closed it and turned on the alarm, but you might want to find out who's leaving your door open. Anyone could have walked in here."

"I'll be sure to check into it. And we should have another job for you soon. In the meantime, why don't you just enjoy your visit to Italy?"

Zoe watched while Weisbaum glanced out at the hallway, then held the door for her.

"Sure, no problem."

‡ ‡ ‡

December 22, CIA Headquarters, Langley, Virginia

"Senator Hemings, nice to see you again." Jeremy Olson nodded. "I understand you want to view the Computer Server Room today."

Hemings smiled and shook Olson's hand. "I'm kind of a wannabe geek, I guess. I've heard you guys have some impressive equipment here."

"Yes, sir, that we do." Olson led Hemings down a wide hallway. "So, you like computers?"

"Oh, I love them. Just don't understand them very well." He laughed. "I majored in political science instead of computer science in school." He didn't add that he'd been a hacker in his youth. He'd outgrown that, but he still played with computers a lot. In fact, he was pretty certain that they'd never let him in the computer room if they had any idea what his capabilities were.

"I'm not much with computers myself," Olson admitted. "I know enough to get around and do my job and that's about it." Olson slipped his key card into the reader, then opened the door.

The room held banks of servers with blinking green and amber lights. One wall was filled with tables that held keyboards and monitors.

"No people?" Hemings asked. "These things run themselves?"

"Almost, from what I understand. But not entirely. The computer operators are housed in the room next door. They monitor everything from there. The workspace in here is only used occasionally."

"Impressive," Hemings said. He walked around the room pretending to look over the equipment. After a few minutes, he paused and leaned against the wall, one hand rubbing his chest.

"Everything all right, Senator?" Olson asked.

"Just a little angina." Hemings shook his head, then gasped for breath. "Maybe I'd better sit down for a minute."

Olson led him to a chair at the worktables. "You sure you're all right? Maybe I should call someone."

"No, it's nothing, really. I'll just take one of my pills and it'll go away." He patted his pockets with a hand and grunted. "Must have left them in my overcoat." He breathed in a way that sounded like he was short of breath. "I hung it up at Susan's desk." His hand rubbed at his chest again. "Think you could go get them for me?"

"Sure. I'll be right back." Olson ran out of the room and Hemings straightened. He pulled a hand-held device from his breast pocket and ran a thin cable from the device to a connection in the back of one of the servers. He tapped commands into the unit with a stylus and waited a moment, then tapped in more commands to find the directory of files he wanted. The unit started to download data and he turned to the door. Olson wouldn't be gone more than four minutes and he wasn't sure how long it would take the files to transfer. The unit beeped just as the doorknob turned. Hemings disconnected the cable and replaced the unit in his pocket as he ran back to the worktable and slumped into the chair.

"Thanks." Hemings didn't have to fake the sheen of sweat on his forehead or the slight tremor of his hand as he took the glass of water from Olson. "The pills are in the breast pocket." Olson found the pills, opened the bottle, and handed one to Hemings.

Hemings placed the pill under his tongue and smiled tremulously at Olson. After a few minutes he straightened. "Damned inconvenient." He stood up. "Fortunately it's nothing serious, just painful until I take one of those little pills. And it doesn't happen all that often."

"That's good to know, sir."

"Well, I don't want to keep you from your duties. Thanks for showing me this." He waved his hand at the equipment. "I wish I understood even a little of it." He laughed and Olson joined him.

"Anytime, sir. And have a Merry Christmas."

"Thank you. Happy Holidays to you, as well."

Hemings shook Olson's hand and walked out with all the files pertaining to The Order tucked in his pocket.

‡ ‡ ‡

December 23, Outside Bern, Switzerland

Dr. Margot Epstein made a notation on her PDA and looked up at the sound of the automatic door swooshing open.

"Capo, has it been three months already, or are you just here for an update?" she asked, dropping her PDA into her lab coat pocket.

"It's time for my booster, but I'd love an update, as well."

"Of course. I must have lost track of time the past few months."

"Time flies." Capo grinned. "But, fortunately, not

for us."

"And it's a good thing. There's so much work to do." But she wasn't complaining. She loved her work. Lived for it, really.

"This is the latest batch?" Capo asked, gesturing to the racks of gallon-sized cylinders.

Margot nodded. "A grand total of three thousand, after the first culling. Pretty evenly distributed between the peacekeepers, domestics, and laborers."

"That is good news, indeed. Over thirty percent of them took."

"Our results are getting better with each batch," Margot agreed.

"When is the second culling?" Capo asked.

"Another two months. By then we'll be able to test each fetus for defects. Hopefully, we'll still have two thousand left after that."

"So we should end up with at least a thousand that will go full-term?"

"At least," Margo said. "Let's get your shot out of the way and then I'll show you our progress."

Capo followed her out of the lab and down a wide hallway to her office. She keyed in a code, and opened the small refrigeration unit behind her desk.

Capo rolled up a sleeve and sat on the small sofa. Margot tied rubber tubing around his upper arm, drew fluid from the vial, and slid the needle painlessly into his vein. She withdrew the needle, pressed a cotton ball to the puncture, and discarded the syringe in a container marked with a biohazard emblem.

"There. You're good for another three months."

"Can you imagine what people would pay for this?" Capo asked.

"Just about anything, I'd think." Margo glanced at her reflection in the glass door of her office. "Aging only one year for every ten? I know I'd pay a lot for it. Fortunately, I don't have to."

"Before, I worried that I'd never live long enough to finish my work." Capo rolled down his sleeve and buttoned the cuff. "Now, I know I will."

"Another hundred years or more for each of us." Margot nodded. The virus she'd injected into Capo's arm carried a special strand of DNA. The virus would attack certain cells, allowing the DNA to invade those cells so that they reproduced differently, eventually replacing the original DNA and slowing the aging process to a tenth of what would normally occur.

"I'm anxious to see our progress." Capo rolled down his sleeve and buttoned the cuff.

"Do you want to see the embryo room again or go to the gestational area?"

Capo laughed. "Embryos aren't all that interesting. Let's have a look at the gestations." He held the door for her and followed her down the hall to an elevator. They rode the elevator down one floor and emerged into a vast space.

"These are just past the final culling." Margot gestured at the Plexiglas cylinders. "I expect at least ninety-five percent of them to deliver." In each five-gallon cylinder, a fetus floated in a special biochemical bath. The fetuses were well formed and appeared much like a newborn infant. They would be transferred to two successively larger cylinders before the process was completed. Margot walked past the line of cylinders to the far end of the room and opened a door.

"These are the two-year-olds." Margot spoke as if she was the mother of the two hundred fetuses. "I just received the report on their development and it's excellent. Normal reflexes, growth, and brain activity consistent with five-year-old humans."

"It seems we are losing fewer with each batch," Capo said.

"True," Margot agreed. "We've had great success in refining the DNA strands used to fertilize the ovum. The next batch will be our first attempt at cloning."

"You expect it to go well?"

"Absolutely. I imagine we'll lose a few more to environmental problems, but we won't be losing the percentage that we normally expect when the ovum DNA is stronger than the fertilizing DNA."

"This looks different from the last time. Have you

instituted changes?" Capo asked.

"You have a sharp eye." Margot nodded. "We increased the movement of the biochemical bath. It gives the fetuses something to work against, which develops their muscles better." She moved to the end of the room and opened another door. "And here are the ones we'll deliver next."

"Your babies."

Margot laughed. "Not all of them are literally my babies, although I think about a quarter of them are." She had used her own eggs for a section of this group of fetuses. The hormone treatments to increase her egg production for several months and the extraction procedure had been difficult, but well worth it. "Twenty of these are my own."

"Which ones?"

"Capo." Margot shook her head and smiled. "I have no idea. There are records, of course, but I'd never personalize this procedure to the point of knowing which ones were created with my ovum." The lie slid off her tongue smoothly, but, in truth, she knew exactly which ones had been created from her eggs. She kept track of them. Not in the computer records, of course. But in her mind. She'd even given some of them pet names. The ones created from her ovum had a substantially higher success rate than the others. She suspected that was due to the anti-aging virus she and

Capo were injected with and planned a series of tests to confirm that.

"How long until delivery?" Capo asked.

The fetuses were about the size of a young teenager. They all showed the beginnings of puberty with the development of secondary sex characteristics. The females were developing breasts although they would never be very large. One of the side effects was that most of them were almost androgynous. The males had all shown an incredibly low sperm count and while the females had ovaries and produced eggs, most had no uterus. Margot had planned to mate some of them, but she'd had to do it in vitro. The first batch had not gone well; she'd lost almost ninety percent of the eggs she'd fertilized, and none had survived past six months in the biochemical bath.

"These will deliver in about five months," Margot said. "I think this is the best batch yet. The Peacekeepers are developing exceptionally well. And the Domestics and Laborers have improved with each batch."

"Psychologically, as well?" Capo asked.

"We haven't had any psychological problems since the first batch that had to be terminated." Margot shrugged. "It wasn't a surprise. We expected some difficulties in the beginning. But we've worked out the kinks now. The last three batches have all been the same psychologically. I'd call it semisentient."

"So, they are self-aware to some degree?"

"It appears so, but they all subvert their self-awareness to the wishes of the masters. They appear to be content with that," Margo said.

"Like a dog, then?"

"Probably a slightly higher level than that. Certainly with more intelligence and ability."

"Good. They will serve us well, then." Capo nodded. "Just as we serve the Legacy."

‡ ‡ ‡

December 24, Iraq

"We are almost ready," Ziyad said. "And slightly ahead of schedule."

"Good. The infidels' next president is proceeding with his inaugural plans," Ayman said.

"He would be an even greater enemy than the last president. But we will prevent that."

"And the virus is ready now?"

Ziyad nodded. "It is even more than I had hoped for. Very fast acting, so the infidels will watch all their leaders suffer and die on television."

"What we are doing will change the face of the world," Ayman agreed.

"But first we must devise the delivery method. The problem is that Rashid cannot carry the device on himself. It's too large and he will have to pass through a security check."

"Then we will have to find another way. There must be somewhere we can plant the device in advance of the ceremony."

Ziyad handed him several photographs of the rotunda of the Capitol Building in Washington, D.C. "This is how it will look, according to past events."

"The podium is really the only thing on the stage. We might be able to hide the device here." Ayman pointed to a column.

"That will be difficult," Ziyad said. "The security that day will be overwhelming, and the Neurotox has to be kept above six degrees Celsius, so planting it ahead of time could be a problem, depending on the weather."

"The podium seems to be the best place. It would be kept inside until that day."

"But how to get to the podium?" Ziyad stood and paced the room. "We have less than a month to accomplish this."

"We will find a way," Ayman assured him. "I have a man working on the maintenance crew at the Capitol Building. He might be able to discover the logistics of the event."

"Impress upon him the importance of acquiring this knowledge."

Ayman nodded and looked at the photos again. "Amazing, isn't it? That all the leaders gather in one rather small space."

"Everyone will be there," Ziyad said. "The president, the president-elect. Same for the vice presidents. As well as the old cabinet and most of the incoming new cabinet."

"Even the Speaker of the House and the president pro tempore of the Senate." Ayman shook his head.

"They assume that their security will prevent an attack of any kind."

"And that is to our advantage. They will never see this coming," Ayman said.

"We will finally take off the head of the snake."

12

December 26, Florence, Italy

Zoe logged on to her computer and opened her e-mail account. The inbox was empty. Not that she'd been expecting anything. This had been the strangest Christmas she'd ever had. The Triumvirate hadn't come up with another heist for her. She'd emailed the pictures she'd taken at the mansion to Ethan and received an acknowledgement and a Merry Christmas from him.

She hadn't seen Logan in several days. They probably had him sequestered somewhere decoding the documents she'd stolen for them. She still hadn't heard anything about the next job. Which meant another day of doing nothing. Probably two days of doing nothing. The inactivity was wearing on her. She'd already worked out at the hotel's gym. There was still time for a run before dark. That was the one thing she'd been skimping on since she'd been in Italy. She pulled on leggings and a T-shirt, laced up her running shoes, and stuffed her key card into her fanny pack.

An hour later, she was leaning over, sucking in gulps of air and glancing across the street at her mother's house. Why had she ended up here? Her mother had told her why she'd left. Because of her brother. And what Mira feared Zeke would do to him. So, her brother had grown up here in Italy. In luxury and wealth, by all appearances. She wondered what he was like. She wondered a lot of things. She pulled her cell phone from her fanny pack and punched in the number she'd memorized.

"Hello?"

"This is Zoe. I thought maybe we could meet again."

"Oh, I'd love to. Do you want to come here? Or I could meet you somewhere? Any time that is good for you."

"Now is good."

"Now? Where are you?"

"Right outside." Zoe walked across the road and stood at the steps to the house. She saw the curtains move and then the door opened. Mira still held the phone in one hand and reached toward Zoe with the other.

"I'm so pleased you called." Mira stood aside to let Zoe through the doorway. "We have so much to talk about."

Zoe wasn't sure about that. But, then, why was she here? She turned to Mira, about to tell her that it was a mistake, when she noticed a young man standing on the stairs.

"You must be Zoe." The man bounded down the stairs and wrapped his arms around her. "I can't believe I have a sister. I used to annoy Mother constantly, asking for a sibling."

Zoe stiffened in his embrace, and he drew back. "Sorry, I forget that not everyone is as emotional as we Italians are." He grinned and his golden eyes twinkled. "You'll have to get used to it."

"Matt, give her room to breathe." Mira pulled at his arm and he finally stepped back a couple of feet. "Zoe, this is your brother, Matteo de Luca."

"I see." She was too overwhelmed to say much more and allowed Mira to lead her into the parlor. Zoe sat stiffly on the edge of the sofa; Matt sat on the other end of the sofa. His posture was relaxed, his body turned toward her, one arm thrown over the back of the couch. Mira took a chair opposite them.

"I can't believe I have a big sister." Matt laughed. "Well, not big," he indicated her small stature. "But older. We even have the same eyes."

"I noticed. It comes from a recessive gene. Our father has dark brown eyes and"—Zoe gestured toward Mira, unsure what to call her—"she has light blue eyes."

Mira smiled in a way that made Zoe want to call her Mom or Mother. With a sickening feeling Zoe realized that what she really wanted was to throw herself into her mother's arms. She wanted to absorb all the motherly affection she'd been denied for so many years. But she couldn't. She wasn't willing to take that kind of risk.

"I have to run." Matt glanced at his watch. "Another meeting. But we'll get together soon, Zoe. I want to hear all about your life." He stood, then leaned down and embraced her again. "*Mi sorella*," he whispered.

"Would you like some tea? Or coffee?" Mira asked after Matt had left.

"No, I'm fine." She paused, looking around the room in order to avoid her mother's gaze.

"What brings you to Italy?" Mira asked.

"I'm on a job."

"Matteo and I would love to have you stay with us while you're here."

"That's not possible. Besides, how would you explain a grown daughter to your husband?"

"I'm a widow."

Zoe refused to feel sympathy for her, refused to give her any condolence. "Explain to me again why you left me." Zoe held up a hand. "I understand why you didn't want Matt to be trained as a thief, and I understand your fear that Dad would do that. But if you didn't approve of what he did, why did you marry him?"

"When I met Zeke Alexander, I was swept away by his handsome looks, his exquisite manners." She lifted a delicate shoulder. "I fell in love with him. I was also just eighteen years of age, and so incredibly naïve."

"You didn't know he was a thief, did you?"

"No." Mira shook her head. "In fact, I wasn't sure of it until after you were born." She waved a perfectly manicured hand. "Oh, I understand that he kept it from me in order to protect me. At least that's what he believed."

"But you loved him?"

"Oh, yes. I loved him so much that I was quite certain I could change him. After a few years, I realized that was impossible."

"So you left him. And me."

"That was possibly the most difficult decision I've ever had to make. I don't know if I could ever make you understand, Zoe, but I felt that by staying I would be sacrificing Matt to a horrible life. At the same time, I knew that your father doted on you. I knew that he would take care of you and love you. And, of course, Nana Phoebe agreed to stay for as long as she was needed." Mira drew patterns on the arm of the chair with a finger. "It wasn't an easy decision, but I did the best I could."

"Nana Phoebe stayed for a long time. She was the mother I never had." Zoe pushed aside the twinge of regret when she saw the pain in her mother's eyes. She hadn't set out to hurt her, but she wasn't going to back down now. Mira clasped her hands together and leaned forward.

"When you were here before, you said something. You said, 'You were wrong.' What did you mean by that?"

Zoe considered her mother for a moment. Part of her wanted to protect Mira from the knowledge that her daughter was a thief. But why should she? Shouldn't the woman know what she'd done to her only daughter? She'd protected one child, but at the expense of another.

"After you left, my father was incredibly morose for a time. But he soon recovered. Part of his recovery was time he spent with me."

"Of course."

"The time he spent training me to be a thief. As I recall, I started by picking pockets. Although, not on the street for several years. After that came training in gymnastics, safecracking, security systems. You know, the usual."

"Oh, God." Tears pooled in Mira's eyes. "I had no idea. I never would have left you if I'd known."

"You never came back for me, either. Was that not an option, or had you just lost interest by then?"

Mira stiffened. "I always wanted to, but my life hasn't always been so luxurious." She gestured at the room. "I spent many years living hand to mouth. When Matt was twelve, I met Francesco de Luca. We were married a year later, and Francesco adopted Matt." She took a shuddering breath. "The first twelve years after I left your father were incredibly difficult. I worked as a maid, in a laundry, as a waitress. Anything I could find to put food on the table."

Zoe steeled herself against the wave of sympathy. "And then you met a rich man and made a deal?"

"No! It was not like that. Francesco and I loved each other. He adopted Matteo as his own son."

"But you never told him about your other husband? You never told him about your daughter?"

"I couldn't. I married him while I was still married to your father. He thought I was a widow. And you were already sixteen when we married. I thought that the last thing you needed was a long lost mother coming into your life. Besides, your father would have never let me take you. And what would it have done to Matteo?"

"I don't know. I only know what it did to your daughter."

"Can you ever forgive me, Zoe?"

Zoe closed her eyes and fought the tears that burned behind her eyelids. She needed to get out of there. She couldn't think straight with all the opposing emotions that were hitting her. She opened her eyes and cleared her throat. "I think it's a little early for that question."

"Are you sure you can't stay with us? We would so love to have you here."

"My job precludes that," Zoe said.

"What kind of job are you doing?"

"I told you," Zoe said, standing, "I'm here on business."

‡ ‡ ‡

December 28, Florence, Italy

"Weisbaum," he answered the phone as he checked the list of documents again. There were only four more documents needed. Hopefully. That's what Capo had decided. Weisbaum wasn't sure of Capo's decision, but there was really nothing he could do about it. There was just no way of knowing until they had the documents and everything assembled.

"Hemings, here."

Karl pulled his attention to the phone call. "Senator Hemings. We haven't spoken since the election. Allow me to extend my congratulations on your victory."

"Thank you. I know Capo insisted that the Legacy document predicted the win, but I was still anxious."

"Understandable," Karl said. "But I'm surprised you aren't swamped with official duties today."

"I am, but I had to call. We have a problem."

"What?"

"I downloaded the files from the CIA computers last week. The thief you hired is working for the CIA."

Karl ground his teeth. "You've had those files for several days and you're just telling me this?"

"Back off, Weisbaum. There were a lot of documents to read through. I couldn't exactly assign it to one of my aides, could I?"

"Of course not. This news is perturbing, to say the least."

"No shit. I don't know what she's found out already. There could be documents that weren't in the files yet. This could bring everything down."

"We will contain it," Weisbaum said, silently cursing Capo for insisting that they hire Zoe. It was just another thing that Capo had screwed up. And there had been a lot of screw ups lately.

"And how are you going to do that?"

"That isn't your concern, senator. We will handle the problem. Just make sure you choose your cabinet carefully. That is your job."

"Don't worry about that. By Inauguration Day, I'll have the right people lined up, and Congress convinced of their acceptability." He chuckled. "And The Order will be one step closer to fulfilling our Legacy."

"I'll take the matter of Zoe up with Capo today."

"See that you do."

Weisbaum listened to the dial tone for a few seconds before he slammed the receiver onto the cradle. He hadn't trusted her from the beginning. But after she'd proven herself on the first few thefts, he'd convinced himself that she really was just a thief. Hell, he'd even checked out her background and she *was* a thief. There had been nothing to indicate that she was associated with the CIA. Not a damn thing.

Leatherman should have found out this information. Then he remembered that the spy had been sent to Italy on a mission shortly after he'd recovered from the beating he'd suffered at Robertson's command. Robertson should have gone easier on him. Then he'd have been back to work sooner and they would have known earlier that Zoe was working with the CIA.

Karl walked to the small bar contained in a paneled alcove of his office and poured two fingers of vodka into a crystal glass. Logan had argued that the other thieves weren't up to the job and the damnable thing was that Logan was right. They probably hadn't been capable of doing the jobs Zoe had aced.

But hindsight only told him what had gone wrong. He needed to resolve the situation. He could just have her taken care of except for the fact that there were more thefts to be done. And they were all tricky. They required a professional. More than a professional. They required the kind of rare talent that only Zoe possessed. What was he going to do about that?

There was no time to recruit another thief—if he could even find one who could handle the jobs they had in mind. Somehow he needed to cut Zoe off from the CIA while still retaining her services. Somehow he needed to secure her loyalty. He sat at his desk and pulled a folder from the top drawer. The folder was labeled *Zoe Alexander* and contained all the information they had accumulated on her. There was her father. But indications were that they weren't especially close and in fact there was frequently antagonism between them. Still, he was a possibility. It was doubtful that she cared so little for him that she would allow him to die.

There was also her mother and a brother. They were estranged, although the information indicated that Zoe either believed or pretended that her mother and brother were both dead. Her mother had left when Zoe was a very small child. That would work in his favor. Would she be willing to do anything for the mother she'd lost so many years ago? He noted the mother's address and made up his mind. He'd start with her mother and brother. If that wasn't enough pressure, he'd send someone after her father. He could keep her working and keep her loyal to The Order. At least for as long as they needed her.

And eventually, he would have to do something about Capo. But not yet. He was still a necessary part of the science team. He had abilities and knowledge, even at his age, that outstripped the other physicists. And there was the matter of the people. The followers.

Of course, they had all been indoctrinated by their fathers, as he had been. It was part of the Legacy. Each father indoctrinated his eldest son, or in rare instances, his eldest daughter, into the beliefs of the Legacy. It began at a very early age and worked unusually well. But Karl knew that the indoctrination still had different degrees of success. Capo had the charisma that beckoned to the followers. The ability to make them want to follow him, to believe every word from his lips. He was the one who had convinced them all that the time was now. That was something he didn't dare disturb.

Yet.

‡ ‡ ‡

December 28, Iraq

Mussad bit into a sweet date and lifted his face to the sun. It was good to be in his homeland again. To feel the warmth of the sun on his skin. Italy had not been extremely cold, but at least twenty degrees cooler than what he was accustomed to. After only one night, he felt relaxed and rejuvenated. Here, at Ziyad's spacious compound, he was not confronted with the foods and activities that were *haram*. Like many of the other members of his cell, Mussad moved around too often to have a permanent residence. He and the others stayed in hotels or with family members or friends when possible. When they returned here, they usually stayed with Ziyad. It was a place to relax between missions. A haven of safety and comfort.

The time in Italy had been especially uncomfortable for Mussad. The days endured at his father's home had seemed interminable. But he had returned with information for Ziyad. And that made it worth it.

"*Salaam.*" Ziyad crossed the stone patio and took a chair at the table.

"*Salaam,*" Mussad returned.

"You rested well?"

"Yes." Mussad nodded. "It is a relief to be away from Italy and my father."

"I understand. Did you receive any new information from him?"

"Some. I don't know how important any of it will be to you."

"I'm sure it will be useful." Ziyad took a date and gestured to Mussad to begin.

"I did as you wished and expressed my interest in joining him in his work with the Order. There were no meetings while I was there, but he spoke of their plans at some length."

"Excellent."

"Unfortunately, he was not very specific. But he mentioned that they are working on an alternate energy source. He indicated that it would be completed soon."

"How soon?" Ziyad asked.

"Several months, perhaps, if all goes as they have planned. He did not tell me what it is, but said that it would end the world's dependency on our oil."

Ziyad nodded, a frown etched across his forehead. Mussad interpreted his silence as a command to continue.

"He also talked about how they will change the world. They believe they can bring peace to the world by using this energy source to create weapons much more powerful and flexible than what anyone has now."

"This is a concern." Ziyad stroked his beard. "We must, of course, prevent them from this. It is another effort to enslave us. I am sorry to tell you that you will need to return to your father's house."

"I expected as much," Mussad said. "I will go gladly. In the name of Allah."

Ziyad nodded. "Allah will bless you."

"My father also told me that the new American president is a member of the Order. It seems that the Order is much larger than we had thought."

"Hemings is a member? That is even more reason to kill him."

"My father told me about him. He is descended from Thomas Jefferson and one of the man's slaves." Mussad shook his head. "One of their most revered presidents, yet he owned slaves." While Islam tolerated the ownership of slaves, which Mussad didn't really understand, it did not approve of slavery itself.

"He also fornicated with his slaves, if Hemings is a descendant. Is this common knowledge?" Ziyad asked.

"I do not know." Mussad shrugged. "I have not heard of Hemings talking about it during his campaign."

"You will stay here for several days, then you will return to Italy. I am sorry you must subject yourself to your father, but it is necessary." Ziyad stood.

"It is no matter. I am happy to serve Allah any way I may." Mussad stretched his feet out and leaned his head against the back of his chair. He had several days to enjoy his homeland before returning to the iniquity of his father's house.

"I will join you later this afternoon." Ziyad walked across the patio with purposeful strides. Mussad's information had planted an idea that could possibly help them resolve the problem of delivering the Neurotox.

In the small room that served as an office, Ziyad turned on the computer and opened his Internet connection. He typed words and phrases into search engines and followed links until he found the information he was seeking. After half an hour, he'd discovered that while Hemings didn't make an issue of his connection to Jefferson, neither did he hide it, and, in fact, he seemed proud of his heritage. He had dedicated a room in his West Virginia home to the Jefferson artifacts and belongings he had collected.

Ziyad smiled as he continued reading. Surely the man would welcome the opportunity to take his oath of office at an antique podium once owned by his ancestor.

‡ ‡ ‡

December 29, CIA Headquarters, Langley, Virginia

"Do you have anything on the photographs?" Ethan asked Leo Buschner, one of the CIA's best computer techs. Leo could get a clear image from a picture that appeared to be nothing but jumbled pixels.

"Oh, yeah." Leo wheeled around in his chair. "First I had to isolate individual photographs of each person. Then I used the program I developed to enhance each picture. When I finally had usable photographs of each person—well, not of every person there—that's even beyond the capabilities of my program. And trust me, it's better than anything else out—"

"So, what did you find, Leo?" Ethan asked.

"Here." Leo handed him several sheets of paper. "The top sheet is just a list of all the people I was able to identify by comparing the photographs to photos we have on file. The other sheets are individual pictures with the names and short biographies of each person."

"My God!" Ethan read down the list Leo gave him. It included ten members of the World Banking Consortium, four members of Congress, several European politicians, and other notables from every industry, including major pharmaceutical firms, international software companies, and manufacturing conglomerates. "How accurate is this?"

"About ninety-nine point eight seven percent," Leo

replied. "You see, what I do is a comparison of—"

"Good work, Leo." Ethan rushed out, ignoring Leo's explanation.

"Don't feel bad," Robyn said. "He does it to me all the time."

"Yeah, well, I figure they're busy, you know?"

"That's one word for it," Robyn agreed.

"You got any plans for New Year's Eve?" Leo asked. "I'm going to a costume party. I've got this great costume. A Wookie. You want to come with me?"

Robyn stared at him for a moment. "No."

13

January 3, Florence, Italy

Mira woke suddenly and sat up. Her mouth was dry and her heart hammered against her breastbone. The clock on her nightstand read three fifteen. She tried to remember the vestiges of whatever dream must have awakened her, but she couldn't grasp even a hint of one. A thump sounded down the hallway. Someone was in the house. Her first thought was for Matteo. He slept like a rock and likely wouldn't wake from a noise in the house. She threw back the covers and pulled on the robe she'd left draped on the foot of the bed. The door opened before her feet were on the floor.

"Stay right there, ma'am."

Mira stood, pulled the belt of her robe tight, and knotted it. The man had shown her a measure of respect by calling her ma'am, and that made her hope that he had no intention of hurting her. On the other hand, he hadn't bothered to cover his face, which made her wonder why he didn't care that she saw him. But mostly, she hoped they had come for her and not for Matteo.

"Why are you here?" she asked, pleased that her voice was strong, because she felt like everything inside her was quivering.

"You're coming with us. Don't resist and it'll go easy. You'll be released later."

"Later?" Mira shoved her feet into slippers. "What's the reason for this?"

"You don't need to know that, ma'am."

"Really? You can come into my house and take me, but you think I have no reason to know why?" She looked the man over. He was tall and big, with a square jaw and unblinking eyes. He held a handgun easily, which made her think he'd done it before—a lot. Her mind worked furiously. The only thing different in her life recently was that Zoe had appeared. And her daughter had been reluctant to tell her why she was in Italy other than she was there on business. Knowing how Zeke had raised their daughter, she could imagine what kind of business that would be. But what it could possibly have to do with her, she couldn't imagine.

Mira sent up a silent prayer that whoever this man was, he would leave Matteo alone.

"This is because of Zoe, isn't it?"

That seemed to surprise the man. He blinked and

grunted. “Yeah. But she’ll come around and then you’ll be released.” He waved the gun in a beckoning gesture.

She straightened her shoulders and walked past him into the hallway. Another man stood outside the open door to Matteo’s room. She stopped, one hand fluttering to her throat, the other reaching out as a second man dragged her son from his room. There was a bloody gash over his left eye, which was already swelling closed. An angry red blotch blossomed on one shoulder, a raised welt on the other.

“Matteo!”

He turned to look at her and shook his head. “No, Mama.”

Mira knew he was pleading with her to not say anything. To do nothing that would make it worse for herself. As if to prove Matteo’s point, the man who’d entered her bedroom gripped her arm and pulled her down the hallway past her son. She stumbled along, turning her head in an effort to see her son until the man jerked her arm painfully and guided her down the stairs. The man led her out of the house and pushed her into the middle seat of a van. He fastened plastic strips around her wrists, then pulled her robe back over her shoulder where it had fallen down to expose the thin nightgown that barely covered her breast. Mira was struck again by his respectful attitude. Perhaps she could reason with him.

"Please. This is unnecessary."

The man turned back to look at her and shook his head.

"I don't know what you're trying to accomplish, but I can assure you that Zoe will not capitulate to your wishes because of me or my son. She doesn't even know us. She only met us a few days ago." The man gave no indication that her words were even heard.

"For God's sake! I abandoned her as a baby!" Mira sobbed and swallowed hard to stop the tears. "She has no reason to care what happens to us." The man stepped aside, and Matteo was shoved into the seat next to her.

Mira raised her bound hands to Matteo's battered face, tears streaming down her cheeks. There would be no reasoning with these men. No matter how polite their leader was.

‡ ‡ ‡

January 4, Florence, Italy

"It's done," Hank Robertson informed Weisbaum.

"You showed them to the rooms we had prepared?"

"The woman tried to reason with me. She indicated that Alexander would be less than concerned about her well-being or that of her son."

Weisbaum waved his hand. "She would say anything at that point. I imagine more to protect her son than to protect herself."

Hank nodded. "That would be consistent with her behavior."

"You administered the drugs?"

"As you ordered. They're both sleeping now."

"And they were not hurt?" Weisbaum asked. "I mean, seriously?"

"No, sir. We proceeded as you ordered. Were you aware that Alexander had contacted her mother since her arrival here?"

Weisbaum lifted his brows. "Really? I had no idea. Perhaps we should have been watching her a bit closer."

"It would be a shame if Alexander isn't persuaded by this."

"Yes. But there's always her father." Weisbaum walked across the room to sit behind his desk. "Has Ms. Alexander arrived?"

"Just before I came in, sir."

"Send her in." Weisbaum expected she would be more than a little put out by the fact that he'd sent two men to her hotel demanding that she accompany them here. It was about time Ms. Alexander learned that she didn't have the upper hand after all.

‡ ‡ ‡

"What the hell is this about?" Zoe shook off the man who was holding her elbow and stomped across the room to stand in front of Weisbaum's desk. "Is there some reason for dragging me out of my hotel room in the middle of the freaking night?"

"Actually, there's a very good reason." Weisbaum gestured at a chair. "Please have a seat. This might take a few minutes."

"What?" Zoe worked at maintaining her anger to disguise the fear that jolted through her. "What might take a few minutes?"

"We can start with the fact that you work for the CIA."

Zoe locked her knees against the weakness that flowed down her legs. "Have you lost your mind? What the hell would a thief be doing with the CIA?"

"That was my question, actually. What would a thief be doing with the CIA? I thought perhaps you could enlighten me."

"You have totally lost your mind. In case it's beyond your power of reason, a thief normally steers clear of involvement with law enforcement of any kind."

"You really should take a seat." Weisbaum picked up a delicate china cup and sipped. "This will evidently take more than a few minutes."

"Fine." Zoe flopped into the chair.

"We have an inside source that has confirmed your work with the CIA. I believe Ethan Calder is your handler?" He waved a hand. "Whatever. I'm assuming that the CIA convinced you to offer your services to us in order to determine exactly what we are doing. I'm also assuming that you have furnished them with information regarding the items you have obtained for us."

"Look, I don't know what—"

"Enough!" Weisbaum tossed several papers across the desk. "Look at those before you continue your denials." He waited while she flipped through the documents.

Zoe swallowed the bile that rose to her throat. The papers were copies of CIA files. Notes about the documents she'd photographed. Reports that Ethan had filed. She scanned the pages quickly, then tossed them onto Weisbaum's desk.

"Now, with that issue resolved, I think I should tell you that we have your mother and brother in our custody. Actually, *custody* is too harsh a word. They are our guests. And they will be treated as such unless you do something that would force us to change that."

"Why didn't you just kill me?"

"Ah. That was a consideration. But the truth is that we still have need of your services. I believe there are two more documents that we require. And even though we could get another thief, time is essential at this point. I'm convinced that it is more expedient to ensure your cooperation."

"Are you threatening me?"

"I suppose you could consider it a threat. But let me put it more directly. If you agree to cease all communication with the CIA—and we will ensure that you do—we will allow your mother and brother to live. After you have obtained the documents, we will release them."

"And if I refuse?"

Weisbaum smiled. "Actually, Zoe, I'm surprised at your association with the CIA. You don't strike me as the sort of person who would be overly concerned with her country's needs or wants. I'd think you were more the type to be concerned about yourself. Your own safety and well-being. And that of your family, of course." He spread his upturned hands. "All I'm really asking is that you sever your relationship with the CIA. You'll still be paid very well for procuring the documents we want."

"I see." Zoe had no problem hearing the underlying threat in his words. If she refused, Weisbaum would kill her mother and brother, and then herself.

"You haven't left me much choice, have you?"

"I prefer to think that I haven't left you any choice at all."

‡ ‡ ‡

January 4, Florence, Italy

Zoe slammed the bedroom door and turned the lock. Like that was going to help. The beauty of the room, with its massive canopy bed, brocade and velvet hangings, and old oak furnishings, only served to fuel her anger. Her suitcases had been placed on the antique dresser. She shuddered at the thought of her personal belongings being handled by the Triumvirate's goons. Of course, her laptop was missing. And Weisbaum had taken her cell phone.

What the hell was she going to do? Sure, she could get out. It would be ridiculously easy for her, actually. Then she could call Ethan and tell him what had happened. Or Drake. Either way, she'd be pulled out. Returned to her father's house in Maryland. Safe and sound.

And her mother and brother would probably be killed. Probably? No, definitely. And a part of her wanted to do just that. Just leave her mother and brother to whatever would happen to them. And why the hell shouldn't she? Her mother had left her, hadn't she? She'd taken Matteo and left Zoe behind. Leaving her daughter to whatever might happen. With no concern for the life that she would be forced to live. What the hell was up with that? Was her brother that much more important than she was? Her father had bemoaned the fact that he had no son to follow in his footsteps even as he'd trained her. And her mother had chosen to save her son over her daughter. Sure, her mother had explained her motives, but Zoe wasn't buying it.

She ripped the covers back on the bed and growled at the luxurious sheets that had to be seven hundred thread count. She had similar sheets on her bed at her father's house. And she'd spent a small fortune on them. She abandoned the bed and headed for the bath, throwing off her clothes as she went. She was too pissed and too confused to think clearly. All she could do at this point was take care of herself. She turned on the shower and stepped in while the water was still cool. Her body absorbed the cold shock of the water, slowly relaxing as it turned warm.

What had she been thinking? Ethan had pointed out that she wasn't an agent. And he'd been right. She was a thief. She stole stuff. She wasn't prepared to deal with her loved ones being threatened.

Loved ones?

Zoe crumpled under the warm spray of water, squatting on the tiled floor of the shower. Her arms wrapped around her knees and she rocked back and forth. She had been playing mind games about how she felt about her mother and brother. About whether she wanted them to be a part of her life. She had even toyed with ways she could make her mother see just how she'd devastated her daughter's life. Just how wrong she'd been. But somehow they'd slipped into her heart when she wasn't watching. Now, the idea of harm coming to either of them sickened her. When had their lives become more important to her than her own? More important than her job?

And she was all about the job. Wasn't she? Of course, she was. She always had been. She was a thief. No, she was the best thief. Since her father had retired, anyway. She could steal anything from anywhere. Anything.

But could she steal *anyone?* Zoe uncurled herself and stood up in the shower. She turned the water off and leaned against the warm tiles. Could she steal her mother and brother from the Order?

‡ ‡ ‡

January 5, Florence, Italy

"What are you doing here?" Logan asked.

Zoe glanced around the large dining room. She and Logan were the only ones there. She piled scrambled eggs on her plate, added three strips of bacon, and moved to the table. Logan sipped his coffee and quirked an eyebrow at her.

"They found out about me."

"What?" Logan looked at the door nervously. "How?"

"Well, I'm glad to know that you didn't out me." Zoe forked eggs into her mouth and chewed. "I don't know how they found out. But that's not even the problem. They took my mother and brother."

"What do you mean they *took* them?"

"Geez, Logan. What part of that do you not understand? They kidnapped them." She bit into a piece of bacon. "Of course, they are assuring me that if I just do a couple more jobs for them, they'll release them."

"What did you say?"

Zoe shook her head. "You just don't get it, do you? Of course, I agreed. But they aren't going to release them. Ever."

Logan pushed his plate away. "Maybe you misunderstood."

"Misunderstood?"

"I thought they'd kidnapped my uncle, too, but he told me last night that he came willingly. He says the Order is going to make the world a better place and he's excited to be a part of it."

"So they aren't holding him against his will?" she

asked.

"Evidently not. He agrees with what they're trying to do. He's working with them to create a new energy source. He says that it'll free the world from the oil cartels. Eliminate pollution." Logan shrugged. "It's hard to argue with the Order doing that."

"You're buying that?" Zoe put her fork down and leaned forward. "They're like all the *good-for-you* laws. It all seems like a good idea in the beginning."

"Good-for-you laws?"

"Sure. Like the seat belt law and the helmet law for motorcycles."

"What's wrong with that?" Logan asked. "I mean, we should wear seat belts and helmets, so what's the problem?"

"Exactly when did you stop thinking for yourself, Logan?"

"Why are you so pissed at me?"

"Look. Anyone who drives a car without wearing a seat belt is an idiot."

"Didn't I just say that?" Logan asked.

"The point is that it's still a *choice*. No one has the right to tell you what you can or can't do as long as you aren't hurting anyone else."

"Yeah, I see your point. But what does that have to do with the Order?"

"The Order says they want to make the world a

better place, but they're going to take away people's choices in order to do that. I think Hitler tried the same thing a while back."

"Don't you think that's going a little far? There's no proof that the Order is doing anything wrong."

"When did you switch sides?" Zoe asked.

"I don't see any of this as being one side or the other." Logan pushed his chair away from the table and stood. "I have a meeting with Weisbaum in a few minutes."

"Mind if I tag along?" Zoe gulped the last of her coffee. "I'd kind of like to know what they have in mind for me."

They left the dining room and walked across the huge entryway past several rooms, and stopped at the third door on the left. Logan paused and looked at her. Zoe took a deep breath and nodded. Logan opened the door and gestured her inside.

"—lucky stroke, really, you being here." Weisbaum looked up as they entered.

"Sorry," Logan said. "I didn't realize you were busy."

Zoe stifled a gasp and tried to control her breathing. What the hell was Drake doing here? Of course. He was the inside source Weisbaum had mentioned.

"No problem. Drake and I were just finishing up."

Drake nodded to Weisbaum. "Just let me know

when." He turned and smiled at Zoe on the way out of the room.

"You said you have a couple more jobs for me." Zoe stepped in front of Logan, physically insisting that Weisbaum deal with her first.

"Yes. The first one will be tonight." Weisbaum picked up a folder from his desk and handed it to her.

"It'd better be a simple one if it has to be tonight." Zoe took the folder and opened it.

"We trust that you will be able to handle it."

"Really? You trust me? That's a hoot." She scanned the pages in the folder and closed it.

"Zoe, there's no need to be snippy with me."

"*Snippy*? Is that a new word for *bitch*?" Zoe turned and walked to the door. "I'll be leaving at ten. Will that be a problem?"

"Actually, we've arranged for an escort for you."

"Whatever." Zoe shrugged and walked out.

‡ ‡ ‡

January 6, Florence, Italy

Zoe pulled on the black bodysuit and zipped up the front. She placed her gloves on the bed next to her fanny pack and sat to pull on her shoes. She wasn't looking forward to tonight, and it wasn't just because of the job, which was going to be difficult enough without having to deal with Drake. This time she was going into an occupied house and retrieving computer files. The other documents had been easy compared to this. And she had to take Drake along as her babysitter.

And he was a traitor.

All the time she'd thought he was working for the CIA he'd been working for the Order. It really pissed her off that she couldn't even let Ethan know. Her head jerked up at the knock on her door. Before she could say anything, the door opened.

"It's generally good manners to wait until someone says come in after you knock."

"Is that what you're wearing?" Drake asked.

"I don't think that's any of your business."

"It is tonight."

Zoe took a breath and held it for a couple of seconds. "This is what I wear when I do a job. It's dark and easy to move around in." She let her eyes travel over his tight jeans, up to the garment bag draped over his muscular arm. "Is that what you're wearing?"

"The bodysuit is fine if you're sneaking in. But there's a better way."

"What would that be? Knocking on the front door and asking to see his computer system?"

Drake shrugged. "Something like that. Here, put this on. I'll be back in fifteen minutes."

She took the garment bag he tossed to her. "What if it takes me longer?"

He lifted a beefy shoulder and quirked an eyebrow. "Take as long as you want. I'll still be back in fifteen minutes." Drake closed the door.

Zoe hung the garment bag on the back of her closet door and unzipped it to reveal a swath of slinky emerald silk. An evening gown. Evidently they were going to a rather elegant affair where she would locate the computer and retrieve the files. She needed makeup. And a hairstyle.

A gold hair clip and some hairspray turned her red curls into a smooth upsweep. She added dark eyeliner and sparkly eye shadow, lipstick, and blush, then found a pair of strappy sandals. She had no idea what Drake had in mind, but she was less than sure of her ability to break into Castagnola's home, download files from his computer, and escape unnoticed when she was clueless as to the electronic security system, the presence of guards, and the location of the actual computer. At least if this blew up, she could blame it on him.

"Very nice," Drake said when he opened the door.

"You didn't knock."

"I told you I'd be back in fifteen minutes." Drake was wearing an Armani tuxedo. She knew because she'd seen one modeled in *GQ*. He looked better in it than the model had. She'd thought his almost-shaved head, muscular build, and tattoos would have made him look incongruous in a tuxedo. They didn't. Of course, she couldn't actually see any of the tattoos.

"Very nice," he repeated.

"This?" Zoe scowled at him. "It's cut down to my navel."

"Yeah, I'd have figured you for a belly-button ring." He glanced at her exposed navel, then let his eyes travel up to her face.

"I wouldn't have figured you for a traitor, so I guess we were both wrong."

Drake's mouth thinned into a straight line. "I'm going to use your bathroom while you finish dressing."

"I'm—"

Drake pressed a finger against her lips and pulled her into the bathroom. He closed the door and turned the shower on full blast.

"What are you doing?" she demanded.

"Do you think that just because this is your bedroom that they haven't bugged it?" he asked. "I'm not a traitor."

"Really? Then you won't mind letting me use your cell phone to call Ethan on our way to this job to verify that?"

"Ethan doesn't know that I'm here."

"But you're not a traitor?" Zoe raised her eyebrows.

"I can't explain it right now. Everything isn't always what it seems to be."

"Sure." She let Drake pull her back into the bedroom after he turned off the shower.

"Turn around." Drake made a twirling motion with his fingers.

"Why?" Zoe eyed him with a measure of suspicion.

"Are you going to argue with everything I tell you to do?"

"Probably. Is that a problem for you?" Zoe turned around as he'd requested.

"Oh, yeah, it's a problem."

"Too bad. I'm not used to anyone telling me what to do."

"Really? Well, tonight will be different for you, then." He draped a gold chain around her neck and fastened it. "I'm in charge."

"Then why do I even need to go?" Zoe looked down at the cloisonné pendant that dangled between her breasts.

"It's a two-person job. We'll attend a party, socialize, enjoy some food and drink. Then we'll slip into Dr. Castagnola's office and download the files. That pendant contains a flash drive."

"I don't see how that requires two people." Zoe lifted the pendant and pulled on the lower half. The pendant parted, revealing a USB plug.

"It might not, but two will make it easier."

"If I'm not in charge, then I need to know what the plan is." Zoe sat down at a small table and leaned her elbows on it. Drake took the chair across from her.

"It's pretty simple. Dr. Castagnola and his wife are having a party at their house. Dante Russo has been invited and he's bringing a guest."

"And you're impersonating Dante Russo?"

"No, I *am* Dante Russo. It's a cover I've used for a few years. You'll be using the name Isabel Landry."

"And we're just going to walk in, find his office, and get the files?"

"Pretty much. His office is located on the second floor. I doubt there'll be guards preventing us from getting there, but it's generally accepted that the guests stay on the first floor."

"You have a plan for getting us to the office?"

"Nope. We'll wing it once we check everything out." Drake stood and held out a hand. "You ready?"

She ignored his hand, stood, and moved to the bed to pick up her small evening bag. "Let's do it."

Less than an hour later Zoe walked into the country villa of Dr. Castagnola on Drake's arm. The structure was even larger and more ornate than the mansion that housed the Triumvirate. The first floor seemed to be dedicated entirely to entertaining. The cavernous entryway held sets of double doors that led to two ballrooms on one side and numerous hallways, parlors, and vestibules on the other. In the middle, a wide, curved staircase of pink marble led to the upper floors. Zoe eyed the staircase. There was no way she and Drake could use that to get to Castagnola's office. Not only was the stairway and entry area well lit, people were constantly arriving or leaving.

Drake guided her into one of the ballrooms and signaled a server who promptly coasted over with a tray of champagne flutes. Drake took two, handing one to Zoe.

"To our success." He lightly clinked his glass against hers and sipped. "You know, this might work better if you pretended to enjoy my company."

"I didn't think that was really necessary. Or are you concerned about what these people will think of you?"

"I'm concerned that everyone believes we are here to enjoy a festive, social event. I'd rather not give them any reason to question our presence."

That he was right just annoyed her further. She smiled, then ducked her head and laughed, glancing up at him through her lashes. She raised her eyes to his and leaned toward him a little while her hand touched his arm briefly, then moved to trace the line of her collarbone. "Is this more what you had in mind?"

"Damn. You're good."

"Thank you. Now what?"

"The office is on the second floor, about thirty feet from the stairs. The first problem is getting to the second floor."

"The stairs in the entrance are out. Too much light, too many people. I'd imagine there's a set of stairs for the servants, but that's probably in the back of the building."

"Let's check out some of those hallways. There's bound to be another way to the second floor besides the main stairs." He crooked his arm and waited for her to slip her hand through, then guided her across the entrance to a wide hallway.

The libraries, parlors, and sitting rooms were a maze of connecting doors and back hallways, but there were no stairs evident. When they left the last room, Drake paused outside the door. Zoe followed his gaze down the stretch of hallway with no doors until the very end.

"It has to be down there." She took his hand and pulled him along the hallway stopping when she heard something behind them. She turned and peered around a potted palm. Two elegantly attired middle-aged men were walking toward them, heads bent in conversation. Zoe glanced up and down the hallway frantically. The meager palm wasn't enough to hide them and the rest of the hallway was empty. They had no explanation for being here. It was well away from the entertainment areas, and their only objective could be the stairs at the end of the hall.

Drake pressed her against the wall, pulled her hand up to rest on his shoulder, and leaned in to nuzzle her neck.

"What the hell are you doing?" She pushed against his chest.

"Just follow my lead." He pulled her other arm around to encircle his waist and pressed his lips against her bare shoulder.

"Oh, sorry to interrupt," one of the men mumbled as they hesitated at the sight of Drake and Zoe, then walked on. The other man snorted and shook his head at the obvious foolishness of the young couple.

When they disappeared up the stairs, Drake pulled away. "See? Works every time."

"You couldn't think of anything else?" Zoe straightened the slender straps of her gown but she couldn't really complain. Hadn't she done the same thing with Logan just the past week when the local police caught them outside the museum in Sardinia?

"Sure. But none of the other options were as enticing."

"Where do you think they were going?" she asked, ignoring his comment.

"Upstairs, obviously. Probably guests of Dr. Castagnola, and they have rooms on the second floor. Or third floor, or fourth."

"So, why can't we just pretend to be houseguests?"

"Like I said, not as enticing."

Zoe rolled her eyes and walked quickly to the stairwell. She stopped on the third step causing Drake to bump into her. "Watch it!"

"Sorry."

He didn't look sorry. Zoe would have enjoyed the mild flirtation if she were convinced that he wasn't working for the Order and a double agent within the CIA. She continued up the stairs and was relieved that the hallway was vacant.

"Where's the office?"

In answer, Drake stepped in front of her and swept an arm back, effectively forcing her to follow him. It pissed her off, but since he knew the location of the office and she didn't, she didn't have much choice but to follow him. He hurried down the hall and stopped at the first door. Turning the knob, he eased the door open and glanced inside a dark room, then closed the door and continued along the hall.

"What are you doing?"

"Finding the office."

"You don't know which room it is?" Then why was she letting him lead? She could open doors as easily as he could.

"Not exactly. But I know what I'm looking for." He opened another door, peered in, then stepped inside and pulled her after him. "This is it."

"Are you sure?"

"Of course I'm sure." He shot her a glance that reeked of indignation. "Over here."

Drake walked across the room to an ornate desk. Behind the desk hung what looked to Zoe like an original Modigliani. The painting swung away from the wall to reveal a recessed safe. "Okay, time to earn your keep."

The safe was a twenty-year-old Juwul with a standard four-digit combination. She'd been cracking safes like this one since she was twelve. She stepped in front of Drake and put her fingers to the dial. It spun smoothly and she quickly picked up the wheels and felt the fence drop.

"Damn, you *are* good," Drake said as she pulled the safe door open. He took out the slender laptop, set it on the desk, and pressed the *power* button.

The screen flickered and glowed, displaying rows of icons. Drake moved his finger over the mouse pad and clicked on an icon. The screen flashed and changed to a blue background with a white box demanding a password.

"Great. We're screwed." Zoe had no idea what to

do now. Give her a nice steel-plated safe with a complicated combination lock any day.

Drake chuckled and pulled a small case from his pocket. He plugged a thin cable into a USB port, tapped a series of commands into the keyboard, and waited. The white box flashed combinations of letters and numbers so quickly they blurred into a gray bar. In less than half a minute the screen flashed again and the program opened.

"One of Robyn's little gizmos." Drake pocketed the device and used the mouse pad to navigate through the computer's hard drive.

"This is it," he said. "Give me the flash drive."

Zoe pulled the flash drive free from the pendant and tried to hand it to Drake. But the drive was still connected to the part of the pendant that hung around her neck by a thin chain. She looked up at Drake frantically.

"It's caught!"

"Just stoop down so I can put this into the port," he instructed. Zoe bent over so Drake could insert the drive into the port.

"How long will this take?"

"Just a few minutes," he answered.

Zoe sighed and knelt on the soft carpet. No reason to kill her back staying bent over. Then she realized that her current position placed her face just inches from Drake's crotch. Just a few minutes, she reminded herself. She turned her head to the side, which was only slightly more comfortable, and glanced up at Drake.

The bastard was grinning.

"Not much longer. I'm almost done." He patted the top of her head. She would have screamed an obscenity at him except for the faint sound of the door opening.

Drake slammed the top of the laptop closed and pivoted to rest his hips against the edge of the desk. His hands closed around her head and one leg came up slightly, blocking her view of the door.

He groaned. What the hell was he doing? Zoe jerked her head free of his hands and looked at the door.

A man stood in the doorway, outlined by the light from the hall. Zoe's eyes widened and she struggled to stand but Drake's hand on her shoulder prevented her from moving.

"Sorry, chap. Didn't mean to interrupt your—" Zoe could see the man's throat move as he swallowed, then backed out and closed the door.

"There, we've got it." Drake pulled the flash drive from the port and closed down the laptop. Let's get out of here."

"That man—"

"What? You recognized him?" Drake asked.

"No! But he thought—he assumed we were—that

I was—"

"So, he has an amusing story to tell about the party and we have the information we came for." Drake shrugged. "We need to mingle a bit and then we can leave."

He was right, damn it. He'd done exactly what needed to be done. He'd saved them from discovery, insuring they got what they'd come for. It would have been easier for her to accept if he hadn't looked so damned pleased with himself. Zoe stood and straightened her gown.

"Still, you weren't the one who looked like a slut."

Drake grinned at her. "Oh, come on. Wasn't it worth it just to see the look on his face?"

Zoe frowned in an attempt to keep her lips from twitching into a smile. The man's expression *had* been funny. "Let's just get the hell out of here."

14

January 7, Florence, Italy

ZOE MOVED THE EGGS AROUND on her plate until they were too cold to eat. She lifted the delicate china cup of tea, but it was cold, as well. When she and Drake had returned last night, he had disappeared into Weisbaum's office and she had climbed the marble staircase to her bedroom, only to lie awake for several hours. She had one more job to do for the Order. Then what?

They would kill her.

There was no doubt in her mind. The remaining job was the only thing standing between her and certain death. If she walked away, her mother and brother would be killed. Of course, the Order planned to kill them eventually anyway. She took a deep breath, trying to still the panic. Everything was closing in on her. She'd lost all control of the situation. She'd been cut off from the CIA. Drake might have thrown his lot in with the Order. Even Logan seemed to think the

Order only wanted to make the world a better place.

"You're looking glum today." Zoe looked up to watch Logan pour a cup of coffee. He sat down, propped his elbows on the table, and let his head rest in one hand.

"You don't look real perky yourself. Reconsidering your affiliation with the Order?"

He pushed his coffee away, untouched. "It's a little warm in here. You want to go outside for a bit?"

"Sure." Zoe followed him to glass-paned French doors that led to the flagstone courtyard. They walked away from the mansion to a small bench. Logan propped a foot on the seat and rested his forearm on his knee.

"What's up?" she asked.

"I was thinking about what you said about the Order abducting your mother and brother."

"Yeah, I've thought of little else myself."

"I really don't think they'd harm them, Zoe."

"I have to disagree." She had better things to do than sit around and listen to whatever Logan had to say about these people.

"Uncle Giovanni told me they're working on developing an alternate energy source. He's really excited about it. Says it'll end our dependence on fossil fuels."

"But at what cost?"

"Look, I'm just saying that maybe they aren't all bad. Maybe they're just a little over the top when it comes to achieving their goals."

"A *little* over the top? Kidnapping people and holding them hostage to get what they want? That's *way* over the top in my book."

"I know it looks bad, but somehow I just don't think they intend to hurt them. Or you."

"Fine. You believe what you want to about them. I hope you're right. I hope everything they're doing is in the best interests of mankind. But I just don't believe it."

Logan raised his hands in resignation. "Whatever. I'll leave you to your new partner."

Zoe turned around to see Drake heading across the courtyard toward them. He waved casually as Logan walked past him, then joined Zoe, dropping down onto the bench. Zoe watched Logan walk back to the villa and wondered why he had changed so much in such a short time.

"Last night was a success," Drake said.

"I'm sure your people are pleased about that."

"They aren't my people."

"Really? It certainly looks like you've tossed the CIA aside for the Order."

"That's not the case. But there's something I have to do here that isn't CIA business."

Zoe shrugged. "All I know is that they have my mother and brother and I need to get them out before I do the last job."

"What makes you think they have them?"

"Weisbaum told me. They discovered I'm working for the CIA and decided they needed to insure that my loyalties switched sides."

"I see. I can find out if they're all right. Would that help?" Drake asked.

"Why would you do that?"

"Maybe to convince you I'm not one of the bad guys?"

"I need to know where they are."

"If I'm correct, they're right here."

"Where?" If her mother and Matt were on the premises, it would make getting them out easier.

"Top floor of the west wing. Of course, I can't be sure, but I noticed brand-new padlocks on a couple of the guest rooms. That kind of hardware tends to stand out in a seventeenth-century villa."

Zoe looked up at the third floor of the west wing, then jerked her head back. Anyone could be watching them from the mansion. "Where exactly?"

"My room is at the end of the hall; the padlocked rooms are right before it."

"Which side of the hall?" she demanded.

Drake hesitated. "Why?"

"Does it matter?"

"You're going to try to rescue them, aren't you?"

"Oh, am I that obvious?" Zoe rolled her eyes. "Of course, I'm going to try to rescue them. I can't leave as long as they're here, and after the next job the Order won't have any use for me or them. You do the math."

"It'll never work. You won't be able to get them out."

"Which side of the hall?"

Drake sighed and stuffed his hands into his pockets.

"Look, I'm going to do this whether you tell me or not."

"This side, second floor." He jerked his head slightly to indicate the direction. "But you can't do that, Zoe."

"Oh, I assure you, I can."

"Wait. Just give me a couple of days to get my business taken care of and I'll help you."

"That's a nice offer. But I don't think I can afford to wait."

"What if they catch you? I've seen a guard in the hallway often enough."

"They won't." Zoe squared her shoulders. "And if they do, they aren't going to do anything to me until after I complete the last job." She shrugged. "I have nothing to lose."

‡ ‡ ‡

January 9, Florence, Italy

Zoe closed the cell phone she'd taken from the maid and slipped it in her pocket. This was the biggest job she'd ever tried to pull off. Stealing jewelry and art was one thing; stealing people was another. She slipped out from behind the shed and strolled back to the mansion wondering if the maid had realized her phone was missing. The maid in question was at the top of the stairs when Zoe walked in. She started up the stairs as the maid descended and when they were just a couple of steps from each other, she pretended to stumble. The maid automatically reached out for her and Zoe slipped the cell phone into her apron pocket. She apologized to the maid and continued up to her room. She'd gotten everything set. All she had to do now was deliver her mother and brother.

She dropped onto the bed and rolled onto her back. She stretched her legs and then her arms, forcing her mind to calm and quiet. She needed to rest while she could. She set a time in her mind to awaken, then let her thoughts drift, concentrating on relaxing the muscles in her feet, then working up her legs and torso. When she reached her neck, her thoughts shimmered into dreams.

When she woke, it was one in the morning. The next hour was spent changing her clothes, stretching, and checking her equipment. A few minutes after two, she turned off the light in her room and slipped out the door. The mansion was quiet and she hoped that meant everyone was sound asleep.

She ran silently down the hallway to the marble stairs. The only light came from the moon shining through the tall windows. At the bottom of the stairs, she glanced around, relieved to see no one about. She opened the closet door where the master control for the alarm system was housed. Pulling the cover off the wall-mounted unit, she held a penlight in her teeth while she plucked at the wires. When she had the correct pair, she cut them with her wire cutters, then pulled out a third wire and snipped it. With the red and black wires twisted together, she snipped the yellow wire, effectively short-circuiting the entire alarm system.

Zoe trotted across the entry area and behind the marble stairs to the French doors that led to the courtyard. She twisted the knob and held her breath as she pulled the door open. No alarm, no floodlights. So far, so good. She looked up at the windows and silently thanked Drake for telling her that a guard checked the doors every couple of hours. Otherwise, she'd have planned to pick the padlocks because that would have been easier than this.

She opened the door to the shed, wincing at the screech of rusty hinges. Hoisting the aluminum ladder on her shoulder, she carefully backed out of the shed. She skirted close to the house, rounded the corner, and leaned the ladder against the wall directly under the last window. It didn't matter if the window led to her mother's room or her brother's. She had to get them both out tonight. She scurried up the ladder, pulled a glove from her fanny pack, and slipped it onto her hand, then used the heavy wrench she'd brought to break the window.

The room was dark when she climbed inside, but leaving the drapes open gave her enough moonlight to see a still form in the bed that was centered on the opposite wall. She crossed to the bed and pulled the blanket back. Her mother. She still hadn't moved, which worried Zoe. She shook Mira's shoulder. Nothing. She placed her fingers on her mother's neck and felt the slow but steady thump of her heart. They must have drugged her. Zoe pulled the covers back, hoping the cool air would rouse her. When that had no effect, she went to the small bathroom and wet a towel with cold water. Bathing her face and neck woke her, but she was still groggy.

"Hi, Zoe. Oh, *bebé.* I've missed you so much," Mira mumbled in a mix of English and Italian, then rolled onto her stomach.

Damn. She was too drugged to even know where she was, much less that she needed to leave. Zoe placed the cold, wet towel on her mother's back and went back to the window. She sent up a prayer that her brother hadn't been as drugged. Hopefully, the wet towel would wake Mira up enough to get her out by the time Zoe came back.

Zoe slipped out the window and down the ladder. She moved the ladder twenty feet and positioned it under the next window, then climbed up. This room was dark, too, when she broke the glass and climbed into the room. The only difference in the rooms was the style of furniture. Zoe moved to the bed and pulled back the blanket.

Matteo was snoring softly. She shook him but got no response. She tried the wet towel trick. Still no response. Damn!

There was no way she could get both of them out of the mansion in their current state. Especially her brother. He was too tall and too heavy for her to lift. Which left her mother. Zoe thought she might have a shot at getting her mother out. Especially if the wet towel had helped wake her up at all.

Zoe moved to the small ornate desk and opened a drawer. As she'd expected, it was filled with notepaper, pens, and envelopes, traditional accessories in guest rooms. She quickly scribbled a note letting Matteo know that he was being drugged and that she would be back for him. Now where to leave it? Anyone who came into the room would see it if she left it on the dresser or nightstand. Under his pillow? What if he didn't move his pillow? No. It had to be in a place that no one else would look, but he would be sure to find it.

Oh, geez, was anything *ever* easy? She folded the note and pulled the blanket back. Matteo wore cotton pajama bottoms but no shirt. Hoping she didn't run into anything that she'd rather not have intimate knowledge of, Zoe slipped the note inside his pants. She pulled the blanket back over his chest and hurried back down the ladder.

Even without looking at her watch, she knew it was a few minutes before three. Years of precisely timed jobs with her father had implanted a constantly running clock in her mind. She moved the ladder and climbed back to her mother's room.

Mira had rolled onto her back. Probably in an effort to rid herself of the cold, wet towel on her back. Zoe pulled the towel from underneath her and ran more cold water on it in the bathroom. She laid the towel on her mother's chest and torso and shook her shoulder.

"What?" Mira's voice was soft and slurred but it was more than Zoe had gotten before.

"Mom. Wake up. You have to wake up." She shook her shoulder again, then lightly slapped her mother's cheeks. Mira's eyes flew open.

"Zoe!" Mira's hand lifted to cup Zoe's cheek. "Oh, baby, I've missed you." Mira's voice slurred and her eyes fluttered closed again.

"Mom. Wake up. Now. You have to wake up. I have to get you out of here." Zoe used the wet towel to wipe her mother's face and neck. Mira stirred again. Zoe pulled her mother's arm over her shoulder and lifted her to a sitting position. She twisted so she could draw Mira's legs over the edge of the bed, then hoisted her up to her feet.

Her mother hung limply against her. Zoe slapped her cheeks again, harder this time. "Mom! You have to wake up!" Placing an arm around her mother's waist, Zoe forced her across the room and back. After half an hour, Mira was stumbling along beside Zoe almost as much as she was being dragged. It was progress.

"Zoe?"

"Yes, Mom?"

"Where's Matteo? You should . . ." Mira seemed to lose her train of thought.

"It's okay, Mom. Just keep walking." Zoe was so relieved that her mother was to the point of talking that she had to blink back tears. It was almost four. The car would wait as long as necessary, but the in-house staff would start to stir in a couple of hours. She needed to get her mother safely away before then.

By five fifteen, Zoe knew she couldn't wait any longer. What the hell had they given her mother and brother? She led Mira over to the open window. It was now or never.

"Mom, we're going to leave now. We have to go down a ladder. Can you do that?"

Mira nodded. "I can do anything." She smiled and touched Zoe's cheek. "For you."

Zoe hoped that was true. She placed the towel on the window to cover any bits of glass and maneuvered herself out to the ladder. She forced her mother to sit on the windowsill and pulled her legs up and over.

"I'm right here, Mom. Just lean on me. I'll make sure you get down all right." Zoe braced herself to take her mother's weight but still faltered when that weight fell against her. Keeping her hands on the rails of the ladder to protect her mother, Zoe stepped down to the next rung, then positioned her mother's feet on the rung above hers. The twenty feet to the ground seemed like a mile or more, but finally Zoe felt her feet touch the ground. She pulled her mother off the ladder and let her sink down to the ground, leaning her back against the wall.

"I'll be right back. Okay, Mom?" When Mira nodded, Zoe collapsed the ladder and trotted across the yard to the shed. When she returned, Mira was still sitting up and her eyes were open, which was a good sign. Zoe pulled her mother to a standing position and wrapped an arm around her waist. They stumbled across the yard to the French doors. Zoe half-carried her mother into the mansion, across the parquet floor to the entryway, and out the front door. She stopped for a minute to catch her breath, then hauled her down the long walkway to the street. Headlights flashed and a car glided up the street, stopping in front of them. The door opened and Zoe shoved her mother inside, then followed.

"Where's your brother?" Ethan asked as the car pulled away.

"Too drugged to get him out. I'll have to do it later." Zoe leaned back against the luxurious leather seat of the limo and closed her eyes. "I don't know what they used but it took me all this time just to get her to a point where I could get her out of the room."

"No one said they were playing nice, Zoe."

"I know." She opened her eyes and rolled her head over to look at Ethan. Mira's head lolled against his shoulder.

"Thanks for coming," she said.

"Zoe, I think it's time we pulled you out."

"Not yet. There's still too much we need to know."

"We'll find all that out after we take them down."

"Ethan, the Order is a lot bigger than we ever thought. You saw those photos. And I think that was just a small gathering of them. We take down the Triumvirate right now and all it does is put them on the defensive. They'll burrow underground and come up later."

Ethan looked like he as going to argue, but Mira interrupted him.

"Zoe." Mira lifted her head from Ethan's shoulder and blinked. "What happened? Where's Matteo?"

"It's okay, Mom. This is Ethan Calder. He's with the CIA."

Mira turned and smiled at Ethan, then looked back at Zoe. "Where's Matteo?"

"I wasn't able to get him out—yet."

"But you took me?" Suddenly her mother was wide awake. "What were you thinking? You should have gotten him out!"

"I didn't have a choice, Mom."

"You always have a choice! I can't believe you left poor Matteo behind."

Zoe felt her face grow warm from the heat in her blood. She tried to tamp it down, then gave up.

"I did the same damn thing you did, Mom," she gritted out through clenched teeth. "I had a choice to make, and I chose to save the one I thought had the best chance of survival."

"The same thing I did? This is nothing like I did!"

"Really?" Zoe asked her.

"Absolutely. I took Matteo because he was the only one I *could* take. And I knew you would be well taken care of. No matter what you think of me, Zoe, it wasn't an easy choice to make. It was the hardest thing I've ever done and I've questioned it every minute of my life since."

Zoe steeled herself against the anguish on her mother's face. "And I took you because there was no way to take Matteo. The difference is that I'm not questioning it because I'm going back for Matteo."

Mira slumped against Ethan. Tears streaked down her cheeks until she sobbed herself to sleep.

"That was a bit harsh," Ethan said to Zoe.

"Shut up, Ethan."

He did for a few minutes, then he continued as if Mira had never awoken. "Have you heard from Drake?"

Zoe shook her head. "Not for a while." She felt guilty about not telling Ethan that Drake might be working for the Order. And she wasn't even sure why she wasn't telling him. Drake had told her that appearances could be deceiving and she wanted to believe that it only looked like he was working for the Order.

She wanted to believe he wasn't lying to her.

"He hasn't checked in with me, either. He's probably pretty deep undercover trying to get information on that terrorist group."

"There's a terrorist group?" she asked.

"It's a completely separate op from the Order. Drake has an undercover persona he's used for a few years. The director thought he might be able to use that to find out what a new terrorist cell is up to."

"So, Drake's doing that *and* being my handler?"

Ethan nodded. "I'd feel better if Drake was close by. I don't like the idea of you being inside the Order all alone."

"I'm fine, Ethan. Besides, they need me for one more job. As long as they need me, I'm safe."

"They'll know you rescued your mother."

"So?"

Ethan sighed. "You go back and then what? You do another job for them and they kill you because they have everything they need."

"Yeah. If I actually give them everything they need." Zoe sat up and leaned over to grin at him. "See, Ethan? I'm getting the hang of this spy thing."

‡ ‡ ‡

January 12, Florence, Italy

Frank Stubeck waited in the small parlor for Capo. He'd taken the express train from Bern yesterday and checked into a hotel for the evening. Of course, he could have phoned Capo with his news. But he'd been working such long hours in the research lab that he felt he deserved a small vacation.

His first night in Florence, he'd dined on pasta and wine at a small restaurant and then taken a walk through the streets. Since he lived at the research facility and it was so far from Bern, he usually ate the food that was brought in. The food was reasonably good, but it didn't compare to the cuisine available in Florence. This was a treat for him, and he planned on staying the rest of the week. He already had tickets to a play, and plans to visit several museums. And, of course, a list of fine restaurants. And besides the mini-vacation, Frank wanted to tell Capo his good news in person. Surely, the leader would be impressed with the millions he'd obtained by creating the Neurotox. And Capo didn't need to know about the small portion he'd reserved for himself. Stubeck believed in what the Order was trying to achieve. But he also knew that it wasn't guaranteed. If they failed, he wanted a cushion to fall back on. He'd earned it, he deserved it, and he'd taken it.

"Taking a break from your research?" Capo asked.

"Yes, Capo. I find I work better if I allow myself a break now and again."

"There's no better place than Florence. Such a beautiful city."

"Oh, yes. Florence is one of my favorite cities."

"And your research on the HIV vaccine is going well?" Capo asked.

"Very well. The constant mutations of the virus are a challenge, but we are making progress."

"I'm pleased." Capo nodded. "Eliminating that virus will be a great service to mankind."

"Actually, I wanted to come here to give you some good news."

"Really? What is that?"

"A few months ago, I met with a man who was seeking a neurotoxin. I was able to produce and refine an existing toxin to his requirements and have just received the final payment. A total of one hudred fifty million euros. All for the use of the Order."

Frank was surprised at Capo's blank expression. He'd thought Capo would be thrilled with the money. Perhaps he hadn't understood.

"What kind of neurotoxin did you develop?"

"It's amazingly effective," Frank explained. "I was able to refine it so that it works immediately. Within minutes."

"Works? How, exactly?"

Frank sat up straighter, eager to explain. "It activates the clotting factors in the blood. Then as the clotting factors are quickly used up, hemorrhaging occurs. First from capillaries and then quickly from the veins and arteries, until the subject bleeds out. The customer was very pleased."

"Who was the customer?" Capo asked.

"He gave the name of William Russell, but I doubt that was his real name. He appeared to be from the Middle East." Frank shrugged. "But the money was wired to our account without delay. That is all that matters."

"No! It is not all that matters." Capo stood up. "I can't believe you did this. You should have checked with me first. Have you any idea what you've done? What these people will do with something like this?"

"But they paid so much money and—"

Capo waved his hand to stop the man. "These people are likely terrorists. They will use the neurotoxin against whomever they disagree with. And we have no idea of who that might be, do we?" Capo paced across the room. "The Order does not support terrorist activity. You should know that. Our goal is to create a peaceful world, not to encourage terrorists."

"I'm sorry, Capo. I thought the money was so important." This was not at all what he'd expected. Instead of gratitude, he was being chastised for his actions.

"Wait here," Capo instructed. He left the room and took a back hallway to Weisbaum's office.

"Karl, we have a slight problem that I need you to handle."

"Of course." Weisbaum stood when Capo entered.

"Stubeck is here from the pharmaceutical research facility in Switzerland. The fool has made a horrible mistake. He developed a powerful neurotoxin and sold it to someone."

"What? Without saying anything to anyone?"

"Exactly. He said the man who bought it appeared to be from the Middle East. I assume he's a terrorist. God only knows what they plan to do with it."

"I don't suppose there's any way to find them?" Weisbaum asked.

"I doubt it. The man used a false name. We might be able to trace them from the money transfer, but they will probably use the toxin before we can find them."

"What do you want me to do with Stubeck?"

"He has to go. It's obvious that he's unsuitable for the Order. This happens occasionally, of course. Not every father indoctrinates his son adequately." Capo shrugged.

"I'll have it taken care of immediately."

15

January 12, Florence, Italy

"HANK. NICE TO SEE YOU again. What's up?" Drake pulled off his leather trench coat and draped it over the back of a chair in the entryway.

"Nice to see you, too." Hank Robertson waved to Drake. "Follow me. I have something to take care of."

"Sure. Can I leave my coat here?"

"No problem." Hank led Drake across the hall and down a hallway. "How've you been? Anything exciting going on?"

"Oh, you know, the usual. Tracking down the bad guys for the CIA. Bummer that they sent me into the field, though. I was really hoping I could get you guys the information you wanted." Like hell. He was mostly hoping that he could get Hank out of this and somehow not destroy his career with the CIA. "What about you?"

"Nothing special, really." Hank opened a door and flicked a light switch, illuminating a narrow stairway. "Just doing my job with the Order."

Drake followed him down the stairs and into a long narrow room. Hank punched a code into a keypad and opened the door, motioning Drake to walk through. On the other side was another long narrow room with five metal doors. Drake recognized it. He'd been held in one of those rooms a few months ago. The nerve endings that hadn't totally healed twitched at the ends of the scars on his rib cage. Hank punched in another code at one of the doors and opened it.

Inside a man sat in a metal chair, much like the one Drake had been chained to. The man was sweating profusely. His head shot up when they entered.

"What?" he asked. "What have I done? I only wanted to help. I obtained a huge sum of money for the Order." His head drooped again. "I don't understand," he whimpered.

"You don't need to understand," Hank said.

"But if I just knew what I did wrong, I could fix it. I swear. I'd do anything."

The man's pleading seemed to have no effect on Robertson. Drake watched as his former commander walked to a table and picked up a Colt .45. He held the gun loosely in his hand and looked at Drake with a half smile, then shook his head.

"I really hate this shit."

Drake forced an answering smile and nodded. What the hell was Hank doing? He figured he must need information from the guy and was trying to scare it out of him. Well, hell. Drake had done the same kind of thing. More than once.

"Try to be a man, for God's sake, Stubeck," Robertson said.

Stubeck's head jerked up. "Yes, of course. I just don't know what you want from me. Just tell me and I will comply."

Robertson shook his head, lifted the gun, and shot Stubeck.

Drake jerked, then immediately tamped down his reaction. Stubeck slumped forward in the chair, held up only by the ropes that bound him, a bullet hole in his forehead.

"Damn. I really hate this kind of shit," Robertson repeated. He laid the gun on the table and turned to Drake. "But you know how it is. Some guys just don't get it. This one took it upon himself to act without the Order's blessing." Robertson shook his head. "Didn't even have the fucking sense to let the Triumvirate know what he was doing."

"Too stupid to live?" Drake asked with a chuckle that he hoped didn't sound as forced as it felt.

"Pretty much," Robertson agreed. He pulled out a chair from the table and sat in it, ignoring Stubeck's dead body behind him. "I'm glad to see how you're taking this."

"What?" Drake asked. "The fact that you had to take care of someone?" He shrugged. "It happens."

"Good to know you feel that way. Time might come that you have to do the same kind of thing." Robertson grinned at him. "Think you can handle it?"

"You think I couldn't?" Drake asked. "Hank, you know me better than that. I can do whatever needs to be done."

"That's what I've told them. In fact, I've assured them you can handle it."

"Well, we've both been there. We know that sometimes you just have to do what you have to do."

"Even if it's someone you know?" Robertson asked.

Drake stared at Robertson. "Sounds like you have someone specific in mind."

"The Order needs one more document. After that, she's a liability. Don't get me wrong. The Order would rather not kill anyone. But Zoe knows stuff that could hamper the Order's efforts. It's for the greater good." He leaned back in the chair. "Since you'll be with her on the heist, they figure you're the best one to take care of her."

"So, I kill her after she gets the document?" Drake asked.

"Well, yeah, but not until the Triumvirate has a chance to check it out. Gotta make sure we don't need her anymore, you know?"

"Sure. Just let me know when," Drake said.

‡ ‡ ‡

January 13, Florence Italy

Zoe jogged the half mile from where the limo had dropped her off and arrived at the mansion shortly before nine. She'd hoped to be back and in her bed before the household arose, but the extra time it had taken to get her mother out had prevented that. Damn, she was exhausted. She opened the door of the mansion and stepped into the entryway, bending over to brace her hands on her knees, trying to catch her breath.

"Ms. Alexander. Out for a morning run?"

Zoe looked up to see Weisbaum standing a few feet from her. Damn it. This day just kept getting better and better.

"You have a problem with that?" She stood up. "I have to stay in shape. Makes my job a lot easier."

"I'm sure it does. If you have a moment?"

Weisbaum gestured toward his office.

"Sure." Every hair on her body stood at attention. Weisbaum was being way too nice, which could only mean they had discovered that her mother was missing. She followed him into his office and slumped into a chair before his desk. "What?"

"Excuse me?" Weisbaum asked.

"You wanted to see me. I'm assuming it was about something in particular. Or maybe you just wanted to share your morning coffee with me?"

"If you want coffee, I can arrange it, but, yes, I wanted to see you about a matter."

"Shoot. I'll have some tea after I have a shower."

"Your mother is missing." Weisbaum sat and leaned his elbows on his desk, lacing his fingers together.

"No shit. I noticed that. No, wait, you told me you'd taken her. Don't tell me you've misplaced her?"

"Your attitude is annoying and unnecessary," Weisbaum said. His hands formed a steeple and his fingertips tapped each other. "Are you telling me you had nothing to do with it?"

"Oh, I'm not telling you a damn thing, Weisbaum."

"You were the only one who knew we had your mother and brother in custody. And you are one of the few persons to possess the skills to get her out of here."

Zoe shrugged. "And your point?"

Weisbaum sank back into his chair. "You're very good."

"I know, but thank you for mentioning it." Zoe stood and walked toward the door, then turned back. "Was there anything else?"

Weisbaum held her gaze for a moment, then looked at a paper on his desk. "Only that we still have your brother." He looked up and smiled at her. "We've moved him to a more secure location, of course."

"Of course."

"One more thing," Weisbaum said.

"What? I'd really like to go take a shower."

"This is your next job. Your last job." He held a file folder out. Zoe strode back to his desk and snatched the folder from his hand.

"You mean my last job for *you*." She ignored the way he raised his eyebrows at her, turned, and walked across the room. She jerked the door open, then kicked it shut and trotted to the staircase. Her foot was on the bottom stair when Drake emerged from a door.

"Zoe," he called. "That's the next job?" He nodded at the folder in her hand.

"Yeah."

"Let's go over it."

"Later." Zoe continued up the stairs.

"Now."

The tone of his voice made her turn around. "I really need a shower and a nap."

"This won't take long."

Zoe gave up. She just didn't have the energy to argue with him. She turned and walked back down the stairs, following Drake to the French doors that led to the courtyard. He walked to a bench on the far side of the flagstones and sat down.

"I'm impressed. You got your mother out."

"But not my brother. And now they've moved him."

"And I know where he is."

"Where?" she demanded.

"Sit. First, some other things. Once you've done this job, they have no further use for you."

Zoe nodded. "I know. I'm sure they have plans for me that include a nice burial."

"You have any plans to prevent that?"

"I don't have any plans at all right now. I've been up all night. I'm too tired to think."

"Well, you'd better start thinking." He held his hand out. "What's the job?"

She handed the folder to him and slumped back against the bench. What the hell was she going to do? She had to get Matteo out. She'd prefer to get herself out, too. And that meant that she'd have to find Matteo before she did the last job for them.

"The Institute of Physics in Prague," Drake said.

"What?"

"That's where the next job is. That isn't going to be easy."

"What are we stealing? Plans for something?"

"A crystal lens." He flipped a page in the folder. "Evidently it's kept in a safe in the basement. It's a backup for the one they use in some special laser."

Zoe took the folder from him and skimmed a few pages. "We'll do it in two days. But, first, where's Matteo?"

"You'll never get him out."

"That wasn't the question."

"I assume Ethan took your mother somewhere. What did you tell him about me?"

"Where's Matteo?"

"Fine. He's in a small room under the villa. There's an electronic lock on the outer door and then electronic locks on each interior door. There are four rooms and I have no idea which one he's in."

"Okay. Do you remember the name on the electronic locks?"

"What?"

"The locks would probably have the brand name on them. Do you remember what it was?"

"Securi something, I think."

"Securitron?" she asked.

"Yeah, that sounds right. Why?" He held a hand up. "Never mind. That was a stupid question."

Zoe smiled. "Yes, it was."

"I take it you're familiar with that brand?"

"Of course."

Drake sighed. "I'll help you."

"Thanks, but it's not necessary."

"You'll never manage it alone."

"That might be true. But I won't be the one rescuing him."

‡ ‡ ‡

January 13, Iraq

Ziyad couldn't stop himself from examining the podium while he waited for Ayman to join him. It was perfect. Constructed in France in 1792, it was just the sort of podium Thomas Jefferson would have stood before to take his second oath of office. And fortunately there were no cameras then, so no one could prove that he hadn't. The Presidential Inaugural Committee had accepted the documentation he'd provided through the mysterious Mr. and Mrs. Randall as authentic.

He ran his hands over the smooth polished surface of the top and underneath where the hidden compartment had been constructed. It was flawless. The compartment, originally constructed to hold a book or sheets of parchment, had been enclosed and would soon contain the Neurotox that would kill and disable the governmental leaders of America. Ziyad was tempted to open the compartment but knew he had to wait for Ayman. He didn't want to take the chance of marring the elaborate piece.

"You are pleased?" Ayman asked as he entered the room.

"Yes. Very pleased." Ziyad could hardly contain his excitement. "Show me how it works."

Ayman crossed the room and placed his hands under the compartment, silently pulling it forward to reveal an empty space. Ziyad eyed the device that had been attached for testing.

"This is where the canister will be attached?"

"Exactly," Ayman said. "And insulation will be packed in to prevent extreme cold or heat from reaching it."

"I almost cannot believe we are so close to achieving our goal. It is a dream come true."

"Has the canister been shipped?" Ayman asked.

"Yes. And the insulation that you requested. Will it really keep the temperature steady?"

"Enough for our purposes," Ayman assured him. "Our agent will attach the canister here, and pack the insulation around it. The podium will ship to France tomorrow and from there to America."

"And you are certain our agent will be able to handle the installation?"

"It will be delivered to the Capitol Building and stored in the basement until the Inauguration. I have a man in maintenance there. He will receive the podium and has already stashed the device and insulation. He assures me that the temperature of the basement is well within our target range of ten to twenty-six degrees Celsius. The day before the Inauguration, it will be brought up and kept inside the building until the morning of the Inauguration. On the day of the Inaugural celebration it will be placed outside on the portico early in the morning, but the insulation will provide more than enough protection from the early morning chill."

Ziyad sighed with relief. "This is the prototype of the actual canister?"

"Yes. And when the device is detonated, this lever releases, which turns this wheel." Ayman pointed at the parts. "Then the Neurotox is sprayed into the air here." He indicated what appeared to be a normal wormhole in the wood but actually hid the nozzle that would deliver the Neurotox to America's leaders.

"We shall test it." Ziyad pulled the white pen from his pocket. Keeping his eyes on the apparatus attached to the side of the hidden compartment, he twisted the cap of the pen and pulled it off.

The lever clicked up, a small wheel turned, and Ziyad imagined he could hear the hiss of the Neurotox being sprayed into the air. The sound of success.

‡ ‡ ‡

January 14, Florence, Italy

Zeke rolled over the top of the stone wall and dropped silently to the ground. He slipped along the side of the wall, keeping to the shadows, until he came to the window with the wood stacked underneath it. He stepped onto the stack, smiling at his daughter's thoughtfulness. His nimble fingers felt around the window casing to make sure Zoe had disabled the electronic sensors. She had. Not that he expected her to be less than perfect, but double-checking was as natural to him as breathing. He took a moment to consider what he was about to do.

Rescue his son. His son! And after that, he'd get his hands on that bitch, Mira. He had more than a few words to say to her about stealing his son. He reached for the window, saw his hand tremble, and pulled it back. He worried that the Parkinson's would cause him to make a mistake. He forced his thoughts to the task at hand. Get in. Get Matteo. Get out. He regulated his breathing and let his thoughts fade away.

He slid the window open, braced his palms on the sill, and hoisted his lean body up and over the ledge. Even though he'd stopped thieving years ago, he'd kept up his training. He was still good. Even with the Parkinson's. Still there was the nagging worry that he might not be up to the job. He stopped that thought immediately. Worry precipitated failure. How many times had he told Zoe that? Plan your work and work your plan. That was the path to success. He'd planned as well as he could with the limited information available. The rest he'd have to trust to fate.

Zeke padded silently down the hallway and turned left. He paused beside a potted palm to assess the area. He could see the entryway bathed in moonlight that filtered in through the floor-to-ceiling windows on either side of the arched double doors. At the other end of the hallway he saw the door that would lead him downstairs. To his son. He moved down the hallway, eased the door open, and padded down the stairs. He opened the door a crack and looked out. The fluorescent ceiling lights were turned off, leaving the room lit only by a series of low-wattage canister lights. Just enough light to see by. He slipped out and closed the door behind him.

Prying the case off the keypad to the security system, he aimed his penlight inside and located the wires. He pulled the white and yellow wires together and took the wire cutters from the fanny pack. His hand fumbled and the cutters dropped to the floor.

Zeke froze. The noise sounded deafening to his ears. He glanced around, waiting for someone to appear. After a moment, he forced himself to breathe normally and concentrated on relaxing his muscles. No one was around. Probably they were so sure of their security system that they hadn't posted night guards. Especially with Zoe out of town on a job. Who else would be interested in rescuing Matteo de Luca? Who else even knew he was here? He chuckled to himself. Their security system, good as it was, wouldn't be good enough.

He picked up the wire cutters, located the white and yellow wires, and snipped them. Then he snipped the red wire and twisted it together with the yellow wire. He said a little prayer as he pushed on the door handle. The door opened. No sound. No alarm. He still had it.

He considered the four doors before him. All he knew was that it wasn't the second door from the right. That left three doors. He chose one on instinct and performed the same wire snipping and twisting. The door opened and for a moment he couldn't even take a breath. He just looked at the long, narrow form lying on the bed, covered with a white sheet and a thin blanket.

Zeke slipped a thin plastic card between the door

and frame to prevent the lock from engaging and moved across the room to the bed. He let his penlight dangle from the cord around his neck and lifted the sheet.

His son was beautiful. A strong jaw and prominent cheekbones, dark eyebrows and thick lashes. Zeke almost chuckled. He'd bet this one had broken a few hearts, even at such a young age. He touched the soft dark curls that fell over his son's forehead. Just like his mother's hair. The bitch.

He unzipped the fanny pack and pulled out the prepared syringe. Calder had assured him this would counteract the drugs they had given Matteo. Zeke wasn't at all sure he trusted the man, but he knew he could never carry Matteo far enough to effect their escape. He removed the plastic cover from the needle and pulled Matteo's arm out, hoping to find a prominent vein. He was in luck. His son's inner arm was traced with the pale blue lines he sought. He plunged the needle into his son's arm just the way he'd been shown and depressed the plunger. Always careful to not leave any evidence, he replaced the plastic tip and shoved the syringe into his fanny pack.

Matteo's eyes fluttered open, then shut again. Zeke shook his shoulder gently.

"Matteo. Wake up."

"Huh? What?" Matteo's eyes opened. "Who are you?"

"It's not important. I'm here to get you out. Come with me." Zeke pulled his son's arm to help him sit up.

"What the fuck happened?" Matteo muttered.

"There's no reason for language like that." Zeke pulled Matteo to his feet. "Can you stand? Can you walk?"

"Oh, sure." Matteo took a step and his legs crumpled under him. "Oh, shit. Maybe not."

"Sit," Zeke instructed. He waited a moment, hoping Matteo would improve. Instead, he slumped back on the bed, his eyes closed.

Zeke pulled the second syringe from his pack and removed the plastic cover. Calder had told him the adrenaline would work immediately. He'd also told him that a second shot might be necessary. Not knowing exactly how drugged Matteo would be, they had sent two smaller doses. He pulled Matteo's arm out for the shot, then he heard footsteps in the hallway. He tossed the sheet and blanket over Matteo and leapt to stand behind the door.

"Just take me a second," a voice said as the door handle moved and the door opened. The plastic card fell to the floor and Zeke held his breath. But the man's voice covered the sound of it hitting the concrete floor and his booted foot covered the card when he stepped into the room. The man held a syringe similar to the one in Zeke's hand.

Dear God. The last thing he needed was to have more drugs in his son. He knew he could take this man down, but what about the other one in the hall? No, it was too risky. The man peered at Matteo, shrugged, and turned back into the hallway.

"He's still out. Doesn't need another shot."

Zeke waited until the last second to grab the door handle and caught it just before it latched closed. He picked up the plastic card and slipped it between the door and frame again, almost sticking himself with the exposed needle. He listened to the men's footsteps as they left. He was too old for this crap.

After catching his breath and calming his heart rate, he moved back to the bed and turned Matteo's arm to expose the inside of his elbow. He found the vein and inserted the needle, depressing the plunger again.

After a few seconds Matteo gasped and sat up. "What the hell?" His breathing was rapid and shallow.

"Again with the language," Zeke muttered. "Come. We must leave."

"Where're we going?" Matteo asked.

"To see your mother."

16

January 14, Prague, Germany

"THAT'S A JOKE, RIGHT?" DRAKE asked.

"What?" Zoe double-stepped to keep up with his long-legged stride down the street. Drake stopped and grabbed her arm.

"Are you serious? You sent a man in his—what, sixties, seventies?—to rescue your brother? I mean, I know you just met Matteo, and I can understand if there's no love lost between the two of you, but really, isn't that just feeding him to the wolves? Along with your father?"

"I sent Zeke Alexander to rescue him. That's not exactly the same as sending a man in his sixties or seventies."

"So how old is he? Your father, I mean."

"Fifty-six or so."

"Same as sixty," Drake said. "They're both dead by now."

"You're full of shit." Zoe hitched her backpack

over her shoulder and stomped off. Drake caught up and walked beside her in silence the last five blocks to the Institute of Physics.

"Over here." He guided her across the street to a bench.

Zoe pulled the miniature floor plan from her backpack and studied it, her forehead creasing in concentration.

"Are you worried?"

"Worry precipitates failure," she said. "Plan your work. Work your plan."

"What's that? An old thieves' saying?" Drake asked.

Zoe grinned at him. "Pretty much." She looked across the street. "The Institute closes in an hour. Let's go."

They entered the Institute and followed the signs to the public exhibits. After wandering through a series of rooms, the museum patrons thinned out, and eventually, they were alone in one of the back rooms. Zoe looked at Drake and then glanced at the cameras mounted in the corner of the room.

"Yeah, I saw them. We need to get to the back hallway anyway." He left the room and headed down a vacant hallway, then pulled Zoe into a small closet.

"Where are we?" She tried to move away so she wouldn't be shoved up against his chest, but the shelves pressed into her back.

"Janitor's closet," he replied. "They don't start cleaning for two hours after the doors close to the public." He pressed a button on his watch to light up the face. "We have half an hour until the doors close."

Zoe settled down on the floor underneath the shelves, straightened her spine, and closed her eyes. She monitored her breathing, forcing herself to take slow, deep breaths. Thoughts of her father, mother, and brother vied for attention, but she let them drift away. She felt the muscles in her neck and back relax and concentrated on that feeling.

"What are you doing?" Drake asked.

Her eyes flew open. "Trying to relax," she snapped. She repeated the process, and felt the relaxation down to her thighs before he spoke again.

"Does it work?"

"Only if you stop talking." She tried again, but it was marred by wondering if Drake was going to start talking. Finally, she unfolded her legs and stood up. That put her in contact with Drake again. This time, his back.

"We should head for the basement now," she said.

"A few more minutes. Just to be sure."

"It's stuffy in here," she argued.

"Well, that's a relief. For a minute, I thought you just didn't like being close to me."

"Ever occur to you I was just being polite?"

"Not really."

They waited in silence for what seemed an eternity to Zoe, then Drake turned the doorknob. "Let's go."

The hallway was dimly lit and silent. They hurried to the ancient wood door that led to the basement. Zoe dropped to her knees and pulled her lock picks from her fanny pack. In seconds the door opened and they crept down the dark, narrow stairwell. The door at the bottom of the stairs was unlocked, and they stepped into a cavernous room filled with old equipment, displays, and office furnishings. Zoe pulled a flashlight from her pack and shone it across the room. At the far end stood a massive Peltz safe. She breathed a sigh of relief. They'd had no information on the type of safe that contained the crystal lens they were after. It could easily have been a modern safe with an electronic lock. Which would have prevented her from getting the lens unless Drake was packing one of his CIA gizmos.

Not that she had any intention of giving the crystal lens to The Order. Unless something went wrong with her father's planned rescue of Matteo. In that case, the lens would be her only bargaining chip.

"So far, so good," she whispered.

"Yeah. Almost seems too easy."

Zoe turned and scowled at Drake. "You never say that to thief. It's like wishing an actor good luck."

"What's wrong with that?"

"It's a superstition. You're supposed to say break a leg."

"I always thought that was stupid."

"Let's just get the damn lens and get out of here." Zoe trotted to the safe. She spun the large dial a couple of times to get the feel of it. The snick of the drive pin thrummed against her fingertips as she detected each wheel in the wheel pack. "This ought to be quick. There's only four wheels. I'd expected a lot more."

"Just how do you do this? Can you hear the lock working?"

Zoe shook her head. "I just have a knack for it. I can feel the vibration when the drive pin touches the wheel fly." She continued turning the dial slowly, picking up the wheels until all four were lined up. The fence dropped and she turned the safe handle sliding the bolt free. The heavy door swung open silently, revealing shelves stacked with papers, small boxes, and other stuff that she couldn't identify.

"It's supposed to be in a box about six inches by four inches," Drake said.

Zoe shined her penlight into the safe, then reached in and handed Drake a box. "Check that one." She pulled out a similar size box and opened it. Nothing. She replaced the box carefully and selected another one.

"I don't know what this is, but it's not a lens."

Drake tipped his box so she could see the small instrument inside. She opened another box.

"This is it." Zoe showed him the lens, resting on a piece of foam. She replaced the foam-padded box lid and tucked the box into her fanny pack.

"What's that?" Drake asked.

"What?"

"I hear sirens."

Zoe tilted her head. "They're getting closer."

"Did we trip an alarm somewhere?"

"No. I checked every door." Zoe closed the safe door and looked up at the window close to the basement ceiling. "Here. Help me up on top of the safe."

She stepped into his cupped hands and he boosted her up to stand on top of the three-foot-high safe. The sirens were even louder now. She peered out the small window to see a fire engine pull up to the curb. A flash of light drew her eye to the building across the narrow alley.

"The building next door is on fire." Within minutes, two more fire trucks, an ambulance, and several police cars had arrived. Zoe hopped down from the safe and glared at Drake. "See, this is why you never say it seems almost too easy. Because it never is."

"Well, at least they aren't here for us."

"We won't be able to leave until they've gone." She nodded at the windows near the ceiling. "That's our only way out. And there's too great a chance we'd be seen with all those people around."

Drake turned to look at the other side of the basement. No windows. "What about upstairs? Aren't there any windows we could use?"

"They're all wired into the security system and I don't know where the controls are to deactivate it. Besides, we don't know how long the cleaning staff is here."

"So we just have to wait until they leave?"

"Or until the Institute opens tomorrow." Zoe flashed her penlight around. "Might as well find something comfortable to rest on."

"It's cold in here. Think that fire will warm the air any?"

"That's just sick."

"What?"

"Wanting someone else's misfortune to provide your comfort."

"You're one to talk," Drake said.

"Over there." Zoe pointed with her light. "Furniture pads." She walked around the old furniture and stacks of files. "There's a lot of them. We can make a bed." She pulled one off the stack and laid it on the floor, then added several more. When she thought it was thick enough, she rolled one up and placed it at one end of the pallet for a pillow, then threw another one on top to cover up with.

"You're quite the little domestic goddess, aren't you?"

Zoe ignored the jab. "Might as well get comfortable. The cops and firemen will be there for hours." She lay down, pulled the pad up to cover her shoulder, and rested her head on the rolled pillow. The pad covering her was thick but did little to keep her warm. Within minutes she was shivering and wishing she'd worn a heavier sweater.

Drake's arm moved across her midriff and she was pulled firmly back to rest against the warmth of his chest and legs. "You never told me what you said to Ethan."

"Why are you working for the Order?"

"I'm not."

"It sure looks that way."

"Like I said, appearances can be deceiving."

Zoe rolled over to look at him in the dim light. "I told Ethan that I hadn't heard from you. Now, tell me something that'll assure me I wasn't stupid to lie to him."

Drake shifted when Zoe laid her head on his arm. "Why not? By the time this is all over, my CIA career will be in the toilet. If I'm still alive."

Zoe waited silently, sensing that any interruption might make him change his mind about talking.

"When I was captured by the Order, Hank

Robertson interrogated me. He was my commanding officer when I was in the Marines. The leader of my Force Recon team. Special Forces teams like the SEALS, Rangers, and Force Recon are different from regular military groups. We have to rely totally on each other. It creates a bond of loyalty."

"So, even though he was working with the Order, you felt an obligation to him?"

"It was more than loyalty. We're taught that you never leave a man behind."

"Alive or dead?"

"Either way. I guess I thought I could get him away from the Order. It seemed like he'd been brainwashed by them or something. So, I agreed to work for them and never told the CIA."

"Ethan is going to have a hard time with that."

"No kidding. But I never would have done anything to compromise the CIA. I just felt that I had to take a shot at getting Hank out."

"Why didn't you just tell Ethan and let him send someone in for Hank?"

"I figured the CIA's concern was shutting down the Order. Rescuing someone who appeared to be working with them wouldn't be a top priority for them."

"That's what Logan said about his uncle."

"So, he really is there to rescue his uncle?" Drake chuckled. "At least he had the good sense to resign from the NSA first."

"You never found a way to get Hank out?"

"No. In my last conversation with Hank, he told me that after we return with the lens, they want me to kill you. That was right after I watched him put a bullet in the forehead of a man who was tied to a chair."

Zoe shot up off the pallet. "You're going to kill me?"

Drake reached up and pulled her back down. "Will you lie down? You're letting all the heat out."

She sheepishly lay down again and pulled the furniture pad over her. Of course, he wasn't going to kill her. If he intended to, he wouldn't have told her, would he?

Zoe shivered. "What are you going to do now?"

"Now?"

"Now that you can't rescue Hank Robertson?"

After a moment of silence, Drake sighed. "I'm going back. I'd really like to find out exactly what they're up to. And maybe if I can, that will keep Ethan from charging me with treason."

"You think Ethan would do that?"

"He should. What I did was wrong. And stupid."

"It was a mistake. But your heart was in the right place. Besides, the CIA doesn't really need to know, do they?"

"Don't they?"

"I don't see why. You didn't give the Order any information; you didn't do anything wrong. Actually, you just went in undercover without exactly clearing it first."

"I'm not sure the CIA would see it that way. Besides, I have to come clean about it. It's the right thing to do."

"Must be a guy thing."

"What about you? What's your next move?"

"When Ethan has my father and Matteo at the safe house, he'll call me. Then I'll join them."

"What if he doesn't get Matteo out?"

"Then I'll use the lens as a bargaining chip to force them to release him."

"I hope your father's as good as you think he is."

‡ ‡ ‡

January 15, Prague, Germany

Zoe opened the door to her hotel room, unfastened her fanny pack, and dropped it on the chair. All she wanted was a hot shower and to sleep in a real bed. But first, she had to check the messages on the cell phone she'd purchased when they first arrived in Prague. God willing, there would be one from Ethan telling her that her father and brother were safely ensconced with her mother. Then she could walk away from the Order. She stopped in front of the dresser and frowned at her appearance. Her hair stuck up at odd angles, and the skin on her face seemed to sag under the weight of her fatigue.

She punched in the number for her voice mail, keyed in her code, and listened. No messages. It was already ten thirty. Her father should have gotten Matteo out of the mansion by three that morning. Zoe pressed the speed dial number for Ethan.

"Ethan Calder."

"Ethan, it's Zoe."

"I was about to call you."

Zoe almost cried with relief. "They're safe?"

"I'm sorry, Zoe. But they never showed up."

She couldn't speak. She could hardly breathe.

"I've still got someone there. But it's been a long time."

"Yeah, I know. Dad had planned to go in around two. He should have been out of there in an hour."

"Zoe, I think it's time for you to come in."

"Not yet. I need to know if Matteo is still there. If they caught my father."

"But they have no further use for you. They won't hesitate to get rid of you, Matteo, and your father."

"I have the lens to bargain with."

"I don't like it, Zoe. It's too risky."

"Well, everything is risky, Ethan. I'm not leaving my brother or my father there for them to dispose of. I'll let you know what happens." She flipped her phone closed and sank down on the bed. Tears stung her eyes as she considered what might have happened to her father. She never should have asked him to do it. A knock at her door interrupted her thoughts.

"Come in," she called.

"Hey, I'm starving." Drake closed the door behind him. "What's wrong?"

"My father never showed up with Matteo. Ethan has someone posted at the rendezvous point, but . . ."

"I see. So, what are you going to do now?"

"Go back. See if Matteo's still there. Hell, for all I know, they might have both of them now." Zoe got up and paced across the room.

"And you think you'll offer them the lens in return for your brother and father?" Drake shook his head. "It'll never work."

"Why not? They have to have the lens."

"Yeah, they do. And they'll take it from you." He held up a hand to forestall her next comment. "And if you think you'll hide it until they release them, think again. These people are masters at torture."

"I have to try."

"I have a better idea. We go back and turn over the lens, just like they expect us to."

"How is that going to help?"

"If you'll listen for a minute, I'll tell you."

Zoe crossed her arms and waited.

"We should have a little time while they verify that we have the correct lens. We can use that time to find Matteo—and your father, if he's there."

"You'll help me?"

"Of course, I'll help you. Probably, your father just couldn't handle the job. He might have realized that and left, or he might have gotten in over his head and been caught."

"You don't think they've already killed them, do you?"

"No. They'll keep them alive until they're sure they don't need you anymore."

Zoe turned toward the window and pulled the drapes aside. Prague was covered in several inches of snow and there was more drifting down. She almost wished it would cause their flight back to Florence to be cancelled. But that wouldn't change anything.

It would only delay the inevitable.

‡ ‡ ‡

January 15, Florence, Italy

Zoe walked into Weisbaum's office without knocking

and placed the case containing the crystal lens on his desk.

"Well, this is certainly a surprise." Weisbaum opened the case, lifted the cloth from the lens, then closed it again. "I'm not sure how you managed to pry your brother from us while you were procuring the lens, but I'm very impressed."

Zoe's knees almost buckled at the news that her father had managed to get Matteo out. Her relief was quickly overshadowed with concern for where they might be now. She had no idea how to find them. And she still needed to escape.

"I told you, I'm the best."

"Yes, and that appears to be the case. But I'm surprised that you came back at all, since we no longer have your mother and brother."

"That's because I agreed to do a job for you. And I keep my word. If that's all, I'd like to get some rest now."

"Certainly, but first you need to accompany Drake. He'll explain everything." Weisbaum opened the leather portfolio on his desk. "Mr. Robertson is waiting for you on the lower level." He drew out a stack of papers and began reading them.

Drake closed his hand on Zoe's upper arm and turned her toward the door. Zoe jerked her arm out of his grasp and glared at him, just in case Weisbaum was watching. Drake opened the door and followed her out, closing it behind them.

"Now what?" Zoe whispered.

"Now we get the hell out of here." Drake turned toward the entryway.

"There you are," Robertson called from the doorway at the end of the hall. "Going somewhere?"

Drake turned and smiled, taking his trench coat off. "Just getting rid of my coat."

Zoe noticed the bulge in Robertson's pocket and decided that running for the front door would be a mistake. Drake grasped her arm again and hauled her down the hallway.

Robertson stepped aside to let them pass, then followed them down the stairs. He keyed in a code at the door and led them into another hallway with four doors, each with its own keypad. He walked to the door at the far end, entered a code, and opened the door.

The room was large and mostly bare. A folding table and two chairs stood against one wall, a scarred wooden desk and chair against the opposite. There was a drain in the center of the tile floor, and Zoe shuddered when she considered what they would need a drain for.

Robertson pulled a gun from his pocket, handed it to Drake, and pushed Zoe to the center of the room. "Take care of it."

Drake hefted the gun in his hand and looked at

Robertson. "Still using the Colt .45? You know the Marines are going to the Sig Sauer P226 now."

Robertson grinned and shrugged. "Yeah, I heard. It's a good gun, but ugly as hell. I'll stick to my Colt. You still partial to that Glock?"

Zoe looked from Robertson to Drake. The camaraderie between the men was unmistakable. They spoke as if they were still buddies together in the Marines. She remembered what Drake had said about the bond that developed between the men on a Force Recon team and wondered if he'd been trying to tell her something. Like, maybe that bond was deeper and more important to him than anything else. God, she hoped that wasn't the case.

"Hey, I love my Glock. But I never had a problem with this one, either. It's a nice, solid piece."

Fear soured her stomach. She tamped the panic down even as Drake lifted his arm and aimed the gun at her, but she couldn't stop herself from squeezing her eyes closed. Her last visual was Drake's hand wavering slightly, then she heard the sharp report of the gun as it fired.

Zoe was so stunned, she couldn't even scream. Her eyes flew open. Drake's features were etched with sadness, the gun still in his hand, now hanging limply at his side. She followed his gaze to Robertson's body. He lay sprawled on the floor, a bullet hole in his forehead, a pool of blood seeping from the back of his head. She shook so hard she could barely move.

"Let's get out of here before they wonder why he isn't upstairs to tell them you've been disposed of." Drake turned and pulled the door open. Zoe ran up the stairs with Drake close behind. They ran down the hall and out the French doors to the courtyard where Logan was sitting on a bench.

"What happened?" Logan rose and trotted after them.

"We have to get out of here and you should come with us," she said.

Logan shook his head. "I can't. My uncle is still here."

"Come with us. We can get your uncle out later. They aren't going to harm him. They need him."

"No, I can't leave him behind. They're moving everyone out in a couple of days. I'll never find him again."

"Where to?" Drake asked.

"I'm not sure. Some place in Switzerland is all I've heard."

"We'll send someone after you and your uncle." Drake boosted Zoe to the top of the wall, then climbed up after her.

They dropped to the ground and Drake took off at a fast clip. Zoe concentrated on keeping up with him as he led her around corners and through alleyways. She ran full-out until a pain in her right side threatened to rip her apart. Bending over, she braced her left hand on her knee, her right hand pressing against the pain in her side. Drake turned and loped back to her.

"Side stitch?"

Zoe nodded, gasping for breath, unable to speak. Drake put his hand on her shoulder and pushed her to a standing position, then pulled her hand away from her side. His big hand pushed into her side just under her rib cage, then pressed upward.

"Just keep breathing." His hand continued to press into her until she stood up straight. "You're exhaling when your right foot hits the ground. It pulls on the ligament that attaches your liver to your diaphragm."

"Where'd you learn that?"

"Looked it up on the Internet. Used to happen to me all the time."

"It's gone. Where are we going?"

"I have a place. It's not luxurious but it's private."

"Can we take a cab?"

"No. We don't want to leave any way to trace our movements. It's not far and we don't have to run anymore."

"Good. Not running would be good. And I'll try to remember that left foot thing." They rounded a corner and a small boy ran toward them.

"*Signore!* You have been gone a very long time."

"*Ciao*, Angelo. Would you like to do me a favor?

"*Si*. Very much so. You pay?"

Drake pulled several bills from his pocket. "I'd like some of that wonderful coffee and a couple of sandwiches. Can you do that?"

"*Si, Signore. Pronto.*" Angelo ran around the corner as they approached one of the tiny houses. Drake pulled out a key and unlocked a side door.

"Come on. It's safe here."

"What is this place?" Zoe asked.

"Signora Romano's house. I rent a room from her."

"What? No fancy hotel?"

"Dante Russo stays in a fancy hotel. I stay here. It's clean, it's quiet, and the people around here know me."

"They know you?"

"Well, not really. But I'm here often enough that I'm accepted. Which means none of them tell anyone anything about me."

"I'm worried about Logan. I wish he'd come with us."

"I wouldn't waste any time worrying about him. Logan has made his choice."

"I don't think so. I think he's confused. He's only seeing one side of the Order."

"Then he's being deliberately blind." Drake held up a hand to keep Zoe from interrupting him. "Don't get me wrong. We'll still try to get him and his uncle out."

Zoe figured arguing with him wouldn't solve anything, and she needed to talk to Ethan. She pulled her cell phone out and punched in the speed dial number.

"Calder here."

"Ethan, it's Zoe. I just found out that Dad did get Matteo out of the mansion. But I don't know where they are." While she listened to Ethan, Angelo showed up with sandwiches wrapped in white butcher's paper and two paper cups of steaming coffee. Her mouth watered from the smell.

"Great. Hold on." Zoe motioned for a pen and paper from Drake, then scribbled the address down that Ethan gave her. "We'll be there soon."

"You told him about me?" Drake asked, handing her the coffee.

"What?" She laughed. "Oh, just that I was with you. But I have the address of the safe house. And Dad and Matteo are there. Evidently, Matteo ran off after Dad got him out."

"He ran off?"

"I guess with all the drugs in him, Matteo didn't grasp that Dad was trying to help him, so he took off. Took Dad a while to chase him down and explain the situation."

"Ethan must be going crazy."

Zoe removed the lid from her coffee, inhaled deeply, and sipped the steaming liquid.

"No doubt."

17

January 15, CIA Safe House, Italy

"THIS HAS BEEN GOING ON forever." Ethan waved toward the living room.

Zoe glanced past Ethan to her mother, brother, and father. They were arguing again. Over what, she had no idea. Her mother said something, then her father, then Matteo seemed to be trying to calm both of them down.

"Don't worry about it, Ethan. They'll work it out eventually." Zoe glanced at her family again. "Probably."

"Oh, I'm not worried about it. I mean I'm not worried about *them*. I'm worried for my own sanity."

"You need to get out in the field more often, Ethan."

Ethan turned his attention to Drake. "Really? So I can go off half-cocked like you did? What the hell were you thinking, Drake?"

"Stop." Zoe held her hands up. Ethan and Drake

had been arguing about Drake's decision to try to save Hank Robertson. Neither of them had seen the other's side of it, although Zoe thought that Ethan probably wasn't going to charge Drake with anything. She was tired of listening to them. It was enough to try to stay out of the conversation between her parents and her brother. "We have more important things to discuss."

"Yeah, like how we're going to stop the Order," Drake said.

"We need to bring in a team and take them down. I've called it in, but we have a minor problem." Ethan glanced at Mira and Zeke, then turned back to Zoe and Drake. "Evidently we need to secure the Italian government's cooperation before we send anyone in."

"Oh, come on, Ethan. Are we back to that shit again? We could go in and take them down and be done before the Italian government even knows we were here."

"I don't make the policy, Drake, I just follow it. Something you don't seem to have a knack for."

"Look. I did what I thought needed to be done. I haven't divulged any secrets. I haven't done anything wrong. But if you want to haul my sorry ass in front of an inquisition, you just go ahead."

"Don't think I'm not tempted. You screwed up, Drake. I don't know why and I don't really care. But you broke more than a few rules. The only thing saving your ass is that you didn't cause any harm and you were actually helpful in the long run. Otherwise, I'd—"

"Enough!"

Both men turned to Zoe.

"I think we can all agree that even though Drake might have made a couple of poor choices, he didn't really do anything wrong and he managed to save my ass in the bargain. The point is, what do we do now?" She glanced over at her family members, who were still in the midst of their argument. Or maybe it was a new argument altogether. Hard to tell.

"Mom, Dad. In case you haven't noticed, Matteo is about to drop in his tracks."

Mira and Zeke both turned toward her, silent for a brief moment. Then they started in on each other again. Each blaming the other for Matteo's condition and their respective lack of attention to that fact.

Zoe walked over to her brother and slid her shoulder under his arm. "Matteo, I think you need some rest. Come on. Let me get you back to bed."

"But if they would just listen." He shook his head. "Either one of them."

"I know, I know." Zoe guided him down the hallway. "The thing is, there's no sense in you getting in between them. Actually, I think it'll go faster if they're just left to duke it out between themselves. In the meantime, you can get some rest." She pushed open the door to the bedroom and guided him to the bed. He slumped down onto the mattress and curled into a fetal position. Zoe pulled the covers over him and headed back to the front room.

"If you two insist on arguing, can you at least not do it in front of Matteo? I mean, you could just give him a little time to get over having been abducted and drugged and finding out that his birth father isn't really dead. Is that really asking too much of you two?"

Her parents looked at her and then at each other, then back to her again.

"That's better. Maybe the two of you could go sit over there and talk—quietly—for a minute?" She walked back to Ethan and Drake, who were speaking in hushed tones in the corner.

"What's the latest on the detonation device we gave to the terrorist cell?" Drake asked.

"We gave a detonation device to terrorists?" Zoe asked.

Ethan scowled. "It's part of a plan. We're tracking it to find the terrorists." He turned back to Drake. "It's somewhere in Iraq. Robyn tries to keep track of it, but there are some problems. She can't always get a lock on it from the satellite."

"Let's hope it stays in Iraq."

"I could use some tea," Zoe said.

"I don't think we have tea. There's coffee," Ethan said.

"Coffee would work."

"I wouldn't mind a cup," Drake said.

"Me, too," Ethan agreed.

Zoe looked from one man to the other. "Are you two telling me that neither of you knows how to actually make coffee?"

Drake shrugged. "I know how. I just don't know where it is."

Zoe turned to Ethan. "I'm assuming you do?"

"You know, Zoe, this is a bitchy side that I've never seen from you before."

"Maybe you just haven't been paying attention, Ethan," Drake said with a grin.

Zoe glared at him. "The question is, what are we going to do about the Order? Logan says they're getting ready to move out."

Ethan shook his head. "I can't do anything until I get clearance."

"Logan said they're headed to Switzerland," Zoe said.

"Can you get clearance for Switzerland?" Drake asked. "'Cause waiting just isn't an option here. Logan said in a day or two. I suspect it'll be moved up once they find that Hank is dead and Zoe and I are missing. I'm going to go back and follow them."

"I'm going with you."

Both men turned to Zoe.

"Why?" Drake demanded.

"Absolutely not," Ethan said.

"Because I'm involved. Because Logan is still there and he needs help. Because we need to take these people down." She turned to Ethan. "Absolutely not?" She held up a hand to stop whatever answer he might have had. "These people have terrorized me and my family. And they're planning on terrorizing a lot of other people. That is not acceptable to me. And it shouldn't be acceptable to you, either."

"I can't sanction an operation when I can't provide backup for you." He sank onto one of the vinyl dinette chairs.

"I don't have a problem with that," Drake said.

Zoe shook her head. "Me, either."

‡ ‡ ‡

January 15, Arlington, Virginia

Hasan and Ali had watched Isaac Jacobs for eight days. Today they were in the back of a utility van waiting for him to leave his house. They had been there for an hour when the kitchen light came on. Ali checked his watch and made a note in a spiral-bound notebook.

"Right on time," he said to Hasan.

"He is very predictable. That will make our job

easier."

Minutes later a light flicked on upstairs. They knew this was Jacobs's bathroom from the floor plans they had been given. The light remained on for nineteen minutes. Ali made another note in the notebook. On previous days the light had stayed on a minimum of eighteen minutes, a maximum of twenty-three. The kitchen light, he knew, would stay on until Jacobs left his house, which normally occurred at a quarter past seven.

Jacobs would then drive his five-year-old BMW to the Supreme Court, where he would work, returning home at six thirty, unless he had made plans to have dinner with someone.

They also knew that Jacobs would be wearing a dark gray or blue suit and a white shirt with a conservative tie. They had videotaped him on several occasions, and the tapes had been sent to Ziyad so Rashid could learn to mimic his movements. Jacobs walked with a mild limp, his head slightly down and forward, left hand usually in a pocket. When the weather was warm enough to not require an overcoat, they could see the white pen in his breast pocket. It was always there.

"He is wearing the gray suit, today," Hasan said as Ali made another note. It was exactly seven thirteen. When Jacobs's car had driven down the street and turned left, Ali and Hasan emerged from the back of the van. They carried rakes and shovels up the walkway and across the yard to the gated fence that surrounded Jacobs's backyard. They closed the gate behind them and approached the back door, protected from the view of the neighbors by the eight-foot privacy fence and surrounding trees.

The first time they had entered the house, Hasan had disabled the security alarm. Later they had gotten a videotape of Jacobs entering the security code. Jacobs was lax in covering the keypad when he punched in the code. He'd never suspected the van marked with the cable company's logo was taping him with a telephoto lens.

Hasan and Ali moved quickly through the house looking for anything unusual or different from the last time they had been there. Nothing. Isaac Jacobs was a man of habit. Highly organized, he kept everything in the same place, did everything at the same time.

And that would be his downfall. Not that there was anything he could have done to prevent it. Hasan and Ali would have found a way, no matter the impediments. They took the apparent ease of their mission as a sign from Allah that it was meant to be.

Ali passed a display of photographs on the wall of Jacobs's home office. A nicely framed photo of Jacobs, his late wife, and their two daughters was surrounded by individual pictures of the family members. Ali remembered the wedding ring Jacobs still wore, ten years after the death of his wife. Jacobs might be an infidel, but he was devoted to his wife and family.

"You will join her soon," Ali murmured to Jacobs's photograph.

‡ ‡ ‡

January 16, Florence, Italy

"You were right," Zoe said. "They're moving out sooner than Logan thought they would." From their position at the end of the street, she and Drake watched several men loading a white moving truck.

"They haven't loaded any furniture. I'm guessing they're taking all their files and whatever equipment they had here."

"So, they must have a facility in Switzerland. Probably where they do most of the work?"

Drake pointed at the mansion. "And now, here come the players."

Zoe watched as Weisbaum, Logan, and an elderly man she thought might be the man she saw speaking to the group got into a Mercedes sedan. "I wonder where von Bayem and Simitiere are?"

"They might already be in Switzerland. I haven't seen them around for a few days." Drake started the BMW and eased out onto the road behind the Mercedes. "Time for a road trip."

"Logan calls Weisbaum, von Bayem, and Simitiere the Triumvirate, but it seems to me that Weisbaum is in charge of everything."

"The Triumvirate is just the front for the leader of the Order."

"The front? You mean there's someone else who's in control?"

"They call him Capo. It loosely means *leader* or *chief.*"

"No other name?" she asked.

"Not that I've heard."

"Wonder who he is?"

"Hopefully they're leading us to him."

Zoe thought they'd lost the car more than once, but Drake would turn a couple of corners and they'd be just a few cars behind them again. When they reached the highway, he dropped back and let more cars fill the space between them.

"You might as well try to get some sleep," Drake said.

"I don't know that I could."

"Try. I'll want you to drive in a few hours so I can take a snooze."

"Okay." Zoe put her seat back, pulled a lap blanket over her, and tried to relax. She really didn't think she'd be able to sleep, but the lack of rest over the past couple of days had taken its toll. The motion of the car lulled her into a much-needed sleep. She woke two hours later when Drake pulled off the highway to get gas.

"Where are they?" she asked.

"Up ahead on the road. Don't worry, we won't lose them. We'll be back on their tail before they can reach the next exit." Drake walked inside to purchase steaming cups of coffee and pay for the gas, while Zoe used the ladies' room.

When she came out, he handed her the coffee and headed for the men's room. She added a package of cookies, some cheese, and crackers to their purchases.

"Good idea," Drake said.

"Do you want me to drive for a while?"

"Nope. I'm fine."

Drake pulled onto the road, gunned the car, and within minutes they saw the taillights of the Mercedes ahead. It was getting dark when they stopped at the Swiss border to pay the toll. They continued on, driving around Lugano. Just past that city, the Mercedes's turn signal flashed. Drake slowed down, letting the distance between them increase. He followed them onto the side road.

"You turned the lights off," Zoe said.

"There's not enough traffic on this road. I don't want them to know anyone is following them."

"Good idea." Zoe had a sinking feeling that she was in way over her head. She glanced at Drake. He seemed relaxed and unconcerned. That was a relief. At least she wasn't in this alone anymore. Up ahead, the Mercedes's turn signal flashed again. Drake pulled off the road and they watched the other car turn onto an even smaller road. After the car had disappeared, he eased forward until they could see where the car had turned.

"Well, that was the easy part," Drake said.

Zoe looked at the chain-link gate across the driveway. It appeared to be operated by a keypad mounted at the side of the drive. From the gate, an eight-foot-tall chain-link fence, topped with razor wire, stretched as far as she could see in the dark. The driveway wound up a slight hill to a massive, modern building.

"Getting past the fence isn't a problem, but I'm betting there's a lot of security in that building." She leaned forward and squinted at it. "Geez, it's huge. What do you think they're doing in there?"

"God knows. But I'm guessing it's nothing good." Drake turned the car around and headed back along the road. "Tomorrow, we'll recon the place."

Zoe gaped at him. How the hell were they going to recon that place?

‡ ‡ ‡

January 17, Outside Bern, Switzerland

"A plane?"

"How else can we get a look at that place?" Drake asked.

"How much can we see from a plane? Not enough to—" Zoe turned at the knock at the door. "You expecting someone?"

"Nigel Blackburn. Let him in." Drake walked toward his bedroom in the suite. Zoe watched long enough to see the towel fall from his hips just before his door closed. She let her breath out and opened the front door. Her first thought was that Nigel looked like a butler.

"Zoe Alexander?" His accent was unmistakably British, which only added to the butler impression. "Nigel Blackburn."

She stood back while Nigel effortlessly lifted a large duffle bag and carried it into the room. He placed the bag on the sofa, unzipped it, and started removing the contents. Individual black canvas cases of varying sizes, which he spread out on the sofa, chair, and credenza.

"What's all this?"

"Tricks of the trade." Drake walked over to Nigel and shook his hand. "Good to see you again. Hope you brought me something good."

"Don't I always?"

"I take it you two know each other?" Zoe asked.

Drake looked up and grinned. "We've done business a time or two."

Nigel shook his head and smiled. "My apologies. I assumed Drake would have told you. I'm in Tech Ops with MI-5."

"I see. You're his Robyn."

"Robyn?"

"Oh, sorry. Robyn is the Tech Ops person I work with."

"Yes, well." Nigel unzipped one of the black canvas cases. "Since she—I assume it's a she—since she isn't here, I will have to suffice."

"What's that?" Zoe pointed to the object Nigel held.

"A camera. A very special camera, actually. With a special lens." He set it down and opened another case. "Electronic decoder." He handed the unit to Zoe. "Oberwerk long-range binoculars." He placed them on the chair.

"Man, this stuff would have made a lot of my jobs easier."

"So, you don't use any equipment, Zoe?" Drake asked. He picked up her fanny pack and unzipped it. "Let's see. Wire cutters, penlight." He set them aside. "Ah, lock picks. Those are handy. And latex gloves."

"It's important not to leave any prints behind," Zoe said.

"I know how good you are with a combination lock, but what about electronic locks?"

"Wire cutters." Zoe pointed to the cutters in Drake's hand.

Drake shrugged and dropped the cutters back into her fanny pack. "And you knew every system well enough to know exactly how to disable it?"

Zoe laughed. "When other teenagers were studying algebra, geography, and English, I was studying security systems."

"I assume you were en excellent student," Nigel said.

Zoe shrugged. "I got by."

"When will the plane be ready?" Drake asked.

"It's waiting for you. Would you like me to come along?" Nigel asked.

"Not necessary." Drake grinned. "But thanks for the offer." He packed most of the equipment back into the duffle bag. "Let's go."

Drake hoisted the duffle over his shoulder. Zoe fastened her meager fanny pack around her waist and followed the men from the room. Nigel drove them to the landing strip, introduced them to the pilot, and said good-bye.

After her stomach settled down, Zoe enjoyed the

lush scenery of the Swiss mountainside. She watched Drake open a case and pull out the camera Nigel had provided. He attached an enormous lens to the camera, then handed her a pair of binoculars and pulled out another pair for himself. Minutes later, the plane dropped down, causing her stomach to crawl into her throat.

"We'll be over the facility in two minutes," the pilot informed them. The plane continued to lose altitude, then evened out.

Zoe could see the building clearly now. Nestled into the side of the mountain, it was almost invisible. But the razor wire on the fence surrounding it glinted in the sunlight. She was surprised at the amount of land enclosed in the fence. The building sat squarely in the middle. There were no towns, villages, or even random houses anywhere close to it. A single lane snaked from the main road up to the building. The surrounding land was heavily forested.

"Did Ethan have any information when you called him?" Zoe asked as Drake focused his binoculars.

"The building appears to be owned by a private corporation. It's called the Institute for Research."

"That's ambiguous enough to be anything." She put the binoculars to her eyes and adjusted the focus. Drake put his binoculars down and hefted the camera with the huge lens, clicking off shots as the plane approached.

"What if they see us?" she asked.

"Not a problem," the pilot informed her. "The call letters on the plane are registered to a tour company. They'll assume we're touring the Swiss countryside. And that's if they even notice us. If you want to go in really close, I can cut the engines and we can coast in."

"Maybe in a while," Drake said.

Maybe never, Zoe thought. She scanned the building with her binoculars, trying to steady them against the movement of the plane. The building was rectangular, looking to be from one to three stories high. Parts of the roof were slanted, and a skylight sat close to one edge.

"There." Zoe pointed. "A skylight."

"Yeah, I see it."

"I'll bet that's their Achilles' heel."

"A skylight?" he asked.

"People will invest a fortune in perimeter security. Fences, electronic alarms on the doors and windows. They forget about skylights."

"They forget about skylights?"

"Weird, but true." Zoe focused on the skylight as the pilot made another pass over the building. "I did a job about eight years ago. Place had the security of Fort Knox. Everywhere but on the skylight over the kitchen."

"Yeah? What'd you get?

"Two mil in gems, eight hundred K in bearer bonds, and an original Botticelli." Zoe grinned at Drake. "In the original frame."

18

January 17, The Order Facility outside Bern, Switzerland

Logan was surprised that Weisbaum had brought him to the facility. He'd finished decoding the last of the documents several days earlier and had assumed that he'd be left behind once he served no further purpose. The drive from Florence to Switzerland had been uneventful and uninformative. Weisbaum had sat in the front with the driver while Logan and his uncle took the backseat. Giovanni seemed more energetic than he'd seen him in years. Almost like he'd turned back the clock. Maybe that was due to him having the opportunity to do work that he felt was important. Logan was having more and more difficulty arguing against what the Order was doing.

The trip had only taken a few hours, and it had felt good to sit and chat with his uncle for a while. Giovanni had even brought out the faceted crystal globe as they reminisced about Logan's childhood. Somehow that sparkling globe always made him feel better. Probably because he associated it with memories of growing up. Whenever his uncle would bring it out they would start talking about the past and before he knew it hours would have gone by.

Logan pulled a sweater over his shirt and opened the door to his room. He was almost surprised that it wasn't locked. Outside the door stood a wheeled cart that held several covered plates, flatware, cups, and a thermal pot.

"Logan," Giovanni called from down the hallway. "I asked to have some breakfast delivered to your room."

"I hope that's coffee in that pot." Logan grinned at his uncle.

"Oh, yes. I remember how you love your coffee. Come, we will talk over breakfast." He held the door open for Logan to wheel the cart inside. Giovanni moved the plates to the small table under the window and poured two cups of coffee. "Here." He handed a steaming cup to Logan. "How do you like your accommodations?"

"They're fine, Uncle Giovanni. A lot more spacious than I'd have thought." His room was almost a studio apartment with its own bathroom and a nook that held a sink, microwave, and mini-refrigerator. "Actually, I'm surprised Weisbaum wanted me to come along since I've finished the decoding."

"You have been an important part of what we're doing. We want you here."

Logan took the cover off his plate and dug into the scrambled eggs. "I'm glad they were pleased with my work. Still, I'd like to know more about what the Order is doing."

"You will. Soon enough." Giovanni pulled the crystal globe from his pocket and held it up. "Look at the light, Logan."

Logan took another sip of his coffee and looked at the prismatic light. He set his coffee cup on the table and moved his hands to his lap.

"We love to look at the light. The light reminds us of everything that is good."

"Yes, it does." Logan's voice was soft. His eyelids fluttered.

"The light tells us everything we need to know. And soon you will know without the light."

"I will know."

"You'll know that together we will lead the Order to where it needs to be. Together we will change the world. Even as I am the Capo of the Order, you will be the next one called Capo."

"The next Capo," Logan repeated.

"You understand how right this is. How we are changing the world for good."

"I understand."

Giovanni continued speaking to Logan in a low murmur. He moved to stand behind Logan and ran his hand through the hair at the nape of his neck. It was still there. The tattoo he'd put there years ago. He smoothed Logan's hair back down and sat in the chair across from him. After a few more minutes of instruction, Giovanni put the crystal globe back in his pocket and picked up his coffee.

"I want you to see what the Order is doing. What you've been a part of. We never could have completed the new energy source without your help."

"It's finished? That's great. Although I have no idea what you actually did. Most of those papers were like reading a foreign language to me." Logan put a forkful of scrambled eggs into his mouth. "Is it a secret or can you tell me how it works?"

"Both." Giovanni chuckled. "It has to be a secret, of course. For now. But you will see it today. In fact, you'll be working in the lab. After breakfast I'll show it to you."

"It's just amazing that the Order has done this. It's going to change the world. No more reliance on petroleum. Although I don't imagine that's making some people really happy."

"The oil was running out anyway. Another twenty years, maybe thirty, and we'd have been riding horses again." Giovanni leaned back in his chair. "I am pleased that you see the rightness of what we're doing. There are some who won't. Not immediately. But eventually, they will all see a better world."

"Is that what the Order is really about, then? Making a better world?"

"Absolutely," Giovanni assured him. "Making the best world. For everyone."

"Then, I'm all for it."

"Good, good." Giovanni picked up his coffee. "Finish your breakfast and I'll give you a tour of the place."

Logan lifted a forkful of eggs. "You keep saying *we*. So, you feel like a part of the Order?"

His uncle smiled. "Absolutely. You'll see. Soon, you'll feel like a part of it, as well."

"Let's go, then. I'm anxious to see the place."

Giovanni led him down the hallway to an elevator. They descended from the third floor to the second sub-level. The elevator opened onto a spacious room with sliding doors on three walls. Logan noticed an electronic keypad and small, flat panel next to each door. Giovanni crossed to the opposite wall and motioned Logan over. "Place your palm on the panel."

Logan pressed his palm against the panel and the screen flashed with a bluish light and the doors slid open.

"See? You have access to everything here." Giovanni

stepped into the lab and waved his hand. "This is where you'll be working. With me."

"But I don't know anything about physics. What will I do?"

"You're smart. You know a lot about computers. There will be much for you to do. But for now, just make yourself familiar with the place."

Logan was surprised at the expanse of the brightly lit space. There were counter-height stainless-steel tables that held a variety of instruments that Logan couldn't identify. One wall was banked in computer screens displaying a variety of graphs with red and yellow bars that moved up and down, and lines of indecipherable numbers and letters. Four individuals in lab coats stood at keyboards, watching the displays and typing in commands. At the far end of the room stood an enormous device behind a glass wall. A purple laser beam shot out from a silver cone into another part of the device contained in a large silver cylinder.

"What's that?" Logan squinted at the device.

"Ah. That is the energy source I've told you about. Come, take a look at what you have helped to create." Giovanni guided Logan across the room to stand before the glass wall.

"How's it work?"

Giovanni laughed. "It's complicated, but basically, the laser beam is aimed at water that has been treated.

Much like cold fusion. But we've applied some quantum physics theories. When you get down to an atomic level, matter interacts with matter differently." Giovanni waved at the glass wall. "That's what all those other scientists were missing. It was necessary to blend the basics of Newtonian physics with what we've learned about quantum physics." He shook his head. "Unfortunately, too many scientists are just not able to cross that line."

"So, what are you doing differently?"

"It sounds simple, but scientists worked on it for years, decades. When we brought all the information together, we found a way to make the laser fuse two extra neutrons to a hydrogen atom."

"Two neutrons? Heavy hydrogen only has one extra neutron."

"Exactly!" Giovanni said. "The two neutrons make all the difference."

"And that's the source of the energy?"

"That's part of it. But the really exciting part is what we can do with the energy. With cold fusion, you get inexpensive, nonpolluting energy. That, in itself, is wonderful."

"And something people have been after for a long time. Since Pons and Fleishmann in eighty-nine."

"Exactly. But we've gone further. Much, much further. Look at that." Giovanni waved his arm at the energy device. "Ten of those will power all of New York City."

"That's incredible, Uncle Giovanni." Logan felt an immense relief. The Order really was doing something good for the entire world. He was amazed that he'd ever thought otherwise. They were secretive, but they had good reason for that. His own government would do the same if they were developing something like this.

‡ ‡ ‡

January 17, Outside Bern, Switzerland

"YES, ETHAN, IT'S REALLY NECESSARY." Drake paced to the window of the hotel room, cell phone tucked between his ear and shoulder.

Zoe watched him turn and pace back across the room. Talking to Ethan about checking out the Order's building on foot was probably a waste of breath. Drake closed his cell phone and sat down on the foot of the bed. Zoe smiled at him in sympathy.

"He said no, huh?"

Drake looked up and grinned. "We're good to go. And we're getting some satellite help."

"You're kidding? You have *got* to tell me how you do that with Ethan. I can never talk him into anything."

"Oh, he has some rules for us to follow."

Zoe snorted. "Rules? Has Ethan ever been in the field?"

"Actually, he was for years. And, from what I hear, he was excellent. Although he also did everything by the book."

"Figures. So what's with the satellite?" she asked.

"He's going to have a tech track us on satellite. They'll also be able to tell us if there's anyone close to us."

"I thought that was just something that happened in movies."

"Oh, no. It's real enough. Although it has its limitations." Drake walked to the window and pulled the drape aside. "Almost dark. You ready?"

"Ready as I'll ever be." Zoe pulled a dark turtleneck sweater over her T-shirt and fastened her fanny pack around her waist. He picked up the duffle bag and held the door for her.

Half an hour later, Drake pulled the BMW off the road and parked a few yards from the chain-link fence that surrounded the Research Institute. He placed an earpiece in his ear and punched a number into his cell phone, then pulled the duffle bag from the backseat and opened it. He handed a pair of heavy-duty wire cutters to Zoe.

"Hey, Ethan. Is the tech ready?" Drake gave Zoe

a thumbs-up sign.

Zoe nodded and walked to the fence. She'd already checked the fence and was a little surprised that it wasn't electrified. Of course, that could mean the place was so well defended that an electric fence wasn't necessary. While Drake talked to the tech ops person, she cut through the chain link and pulled back a section big enough for them to enter.

"Ethan says they aren't detecting anyone outside the building. We're to recon the exterior security and try to find a place where the team can enter."

Zoe looked up at the sky. "And they can see where we are?"

"They use infrared to see our heat signatures. They can't see much inside the building, but anyone outside the building will show up."

Drake carried the duffle bag over his shoulder as they loped across the half mile of ground to the building. They stopped next to a tree about a hundred feet from the building. It was bathed in a soft glow from the footlights that surrounded it. Zoe hoped that meant there were no motion-sensitive lights. The remaining distance to the building was smooth lawn and that made her nervous. Even though there didn't appear to be any guards, she didn't like the idea of just walking out in the open. Unfortunately, there didn't seem to be another option.

"Ethan says there's a large heat source at the rear of the building."

"Large? Bigger than a person?"

"That's what he says."

"Bigger than a group of people?"

Drake grinned. "I guess we'll find out."

"I'm getting the impression that you really *like* living on the edge, Drake."

"And you don't? Let's go." Drake trotted down the line of trees until he reached a point that lined up with the corner of the building, then cut across the expanse of lawn.

Zoe swallowed her aversion to the open space and loped after him. She stopped just behind him in the deep shadow between the footlights. She peered around the corner and breathed a sigh of relief that there were no people. Instead, she saw a metal rectangle with two vents on top. In the cold air, she could see the waves of heat emanating from the structure. Must be an incinerator of some kind. She turned to Drake, who was speaking softly into the microphone of his cell phone headset.

"Yeah, it looks like an incinerator, Ethan." He pulled her back into the shadow. "Right. I'll let you know what we find."

"Where to now?" Zoe asked.

"Now we check out the security of this place. You

see anything that grabs your attention?"

"From what I can see, they have the windows wired. No motion-activated devices. The keypad on the front door is a Saf-T-Max. It's a good system, but not impossible to circumvent. The only cameras I saw were at the front entrance." She paused and looked at Drake. "Do you want me to speculate on the interior security? Considering what's out here, I'd expect more security on the inside. Cameras, some motion-activated alarms, although they're probably only turned on after normal working hours."

"You picked up all that just from running around the side of the building?"

Zoe shrugged. "It's what I do."

Drake snapped a few photos, then tucked the camera into his pocket. "Let's check out the other side of the building."

Zoe followed him, stopping when he paused to snap more photos. This side appeared pretty much like the other. She looked at the building with a critical eye. There was no easy egress into the building from the ground. The windows and doors were alarmed. She looked up at the second floor. Probably alarmed, as well. The only other entrance she saw was a door set a couple of feet into the ground with three steps leading down to it. Probably led to a basement. If she were going in, she'd still bet on the skylight.

They rounded the corner and Drake halted, holding out an arm to stop Zoe. "Look at that." He pointed to an area a couple hundred yards from the building. "Let's check it out."

"I don't remember seeing this from the plane."

"The trees blocked the view." Drake loped across the ground and stopped at a structure made of tall poles with cargo netting draped between them. Farther out were other structures that looked vaguely familiar to Zoe.

"Ethan, we've found an area a couple hundred yards from the building that looks like a training setup."

"What is this?" Zoe asked.

"Exactly, Ethan. This looks a lot like boot camp. There's an obstacle course, firing range, workout area."

"They're training soldiers?" Zoe looked at Drake.

He nodded. "Let's get back to the building. There's a patio with some floor-to-ceiling windows on this side."

They trotted back to the building and across the large patio. Zoe peered into a window and was surprised to see a classroom. Moving to the next window, she saw another classroom. From the low tables and small chairs, this one appeared to be geared for small children.

"This is just strange. Classrooms for small children and a training area for soldiers just a few yards away? It makes no sense."

"I'm sure it will when we find out exactly what the Order's plans are." Drake jerked his head toward the rear of the building. "Let's go back. I want to check out that door on the back of the building."

"Right," Zoe said.

"Ethan, we're going to check out a door at the rear of the building. It's recessed into the ground and I'm thinking it leads to a basement." He paused. "It might be the best way for the team to come in."

They ran around the building and stopped at the door. It was steel, no window, with a metal plate where a doorknob would normally be.

"The team might be able to get in here," Drake said.

"You'd have to blow the door and I'd assume it's alarmed. Not exactly subtle."

"Subtle isn't always an option. This might be our only option. I think we've done everything we can without going inside. Let's get back." His hand moved to the earpiece of his cell phone. "We're done here. Did you get everything?" He nodded and gave Zoe a thumbs-up. "Right, we'll check with you when we're back at the hotel."

They turned to leave and Zoe heard the door squeak open.

"Wait. What? I didn't get that, Ethan."

‡ ‡ ‡

January 17, Washington, D.C.

Abdul waited with the forklift while another man unlocked the back of the container. The man pocketed the key, and pushed the door open. "There ya go," he said stepping to the side. Abdul pushed the forklift forward and carefully inserted the forks into the open slots of the palette. He pushed the handle forward lifting the crate, then backed the lift several feet away from the container.

"Thanks," he called. The man closed the container door, half-turned, and waved as he jogged back to the cab of his truck.

Abdul turned the forklift and guided it to the predetermined place for the crate. He lowered it to the floor, backed up until the forks were free of the palette, then turned and drove to the supervisor's small, cramped office.

"This just arrived." Abdul tore the lading bill off his clipboard and handed it to the supervisor.

"About time. Meredith's been bugging the hell outta me about it." He picked up the phone and punched in a number.

"Hey, Meredith. It's here."

Abdul waited outside the office, pretending to look at his clipboard, listening to his supervisor's conversation.

"Yeah, I know. Thought you'd want to know right away." The man picked up his coffee cup and sipped. "Sure. No problem." He replaced the receiver.

"Hey, Abdul. I need you to open that crate and take the podium inside up to the main floor. Ms. Gavin will meet you up there."

That was exactly what Abdul had expected. He nodded to the supervisor and walked back to the crate. Using a crowbar, he carefully pried the crate apart and removed the insulation, then loaded it onto a dolly and steered it to the freight elevator.

When the elevator doors opened, Meredith Gavin was waiting for him. "Over here," she instructed. Abdul obediently pushed the podium to the spot she indicated and settled it gently to the floor.

"Oh, my. It's just beautiful." Meredith ran a graceful hand over the smooth wood. "This will absolutely make the Inauguration." She laughed. "I was getting worried that we'd have to use the other one. But it's finally here. And worth the wait."

"Yes," Abdul agreed. "It is splendid, is it not?"

"Security cleared it?" she asked.

"Yes, it was examined at the airport, then delivered directly here. Do you wish to see the security tag?"

"Not now. Just send it to my office tomorrow and make sure the podium is locked up downstairs."

"Of course." Abdul nodded pleasantly, leaned the dolly back, and wheeled it onto the elevator.

When the doors opened in the basement, he wheeled the dolly over to the supervisor's office and asked for the key to the security room. On the way to the security room, he stopped and retrieved a package he'd stashed behind a trash bin. Inside the room, he closed the door, then unwrapped the package. In fifteen minutes, he had the device installed. He pulled out his cell phone and punched in a long series of numbers.

"Yes?"

"I thought you would like to know that Martha has delivered a baby boy," Abdul said as he'd been instructed.

"That is good news. Is he healthy?"

"Oh, yes. Perfect in every way."

"I'll let everyone know. I'm sure they will want to celebrate the birth."

"Of course. I have to get back to work now."

19

January 18, CIA Headquarters, Langley, Virginia

"What the hell is that?" Ethan demanded over the crackling static. "Drake? Drake!" He was answered with total silence. No response. No static. Nothing. He pulled his headset off and tossed it onto a desk. "What do you see, Leo?"

Leo Buschner tapped commands into a keyboard and watched the screen. "I'm trying to get a better resolution, Ethan."

"Just tell me what you see."

"Well, it's a little difficult because there was a blur." Leo looked up at Ethan and cleared his throat. "If I had to guess, I'd say that a door opened. That would have let heat out of the building. That was the blur there for a few seconds. Then there were more separate heat signatures."

"So, someone came out of the building?" Ethan stared at the screen. The flashing red dots blurred together, then separated. "What was that?"

"That spark?" Leo asked. "I have no idea."

"It was a momentary heat flare," Robyn said. "I've seen it before. Probably from a gun. See." She pointed to the screen. "One of the heat signatures was moving, then stopped when the heat flare occurred."

Ethan stared at her for a moment. "Someone fired a gun?"

Robyn nodded and pointed to the screen again. "Look, the heat signature that stopped is moving again. Back toward the others."

The flashing red dots separated into two groups. Two flashing dots, followed by three other dots. Then they all disappeared.

"What happened now? Where did they go?" Ethan demanded.

"Into the building. That's the only thing that would mask the heat signatures like that," Robyn said.

"Shit!" Ethan slammed his fist against the wall.

Leo looked like he might cry. Robyn patted his shoulder and looked at Ethan. "What can we do?"

Ethan just shook his head and rubbed his forehead. "Keep an eye on that place. Anything you can see will help."

Robyn turned to Leo. "Let's bring up the video from the secondary satellite on this monitor, then overlay both displays here."

"There's a secondary satellite?" Ethan asked. "Will that tell us anything?"

"The secondary gives us a deeper penetration into the building, but the heat signatures aren't as defined. Anything we see, well, we won't know who or what it is. Still, it's something."

"Do it." Ethan walked out of the room and headed down the hall to his office. This situation was totally unacceptable. He'd sent an untrained person in to do the job of an agent. He'd let her talk him into going in deeper than he ever should have allowed. And he didn't know what the hell Drake might do. Ethan picked up his phone and punched in a number.

"Calder here. Sorry to wake you, sir, but we have a situation in Switzerland. I have two agents down."

"Are they dead?" Kevin Bolton asked.

"Unknown, sir, but I have reason to believe they are still alive. We need to go in. Now."

"Can't do it, Ethan. We're twenty-four hours from a go. At the least."

"That's not acceptable. The agents will almost certainly be dead by then." Ethan took a deep breath. "And the Order could be gone. We need to move now."

"I understand. But again, we're at least twenty-four hours from a go. I have to get an okay from our contact in Switzerland, and he's not reachable until tomorrow. Even then, he'll have to talk to his people. I have no doubt it'll be a go, but we simply cannot go in until then."

"I see."

"Ethan, I'm sorry. I'll move this along as quickly as I can. But until we get word, we have to stand down. You got that?"

"Yes, sir. I understand." Ethan replaced the receiver in the cradle and walked back down the hall to the ops room.

"Ethan, we've got something," Robyn said when he entered the room. "See these two heat signatures? They've been in this area since you've been gone. They move occasionally, in a limited way. The other three heat signatures that we believe were outside escorted them here and then went away."

"You think that's Zoe and Drake?"

"It would make sense. See that?" She pointed at the screen. "They're still moving, but not much. Like they're in a confined space."

"And since the other heat signatures left, you think the others were whoever came out of the building?" he asked.

"It's our best guess."

"Call Cournoyer, Timmens, LaCaria, and Schufreider. No, wait. I'll call Timmens myself. Tell the others to be ready to go."

"We've got clearance to send the team in?" Robyn asked.

Ethan looked at her for a moment. "We go wheels-up in one hour. I'll brief them on the plane."

‡ ‡ ‡

January 18, The Order Facility outside Bern, Switzerland

"Is it me or is there something just incredibly creepy about those guards?"

"You mean the blank eyes? The total lack of emotion?" Drake sat down on the cot next to Zoe. "Yeah, I noticed."

"Maybe the Order brainwashed them." Zoe shuddered and walked across the small room. "We need to get out of here."

"Good idea. But I don't see any way out." Drake looked at the windowless walls and solid door.

"I do."

Drake followed her gaze to the small vent high on the wall above the cot. "No way. It's too small."

"For you. Not for me."

"Even for you."

"Wanna bet?" Zoe stepped onto the cot and ran her fingers around the edge of the metal vent covering.

"Excellent. It's not screwed in."

"I still don't think you're going to fit through there."

"I'll fit." Zoe worked her fingers around the edge of the vent, slowly pulling it off the wall. "The question is, where do I end up and how do I get you out of here?"

"You'll figure it out."

Zoe stopped and looked down at him. "You sound pretty positive."

"Does that surprise you?"

"Well, yeah. I mean, what if I don't come through?"

"You will."

"Great. No pressure." She dropped the vent cover into his hand and peered into the opening. "It opens up to a larger vent not far from here."

Drake stood on the cot next to her and looked into the duct. "Good thing you're not claustrophobic."

"Yeah. I'll go left when I get to the larger duct, then look for a vent that opens someplace I won't be seen. Then I'll come back to get you."

"Good plan," Drake agreed.

"You really think I can take out the guard and get to you?"

"I don't see why not." Drake grinned and then leaned in to brush his lips across hers.

"What's that? A kiss for luck?" she asked.

"Maybe I can do better."

He captured her lips again, running his tongue around the edges, nipping at the corners. Zoe responded by fitting her body against his. She relaxed into the arm that wrapped around her back. Her lips softened under his as an unbidden energy flowed through her.

"This is really bad timing." Zoe pulled back a few inches.

"Yeah, we should have thought of doing this a long time ago." Drake grinned. "Well, actually, I did think of it."

"Hold on to that thought. And give me a boost up."

Drake cupped his hands for her foot and lifted her up to the vent. Zoe put her arms through first, twisting to get her shoulders into the opening. The duct was just slightly larger than the opening and she was able to squirm the ten feet to the larger duct. She glanced back, waved, and crawled down the larger duct. She had to make two more turns before she saw another vent she could fit through.

She pressed her face up against the vent cover. An empty hallway. Exactly what she needed. Her internal clock told her it was close to midnight and she hoped that meant everyone was bedded down for the night. She pushed against the vent cover but it was screwed into the wall. Damn it. She'd have to kick the cover off and hope there was no one around to hear. Maneuvering around, she braced herself as best she could and pulled her legs back for the thrust. Then she heard voices. She lowered her legs and waited a few minutes. The voices faded and she heard nothing more. It was now or never. She pulled her legs back and thrust out with all her strength.

The vent cover flew out and hit the far wall of the hallway. Zoe dropped from the opening, picked up the metal vent, and shoved it back into place. She ran down the hallway, stopping at the corner to make sure she was alone and unobserved. Unless there were cameras. A quick glance behind her revealed a camera in the far corner. She might have been within its range. Another glance down the connecting hallway showed another camera. Were these people paranoid or what? She turned into the adjoining hallway and sprinted to the first hallway on her right. If they were watching all the cameras, they'd already have seen her. Speed was her only option if that were the case. Another turn and she stood a few yards from the door that led to the guard.

Zoe ducked and moved to the small window in the door, popped up for a quick glance and then down again. The guard still looked creepy to her. He sat at a desk, back straight, eyes focused into the distance.

Now what? The hallway was empty. Except for a fire extinguisher. She slinked away from the door, pulled the fire extinguisher off the wall, and crept back. Taking a deep breath, she banged the red cylinder against the door. The guard looked up, then moved from behind the desk. He looked back to check the monitor on the desk, then walked to the door. Zoe knocked the fire extinguisher against the door again and stepped back.

The guard opened the door and stepped outside. Zoe didn't hesitate. She lifted the red cylinder and threw herself into the air to bring it down on his head. The guard crumpled to the floor. She barely caught the door before it closed behind him.

Using his foot to brace the door open, she stepped over his body and sprinted to the room she thought Drake was in.

There was no doorknob. Just a flat glass panel next to the door.

Damn it!

She went back to the guard and put her arms under his shoulders. He weighed a ton. She pulled him a few yards inside the guard room and the door closed behind them. She'd dragged him within a few feet of the room when he moaned. No! She didn't want to have to hit him again. His head moved, then lolled to one side again. She pulled him closer to the door and tugged on his arm, pressing his palm against the panel.

When she heard the soft snick of the lock releasing, she dropped his arm and pushed on the door.

"What took you so long?" Drake demanded.

"Ten minutes is a long time for you? I find that a little disappointing."

Drake dragged the man into the room and pulled both guns from the guard's holster. "We'll talk about that later." He handed one gun to Zoe, tucked the other one into his belt, stepped outside, and let the door close. "And I'll win."

Zoe grinned at him. "Where do you think Logan is?"

"What?"

"Logan. Where do you think he is?" She took her fanny pack off the shelf above the guard's desk and fastened it around her waist.

"What difference does that make?

"We need to find him," Zoe explained patiently.

"There's no time. We need to get the hell out of here."

"We can't leave Logan here," she objected.

"Look. There comes a time when you have to consider the options and make the best choice. Logan's already made his."

"No!" She didn't want to believe Logan was truly a part of the Order. Not a willing part anyway.

Drake put his hands on her shoulders and stared

into her eyes. "You'd put our lives in danger because of Logan Forrester? Face it, Zoe. He's one of them."

Zoe shook free of his hold. "You can't prove that."

"I can. Given time."

"Well, we don't have that time, do we?" Zoe crossed her arms over her chest. "I'm not leaving without him."

‡ ‡ ‡

January 17, Over the Atlantic Ocean

Ethan checked his watch again. They had been in the air for an hour and would land in Bern in just over three more. Drake and Zoe had been inside the Order's Swiss facility for over two hours. He turned and motioned Timmens, Cournoyer, LaCaria, and Schufreider to join him. They all moved forward, leaving the other eight men in the rear of the Learjet Bombardier XRS.

Ethan unrolled the satellite map and pointed to the outline of the facility. "This is our target. We have two agents inside. Primary goal is to extract the agents."

"What do we know about security?" Timmens asked.

"Precious little," Ethan answered. "But we can expect it to be good. Guards, electronic locks and alarms, at the least."

"Damn, what do they do in there?" Schufreider asked.

"They're building a better world for us," Ethan said.

"Oh, that again." LaCaria laughed.

"Do we know where the agents are being held?" Cournoyer asked.

"No." Ethan indicated a spot on the map. "We suspect this area. And they might have already been moved. We have no contact with them, no way of knowing what their condition is."

"Great. Just who are they?" Timmens asked.

Ethan turned his laptop around so the team leaders could see the screen. "Drake Leatherman. Six feet three inches, two hundred ten pounds. Green eyes, shaved head, assorted tattoos."

"Damn. I've worked with him before." LaCaria shook his head.

"Also, Zoe Alexander. Five feet one inch, one hundred five pounds. Amber eyes, curly red hair. Both agents are in exceptional physical condition, so even if they've been injured, they're still probably mobile."

"That would be a plus." Timmens pointed at the map. "So, this is the facility. Looks like there's nothing around it, so we don't have to worry about any citizens in the area. That's good. It won't limit our use of artillery."

"Any idea of the best place for us to gain egress?" Schufreider asked.

"Once we land in Bern, we'll take a helicopter to the site. After we're there, you go in any way you can." Ethan looked at the men. "We know nothing about the facility, so you'll have to wing it."

"I'll set up the snipers here, here, and here." LaCaria pointed to three places on the map. "Of course that's a guess. It could change depending on what we find when we get there."

"My men will go in first. They can blow an exterior door and use flash bangs if necessary. LaCaria's snipers can give us cover," Schufreider said. "Since we don't know anything about the facility, I'd suggest we go in through the front doors. That'll give us the best access routes once we're inside."

"My men will provide backup with heavy artillery. We'll go in right behind you." Timmens said.

Cournoyer nodded. "I'll link up to Robyn and get the satellite download. I can let everyone know where there might be personnel. Unfortunately, we won't know if they're friendly or not."

Timmens shrugged his massive shoulders. "I'll go make sure everyone's eaten and had plenty of water."

"Great," Schufreider said. "They'll all have to stop to take a piss."

"I don't care if they piss their pants as long as they aren't slowed down by a muscle cramp." Timmens moved to the rear of the plane.

The copilot opened the door of the cockpit and motioned to Ethan. "Sir? You have a phone call. You can take it on that phone."

Ethan nodded and picked up the phone. "Calder here."

"Ethan, where the hell are you? I called your office and it took almost five minutes for them to route me to this phone."

Ethan swallowed hard. "I'm working off-site, sir. Do you have an update?"

"Actually, I have good news. We have the go-ahead to proceed. How soon can you have a team in Switzerland?"

"Before you know it, sir." Ethan glanced to the rear of the plane where the team leaders were informing their men. "Everyone's on standby."

"I can hardly hear you, but I got that. Sounds like you're on a damn plane or something."

"I'll contact you as soon as I know something, sir."

‡ ‡ ‡

January 18, The Order Facility Outside
Bern, Switzerland

"Okay. You check for a way out and I'll go find Logan." Zoe ran out of the guard station and headed up the first flight of stairs ignoring Drake's hissed command for her to return. Maybe by the time she located Logan, Drake would have found a way out of the facility that wouldn't alert anyone to their escape. She paused at the top of the stairs and looked down the hallway. To the left the hallway was dark. To the right she saw a partially open doorway. Zoe approached the doorway cautiously. She peered around the door jamb but the room was empty.

"He has to be here somewhere," she muttered to herself.

"I imagine you're looking for Logan?"

Zoe jerked and turned at the unexpected voice.

"Giovanni Castiglia. I don't believe we've met." He chuckled as he moved into the room. "Although I know quite a bit about you."

"Sorry I can't say the same."

"Of course. But you know that I am Logan's uncle."

Zoe nodded. From what Logan had told her, Giovanni was an elderly Italian man. This man appeared to be in his sixties, but he moved like a younger man. And he didn't sound especially Italian. Her eyes darted about the room, looking for another way out.

"I'm afraid I'm blocking the only door." Giovanni shook his head. "You can probably get past me but the Peacekeepers will stop you."

"Peacekeepers?" Zoe asked.

"The guards," Giovanni explained. "They've been specially trained. Actually they've been bred for the job. They're very good at what they do. Exceptionally good."

"I'll bet." Zoe hefted her gun. "But I'll also bet that I can get out of here without a problem. With you as a hostage."

"Me?"

"Yeah. They still need you, don't they? For whatever they're doing? The alternative energy source?"

"Ah. I didn't realize you knew about our energy source." Giovanni didn't appear to be very upset about it.

"What she knows is of no importance, because she won't be alive to tell anyone."

Zoe's attention flew to the sound of Weisbaum's voice. He stood in the hallway, a few feet behind Castiglia, and behind him, one of the Peacekeepers that gave her the willies. Damn it!

"Take care of them, then meet me in the lab." Giovanni started toward the door.

"We still don't know where Drake is," Weisbaum said. "I'd rather keep her alive until we have him, too. Besides, I have a few questions I want answered before we kill them." He waved a hand toward the door, then held it out for Zoe's gun. Zoe slapped the gun into his hand and strode past him.

"Please join us." Weisbaum motioned toward the door with the gun, then handed it to the guard, who tucked it into his belt. "Really. I insist."

Zoe followed Weisbaum down the hall, extremely conscious of the man behind her with the guns. Where the hell was Drake? And where was Logan? She glanced back at the Peacekeeper. No expression on his face. Zoe wondered if there ever had been.

"Here we are." Weisbaum pressed his palm against a glass panel and the metal door slid open.

Zoe did *not* want to go into that room. Every fiber of her being resisted crossing that threshold. The Peacekeeper placed a hand on her shoulder and pushed. She stumbled and Giovanni put his hand under her elbow.

"This is very much the heart of the facility. Let me show you." He walked over to a control panel.

"Really, Capo, is this necessary?" Weisbaum asked.

Giovanni shrugged. "There's no harm in it. I just want her to see what we're really about. To understand the service we are giving to humankind."

Zoe shivered and looked around the vast area. At the far end of the room a glass wall separated them from a huge device. "Capo? I thought your name was Castiglia."

Giovanni shrugged. "It's a term. It means *leader*."

"You're the leader of the Dominion Order?" Zoe asked.

"Even the Order needs leadership. Someone who sees the big picture. Someone who sees the vision. And puts it into action."

"Does Logan know you're the leader?"

"Not really." Giovanni waved a hand. "Logan is like a son to me. I never had a son to bring into the fold. Not even a daughter. But by the time I realized that it just wasn't going to happen, Logan was already eight." He shook his head. "Most Legacy children are indoctrinated from birth."

"Indoctrinated?" Zoe had a really bad feeling about that.

"Just a term. We are all descended from original members of the Brotherhood. Of course, the Brotherhood disbanded at the end of the eighteenth century." Giovanni held up a finger. "But that doesn't mean the ideals were abandoned. Some of the members knew that this way of thinking was right. That it would save the world."

"And we will," Weisbaum added.

"Yes. The time has come." Giovanni turned back to Zoe. "Our forefathers created a Legacy for us. After a while, they wrote down the instructions, the prophecies. They told us what would happen and when it would happen and how we would know the time was right."

"Yeah, that's gotta be handy." Zoe glanced back at the Peacekeeper but he stood at attention, oblivious to everything. "But how does Logan figure into this?"

"Ah, yes. Logan. If he'd been my son, he'd have been indoctrinated at a much earlier age. But, as I said, I didn't realize that I would have no children of my own. Still, I started when I could. I'd visit his mother and father every summer." Giovanni chuckled. "But even I am not immune to doubt. Until recently, I doubted I'd be able to bring him in. To make him see the rightness of what we are doing."

"Until recently?" Zoe asked. Where the hell was Drake? He should be here by now. She didn't know how much longer she could keep him talking.

"Logan is almost ready. He doesn't know that I'm the leader of the Order. Not yet. But he will. Soon. He's almost ready to learn everything. Almost." Giovanni pulled a small cut crystal globe from his pocket. He dangled it from the attached silver chain. "One more session. Maybe two. Then he'll be ready."

"You really think your little group is going to make

a difference?" she asked.

"Our little group?" Weisbaum laughed. "We aren't so little, my dear. But more importantly, we are powerful."

"Because of your gizmo here?" Zoe gestured at the cylinder.

Weisbaum shook his head. "Our members are powerful. We have senators, princes, prime ministers, heads of powerful international corporations. We even have the next president of your country."

"President-elect Hemings is a member of the Order?" Zoe's stomach twisted with nausea.

"Ah, here we go." Giovanni typed on the keyboard again, then pointed to the cylinder.

Zoe watched as a purple light shot out from a cone into the silver cylinder. Lights flashed on the bank of computer screens.

"This is the source of an energy such as man has never seen." Giovanni's fingers flew across the keyboard. "And we can end the threat of nuclear war. The energy can be converted into a weapon that can intercept and annihilate a nuclear device, rendering it useless."

"Impressive. How's it work?" Zoe asked. Surely Drake would be here soon. Unless he'd escaped and just left her behind.

"I doubt you'd understand the complexities, Zoe."

Weisbaum stepped over to one of the computers and typed in a command. "No reason you can't see the demonstration video, though. It's not like you'll be able to tell anyone about it." He nodded at one of the monitors as the video began. "This was all done from a satellite."

Zoe watched as the camera zoomed in on an old barn. Nothing happened for several seconds, then the barn exploded, throwing splintered wood into the air. Zoe flinched and watched as the camera panned to an old truck. After a moment, it burst into flames.

"Of course, these are small-scale demonstrations," Weisman said. "The weapon can be targeted at a single person or an entire city."

"Impressive. And Logan thinks this is a good idea?" Zoe asked.

"He doesn't know all the particulars just yet." Giovanni waved his hands in the air. "But you are only looking at this as a negative."

"And there's a positive side to this?" Zoe asked.

"It is our wish that the weapon never be used."

"Of course. You just have it for what? A back-up plan in case the passive path to world domination doesn't work for you?"

"It is there to ensure that others don't use their weapons."

"Sure. Just another Peacekeeper, right?" Zoe asked.

She glanced at the guard, then yelped at the sharp report of a gunshot. The Peacekeeper dropped his gun and fell to the floor.

20

January 18, The Order Facility, outside Bern, Switzerland

"I GUESS I OWE LOGAN a big apology." Drake stood in the doorway, his gun aimed at Giovanni. "All this time, I just thought he was one of the regular bad guys."

"Took you long enough to get here," Zoe said.

"Yeah, I got a little lost. Saw some interesting stuff, though. Seems the Order is involved in a lot of unsavory activities." He looked at Weisbaum. "You want to explain what's in those tanks?"

"You got into the Genetics Lab?" Weisbaum asked. "How?"

Drake grinned and shook his head. "It's really not that hard. So, what are you doing in there?"

Giovanni shrugged. "Experiments."

"On humans?" Drake asked.

"We believe they will be classified differently than

humans." Weisbaum crossed his arms over his chest and leaned against a table.

"You don't understand," Giovanni said. "They've been created to help humans. To free us from drudgery, from dangerous work. The Domestics will take care of our homes and rear our children with more patience than we could ever muster. The Laborers will work longer hours than we possibly could. The Peacekeepers will ensure our safety. And they'll do all that happily, because it's what they've been bred to do."

"You're breeding slaves?" Zoe asked. "That's disgusting."

"You sick bastard." Drake looked at Zoe. "We need to find a way to contact Ethan."

"I don't think so," Weisbaum said.

"You plan on stopping us?" Drake asked.

"No, I plan on Messieurs von Bayem and Simitiere stopping you."

Zoe looked past Weisbaum where von Bayem and Simitiere stood, both holding guns. Von Bayem lifted his gun and fired. Drake fell to the floor, rolled over, and aimed his gun at von Bayem. Zoe dove for the automatic pistol the Peacekeeper had dropped and saw Logan step out from behind a bank of computer servers holding a metal stool.

He brought the stool down on Simitiere's back causing him to stump forward. Simitiere caught himself, pulled up his gun, and fired. Drake emptied his pistol in the general direction of Weisbaum and Castiglia. Von Bayem fired repeatedly and Zoe did the same.

Zoe's ears rang in the sudden silence. She pushed herself off the floor and looked at the bodies. Logan still held the stool he'd hit Simitiere with. His shoulders sagged and tears streamed down his face. Castiglia lay on top of Weisbaum, blood flowing freely from the gaping hole in his back. A few yards away, von Bayem's arm was shot off above the elbow and the top half of his head was missing.

Drake stood up holding his bleeding side. They both heard the noise at the same time. Drake pivoted and fired a final shot into Simitiere's forehead.

Zoe ran over to him. "How bad is it?" She pulled Drake's sweater up. The bullet had gone through his side. Blood seeped from the wounds.

"I think it nicked a rib, but I'm okay." Drake hobbled to a stool and slumped down on it.

"What about you, Logan?" Zoe moved over and touched his hand. "You okay?"

"He was mentally programming me and I didn't even know it." Logan pulled his eyes from the sight of his uncle's body and wiped his sleeve across his face.

"But it didn't work. Not totally. When you found out, you overcame it." Zoe grinned at him. "You were stronger than the programming."

"What's that?" Drake pointed to one of the computer screens that was emitting a high-pitched beep.

"Oh, God, no!" Logan rushed to a console and typed in commands. "The energy source is overloading." He typed in more commands and watched the screen. The bars were all flashing red. He turned to Zoe. "You need to get him out of here. I'll stay and shut this down, then join you."

"We'll wait for you. Then we'll all leave together."

"No," Logan said. "Drake can't move very fast. You need to start now. Once I'm done, I'll catch up."

Zoe tucked her shoulder under Drake's arm to support him.

"Go out that door and turn right. There's a door marked *Emergency Exit*. It leads to a tunnel that will take you outside behind the tree line."

Zoe nodded. "Hurry." She pulled Drake to his feet and helped him across the room and out to the emergency exit. The tunnel was dimly lit and had been built as a switchback, turning every twenty yards or so, sloping up to the ground level. Zoe looked over her shoulder at each turn to see if Logan was following, but there was no sign of him. They made the final turn and she could see a door at the end.

Zoe's hand was only inches from the door handle when the explosion threw her and Drake to the floor. The concussion rolled through the tunnel like an earthquake. Behind them the ceiling cracked and a beam fell down. Zoe crawled through the dusty air to the door and pulled it open. She sucked in the fresh air and turned to help Drake up. They struggled up the steps and onto the ground.

"I can't see the building from here because of the trees," Zoe said.

Drake shook his head. "I doubt there's any building left."

"Do you think Logan got out in time?"

Drake looked up at the sky. "You hear that?"

Zoe looked up. "A helicopter?"

"That's what it sounds like to me."

Zoe stood and pulled a flashlight from her fanny pack. She turned it on and waved it at the sky. The huge helicopter flew over them, then turned and flew back. After a moment of hovering, it moved off and started descending.

"I think they saw us," Zoe said. She helped Drake up and they walked slowly toward the clearing. Minutes later, two men in fatigues trotted toward them.

"Leatherman? Alexander?" one of them asked.

They both nodded. "That's us," Zoe said.

"I'm Timmens and this is Cournoyer." The man nodded. He gently pulled Zoe away from Drake and took her place. Cournoyer took the other side and they almost carried Drake. Zoe trotted along behind them. In the clearing, a dozen other men stood next to the helicopter.

"Ethan!" Zoe threw herself at him. "I've never been so damn happy to see anyone."

Ethan patted her back, then pushed her away to look at her. "What happened?"

"The energy source overloaded. When we left, Logan was trying to shut it down."

"Obviously that didn't happen," Ethan said. "Let's get you two some medical attention."

"We need to go back and find Logan," Zoe said.

"There's nothing left, Zoe. If Logan was in the building . . ."

One of the men in fatigues lifted her into the helicopter and the others piled in. They rose in the air and Zoe looked out the window. The stone and glass facility was a mass of smoking rubble. Nothing was left standing. She turned to Ethan. "Maybe he made it to the tunnel. He could still be alive."

‡ ‡ ‡

January 19, Arlington, Virginia

Ali, Hasan, and Rashid sat quietly in the utility van. Ali's hand had twitched for a pen when the lights came on in the kitchen, and again when the bathroom window lit up. But there was no point in taking notes now about Isaac Jacobs's routine. Because this was the last day of Jacobs's life.

All they had to do now was wait.

Ali glanced at Hasan sitting next to Rashid. His elbows were propped on his knees, his fingers lacing together and separating rhythmically. In contrast, Rashid was still, his hands lightly clasped in his lap. Ali marveled at how calm Rashid appeared, then remembered that Rashid had prepared for this for over a year. He was obviously secure in the knowledge that he would accomplish his mission in less than thirty-six hours. Then Rashid would be in Paradise. Meanwhile his and Hasan's mission would begin today. And then there would be other missions on other days before they went on to Paradise. If all went as planned.

The kitchen light went out and minutes later the garage door opened. Jacobs's BMW rolled out, turned left out of the driveway, and motored down the street. Ali checked his watch and waited an excruciating five minutes. Then he forced himself to wait two more.

He opened the back door of the utility van that had the same logo as the company that regularly serviced Jacobs's yard. The three men climbed out, taking rakes, shovels, and clippers with them. They followed the walkway to the front of the house and across the neatly manicured lawn to the gate that led to the backyard. This was the easy part. None of the neighbors would think anything of the men because they had seen two men do the same thing many times over the past few months. That there were three men instead of two wouldn't be thought unusual. It probably wouldn't even be noticed.

Ali punched in the code for the security system and opened the door that led from the patio to the kitchen. Inside, the men separated. Rashid went to the master bedroom and laid down on the bed, which Jacobs had made before he left for the day. Ali and Hasan moved through the house, making their regular rounds, checking that nothing had changed. Which, of course, nothing had. When they were done, they met in the living room and sat down to wait. Their entire day would be about waiting. Knowing that made it less frustrating.

After a few hours, Hasan checked the kitchen for something to eat, but found only cheese and bread. Refined, sliced bread in a cellophane package. But the cheese was good. A smoky provolone. He and Ali washed it down with water from the filtered spout on the kitchen sink.

And they waited more. Rashid remained upstairs. Ali assumed he was meditating and praying. He certainly would have been, knowing that his life would end in the next twenty-four hours. But Rashid was assured a place in Paradise, so he could be at ease. Of course, he still had his mission to accomplish tomorrow. But even if the mission failed, Rashid was assured of his place in Paradise as long as he did his part.

When the afternoon light faded with the sunset, Ali and Hasan moved into the kitchen. There was still an hour before Jacobs should arrive but they wanted to be ready. Even though he'd never arrived home before six fifteen, something could happen to make him early. They'd chosen the kitchen because that was where Jacobs would enter the house after parking his car in the garage. Hassan would use a garrote to kill him because it would be quick and noiseless.

They knew that Jacobs would lose control of his bowels when he died, and the tile floor of the kitchen would be easy to clean up. They didn't want to spend the night in a house that smelled of offal. Ali had to smile at the thought of sleeping in the man's home the night before they killed the infidels.

It was another sign from Allah that it was all so easy to accomplish. Jacobs's two daughters lived far away and usually called him on Sunday. He wasn't socially active so no one would be stopping by the house. Especially since they knew he would officiate at the Inauguration tomorrow. But when the kitchen clock showed 6:45 and Jacobs still hadn't arrived, Ali worried.

"He should have been here by now," Hassan whispered harshly.

"It is nothing. Perhaps he worked late." Ali hoped it was something that simple. They were so close now, so very close. Ten minutes later, they heard the garage door open and Ali smiled. He had been right. Jacobs had only been delayed for a short time. Hassan positioned himself by the door that led to the garage and Ali stood about ten feet in front of it. Jacobs would be startled by the sight of Ali, Hasan would move behind him and tighten the garrote around his throat. It would all be over in minutes.

Hasan almost dropped the garrote when the doorbell rang. Ali saw the knob of the door to the garage turn and leapt toward Hassan, jerking the door to the pantry open. They squeezed into the small dark closet just as Jacobs stepped into the kitchen. He walked through the kitchen, laid his briefcase on the dining table, and continued to the front door.

"Good evening, Marion."

"I made lasagna tonight and there's so much left over, we'll never eat it all. I thought you might like some."

"Wonderful. I love lasagna. And I know that you make the best. It's freezing out here. Come in."

"Thanks, but I can't. I have to get back to the house and help Ronnie with his science project. Enjoy the lasagna."

Ali and Hasan waited until the door had closed, then eased out of the pantry. Ali motioned Hasan to stay behind him, then walked into the living room to stand before the fireplace. Jacobs stepped into the living room and turned on a lamp, the lasagna balanced in one hand.

"Mr. Jacobs," Ali said to get the man's attention.

"Who are you?" Jacobs jerked and turned toward Ali, the lasagna flying out of his hand and spilling on the carpet. "What are you doing in my house?"

Hassan stepped forward and slipped the garrote over Jacobs's head. He crossed his hands and pulled on the wooden handles, watching the wire cut into the man's neck. Jacobs's hands clawed at his neck, trying to pull the wire away. Hassan tightened the garrote.

The stench of Jacobs's bowels filled the room.

‡ ‡ ‡

January 19, CIA Headquarters, Langley, Virginia

The debriefing hadn't been as taxing as Zoe had feared. She'd had a shower and changed into jeans and a T-shirt that Robyn lent her and was settled on a sofa in Ethan's office with a cup of tea.

"Congratulations, Zoe," Ethan said. "You were instrumental in our success."

"Did they find Logan?"

"No. There was no sign of him. They checked the tunnel. It'll take some time to go through the rubble. But all the indications are that everyone died."

She didn't like to think of Logan dying after all he'd done. She wanted to hear that he was alive and well. But she'd wanted a lot of things in life that hadn't turned out.

"I'd like to think that Logan survived, but I really don't see how he could." Drake walked in and sat next to her on the sofa. "He did a good thing, staying to try to shut it down. And I think he knew exactly what he was doing."

"Yeah, I guess he did." She swallowed the lump in her throat.

"What about Hemings?" Drake asked.

Ethan cleared his throat. "There's no evidence that he was involved with the Order or that he did anything detrimental to the United States. The decision has been made to leave it at that."

"Leave it at that?" Drake shook his head. "Ethan, tell me that's your idea of a fucking joke."

"Drake, there's nothing we can do. Hemings has been questioned at length and he's denied all affiliation with the Order."

"So, Hemings just goes on and becomes president?" Drake asked.

Ethan held up his hands. "I believe Mr. Hemings is aware that he will be scrutinized closely. We can only hope he keeps that in mind when he takes the oath tomorrow."

Drake rolled his eyes and Zoe sighed heavily.

"I know you two must be exhausted after your ordeal and then the flight and debriefing. Zoe, I have a car waiting to take you home. I understand that Mira and Matteo are at your father's home for a prolonged visit."

"They are?"

"Evidently Matteo wanted to get to know his father, and Mira—well, she wasn't willing to have the visitation be unsupervised. Now, I have a lot of paperwork to do to explain all this to our superiors, so if you'll excuse me?"

"Sure." Zoe stood and walked to the door, Drake right behind her.

In the elevator, she leaned her head against the wall. "This is going to be like going from one war zone to another."

"That bad, huh?"

"You've seen them."

"Maybe you could spend the night somewhere else."

"I guess I could go to a hotel," Zoe said.

"Or you could spend the night at my place."

Zoe opened her eyes and looked at him. "You live in an apartment, right?"

"Yes." He leaned down and kissed her neck above the too-large T-shirt.

"You have a guest room?" She shivered as his lips traveled up her neck and nibbled at her mouth.

"No, it's a one-bedroom."

"Perfect."

21

January 20, CIA Headquarters, Langley, Virginia

"I JUST WANT TO RUN in and check my messages," Drake said as he pulled his car into the parking garage. "You want to come in?"

"Sure. I've only seen Ethan's office, the debriefing room, and the showers." Zoe unfastened her seat belt and followed Drake to the elevator. He took advantage of the privacy to nuzzle her neck, sending a flash of heat into her belly. When the door opened, he took her hand and pulled her down a hallway. He punched a code into a keypad and opened the double doors.

"Robyn, what are you doing working on a Saturday?" Zoe asked.

"Trying to get a location on that detonation device we put into an ink pen and gave to the terrorists. What are you guys doing here?" She glanced at Drake and back to Zoe, then grinned. "Maybe I shouldn't ask."

"An ink pen?" Zoe asked, ignoring Robyn's

comment.

"A white Waterman L'Etalon, to be exact," Robyn said.

"Where was the last location you got on it?" Drake asked, leaning over to look at her computer screen.

"I tracked it from Iraq to France, then to London. Then I lost it."

"Let me know if you find it again." Drake patted Zoe's butt and turned to go to his cubicle.

"So, what's up with you and Drake?" Robyn asked.

Zoe shrugged. "I'm not sure, but I'm enjoying it."

Robyn laughed and shook her head. "I don't know. I hear that relationships started under extreme circumstances don't last."

"Really? I haven't thought much beyond the next week. Or two."

"Yikes! I think I've found it again."

"The device?"

"Yep. Hey, Drake, I'm getting a location on the pen," Robyn called.

Drake came out of his office and leaned over Robyn's shoulder. Zoe stepped out of the way and focused her attention on the television set. She'd forgotten that today was the Inauguration. Zoe shivered at the thought of Hemings becoming president of the United States. The television showed a view of the

Capitol Building, then zoomed in on the arriving dignitaries.

"I can't understand what you're looking at," Drake said to Robyn.

"The satellite is closing in on the latitude and longitude of the device. Those are the numbers you see flashing on the screen. When it locks in on an exact location, it'll display more information."

"Can't you hurry it up?" Drake asked.

"Sorry, there's no *go faster* button on this." Robyn's fingers flew across the keyboard. "It's closing in. Just another few seconds."

Drake stared at the computer monitor with an intensity that made Zoe think he was mentally willing it to work faster. She looked back at the television screen. A reporter was making her commentary of the occasion.

"Shit. I'm losing it!" Robyn typed in more commands and the computer screen flashed more numbers.

"Where is it?" Drake demanded.

"You're not helping, Drake." Robyn watched the computer screen. "There! It's defining the location. Oh, God, it's in the U.S."

"Where?"

"Stop asking me that! It's working," Robyn said. Her fingers were still on the keyboard, and the three of them watched the computer as it displayed the location on a split screen. The left half changed from a map of the United States to the Eastern states, then closed in farther. The right half flashed letters and numbers so fast Zoe couldn't keep up with them.

"It's here," Robyn said.

"Here where?" Drake asked.

"Here in D.C." Robyn pointed at the map that had focused on the area. The right half of the screen flashed more data, then stopped on an address.

"Capitol Hill," Robyn said. "It's on Capitol Hill."

"The Inauguration." Zoe pointed to the television set.

Robyn picked up the remote and pushed the button to bring up the sound.

"We're speaking with the Chief Justice of the Supreme Court, Isaac Jacobs, who will swear in President-elect Jefferson Hemings as our next president." The camera pulled back to include the Chief Justice in the shot. He patted the breast pocket of his coat and fingered a white cylinder.

"That's it!" Drake ran down the hall to his office and came back with a white cigar-shaped pen in his hand.

"What's that?" Zoe asked.

"It's the pen the terrorists gave me to have the detonator put in. Robyn used an identical pen and I kept this one."

"Chief Justice Jacobs?" Zoe asked. "He can't be a terrorist."

"Anyone can be a terrorist," Drake said.

The news reporter asked Jacobs questions about

the event but he shook his head and patted his throat, shrugging apologetically. "It seems Chief Justice Jacobs has a throat infection and wants to save his voice for the ceremony." The reporter smiled at the older man. "We understand, Mr. Jacobs. Perhaps we can have an interview later?"

Chief Justice Jacobs smiled and nodded, his right hand moving again to the white pen in his pocket. He pulled the pen out and rolled it in his fingers, then slipped it back in the pocket.

"That's not him," Zoe said. "It can't be."

"Like I said, anyone can be a terrorist." Drake threw the pen down on Robyn's desk and ran a hand over his head.

"No. That's not what I mean. Look at his hands." Zoe picked up the pen and tapped the television screen.

"What?" Robyn asked.

"His hands are smooth. No wrinkles. They don't look like they belong to a man in his late sixties." Zoe watched as the Chief Justice returned the pen to his breast pocket. The man's face was flaccid with pronounced wrinkles around his eyes and mouth, yet his hands were smooth and supple.

"Robyn, don't lose the satellite feed. I'm going to the Inauguration." Drake pulled out his cell phone. "I'm dialing into your cell phone. Bring up the floor plans of the Capitol Building. And call Ethan."

Robyn put her headset on, punched a button on her phone, and typed in the commands to display the floor plans of the building. Zoe dropped the pen into her pocket and ran down the hall behind him, sliding into the elevator just before the doors closed.

"No," Drake said shaking his head.

"What?"

"You're not coming with me."

"Oh, I am absolutely going with you." Zoe grinned at him. No way was he talking her out of this.

"Look, it might be dangerous."

"I think I can handle it.

"You're wrong. This is serious, Zoe."

"Besides, you might need help."

"Need help?"

"I'm coming with you."

Drake sighed. "Just do whatever I tell you. No questions."

"Sure." Zoe closed the car door and fastened her seat belt.

Drake ignored the speed limit and sped the few miles from Langley to Washington, D.C. But as they approached the city, traffic ground to a halt, every street choked with citizens wanting a glimpse of the Inauguration.

"We'll make better time on the Metro," Zoe said.

Drake turned onto a side street and wound his way to the White Flint Metro station. He stopped the car at the curb and jumped out. Zoe trotted behind him into the station.

The station was crowded, but Drake and Zoe elbowed their way through the crowd and onto the next train into D.C., garnering more than a few disgruntled glances. By the time the train pulled into Metro Center, they'd been shoved to the rear of the car and had to wait while everyone else exited.

Drake put a wireless earpiece on his ear and pushed people aside as he left the station. Zoe trotted along in his wake.

"Robyn, where do you show the device now?"

"It's in the Capitol Building. Looks like the south end of the building."

"What do the floor plans say is there?" Drake asked.

"The second floor has the president's room in that location."

"What about the first floor?" Drake asked.

"I'm still checking. And I couldn't locate Ethan. Do you want me to call Bolton?"

"No. Not yet."

Drake pushed through the throng of people and finally reached one of the ticket gates. He pulled out his CIA identification and showed it to the man at the gate. "We need to get to the Capitol Building. Now."

"Do you have a ticket?" the man asked.

Drake leaned closer. "What part of a CIA ID do you not understand?"

"Yes, sir." The man stopped the line of people and let Drake and Zoe through.

Drake broke into a run, and Zoe's shorter legs pumped to keep up with his long stride. They had to stop twice more to show his ID before they reached an entrance to the building.

"What now?" Zoe asked when Drake paused to look around.

"Now we have to convince the Secret Service to let us into the building."

"Is that going to be hard?"

"Probably. They take the job pretty seriously." Drake walked over to a man in a gray suit. He wore dark glasses and had an earpiece with a curly cord running down his neck and disappearing under his jacket.

"Can I help you?" the man asked.

Drake showed him the ID. "We need to get into the building. It's a matter of national security."

"Sorry, no can do. No one goes in that isn't on the list."

"I realize that, but like I said. It's national security."

The man was shaking his head again when another

Secret Service approached him. Drake grinned when he recognized the agent. He'd been CIA before he went to the Secret Service. Drake had saved his life on an op. If anyone would let them into the building, it would be Antoine Stewart. "Antoine. I really need to get into the building."

"So do a lot of people. What's up, Drake?"

"It's a matter of national security."

"Seriously?" Antoine asked.

"Yeah, I need to get to the president's room."

Antoine's eyebrows lifted. "That's where Chief Justice Jacobs and Justice Greene are."

"Exactly."

"I can't do that, Drake."

"National security. I'm not kidding about this."

"Tell you what. I'll let you in, but it's gotta be quick. The ceremony starts in half an hour."

"Thanks. When this is all over, I'll tell you what a hero you are." Drake grabbed Zoe's hand and they hurried into the building. At the top of the stairs, Drake stopped and ducked into an alcove.

"What's the plan?" Zoe asked.

"Excellent question. I thought I'd just go in there and take the damn pen away from him."

"That could work," Zoe agreed. "But we don't know what it's going to detonate or where it is. What if he's able to detonate it before you get the pen?"

"That's a chance we'll have to take."

"I could take it away without him knowing," she suggested.

"No." He shook his head. "Too dangerous."

"Then we could get it far enough away that it won't detonate anything," she continued.

The problem was he didn't have any better ideas. "What are you going to do, just walk up and ask him for it?"

Zoe rolled her eyes. "I'm a thief, remember? I could take his underwear without him knowing."

"He'll know when he reaches for the pen."

"So?"

"He's been touching that pen every time we've seen him. If he realizes it's missing soon enough, they might have a backup plan."

Zoe held up the pen Drake had tossed on Robyn's desk. "Then I'll replace it with this one."

Drake considered the situation. It might work. If she could really switch out the pens without him knowing.

"Drake, we have to do something. It's almost time for it to start."

"Okay. Let's go. What do you want me to do?"

"Just stand back and watch." Zoe turned and walked to the double doors of the president's room.

Justice Greene was settled in a burgundy leather

chair next to the fireplace watching a television that had obviously been brought in for the occasion . She looked up when they entered, set her coffee cup down, and stood.

"Time for me to swear in the new vice president. I'll see you in a bit, I suppose." She smiled at the phony Jacobs, and nodded to Drake and Zoe on her way out. Zoe nodded and walked over to the imposter.

"Chief Justice Jacobs?" She held her hand out. "I'm Zoe Alexander. I can't tell you what a thrill it is to meet you. I'm a law student and you're just like my hero, you know? I follow all your decisions and everything and I just wanted to meet you."

He glanced around, catching Drake's eye for a moment. Drake smiled and shrugged. Zoe smiled broadly at him and jumped up and down on her toes.

"I graduate this year and I'm so totally nervous about taking the bar, you know?" Zoe leaned in from the side, hovering over him. Predictably, he rose to take a step away from her. As soon as he stood, Zoe stumbled and put her hands up against his chest. The startled man automatically put his hands under her elbows to steady her.

"Oh, I'm so sorry. I'm just so excited to meet you and everything. I must sound like an idiot."

His eyes flickered to the clock and he nodded. Zoe followed his gaze, then gasped. "Oh, my God! I'm holding you up, aren't I? I'm so sorry." She grabbed his hand and pumped it with hers. "This has been such an honor. Really."

Drake watched the man pull his hand away from Zoe's and move it to his breast pocket. He patted the white pen and smiled at Zoe, then stepped around her. Drake nodded when the man passed him to open the door and step out into the hallway.

"Did you do it?" Drake asked after the door closed.

"You didn't see it?" Zoe asked.

"I saw you stumble against him. Is that when you switched the pens?"

"Of course. I thought I was a little slow. Worried me for a minute." She held the pen out to Drake. "What do we do with this?"

Drake took the pen from her hands gingerly. "Robyn? You still there?"

"I'm here. You have the pen?"

"In my hand."

"Don't open it. Removing the cap activates the detonator."

"What's the range?"

"Ten meters. Maybe a little more."

"We're heading back. I want this thing as far from here as I can get it."

"Wait. I've got Ethan on the other line. I'll patch

him through."

"Ethan?"

"Robyn filled me in. You have the pen?"

"Yeah, I've got it, but I don't know what it's supposed to detonate or where it might be."

"I have a team on the way and I've alerted the Secret Service. Just stay put and don't let anyone touch that pen. Let's hope there's no backup device."

"That's a comforting thought."

The doors opened and Antoine walked in. "Drake, you want to tell me what the hell this is all about?"

"Yeah, that's probably a good idea." Drake gave him a brief version of what had happened.

"So, there's still something that might be detonated, but we don't know what it is or where it is?"

"Pretty much."

"Fuck! You couldn't tell me this earlier?"

"I wanted to get the detonation device before we started with the general pandemonium."

"Is the president-elect in any danger?"

"In my opinion, no." Drake didn't really care if the president-elect was in any danger because he didn't particularly care for the president-elect, but he wasn't about to tell Antoine that.

"Look! They're starting the swearing-in." Zoe pointed to the television set. Drake and Antoine both turned. Hemings was standing before the podium with his wife and what appeared to be Chief Justice Jacobs. Drake held his breath.

The imposter coughed, then reached into his breast pocket. He pulled out the pen and smiled.

The television showed the reporter in a small frame inset into the picture. "Chief Justice Jacobs is preparing to swear Jefferson Hemings in as the next president of the United States. Earlier we learned that Justice Jacobs has been suffering from the flu and has had problems with a raspy throat."

Drake clutched the pen tighter as he watched the imposter twist the top off his pen. Zoe sidled closer and held his arm. The imposter pulled the top off the pen and looked at the podium.

Seconds passed before the reporter spoke again. "There appears to be a problem. I'm not sure what it is, but the Chief Justice seems to be delaying the swearing in. The future First Lady is holding the Bible and President-elect Hemings appears to be ready. As we reported earlier, Chief Justice Jacobs has been ill with the flu."

The camera zoomed in on the imposter and Drake saw the man's jaw working. He looked at the two pieces of the pen, then put the cap back on and twisted it off again.

The reporter's voice started again. "We don't know what the problem is. Chief Justice Jacobs appears to be having a problem with his pen. Of course, everyone knows that Jacobs uses that pen to sign all his decisions and has for years. There's no reason he needs the pen at this time, but there still seems to be a problem. The swearing in still hasn't begun." The reporter looked nervous, touching his earpiece and glancing at the camera and then away.

Tears started to flow down the imposter's cheeks as he repeatedly capped and uncapped the pen. He reached into his pants pocket, then put something into his mouth. Within seconds he was gasping for air. His eyes rolled back into his head and he slumped down to the floor.

"What happened?" Zoe asked. "What's he doing?"

"My guess is that he just ate a bullet," Drake said.

22

January 22, CIA Headquarters, Langley, Virginia

"ANYTHING ON THE IMPOSTER?" Drake asked.

Ethan nodded. "We traced him to Ziyad Al-Din. The plan was to kill everyone in the vicinity at the Inauguration. The podium contained a device that would have emitted a deadly neurotoxin if the imposter had been able to detonate it."

"How did they get the device past security?" Drake asked.

"We're still checking on that. One of the regular maintenance workers in the Capitol Building has disappeared. We suspect he was involved. It'll take a while to trace everything. But we will."

"So, everyone would have been killed?" Zoe asked.

Ethan nodded. "Everyone within a fifty-meter range would most assuredly have died. Beyond that, we aren't sure yet, but it would have been devastating."

"That would have been almost everyone in line for the presidency." Zoe shook her head.

"Actually, it *would* have been everyone in line. The

country would have been literally without a leader."

"How did he die?" Zoe asked.

"Cyanide," Ethan said. "Most likely a capsule he'd been given just in case everything fell apart, which, thanks to you two, it did."

"What about the team in Switzerland?" Drake asked. "Any more news from them?"

Ethan shook his head. "I'm afraid not. It looks like everyone in the facility was destroyed at the time of the explosion."

"There was no sign of Logan anywhere?" Zoe asked.

Ethan shook his head. "The team scoured the area, but there were a lot of body parts that can't be identified. There's just no way of knowing if anyone survived, although indications are that everyone perished."

"How awful," Zoe said. "Logan sacrificed himself for his country, for everything he believed in and there's not even anything left to bury."

"We believe that his efforts were key in taking down the Order. He'll be remembered for what he did," Ethan said.

"But there are thousands of people out there who are still part of it. What about them?" Zoe asked.

Ethan shrugged. "It's not illegal to believe a certain way. A man—or a woman—has a right to rear their children to believe anything they want." The phone on Ethan's desk rang. "Excuse me."

Like her father had raised her to be a thief. She'd willingly followed him most of her life. Just like these children would follow their parents. Damn, she needed a vacation.

"What?" Drake looked at Zoe.

"I was just thinking I need a vacation. Maybe a nice, almost deserted island with sun and sea and not much else."

"Yeah? That sounds nice. Would you like some company?"

"I wouldn't mind some company."

Ethan hung up the phone. "I have to go. Director Bolton wants to see me."

"Oh," Zoe said. "Are you in trouble?"

"Most likely." Ethan gathered up the papers on his desk and stacked them into a neat pile. "But my team saved the world. How pissed can he be?"

Drake grinned at Zoe. "You have any particular island in mind?"

"Hawaii is too crowded. Fiji, maybe?"

"Sorry, Zoe, you don't have time to go to Fiji."

Zoe turned toward the familiar voice. "What are you—"

"I know you deserve a vacation, but I need you on this job."

Zoe gave Drake an apologetic shrug. "Okay, but what's with the platinum blond hair, Shelby?"

BREEDING EVIL

Liz Wolfe

SOMEONE IS BREEDING SUPERHUMANS . . .

. . . beings who possess extreme psychic abilities. Now they have implanted the ultimate seed in the perfect womb. They are a heartbeat away from successfully breeding a species of meta humans, who will be raised in laboratories and conditioned to obey the orders of their owners, governments and large multi-national corporations.

Then Shelby Parker, a former black ops agent for the government, is asked to locate a missing woman. Her quest takes her to The Center for Bio-Psychological Research. Masquerading as a computer programmer, she gets inside the Center's inner workings. What she discovers is almost too horrible to comprehend.

Dr. Mac McRae, working for The Center, administers a lie-detector test to the perspective employee for his very cautious employers. Although she passes, the handsome Australian suspects Shelby is not what she appears. But then, neither is he. Caught up in a nightmare of unspeakable malevolence, the unlikely duo is forced to team up to save a young woman and her very special child. And destroy a program that could change the face of nations.

But first they must unmask the mole that has infiltrated Shelby's agency and stalks their every move. They must stay alive and keep one step ahead of the pernicious forces who are intent on . . .

NATURAL SELECTION

A Liz Wolfe Novel

Paige Blackwell needs a vacation. She's been working hard as a partner in Shelby Parker's PI agency. When she's offered a chance to be on a survival type reality television show that takes place on a tropical island, she jumps at the opportunity.

On the island Paige meets her fellow competitors, including one it might be fun to share a sleeping bag with, should things work out. It looks like the week is going to be even more enjoyable than she had thought. And then the first shots are fired. At them.

There's no reality TV show. Just reality. They're being hunted. Survival takes on a whole new meaning. But Paige and her companions are not the only ones in jeopardy.

Back home, Shelby and new associate Zoe are racing against the clock to stop a plot by the shadowy and sinister Dominion Order to control the U.S. guided missile system.

Who wants the carefully selected contestants on the island dead? What do they all have in common? And why are Shelby and Zoe now targets, too?

Clearly, only the fittest will survive.

ISBN#9781932815221
Mass Market Paperback / Suspense
US $6.99 / CDN $9.99
Available Now
www.lizwolfe.net